"Susan Johnson is a queen of erotic, exciting romance who soars to new heights with each novel." —*Romantic Times*

"Johnson delivers another fast, titillating read that overflows with sex scenes and rapid-fire dialogue."

—*Publishers Weekly*

"A spellbinding read and a lot of fun . . . Johnson takes sensuality to the edge, writing smoldering stories with characters the reader won't want to leave."

—*The Oakland (MI) Press*

"Smart . . . sexy . . . sensuous . . . [Her] books are legendary!" —Robin Schone, *USA Today* bestselling author

"Sensually charged writing . . . Johnson knows exactly what her devoted readers desire, and she delivers it with her usual flair." —*Booklist*

"Fascinating . . . The author's style is a pleasure to read."

—*Los Angeles Herald-Examiner*

"Flat-out fabulous, sexy [novels] so textured they sometimes compare . . . to the phenomenal Judith Ivory."

—*All About Romance*

Berkley Sensation Books by Susan Johnson

SWEET AS
THE *Devil*

SUSAN JOHNSON

BERKLEY SENSATION, NEW YORK

THE BERKLEY PUBLISHING GROUP
Published by the Penguin Group
Penguin Group (USA) Inc.
375 Hudson Street, New York, New York 10014, USA

Penguin Group (Canada), 90 Eglinton Avenue East, Suite 700, Toronto, Ontario M4P 2Y3, Canada
(a division of Pearson Penguin Canada Inc.)
Penguin Books Ltd., 80 Strand, London WC2R 0RL, England
Penguin Group Ireland, 25 St. Stephen's Green, Dublin 2, Ireland (a division of Penguin Books Ltd.)
Penguin Group (Australia), 250 Camberwell Road, Camberwell, Victoria 3124, Australia
(a division of Pearson Australia Group Pty. Ltd.)
Penguin Books India Pvt. Ltd., 11 Community Centre, Panchsheel Park, New Delhi—110 017, India
Penguin Group (NZ), 67 Apollo Drive, Rosedale, North Shore 0632, New Zealand
(a division of Pearson New Zealand Ltd.)
Penguin Books (South Africa) (Pty.) Ltd., 24 Sturdee Avenue, Rosebank, Johannesburg 2196,
South Africa

Penguin Books Ltd., Registered Offices: 80 Strand, London WC2R 0RL, England

This is a work of fiction. Names, characters, places, and incidents either are the product of the author's imagination or are used fictitiously, and any resemblance to actual persons, living or dead, business establishments, events, or locales is entirely coincidental. The publisher does not have any control over and does not assume any responsibility for author or third-party websites or their content.

SWEET AS THE DEVIL

A Berkley Sensation Book / published by arrangement with the author

PRINTING HISTORY
Berkley Sensation mass-market edition / March 2011

ISBN: 978-0-425-24041-0

BERKLEY® SENSATION
Berkley Sensation Books are published by The Berkley Publishing Group,
a division of Penguin Group (USA) Inc.,
375 Hudson Street, New York, New York 10014.
BERKLEY® SENSATION and the "B" design are trademarks of Penguin Group (USA) Inc.

PRINTED IN THE UNITED STATES OF AMERICA

10 9 8 7 6 5 4 3 2 1

SWEET AS
THE *Devil*

CHAPTER 1

London, May 1893

"JAMIE, DON'T YOU *dare* leave! I *need* you. *Jamie!*"

Already sliding from the bed, James Blackwood turned back, leaned over in a fluid ripple of honed muscle, and kissed the countess's pouty mouth. "I would stay if I could, darling," he said, sitting up and smiling at her. "But I'm already late. Drinks at eight. John's new wife was quite emphatic."

"Pshaw on little Vicky," Countess Minton peevishly noted. "What about me? I haven't seen you in almost a year. And it's only drinks. You won't miss dinner, I promise. You can't say you're not *interested*," she murmured, her sultry gaze drifting to Jamie's blatant erection, her smile sly and knowing.

"You keep a man interested, Bella—no doubt about that." The voluptuously nude woman sprawled in the shambles of the bed was well aware of her sensual allure. And her charming capacity for innovation was also an accomplishment of no small merit. "Unfortunately," he said with a truly regretful sigh, "duty calls." There were degrees of lateness and politesse apropos his cousin's wife, and he was pressing the boundaries of both. He began to turn away.

Rolling up on one elbow with breathtaking speed, Isabella seized Jamie's upthrust penis in her pink-nailed grip, swiftly bent her head, and seized the moment.

Christ! Jamie's breath hissed through his teeth, his cock oversensitive after hours of fucking, Bella's assault a shock to his nerve endings. But a heartbeat later, his twitching nerves adjusted with indecent speed to licentious pleasure and he softly exhaled. *Now what?* With Bella performing fellatio in her usual masterful fashion, assessing the relative merits of duty and lust required a degree of rational observation that was fast eluding him. Yet—a modicum of reason still remained in the nether reaches of his brain; he glanced at the clock.

Bella suddenly nibbled a trifle overzealously or perhaps deliberately, and an unexpectedly sharp jolt mauled his senses.

He gasped, the fine line between pleasure and pain not only taking his breath away but also effectively ending his debate. *What the hell.* Shutting his eyes, he gave himself up to prodigal sensation.

One good turn deserved another, et cetera, et cetera, and an hour later, lying facedown on the bed, panting, Bella gasped, "No more."

Sprawled on his back beside her, laboring to drag air into his lungs, Jamie finally became aware of the censorious voice inside his head that had been trying to warn him for a considerable time that—*Vicky's going to be furious!* Silently swearing, he lifted his head from the pillow, took a disgruntled breath, and sat up. Why had he made plans? He never made plans. Raking his fingers through his dark, ruffled hair, he wondered how much time had passed since he'd been so felicitously persuaded to tarry.

Oh Christ. The face of the small bedside clock jerked him back to reality. Swinging his legs over the side of the bed, he scanned the floor for his trousers.

"Don't go."

He glanced at the flushed woman who could keep his cock hard indefinitely. "You said no more."

Her smile was Circe's. "I take it back."

His dark lashes lowered slightly. "Be reasonable. I'm already later than hell."

"I don't care. Stay—*please, please.*"

For a moment he actually debated staying; it was incredibly late. He still had to return to his apartment and change—which would make him even later. Dare he ignore Vicky's invitation? And risk his cousin's displeasure? Knowing the politic answer, he twisted back with the fluid grace of an athlete, whispered in Bella's ear, and quickly quit the bed before his libido regained the upper hand.

He found his trousers where they'd been hastily discarded that morning after he'd stopped by to talk to Charlie about a prime cavalry mount he wished to buy and had found Isabella in dishabille instead.

Charlie was out of town, she'd explained with a seductive smile. "But there's no reason to hurry off, Jamie dear," she'd purred. "We haven't seen each other in ages. Do tell me all the gossip from Vienna."

She hadn't meant it of course.

She'd meant something else entirely.

And now he was damnably late for Vicky's dinner.

HE MADE HIS excuses to Vicky and his cousin, John, Baron Reid, and to all the guests who'd looked up from their desserts as he'd entered the dining room and greeted him with sly smiles and curious gazes. No one believed for a minute that he'd been detained because of an accident on the Windsor road, since Vicky had chanced to mention over drinks that Jamie had gone to see Charlie Bonner on the matter of a horse, to which Freddy Stockton had pointed out that Charlie was in the country. Everyone also knew that Isabella had a penchant for handsome men and Jamie Blackwood in particular.

But since the fashionable world viewed fidelity in marriage much as they viewed children—as something to be ignored—amorous peccadillos were not only commonplace but also generally regarded with amusement.

So after the initial raised brows and roguish scrutiny, conversation reverted to the usual tittle-tattle and gossip that passed for social intercourse in the frivolous world of the beau monde. Several earlier courses were brought up from the kitchen for Jamie while the other guests indulged in a sumptuous variety of sweets. John's chef was superb, the wine free-flowing, and famished after having exerted himself at stud all day, Jamie tucked into his meal with gusto.

"Worked up an appetite, I see," Viscount Graham sportively noted.

Jamie turned a bland gaze on the man to his left. "There's no opportunity to eat when your carriage's stalled in traffic."

"The road to Windsor, you said?" the viscount pronounced with unsullied cheer.

"Yes, Windsor." Jamie set down his knife and fork, his dark brows lifted faintly. "Would you care to ask me something?"

Graham smiled widely. "Hell no." While Jamie served officially as attaché to Prince Ernst of Dalmia, he was, in effect, bodyguard to the prince, and in that capacity had gained a reputation for efficiency, or more pertinently, violence.

"I didn't think so." Jamie signaled to have his wineglass filled, and returned to his meal.

MUCH LATER, WHEN all the guests had departed and Vicky had gone off to bed, Jamie and his cousin retired to John's study to share a decanter of whiskey.

"Allow me to apologize again for arriving so late," Jamie immediately said. "It was—"

"Bella's engaging charm?" his cousin interposed with a grin. "Along with her inexhaustible desires?"

"Indeed." Jamie dipped his head. "Not that I'm complaining. You no doubt speak from experience."

"Previous experience. I'm a happily married man now."

Jamie raised his glass in salute. "To your brilliant marriage. You love Vicky and she obviously loves you. A nice change from the beau monde's penchant for marriages based on balance sheets and quarterings." With a smile for his cousin, he drank down his whiskey.

"Thank you. I consider myself very fortunate. *You* should consider marriage. I heartily recommend it. Women are always in hot pursuit of you," John said with a lift of his brows. "Why not let yourself be caught?"

"No thanks." Swift and certain. "The Isabelles of the world suit me just fine."

"So it seems. My personal bet was you wouldn't make dinner."

"I almost didn't. It was a matter of not wanting to disappoint your lovely new bride."

"And you were fucked out," his cousin perceptively remarked.

Jamie smiled. "That, too."

"Someday the right woman is going to change your mind about marriage."

Jamie gently shook his head. "Don't waste your breath. Unlike you, I've never been enthralled with the concept of love. Several of your youthful infatuations come to mind," Jamie added with a grin, "if you'd like me to refresh your memory."

"God, no. In any case, Vicky's different."

"Which is why you married her. I'm not questioning your sincerity. I just lack the necessary sense of devotion."

Leaning forward, Jamie picked up the decanter and re-filled his glass.

"I used to think as much."

Jamie shot his cousin a jaundiced glance, but rather than argue his cousin's past history with women, Jamie set down the crystal container and politely said, "Even if I were inclined to endorse the notion of love and marriage, *at the moment*, I'm up to my ears in risky ventures. As you well know, the Habsburg Empire's in decline; every petty despot with influence or an army at his back is jockeying for position."

"Including Prince Ernst."

"Including him." Leaning back in his chair, Jamie met his cousin's gaze with his usual immutable calm. "He's as ambitious as the rest. And why shouldn't he be? Twenty generations of Battenbergs have ruled that piece of prime real estate, offered up their resources and sons to the emperor when needed, and played a significant role in the Habsburg prosperity."

"As your family has for the Battenbergs." Jamie's fore-bears had fled Scotland after the '45 defeat and sold the services of their fighting clan to the duchy of Dalmia.

"With due compensation," Jamie serenely said, John's red hair gleaming in the lamplight always reminding him of his mother's. Shaking off the melancholy that always overcame him on recall of his mother's unnecessary death, he pushed up from his lounging pose and said, "You heard, of course, that Uncle Douglas came back from India with a fortune."

"And a native wife."

"A very beautiful wife. He's looking to invest his money. I told him to talk to you. You've guarded my investments well," Jamie said with a grin.

"Anyone could. Other than upkeep on your Dalmian estate, you don't spend any money."

"I don't have time. Guarding Ernst is a round-the-clock commission."

"Speaking of guarding, who's protecting Ernst in your absence?"

"He's on holiday with his newest paramour, who rules a principality of her own with a small army and a top-notch palace guard." Lifting his glass to his mouth, Jamie arched his brows. "Adequate deterrent to any assassin," he murmured and drank down half the whiskey.

"Which explains *your* holiday in Scotland."

"A much needed holiday," Jamie softly replied, lowering his glass to the chair arm.

John looked surprised. "Do I detect a modicum of frustration? Is Ernst spending too much time in libertine pursuits—silly question."

"Let's just say he doesn't have his father's sense of responsibility."

"Or any responsibility at all."

"He was perhaps too indulged." Jamie shrugged. "A problem at a time when Dalmia could use a ruler of insight and diligence."

"What of his heir? Rupert appears to be of a sensible nature."

"He's still young, and tiger hunting in India at the moment with his friends. But even if Rupert wished to take a hand in the administration of the duchy, Ernst wouldn't let him. Like your queen, Ernst has no wish to share power." The Prince of Wales was almost sixty and still not allowed to participate in Queen Victoria's government. "In any event, at twenty, Rupert's probably too young to effectively deal with the political scheming in our corner of the world. It's reached new, ruthless heights."

"How so? Haven't the Balkans always been a tinder-box?"

"It's worse now. The emperor's totally oblivious to the political realities of the world. He's a blundering dyed-in-the-wool reactionary with fifty million subjects from a dozen nations itching to rise in revolt. His enemies are simply waiting in the wings, nurturing their ambitions. With the crown prince dead and the new heir a witless dolt, once Franz Joseph dies, all hell's going to break loose. And after three assassination attempts in the past few years, the emperor's death may come sooner rather than later."

"Like Rudolf's. Some say it wasn't suicide."

"More than some. The crown prince was too liberal for those in power. His advisors were impatient for him to depose his father and take the reins of empire. Rumor has it that he and his mistress were shot with a sniper rifle while they slept"—Jamie arched one brow—"or were passed out. Rudolf was addicted to morphine."

"Because of his unpleasant disease."

"Yes—a bright young man killing himself slowly." Jamie grimaced. "But screw it. I'm not in Vienna, I'm here. Tell me about your thoroughbreds instead. I heard that your chestnut brute's going to take all the major races next year." The last thing Jamie wished to dwell on was the crumbling Habsburg monarchy.

"You should plan on being here for the derby next year," John pleasantly said, urbanely shifting topics. "Shalizar's going to win by ten lengths. You can bet on it."

"In that case," Jamie drawled, "I shall—heavily."

"As will I. A pity you don't have time to see my stud at Bellingham."

"Next time. I promised Davey I'd meet him day after tomorrow. He's coming down from the hills to meet me."

The two men, long friends—their family resemblance clear despite their disparate coloring—went on to discuss the merits of various horses and trainers, bloodlines and jockeys. The quiet study was peaceful, a temporary hermitage in a quarrelsome, perilous world, and the fine Highland whiskey served its purpose well in lessening Jamie's disquiet. Neither touched on the serious or personal, both careful to keep the conversation companionable, and toward dawn, cheerfully drunk, the two men parted ways.

John went upstairs to his wife.

Jamie strolled to Grosvenor Square, entered a large house through a back door, conveniently unlocked, took the servants' stairs to the second floor, and entered a shadowed bedchamber.

"I didn't know if you'd come," Isabella drowsily murmured, gazing at Jamie from under her lashes.

"I said I would." Quietly closing the door, he slipped off his swallowtail coat, dropped it on the floor, and pulling his shirt studs free, moved toward the bed.

"How nice." Pushing up on her elbows, Isabella smiled. "I don't believe I've ever met an honest man."

Jamie grinned. "I have an excuse. I live outside the fashionable world."

"Too far outside at the moment," she purred, tossing the covers aside. "Do come in . . ."

CHAPTER 2

THE NEXT MORNING, the air heavy with the promise of rain, Sofia Eastleigh was cooling her heels in a small drawing room off the entrance hall of Minton House and becoming increasingly agitated. She didn't as a rule agree to paint society portraits, finding those in the fashionable world too spoiled or difficult to sit the necessary hours required to complete a painting. But Isabella, Countess of Minton, was one of the reigning beauties of the day—not to be discounted when it came to publicity—and she was generous as well in terms of a fee.

She'd give her five minutes more, Sofia resentfully decided, and then the countess and her money could go to hell. With her artwork much sought after, Sofia didn't *need* the money. Nor did she appreciate being kept waiting like a servant for—she glanced at the splendid Boulle clock on the mantel—damn it . . . *thirty-five* minutes!

Rising to her feet, she was slipping on her gloves when the drawing room door was thrown open by a liveried flunkey, Isabella was announced, and a moment later, a radiant, blushing countess, obviously just risen from bed, swept into the room, trailing lavender mousseline and a cloud of scent.

"Good, you're still here. A matter of some importance delayed me."

The countess's partner in that important matter strolled into the room behind her and offered Sofia an engaging smile. "I'm sorry you had to wait. Please, accept my apology. Bella tells me you're an artist of great renown."

"The baron will keep me company while you paint," the countess briskly interposed, ignoring Jamie's apology. "We're quite ready if you are."

Understanding that Bella viewed an artist as a trades person, consequently not due the courtesies, Jamie introduced himself. "You're Miss Eastleigh, I presume. James Blackwood at your service."

Even with her temper in high dudgeon, Sofia couldn't help but think, *Wouldn't it be grand to be serviced by a big, handsome brute like you.* The man was splendid—tall, dark, powerfully muscled, and all male, with the languid gait of a panther and the green eyes to match. Now there was a portrait worth painting. She'd portray him as he was, casually dressed in the remnants of last night's evening rig, his dark hair in mild disarray. He wore a cambric shirt and black trousers, the shirt open at the neck, his long, muscular legs shown to advantage in well-tailored wool, his feet bare in his evening shoes.

A faint carnal tremor raced through her senses.

Commonplace and not in the least disconcerting.

She found handsome men attractive and in many cases, useful.

A modern woman, a bohemian in terms of cultural mores, Sofia enjoyed lovemaking. But on her terms. She decided if a man suited her; she decided when and if to make love and whether to continue a relationship—mostly she didn't, preferring men as transient diversions in her life. Although, for a gorgeous animal like Blackwood, she might be inclined to alter her rules and keep him for a time. He had the look of a man who was more than capable of satisfying a woman. And the fact that the countess—who had a reputation for dalliance—was obviously captivated by him was testament to his competence.

Taking jealous note of Sofia's admiring gaze, for a brief moment Isabella debated canceling the sitting. On second thought, the pale, slender artist was hardly the type of woman to appeal to Jamie, who preferred women of substance who could keep up with him in bed. The little painter looked as though a good wind would blow her away. "Come, Miss Eastleigh," Isabella crisply commanded. "I have another appointment after your sitting."

Following the women from the waiting room, Jamie contemplated the stark differences between the two beauties, the lively contrasts of blonde femininity intriguing. Miss Eastleigh was slender with hair the color of sunshine on snow, her pale loveliness poetic and ethereal—like an Arthurian Isolde who might bruise with the slightest touch. Isabella, on the other hand, didn't bruise at all, as he well knew after two days of wild, untrammeled sex. Bella's golden splendor was that of a robust flesh-and-blood Valkyrie, passionate, impatient, demanding. He understood why Charlie preferred his sweet, young mistress in Chelsea from time to time if for no other reason than to rest.

A few minutes later, they entered the small conservatory where Sofia had set up her easel. Isabella disposed herself on the chaise in David's *Madame Recamier* pose, waved Jamie into a chair opposite her, and sweetly cajoling, murmured, "Darling, tell me how I might tempt you to stay. Surely, your Highlands can wait for a day or so." She spoke as if Sofia didn't exist. "And don't say you must go immediately because you don't when you're here for an entire fortnight."

"If Davey wasn't coming down from the hills to meet

me, I could change my plans, but it's a long, rough trek for him. It wouldn't be fair to waste his time."

"He's your gillie for heaven's sake. Send him a telegram. He can wait for you in Inverness for a day or so."

"We can talk about this later," he quietly said.

"Why? Oh, you think Miss Eastleigh is mindful. Of course she isn't." A duke's daughter would, of course, hold such an opinion; servants were invisible.

"That's enough, Bella."

The countess offered her lover a sultry smile. "Will you beat me if I don't obey?"

"Of course not."

He spoke with soft restraint, but something in his tone apparently struck home, for the countess said with a complacent sigh, "Very well. You must always have your way." She smiled. "For which I've been extremely grateful on any number of occasions, my masterful darling."

"Are you quite done?"

"I suppose I must be with you frowning so. Was Vicky pleased last night that you finally arrived?" She knew when to be accommodating, particularly with Jamie. While they shared mutual pleasures, he wasn't in the least enamored or adoring like so many of her lovers.

"Vicky was very pleasant," he said, relieved Bella was finally minding her manners. "John's a lucky man."

"His wife is lucky as well. You and your cousin share a certain charming expertise. I was surprised when he married."

"He's in love."

"You don't say. How quaint."

"It happens."

"But fortunately not to you"—she smiled—"or me."

"Could we talk about something else?" *Or not talk at all?*

"Of course, darling. Did you hear that Georgie Tolliver left his wife for his children's governess? Isn't that droll?" At which point, Bella lapsed into a gossipy discussion of their various acquaintances who were involved in affaires of one kind or another—the favorite amusement of the aristocracy.

Sliding down on his spine, his eyes half shut, Jamie replied in a desultory fashion to her comments. He was tired; two days of carnal sport and little sleep had taken its toll.

Bella seemed not to notice, absorbed as she was in her frivolous recital, or perhaps she was simply content to have Jamie near.

It was like watching a bored animal, Sofia thought as she captured the countess's pretty features on the canvas, Countess Minton's lover politely biding his time, listening with half an ear to the countess's chatter, appearing to doze off on occasion. Although, apparently, he didn't, for he always managed to respond when required. Politely. With a cultivated civility at variance with his lassitude. He'd open his eyes and answer even the most banal queries with good humor.

The conservatory armchairs were gilded faux bamboo, the attenuated metal dangerously light for a man his size.

Would or wouldn't the chair collapse beneath his weight?

Would he or wouldn't he actually fall asleep? Sofia wondered as if she were somehow his keeper. Or the countess's. As if either of them cared what she thought when they apparently dealt very well together.

Wresting her gaze from the stunning couple, Sofia curtailed her contemplation of the two lovers and applied herself to her work.

And so the sitting progressed, Bella chattering, Mr. Blackwood largely inanimate, Sofia finishing the depiction of the countess's large blue eyes and beginning to sketch in her nose with quick, sure strokes. Having defined the shape to her satisfaction, she was gathering a dab of pale pink paint from her palette for the highlights when the door to the conservatory abruptly opened.

A stylish young lady dressed in ruffled, beribboned

white muslin burst in, using her parasol to shove aside a flustered servant who'd arrived in her wake.

"Your man, Walters, wasn't going to let me in, Bella," she irritably proclaimed, casting a censorious glance on the innocent footman who'd followed her on the butler's orders. "I knew perfectly well that you were at home with Jamie in town." She swung around in a rustle of silk. "Hello, Jamie, *darling*." Her smile was both dazzling and gloating; she'd successfully run her fox to ground. "You're looking utterly gorgeous as usual. Do give me a kiss."

While the countess scowled, Lady Winterthur, flushed with triumph, swiftly advanced on her prey, her parasol swinging from her wrist. "I should be in a pet with you, darling," she sweetly said with feigned chagrin. "You didn't stop by to see me."

James Blackwood had come to his feet before the lovely brunette reached him and, taking her hands in his, suavely saved himself from her embrace. Bending, he bestowed the requested kiss, held her at arm's length, and smoothly lied. "I'm just passing through London or I would have called."

"Since you've chosen to disturb our sitting, do sit down at least, Lily," Bella ordered, anxious to separate her rival from her lover. "And don't distract the painter," she said with annoyance. "We are under a time constraint. I have another appointment after this."

Taking a seat next to Jamie, Lily Chester slanted a sly glance at the countess. "How perfect! I'll take Jamie off your hands then. We'll find something to do to amuse ourselves, won't we, darling?" she brightly said, smiling at her quarry.

"You'll do no such thing," Bella snapped. "He's staying here!"

"Ladies, I prefer not being handed around like a Sacher torte," Jamie drily said. "I'm off to Scotland at five in any event."

"What a shame. We won't have time to *play*," Lily murmured. "You've been terribly selfish, Bella," she chided, turning on her hostess, "keeping him all to yourself." She glanced at Jamie, her gaze openly avaricious. "Perhaps on your return to London, darling, we could share a *moment or two*."

"We're done here," the countess rapped out, her color high.

It was unclear to whom she was speaking, until she rose from the chaise and dismissed Sofia with a flick of her fingers. "Really, Lily, have you no shame?" she hissed, turning a vengeful eye on her guest. "Do I intrude when you have company? We are *done*, Miss Eastleigh," she repeated, sharply.

"She's putting her brushes away, Bella. Be civil." Rising from his chair, Jamie walked toward Sofia, stopping just short of her easel. "Ignore her," he softly said. "May I help?"

"Thank you, no," Sofia replied, wiping her brushes. "This will take just a minute." Dropping her brushes one by one into a jar of turpentine, she closed the lid on her paint box.

"I apologize for them both."

"You needn't. I'm familiar with—"

"Outspoken females?"

He'd formed the word *bitches*, Sofia noticed, but changed his mind. "Yes," she said, giving her hands a last wipe.

He nodded toward the painting. "The likeness is superb."

"The countess is very beautiful."

He smiled faintly. "Let me see you to the door. I'll be right back, Bella," he called out, ignoring his lover's scowl, offering Sofia his arm.

As they exited the room, he said, "My apologies again. Lily is always troublesome, and Bella is—well, Bella. She's a spoiled child."

"And yet?" Sofia shot him an amused glance, the faint scent of the countess's costly perfume lingering on his clothes.

He grinned. "I have no excuse. Have you been painting long? You're very good."

"All my life if you count amateur efforts. Both my parents are artists."

"Ah. That explains it then. My forebears were all soldiers."

"That explains it then," she said, echoing him. "You have a powerful physical presence. As an artist, I notice such things."

He could have said most women noticed his size, but on his best behavior, he said, instead, "I hope Bella's paying you well for her discourtesy."

"Yes, very well. I'm quite content, and no offense, but I don't really listen to women like her. Aristocratic women are entirely wanting in occupation." She grinned. "Which is where you come in I expect."

"It does pass the time," he said with a broad smile.

"But you're on your way to Scotland."

"Yes, and none too soon."

"I noticed your boredom."

"Too much of a good thing," he drolly replied. "I'm looking forward to little conversation and fewer people at my home in the Highlands."

"Then I wish you safe journey."

They'd reached the front door, where two flunkeys were waiting.

Jamie nodded to them.

The door was opened, and with a graceful bow he sent Sofia on her way.

CHAPTER 3

WHETHER IT WAS her artist's eye, Jamie's dark good looks, or the fact that she'd been celibate for the rare interval of a fortnight, Sofia found herself dwelling on the splendid James Blackwood as she walked home.

He was exceptionally kind and well mannered as well.

Not that either of those qualities necessarily prompted her reverie apropos the darling man. Rather, it was his undiluted sexuality on display in the countess's home, as if it were unremarkable for him to serve as stud to female passions. Common and habitual in fact. His composure told the tale.

He knew women wanted him.

In this case, two women.

And Sofia didn't doubt if he hadn't had a train to catch, he would have satisfied them both.

Now *that* would have been a fetching painting—the large, powerful, dark-as-sin Jamie Blackwood engaged in carnal congress with a voluptuous blonde and brunette.

A shiver of arousal rippled through her vagina.

She *could* represent them in mythological guise, him in full rut with two nymphs or goddesses. Perhaps the Judgment of Paris would serve, although she'd have to add another woman. She drew in a sharp breath at the thought of Jamie Blackwood servicing three women, an involuntary flush warming her body. Quickly glancing around, she took note of the pedestrians in her vicinity and heaved a sigh of relief. Thank God, the nearest was several yards away.

Heavens! How long had it been since she'd made love? Too long if she was indulging in such lewd fantasies!

There was no point in any event in fantasizing about Jamie Blackwood; he was leaving London. And unlike the interfering Lily, she most definitely could not expect a visit upon his return. Although, she rather doubted he'd be calling on the lovely Lily either. *Too much of a good thing*, he'd plainly said.

Unlike most aristocrats with excess leisure, he did not appear to construct his life around sexual amusements. The countess *had* referred to him as *baron*. A Scottish title most likely with a name like Blackwood.

Not that it mattered.

She'd never see him again unless he happened to be at another of the countess's portrait sittings. Which was unlikely.

So there was absolutely no earthly reason for her to detour to Bruton Street Books to query Rosalind about the baron James Blackwood. But she knew the Duchess of Groveland was originally from Yorkshire—which bordered Scotland. Oh hell, he'd said he was from the Highlands not the Lowlands. Perhaps Fitz knew him.

She found not only Rosalind in her office at the store but also Isolde, Oz Lennox's wife who'd become a good friend the past year. Rosalind's small son was asleep in a crib, a nursemaid at his side.

"Come in, sit down, Sofie. I've been telling Isolde

you've been spending considerable time with Bella Bonner, making her more beautiful than she already is."

Sofie smiled. "Isn't that the point of having your portrait painted?"

Rosalind turned to Isolde. "Bella's paying Sofie a fortune or she wouldn't do it."

"I'm going to spend my windfall in Paris enjoying the pleasures of wine, men, and song. Or just wine and men," Sofie added with a grin. "The music halls and opera will have to do without me."

"While we two old married women will live vicariously through your pleasures," Isolde teased.

Sofie snorted. "Married to your husbands you have pleasures enough I don't doubt."

Rosalind and Isolde exchanged smiles, both inexpressibly content in their marriages.

"So how did Bella annoy you today?" Rosalind asked, up-to-date with all of Sofie's complaints about her new client.

"She was no more annoying than usual. But she had someone keeping her company during her sitting whom I'd not seen before."

"A man no doubt," Rosalind said. She recognized a certain excitement in Sofie's tone.

"A very beautiful man."

Rosalind came to her feet. "Maud, if you'll excuse us for a moment. I think we ladies will have tea in the gallery."

"I don't want tea," Sofia said as they exited Rosalind's office.

"Nor do I. Come, we'll sit over there." Rosalind indicated a sofa and chairs in a corner of the gallery. "Now, tell us about this lovely man. He's obviously piqued your interest."

"I suppose he may have just a little," Sofie said, dropping into a jonquil yellow chintz-covered chair that complimented her simple gown of green sprigged muslin.

Having been the recipient of Sofia's lascivious accounts of her lovers over the years, Rosalind smiled faintly as she sat beside her in a matching chair. "Just a little? You're practically twitching, darling. He must be very special."

"I don't twitch."

"Exactly. I'm intrigued." She glanced at Isolde, who was curled up on an equally flamboyant sofa upholstered in a brilliant tomato red Liberty of London fabric. *"We're* intrigued, aren't we?"

Isolde grinned. "Indeed. Give us every little detail of this paragon down to his shoe size."

"Or other sizeable assets of which you no doubt took notice," Rosalind sportively added.

"I did. He's sizeable in every vividly masculine way. Not that it'll do me any good." Sofia sighed. "I'll never see him again."

"I doubt that very much," Isolde said. "Men always pursue you."

"Not him. He was only civil."

Rosalind frowned. "Does this apparently undiscerning man have a name?"

"His name is James Blackwood, a baron it seems. He was at the countess's portrait sitting—clearly at her request. From all appearances, she didn't want to let him out of her sight." Sofie's brows rose. "The scent of sex was pungent in the air. And he's leaving for Scotland at five."

"Should I know him?"

"I was hoping you might since you're from Yorkshire."

After Sofia explained all she knew, Rosalind pursed her lips. "I know the border families, but I'm not familiar with the Highlands beyond the most prominent names. Let me call Fitz. He might know something of this baron."

After several calls, Rosalind had tracked her husband from their home to his club to his architect. Setting down the phone, she turned to Sofia with a smile. "Fitz is on his way here."

"He'll think me juvenile."

"Not in the least. We can be curious, can't we? Don't men forever talk about women in and out of society?"

"I don't."

"Nor do I."

The deep, amused voices came from the doorway.

"Then you're the exception," Rosalind said, turning to her husband who was advancing into the room, followed by Oz carrying his baby daughter in the curve of his arm. "For which I thank you," she added with a smile.

"You'd better. I'm a constant target of ridicule for my indifference to other women. Hello, Sofia. How went your sitting with Bella?"

"How did you know?"

"We ran into Lily on the street. She was delighted to have obstructed Bella's little tête-à-tête with Blackwood. We had to listen at some length to her crowing. You must have been amused."

While Sofia debated how best to reply, amusement having not been her reaction to James Blackwood, Rosalind stepped in. "As a matter of fact, I've been calling around to find you specifically because of Lily's little contretemps with Bella. We'd like some information on James Blackwood."

"We?"

"Me," Sofia said with a rueful grimace. "Don't laugh. He's quite beautiful. I was thinking about painting him."

Oz grinned. "With or without clothes?" Taking a seat beside Isolde, he settled the baby in his lap, untied her bonnet, and tossed it aside.

"I haven't decided yet," Sofie said, smiling back at the young man who prior to his marriage had cut a wide swath through the boudoirs of London. "I'm intrigued, though. He's obviously the countess's lover."

"They're old friends." Fitz drew up a chair beside his wife. "What do you want to know?"

"Why haven't I seen him before? Is he a recluse?"

"No, but he lives abroad. He's attaché to Prince Ernst, as were his forebears. The family estate is in Dalmia—"

"Sofia thought it was in the Highlands," his wife interposed.

"There's land there as well. He holds two baronies. He must have only recently arrived in town."

"I don't know," Sofie said. "But he's leaving this afternoon and taking a train north."

"That's why Lily was so pleased to have interrupted Bella's plans. Their little catfight must have been irritating for Jamie."

"You speak from experience?" his wife playfully queried. The duke had been a much-pursued bachelor until his midthirties.

"Actually he seemed unperturbed," Sofia offered, knowing Fitz would prefer not answering.

Fitz shot her a grateful look. "Come to think of it, I never have seen him rise to anger."

"And yet he's a soldier."

"Perhaps that's why he controls his emotions. I expect he's seen his share of nastiness in that volatile region. Someone is forever assassinating or attempting to assassinate someone."

"Then he doesn't live in Scotland at all?"

Fitz shook his head. "When the clans regained their lost lands, his family stayed in Dalmia. What else do you want to know? Or should I say," he added with a grin, "*why* do you want to know, my dear Sofia? I doubt it's about a painting."

"I'm not entirely sure."

"You're blushing." He was surprised; Sofia was a sophisticated woman who treated men with nonchalance.

"I admit something about him beyond his obvious beauty engaged my interest. He exudes a quiet power and authority, although perhaps that intrinsic air of command comes from his military background. In any case, I found him fascinating." She smiled at Rosalind. "Like one of your romantic heroes." Rosalind had written erotic romances before her marriage to Fitz.

The duchess grinned. "Perhaps you should think about a holiday in Scotland."

Sofia laughed. "I *could* appear on his doorstep and ask for directions."

"If you could find his doorstep," Fitz drolly noted. "His estate in the Highlands is beyond the rail lines and normal roads. The last few miles require a trek on horseback."

"It sounds as though you're going to need a good tracker," Oz playfully observed. "May I offer my services?"

"Certainly not," Sofia said with a moue. "I'm intrigued, not deranged. I *shan't* be stalking the elusive baron."

"Nor would you be successful even if you did," Fitz remarked. "Jamie's an excellent tracker himself, a world-class shot, not to mention Prince Ernst's savior from assassination on several occasions. You wouldn't get within a five-mile radius of his house without being seen."

"A true professional," Sofia murmured, picturing the splendid Jamie as some warrior of old defending his lands—dressed in a kilt or perhaps in the chain mail of the Balkan mountain tribes. "Obviously the man's beyond range," she added with a small sigh, "in every sense of the word."

"Perhaps not," Fitz rebutted. "Consider, he has to pass through London on his way back to Dalmia. Something can be arranged. He's single, by the way; did I mention that?"

"Hardly a requirement for amorous amusements in the ton," Sofia returned with a cynical lift of her brows.

"True. But he prefers his bachelor state. Or so he's told me on more than one occasion."

"As if," Isolde waggishly noted, "any of you men are interested in relinquishing your bachelor state until such a time—"

"As we are." Leaning over, Oz kissed his wife's cheek. "For which good fortune I constantly thank the gods," he added with an affectionate smile. "Now then, I say we put in a good word for you, Sofia. Fitz and I both know Jamie; I became friends with him a few years ago in Trieste."

"Sharing common amusements no doubt," Isolde quipped, gently patting her husband's hand, careful not to wake the baby, who'd fallen asleep on her papa's lap.

Oz grinned. "Since it was long before I met you, I'm allowed to say yes. I was invited to join his yachting party, and we spent a fortnight sailing the Adriatic. He has a home on one of the islands that was built by an ancestor enamored with Diocletian's palace at Split."

Fitz glanced at Oz. "The pool is unusual."

"Very. Another ancestor apparently had a taste for Byzantine excess."

"Gold mosaics," Fitz interposed with a smile for the women. *Along with murals depicting explicit sexual acts.*

"A home on the Adriatic? He sounds even more enticing now," Sofia grumbled. "And I don't have a chance in hell of seeing him again."

"Anything is possible, darling," Oz drawled with the certainty of an extremely wealthy man. "You need but ask."

Sofia laughed. "You would dragoon him into my bed?"

"Since he's met you, I doubt dragooning is required," Oz pleasantly replied. "I was thinking more along the lines of a polite invitation to stop by for drinks on his way back to Dalmia."

"Please, spare me the embarrassment. I mean it," she firmly said to the mischievous gleam in Oz's eyes. "Now, I'm quite finished with this entire conversation."

"In that case, Dex is still in the running," Fitz roguishly offered. "He was hoping for an introduction."

Sofia's eyes widened. "Dexter Champion?" The earl was a champion not only in name but in sport as well: his prowess on the polo field had won England the world title three years running.

Fitz winked. "He's been pining from afar."

"Apparently not for long. Didn't he just leave his wife?"

"It was a bad marriage from the start," Fitz dismissively noted. "His mother had a hand in it."

"And he wasn't capable of saying no?"

"He did for some time, and then Helene claimed she was pregnant and he stopped protesting."

"She wasn't?"

"No, just devious."

"They don't have children, do they?"

"Not his at least. Rumor has it her recent holiday in Italy resulted in the child she brought home and has since referred to as her niece. So, would you like to come to dinner and make his acquaintance?" Fitz glanced at Rosalind. "If that's all right with you, dear?"

"It's up to Sofia. Dex is a lovely man, though." Rosalind turned to her friend. "You should think about meeting him."

Sofia hesitated briefly before saying, "Maybe I will. I'm not likely to be painting Jamie Blackwood in this lifetime."

Oz chuckled. "I haven't heard that euphemism used before. Painting, you say."

She sent him a lowering look. "Very amusing."

"You could paint Dex." Oz grinned. "As runner-up."

"Not likely. Lord Wharton may be handsome, but he has none of the captivating intangibles of Blackwood."

"You *could* paint Jamie from memory," Rosalind suggested.

Sofia's eyelids lowered slightly. "Now why would I want to do that?"

CHAPTER 4

WHILE THE TWO couples and Sofia were discussing Jamie Blackwood, several blocks away, Countess Minton and the subject of that conversation were engaged in a hot, sweaty, vigorous farewell. Bella was demanding in bed, and considering this tryst would be his last for a fortnight, Jamie was willing to oblige her.

He planned on spending a celibate holiday at his hunting lodge. His preference for solitude was well-known by his troopers and the small staff who managed his estate. Scotland had always been his sanctuary—from excess on occasion, more so in the past than now, although, no question, Bella was definitely putting him through his paces. In recent years, Blackwood Glen also served as a hermitage from the corruption of the world and more particularly from Ernst's Machiavellian political machinations that might kill them both in the end.

Revolutionary fervor was spreading like wildfire in the Habsburg Empire, the price of power traded openly. And Ernst was deep in the game. Magyars, Serbs, Croats,

Slovaks, Czechs, Bohemians, Poles, Ruthenes, Germans—
each with unique national interests and diverse loyalties—
were maneuvering for advantage. Some were lunatics, all
were dangerous, and while Prince Ernst thought he was
skilled in this dirty business, his ideas of suave diplomacy
weren't always masterful.

When Franz Joseph had been invited to ascend the
throne forty-six years ago by a consortium of powerful
magnates who'd deposed his uncle, the eighteen-year-old
archduke had recognized how precarious his crown was.
Mindful of the naked tyranny that had brought him to the
throne, he viewed with suspicion any assault, however minor, on his prerogatives. He nurtured the goodwill of the
military as a bulwark against sedition, surrounded himself with sycophants and biddable bureaucrats, and promoted
the fiction that he ruled by the grace of God. The truth was
rather less romantic than the ideal of a God-given authority.
It was the ubiquitous presence of his secret police that kept
his nobles in line and preserved him from the mob.

"Stop, stop, *stop*! You can't *do* that!"

Recalled to reality by the sharp cry, Jamie instantly
curtailed the forceful thrust of his hips, automatically said,
"Forgive me," and only then glanced down to discover the
origin of the complaint. Ah—Bella, apparently she did
have limits. "Sorry, darling," he gently added as he un-
twined her legs from around his neck and withdrew from
her body. "Did I do damage?" Inhaling deeply to bring his
breathing under control, he dropped into a sprawl beside
her, slowly exhaled, and schooled his expression to one of
contrition.

"You might have," Bella pettishly said, turning to him
with a frown. "I'm not a bloody contortionist."

Sometimes you are. "My mistake," he said instead, offering her a conciliatory smile. "Tell me what I must do to
make amends." Selfishly, he meant it. He'd been damned

near to climax once again, his cock was still rock hard, and his train didn't leave for another hour. He was quite willing to pay whatever penance was required. "I'm completely at your disposal, my sweet," he murmured.

"Umm," she said with a little pout, debating whether to tell him he must stay as the price of atonement.

He smiled faintly. "Anything within reason, puss." He glanced at the clock. "You have forty minutes to order me about."

She softly exhaled, recognizing her momentary lapse, recognizing as well why Jamie had discerned her thoughts. Women always wanted him to stay. "Very well, kiss me," she said with the merest touch of imperiousness to soothe her ego. "Nicely."

"Where?"

His grin was sweetly boyish, damn him; she couldn't help but smile in return. "Someplace I'll like, you incorrigible rogue."

Coming up on one elbow, he leaned over and kissed her softly on her pouty mouth. "How's that?"

She gave a little shrug. "Lovely, if we were thirteen."

"Ah—you have something more carnal in mind." His gaze was angelic as a choirboy's. "Here for instance?" He slid his middle finger delicately up her sleek cleft. "Would you like a kiss here?"

It took her a moment to answer, for he'd gently invaded her vagina, slipping two slender fingers deep inside her slick passage, touching a particularly sensitive spot with exquisite delicacy. When she found the breath to speak, she whispered, "Do you really have to go?" Every frenzied sexual receptor, every overindulged nerve ending, every pulsating bit of flesh was loathe to relinquish his virtuoso talents.

"Not just yet," he whispered back, and moments later when she was begging for more, for him, for his glorious cock inside her, he accommodated her frantic desire in a thoroughly conventional fashion, choosing the missionary position as most respectful of her comfort.

An orgasm was an orgasm after all. Several of which he afforded her in rapid succession, himself as well with less frequency, until time and his train schedule intervened.

With a light kiss, he slipped from the bed and quickly dressed under her sulky regard. Apologizing profusely, a custom of long standing on taking his leave, he moved toward the door, and in answer to her sullen query, promised to visit again soon. "Provided the empire doesn't explode or some demented revolutionary doesn't decide I'm the cause of his oppression. In which case, send flowers to my funeral."

Then he blew her a kiss, opened the door, and escaped. He immediately broke into a run, traversing the long upstairs corridor in seconds. Reaching the stairs, he descended them in flying leaps and exited Minton House as though the demons of hell were on his heels. Dashing into the street, he brought traffic to a halt at some risk to his life and found a hackney cab to take him to Euston Station. "Get me there by five and I'll give you fifty quid," he called out and leaped inside.

After several near-death experiences, the cab reached the station, and Jamie jumped out before the vehicle came to a stop. Tossing the folded banknote into the driver's outstretched hand, Jamie sprinted through the crowded station to the platform from which the London and North Western Railway departed. Gasping for air, he saw the caboose nearing the end of the platform and, racing headlong after it, managed to leap aboard. A fellow passenger out enjoying his cigar had kindly held open the back gate.

"Many thanks," Jamie gasped, collapsing against the caboose wall.

"Dinna think ye were up to that leap," the elderly Scotsman said blandly. "A right daredevil ye are."

"My gillie's—coming down . . . from the hills—to . . . meet me."

"At Inverness?" Inverness was the gateway to the hills.

Dragging air into his lungs, Jamie nodded.

"Ye dinna live up that way, do ye?" He tapped his ear. "A bit o' accent I ken."

"I visit in the summer." Jamie's breathing was partially restored. "May I buy you a drink?"

The elderly man smiled. "Ye're a closemouthed scamp. Ye can share a drink with me"—he held up his cigar—"once I've smoked me fill."

"My pleasure, sir. I'll see you inside." With a bow, Jamie opened the caboose door and made for the club car. The moment he entered the crowded lounge, he was hailed. "Blackwood, over here!" Lord Rothsay waved from the bar.

Threading his way through the throng to the bar, Jamie smiled and took the whiskey Rothsay held out to him.

"You smell of cunt," the earl said with a smirk. "And you're still in last night's evening rig. She must have been good."

"Afternoon, Dougal. Nice day. Traveling home to the wife and family?" The men knew each other from the summer war games they'd both competed in as youths. Rothsay was a Sandhurst fellow.

The earl grunted. "Have to occasionally." He reached out and plucked a golden hair from Jamie's shoulder. "Anyone I know?"

"I'm sure you do." Jamie raised his glass. "Cheers." He drained the liquor, set the glass down, and signaled for another.

"You're not going to tell me, are you?"

"No."

"Bastard."

"That's my job." Jamie turned to smile at the bartender, who held out another glass of whiskey.

"Speaking of bastards, how is that aging libertine Ernst doing?"

"Same as ever. Cheers." Jamie tossed off the whiskey.

"I heard rumors he's making himself amenable to Banffy in Hungary and the powers that be in Germany."

Jamie nodded at the bartender and pointed to his empty glass before answering. "Ernst thinks he's another Bismarck," he said. "I keep reminding him that even Bismarck eventually overplayed his hand. Leave the bottle." He handed the young barman a large banknote and picked up his refilled glass.

Rothsay's brows rose. "Keep that up and you'll have to be carried off at Inverness."

Jamie grinned. "Care to wager?"

"Five hundred says you won't last."

"You're on."

"With most men I'd say they were drinking away some female entanglement, but with you I know better. Did you discover your conscience?" the earl asked with a chuckle.

"Not unless you discovered yours." Rothsay preferred opera tarts, cancan girls, and his pretty maidservants more than his wife, not exactly uncommon in the fashionable world. Dougal and his wife had agreed to disagree in the civilized way of the upper classes and lived on friendly terms. Gossip had it Lady Rothsay found solace with a parade of young, handsome grooms, which might account for the increasing size of Rothsay's family.

"Don't have a conscience," Dougal complacently replied. "Take after my father, who couldn't remember our names or that of my mother come to think of it. We Rothsay men are a ramshackle lot all bound for hell, but in the meantime," he said in the frank, easy way he had, "I'm indulging in my pleasures—the lovely ladies foremost—and the devil be damned."

Jamie raised his glass. "A fair exchange. I'll drink to that."

"Amen and God bless all the willing jezebels," Dougal returned with a lecherous wink.

In the end, Rothsay lost his five hundred, although Jamie was definitely feeling no pain when he quit the train at Inverness.

Davey Ross was waiting on the platform, his cap in hand, a broad smile on his face. "Mornin', sair. You look mighty happy."

"Damn right. I'm escaping civilization—and I use the word loosely."

"You've come to the right place, sair. The ends o' the earth we are. This way, sair," he said, leading him toward the stables. "Yer flask is in yer saddlebags and a change of clothes if ye like." This wasn't the first time Jamie had come north from some woman's bed. "Our sour mash turned out damned near perfect this season if I do say so meself."

"Excellent. Perfect whiskey, comfortable clothes, and your fine company. Surely the gods are in the heavens."

"Don't know aboot that, sair. But the coverts and the salmon are prime this year. Along with that devil of a horse you like. He knew ye were acomin' afor we did. He's been right frisky of late." He lifted his hand in the direction of the large black snorting and pawing the ground. "As ye can see."

"Hello, Athol laddie," Jamie softly said as he came up to him and gently stroked the stallion's powerful neck. He briefly rested his forehead against the soft coat and inhaled before raising his head and smiling widely. "Ah—the smell of heather. Now I know I'm home. Hey, hey," he said as Athol nuzzled him. "You think I brought you something?" Pushing the horse's nose away, he slipped his hand in his pocket, withdrew some sugar lumps he'd obtained from the bartender on the train, and held them out on his open palm.

"That there brute squealed like he caught the scent of a filly in heat when I saddled up my mount. He weren't about to be left behind."

Jamie had raised Athol from a colt. "We're friends," Jamie murmured, "aren't we, laddie?"

As if he understood, Athol lifted his head and softly snorted.

"There, you see?" Rubbing the stallion's ear, he grinned at Davey. When the thoroughbred was finished eating, Jamie wiped his palm on his pants, unbuckled his saddlebag, and extracted his worn flask. Drinking a long draught, he handed it to Davey, undressed in the stable yard, and soon was wearing his Highland uniform: buckskin pants, riding boots, a homespun shirt, and a jacket made from his family's hunting plaid. "There now. I feel whole again," he said with a smile, taking back his flask and shoving it in his pocket.

"Ye'll feel even better, sair, once you get a good night's sleep. Ye're a wee peeked, sair, from a tad too much o' civilization—eh?"

"A tad too much of everything, Davey," Jamie said, swinging smoothly into the saddle and nudging his mount into a turn. "I'm looking forward to a good long rustication."

The two men rode slowly through town. Once into the open country, Jamie set Athol into a canter, a pace their mounts could sustain for the hours necessary to reach the hunting lodge. Travelers didn't as a rule brave the high mountain trails, but then none of them had Davey Ross for a guide, nor bloodstock that could navigate the treacherous paths with sure-footed competence. Although the owner of Blackwood Glen could have found his way to his hunting lodge blindfolded and drunk as a lord.

The latter very much the case that morning.

As THE SUN rose high in the sky over the spring green hills of the Highlands and the two riders had finally entered Blackwood land, events were unfolding halfway around the world that would seriously impact Prince Ernst.

By extension, Jamie. And more extraordinarily, Sofia East-leigh.

Earlier that day, Rupert, Ernst's heir, along with a small party from Vienna, had been feted with all the pomp and circumstance of the Nizam of Mysore's opulent court. The Europeans had been splendidly entertained with sport commensurate to their rank and particular to India—a tiger shoot.

Before dawn, Rupert and his companions had been transported in gilded howdahs atop richly caparisoned elephants through a jungle teeming with blooms and redolent with sweet scent, finally coming to a halt in a clearing cut from the lush undergrowth. A limpid pool lay beyond a screen of bamboo. It was the water source for the animals in the surrounding area, and just prior to the rainy season, with water scarce, a great variety of game came to drink.

Skillful organization was required for a tiger hunt, along with accomplished shikaris (hunters) who knew the country and the animals' habitat and temperament. Most crucial was the necessity of safeguarding the nizam and his guests. Nothing was more dangerous than a snarling tiger breaking from cover at a full gallop. The man-eating beasts were known to attack elephants, even charge the howdahs in a flying leap, and they could carry off a man at lightning speed. A mother with cubs was particularly fierce, liable to take the offensive without provocation. The Europeans had been warned.

At the sound of a single gunshot signaling the beginning of the drive, a sudden tension filled the air. And a moment later, blaring horns and banging drums indicated that the nizam's vassals were on the march, forcing the beasts of the jungle to flee before them.

As Prince Rupert and his colleagues waited under the blazing sun, a native shikari stood behind each howdah, ready to hand over the loaded guns. The elephants had been prodded by their mahouts into a line facing the oncoming drive. Regardless of the oppressive heat, the advancing drumbeats prompted a cold sweat on tyro brows.

After what seemed an eternity to the novices from Europe, flocks of frightened birds abruptly burst from the jungle in a frenzied cloud, the shrill cries of monkeys terrorized by the tigers underfoot rose into the air, and the hunters were warned of the imminent approach of game.

The shikaris quickly passed over the guns, and short moments later eight roaring tigers broke from the jungle and scattered in every direction. The well-trained elephants stood firm, a dozen guns opened fire in a wild explosion, and the indiscriminate slaughter commenced.

The bag that day was thirteen tigers, six leopards, four cheetahs, and several score lesser game. Afterward, pictures were taken by the nizam's court photographer; the smug foreigners, their guns in hand, lined up behind the splendid array of exotic animals spread at their feet.

As the nizam intended, his tiger shoot afforded peerless pleasure to his guests. Regardless that British rule was universally hated in India, he was obliged to offer his hospitality to them and their European compatriots for the sake of the dominions his family had ruled for a millennium.

Better artifice than prison.

And he had many sons to advance.

The return to the palace was a raucous affair as the young aristocrats shared and compared shooting experiences, the exhilaration of danger met and conquered adding a piquant satisfaction to the lively discourse. Servants riding alongside the elephants served cool wine to the guests, the drink quaffed down like water in the blazing heat.

After the party alighted at the palace and everyone had rested and bathed, a sumptuous dinner was served in the nizam's cool, perfumed garden lit with hundreds of lanterns strung from the trees. Endless courses and wines, fruits and delicacies were served while poets recited *ghazals*—the Urdu or Persian love lyrics intrinsic to an evening's entertainment.

In due course, musicians arrived, accompanied by beautiful, shapely dancers who launched into an enchanting performance of indigenous dances. The young men from Vienna were captivated by the sensuous, overtly erotic choreography and particularly enticed by the ladies' diaphanous garments that left nothing to the imagination.

Wine continued to flow copiously, a servant always at the ready to refill the guests' cups; golden hookahs were lit and passed around, affording bliss of another kind. Before long, couples began to wander off to indulge their passions.

An extremely voluptuous natch girl had attracted Rupert's notice, her curvaceous body a potent lure to the eye, her explicit sexuality appealing to more carnal sensibilities. She was ravishing and available, and he'd never denied himself the pleasures of the flesh. What handsome young man of wealth had? Not that the scantily clad, bejeweled dancer wasn't an extraordinary treasure; she put his former lovers to shame, her scent alone a tantalizing aphrodisiac. It was inevitable that when she said in charmingly accented English, "Show me, how do you say, your virile member," Rupert laughed and replied in unaccented English, "It would be my pleasure."

Once they were ensconced in his commodious bed and had gratified their carnal appetites for an enchanting period of time, Rupert decided she was quite remarkable—a tantalizing vixen with an incredible gift for sustaining sensation. He would remember this night with fondness. Then she gently nibbled on his cock, curtailing his musing, his erection quickly rose once again, and he softly groaned as every delicate nibble and piquant lick brought his blood to boiling point. But when he climaxed that time, a strange lethargy overcame him—not unpleasant . . . comforting in a way, like falling asleep in a bed of jasmine. Ah—that was her scent, he thought as he drifted off. Jasmine . . .

The instant Rupert's breathing slowed into that of deep sleep, two men who'd been watching the couple from behind a half-closed door quietly entered the room. One remained at the door, the other moved soft footed toward the bed. With a curt nod he dismissed the woman lying beside Rupert. The dark-haired beauty sat up, pushed aside the sheer silk curtains enclosing the bed, rose to her feet, gathered up her jewelry, and nude and splendid, walked from the room without a backward glance.

Rupert didn't stir, the slow-acting sleeping potion she'd slipped into his wine having taken effect.

Von Welden's agent glanced over his shoulder. His accomplice dipped his head, signaling that they were alone. The trim, middle-aged man who traveled with the party as a factotum for Prince Reiger turned back to the fair-haired youth resting peacefully on his back. Pulling a coil of silk cord from his pocket, he slipped the garrote around Rupert's neck and expertly strangled the heir to the duchy of Dalmia.

It was not a random act.

Rupert had been a marked man since he departed Vienna.

While Rupert had no personal enemies, a number of impersonal circumstances had led to his death. An ancient covenant certified that the duchy of Dalmia would revert to the Habsburg crown should the Battenberg line expire. Prince Ernst *could* remarry and sire a child, but he was in his fifties, which suggested that even should a child result, that child would likely be a minor on Ernst's death. The obligatory regency would ensue, which was even more likely to prove unsuccessful if history in that unstable region followed convention.

However, the need to hasten the end of the duchy of Dalmia was prompted by more than ancient covenants.

Quite apart from Ernst's imprudent meddling in Austrian politics, and more pertinent, was the fact that gold had been clandestinely discovered in the Dinaric Alps that formed the eastern border of Dalmia.

As minister of police and virtual dictator of Vienna, Count Von Welden had naturally been privy to the report. Venal to the core and in need of sizeable funds to finance the Versailles-like estate he was building in Hungary, he'd calculated that the transfer of Ernst's lands sooner rather than later would better serve his purposes.

Von Welden was prepared to make Prince Ernst an offer he couldn't refuse, and he rather thought the prince would accept. Ernst was a selfish man, and left without an heir, he'd likely see the wisdom in the old saw about a bird in the hand. Or so the minister of police confidently surmised.

When the coded telegram from India was placed in Von Welden's hand, he read it and subsequently allowed himself a moment of self-congratulation. Then he called in his secretary and dictated a message to be delivered to Prince Ernst.

Von Welden's spy network was pervasive. Very little apart from the occasional whispered comment was free of censorship or the watchful eye of the secret police.

The minister knew exactly where and with whom Prince Ernst was taking his pleasure.

CHAPTER 5

RUPERT'S BODY HAD been packed in ice and shipped home on a swift steamer via the Suez Canal. When the container was opened wharfside in Dalmia and Prince Ernst saw the ligature marks around his son's neck, he immediately began to compile a list of his enemies. He wasn't naive enough to believe that Rupert had been killed by a native in some capricious act of violence. Especially when the cable had come from Prince Reiger, who was one of the most reactionary of the government's advisors and no friend of his.

Directly after the funeral, Ernst took himself up to Vienna in search of answers. The conspiracy to murder Rupert would have originated in the capital.

Stepping down from his carriage in the courtyard of the palace that had been in the Battenberg family for centuries, he was overcome by a rare melancholy. He was not by nature an emotional man, but with Rupert's grievous death, he faced a stark reality. Barring a precipitous marriage resulting in an heir, he was the last Battenberg. No brothers or uncles, sisters or aunts, no cousins survived.

Merde. The last thing he wished to do was remarry, he thought, walking across the ancient cobbles toward the massive bronze entrance doors.

His marriage hadn't been congenial.

Marie had chosen to live apart from him, and her death, while not a surprise, had, in truth, been a relief. The invalid role she'd adopted so as to avoid not only his company but also Rupert's had killed her in the end—or perhaps it was the incompetence of her *cher ami*, Doctor Meynert, who prescribed opium for any or no ailment.

As the huge double doors opened before him, the suits of armor standing row upon row in the entrance hall met his gaze, as did the scores of swords and shields decorating the walls, memorials all to his long-ago ancestors. And other things never changed as well, he thought as his indestructible butler approached. "Good afternoon, Heinrich."

The tall, regal butler bowed. "Good afternoon, Excellency. May I offer you the very deepest condolences from myself and the staff."

"Thank you, Heinrich. These are troubled times—no question." Ernst would never display his feelings before servants. "Someone should go through Prince Rupert's things and distribute whatever would be appropriate to charity. I'll leave it up to you."

"I'll have Renner make an accounting, sir." The majordomo opened his mouth, then shut it.

"Speak up, Heinrich. I needn't be coddled."

"A small quandary, Excellency. I was uncertain whether to give this to you." Taking an envelope from a console table, the butler held it out. "It was delivered by a vulgar little man with instructions to see that you receive it promptly. A most unsuitable person," he noted with a sniff, "to be giving orders."

Ernst smiled faintly; Heinrich was a stickler for rank. "Unsuitable, you say? Let's see." Taking the envelope, he tore it open, pulled out the heavy monogrammed card, and quickly perused an invitation from Von Welden for drinks. He looked up. "When did this arrive?"

The grey-haired butler raised his brows an infinitesimal distance. "Ten minutes ago, Excellency."

Bastard. He's having me followed.

"Will there be a reply, Excellency?"

Heinrich was clearly hoping he'd say no. But prudence required a response. "Send my acceptance tomorrow. Late tomorrow." He could at least return Von Welden's insolence with equal bad grace.

"Very good, Excellency. Will you be dining in tonight?"

Ernst shook his head. The principessa with whom he'd been holidaying had followed him to Vienna. "Dispose of this." Handing over the note, he moved toward the ornate staircase. He supposed he could have been rude to Antonella and rejected her company. Not that he was entirely sure she would have complied. The principessa was charmingly willful, *a woman of parts*, the English would say. Wealthy enough to do as she pleased and what she pleased.

Which generally—almost always, he amended—managed to please him, too.

TWO DAYS LATER when the prince set out for his visit with the minister of police, he took the precaution of arming himself with a small silver pistol. Men were known to disappear into the bowels of the prefecture building that served as headquarters for the secret police—even men of substance. He'd shoot Von Welden if it came to that, he decided with the casual disregard for the law habitual to men of wealth and power.

Karl Otho, the majordomo of the exclusive men's club where Ernst served on the board, greeted the prince warmly and offered his sincere sympathy for his loss. "We will all miss the young prince, Your Excellency. He was a true gentleman."

"Yes, he was. Thank you very much, Otho." He handed his hat and gloves to a flunkey. "I have an appointment with Von Welden. Has he arrived?"

"Yes, Excellency. He's in the Europa Room."

Was Von Welden making some symbolic point in selecting that particular venue? Ernst wondered. Were they engaged in some mysterious battle of which he was unaware?

The majordomo chatted with the customary informality that endeared him to many of the club members while he personally escorted the prince to the private room. "If you should need anything, Excellency," he offered as they reached the door, "I'll have a man outside."

Ernst smiled faintly. "Armed I hope." Everyone knew Von Welden's reputation for malevolence.

The plump little man met his gaze. "Of course, sir."

"In that case," Ernst said with a flicker of his brows, "two of us will be armed."

"Very prudent, Excellency." He signaled forward the man who had followed them.

"I'm quite ready," Ernst quietly said.

The majordomo opened the door and announced Prince Ernst with all his many titles—a not so subtle discourtesy to Von Welden, whose title was new and inferior.

Ernst entered the room, and the door shut softly behind him.

Von Welden had come to his feet, and with a bow and a military click of his heels he punctiliously observed the courtesies. "How good of you to come, Your Excellency," the count said as if he hadn't waited two days.

"How kind of you to invite me," Ernst replied with equal mendacity, glancing at the large painting of the dramatic Battle of Vienna that dominated the room. The Ottoman advance into Europe had been stopped at the gates of Vienna in 1683.

"I apologize for imposing on you at this painful time. Please, come sit." The minister waved Ernst to a chair, then nodded to a footman.

The men sat and waited in silence while the liveried servant poured two cognacs and placed them on a table between their chairs. After placing the decanter and a silver tray of cigars on the table, he glanced at Von Welden.

"Leave us," Von Welden ordered.

Once they were alone, the count leaned forward and picked up the glasses. Handing one to Ernst, he glanced at the black armband circling the prince's upper arm and softly sighed. "My dear Ernst. Such a crushing blow. How are you coping?"

"Well enough."

"A tragedy," the minister murmured, leaning back in his chair. "If there's anything I can do to help."

Choke on your drink. "No, nothing, thank you."

"India's a barbaric country. Rabble everywhere, no law to speak of, the British army notwithstanding. But they can't police every native enclave. Were you given any indication of the identity of the vile perpetrator?"

"The colonial administrator is continuing the investigation, I'm told."

"Good, good—excellent. The British can be dogged in pursuit. They recently captured the villain who attacked Wales five years ago—or was it six? The brute was tracked down through émigré circles. Although if you ask me, England's leniency toward emigrants is not only foolish but dangerous," he said with a sneer. "Anarchists, the lot of them."

"You're not referring to Napoleon III or Empress Eugénie?" After France's defeat by Germany, both had fled to England; the empress had a home there still.

Von Welden shot him a narrowed look over the rim of

his glass. "Theoretically, no, although Eugénie interfered more than necessary in her husband's affairs."

"Ruling Europe has always been a family business," Ernst noted. "Everyone's related; everyone feels obliged to participate in some fashion."

"Then again, fashions change, Your *Excellency*," Von Welden said with mocking emphasis. "Modern times require modern means. Innovative technology, fresh economic ideas, banking capital from new and diverse sources—we're progressing toward a social structure free from the outmoded principles of noblesse oblige."

The prince lifted his pale brows. "I didn't realize you had such liberal convictions."

"Surely you jest." Whether the prince's comment was sarcasm or levity, neither pleased Von Welden.

"I stand corrected." Smiling faintly, Ernst raised his glass and drank.

The silence lengthened.

"How did we get on such a dull subject?" Von Welden interjected with bluff good humor. "Technology and economics, bah! Try one of my cigars." He leaned over and nudged the tray closer to Ernst. "They're made for me in Havana," he smugly said, calling attention to his affluence and good taste.

It took Ernst a fraction of a second to respond to the arriviste thug with his new title and stolen wealth who was flaunting his status like some ill-bred parvenu. The Battenberg princely title had been bestowed a thousand years ago, the family's wealth amassed long before that. "I'd be delighted," Ernst said with impeccable courtesy to a man he despised.

While Ernst had a propensity for vice and pleasure, for fine tailors and wines, for a sybaritic life of luxury, he was at base a man of rigid beliefs. He believed in nobility, pedigree, and family wealth. He believed in the power of the sword. He believed there was no substitute for victory.

As the men drank, smoked, and urbanely chatted about current affairs, the prince waited to be apprised of the reason for his invitation. This was no friendly or consoling visit, both adjectives meaningless to a man of Von Welden's ilk.

When at last the minister of police expressed his desire to purchase Ernst's ancestral lands in Dalmia, Ernst responded with a degree of calm that was testament to his father's conviction that dignity was a requirement of their rank. "You surprise me," he said. "I was of the opinion your interests were in Hungary."

The minister smiled. "I've always loved the sea."

An outrageous lie. "Naturally, I'll need time to consider your generous offer," Ernst coolly replied, betraying nothing of his fury at the man's brazen greed. While Ernst had never been an affectionate father, he was no less a father than any other aristocrat.

More to the point, Rupert had been his only son.

"I understand," Von Welden returned. "If I wasn't about to leave for Hungary on a mission for the emperor, I would have been less precipitous in my approach. But I'll be away for some weeks."

"The duchy has been in the Battenberg family since medieval times. A decision will be difficult," Ernst noted. "Why don't we talk again on your return?"

"Of course, all in good time." Von Welden's smile was innocent of warmth, but then no one would accuse him of benevolence. "Let me refill your glass. This cognac is from my private reserve."

Ernst had spent a lifetime in a society where passive cruelty and overt vice made a cynic of everyone. He was well versed in the game. "It's excellent cognac," he said, smiling at the man he suspected had ordered his son murdered. "I'll send over a bottle of my Tokaji for your enjoyment."

Poisoned no doubt. "How kind. Your vineyards are celebrated."

The men conversed over fresh drinks, both capable of the necessary artifice for the occasion. The emperor's penchant for hunting afforded them several minutes of discussion; Empress Elisabeth's latest journey to England briefly engaged their interest. They agreed that her frequent absences from court gave her as much joy as they did the Austrian court that loathed her. In the midst of an analysis of German military preparations—which were making much of Europe uneasy at the moment—Ernst experienced a sudden blinding epiphany. Had he actually believed in religion, he would have characterized it as a miracle—like Paul's vision on the road to Damascus.

Suppressing his rush of elation, Ernst instead posed a question concerning the readiness of the cavalry division Von Welden had commanded prior to his current position. Von Welden, while no longer the dashing figure of his youth, still wore a cavalry mustache and took a keen interest in his hussars.

The question elicited an immediate scowl from the minister. "As a matter of fact, I finally had it out with Wittelschlag last week, damn his slovenly procrastination. He has orders to purchase twenty thousand mounts in Hungary. Not enough, of course," the count grumbled. "But a start. The bureaucrats never understand the necessity of military procurement. They only reckon florins like boorish shopkeepers."

"What of the levies from Bohemia?" Ernst asked, indifferent to the answer, merely playing a part until he could leave. "Will they perform?"

"Perhaps with a gun to their head they will." Von Welden smiled. "I'm not sure the reserves from your region are any more compliant."

Ernst shrugged. "Such are the risks of broadening education. It often gives rise to revolutionary principles."

"Never fear," the count firmly declared. "We shall dispatch revolution wherever it rears its ugly head."

"Only with good discipline in the army." The custom of quartering regiments far from their home regions was becoming a problem with nationalistic sentiments on the rise.

And so it went—a totally useless conversation now that Von Welden had played his hand. But Ernst maintained his role even as he mentally made plans to depart for England posthaste. He was careful not to appear hurried, conversing with aplomb, politely accepting another drink, allowing Von Welden to determine the moment to end their meeting.

When the men finally parted, Ernst embraced the minister with a display of cordiality that would have earned praise from the most accomplished thespian.

It was only after he'd exited the club and was standing on the sun-dappled pavement outside that he quietly swore revenge. By all that was holy or unholy—it mattered little to him. The Battenbergs had not survived twelve centuries by turning the other cheek.

Two hours later, he was on the night train to Paris, more heavily guarded than usual.

From there to the coast and then to England.

He would reach London by afternoon tomorrow.

CHAPTER 6

THE FOLLOWING DAY, under the last rays of the midnight sun, Jamie was half dozing on the hill behind his house, a flask at his side, doing much as he had for most of his holiday. Very little.

The simple rhythms of his country estate had restored and demilitarized him, giving him the respite he needed from the outside world. Far removed from any sense of urgency, he'd fished the salmon streams, rode the estate when the mood struck him, helped plant ten acres of pine seedlings, purchased two new breeds of sheep that would produce high-quality wool, and frequently availed himself of his fine estate whiskey.

Having temporarily relinquished the constant vigilance required of him on the Continent, where he instinctively took note of an unusual sound, the expression on someone's face in a crowd, a workman or servant where they shouldn't be, he'd slept like a baby. Not once had he suddenly come awake and found himself drenched in sweat with his heart pounding.

He was rested.

Recharged.

In fact, he was so much in charity with the world that he briefly considered the old maxim about beating swords into plowshares a possibility. Ever practical, however, saner judgment quickly prevailed, and dismissing illusion, he raised his flask to his mouth, drank deeply, and emptied his mind of useless imagery.

"Jamie! Jamie!"

Coming up on his elbows at the sound of his name, Jamie glanced downward and frowned. One of his gillies was clambering up the steep hill waving what appeared to be a letter. Sitting up fully, he waited with an outward calm that belied his quickening pulse. What the hell was so important at this time of night?

"It be a cable, sair," the red-faced man panted on reaching him.

"I'll trade you." Jamie handed him his flask, took the cable, glanced at the Paris postmark, and tore it open. He read it swiftly, swore, then muttered, "Poor boy," and came to his feet.

"Bad news, sair?"

"Yes. Prince Rupert is dead." He didn't question why Ernst hadn't informed him before. He was his ADC, not a boon companion. The telegram merely read, *Rupert buried last week. Meet me in London.* "Have Davey saddle up our mounts," Jamie ordered, then he ran and slipped and slid down the hill, intent on reaching Inverness in time for the early train.

THE FOLLOWING MORNING, after a breakneck race over the hills, while Jamie was boarding the train, Prince Ernst was embarking from the port of Calais on a chartered yacht. He had a full complement of his Scots guard with him, the troopers like him, in mufti, posing as his entourage.

Meanwhile, in London, after supervising the hanging of two of her new paintings in the gallery of Bruton Street Books, Sofia was having a light breakfast with Rosalind and politely refusing the duchess's persistent urging that she meet Dex Champion at dinner. She had to be in the mood and she wasn't.

"Don't keep saying you're busy," Rosalind objected, looking up from pouring them another cup of tea. "You don't work at night."

"Sometimes I do." Sofia plucked another cream pastry from an assortment on a tiered plate and licked the topping.

"Dex constantly asks about you. If you continue this silliness, I wouldn't be surprised if he comes knocking on your door."

"Tell him not to." *Hmm . . . apricot jam under the cream filling.*

"You tell him. It's only a dinner, not a marriage proposal."

"Which would be difficult since he's married," Sofia said through a mouthful of pastry.

"Not for long. He's started divorce proceedings."

Sofia swallowed. "Good," she crisply said. "Then he'll have droves of women after him and he can forget about me."

"There's no point in saying you're playing hard to get because you generally do, but seriously, I think you'd like him. He's very sweet."

"I don't like sweet men."

Rosalind sighed. "I only meant he's not a complete rake."

"There are times when rakes appeal."

"Hush, you troublesome child! I'm done arguing. Come to dinner tomorrow. You know everyone, and if you don't come, I won't speak to you for a month. Maybe two."

A worthless threat; they'd been friends too long. "Dex will be there, I presume," Sofia muttered, looking very much the petulant child of which she'd been accused.

"Fitz invited him, not I. Something about making plans for Cowes. Wear your lovely Worth gown that you bought the last time you were in Paris. The one with those pretty little rosebuds on the décolletage," Rosalind coaxed, shifting from threats to cajolery, hoping to better persuade her reluctant companion.

Sofia lifted one brow. "Now you're telling me what to wear?"

"Yes, as a matter of fact," Rosalind said with a grin. "I know what's best. The low décolletage will distract from your acid tongue."

"And my sharp claws."

"Exactly." Rosalind waved a half-eaten scone in Sofia's direction. "I want you to beguile and bamboozle like any other self-respecting female."

Sofia laughed. "I still should say no."

"Oz wagered me you wouldn't come."

"He did, did he? How much?"

"You know Oz. I'm not as extravagant. We settled on three hundred."

Sofia leaned back in her chair and smiled. "Surely we can't let a man win now, can we?"

"That's what I was thinking."

"Manipulative schemer."

"I believe the phrase is *I'm doing it for your own good*," Rosalind sportively countered. "Now remember, the Worth gown." Then she quickly changed the subject, having successfully accomplished her mission. It wasn't that she was seriously matchmaking. Sofia was beyond such foolishness. Rather, Rosalind felt that Dex would offer her dearest friend the kind of informal relationship she preferred. Sexual, unpredictable, spirited. Also, anyone who had put up with Helene for so many years was either indifferent to his wife or eligible for sainthood. Neither exactly the style of man Sofia fancied, but Dex was also incredibly handsome, charming, and most important, according to Fitz, a favorite with the ladies who were partial to sexual amusements.

AFTER ARRIVING IN London, Jamie took a cab directly from the station to Ernst's home in Belgravia, and jumping down from the carriage, crossed the pavement and greeted the two guards at the front door. The men were in uniform and heavily armed. "Ernst must be expecting trouble. How many of you came to London?"

"Twenty," his cousin Douglas replied.

"Stationed?"

"Front door and back, at the garden gate, two at the stables. The others are resting between watches."

"How is he?"

"The same." Another cousin shrugged. "You wouldn't know anything had happened—no surprise there. You arrived just in time. He's about to go out."

"We'll talk later." Jamie lifted the knocker, let it fall, and shoved the door open.

"Ah, there you are." The prince was in the entrance hall putting on his gloves. "You made excellent time." Stripping off his gloves, he handed them to a servant and shrugged out of his coat. As a flunkey took his coat, he waved Jamie forward. "We'll go into my study."

Moments later, Jamie closed the study door behind him. "My condolences, sir."

"Thank you," Ernst replied with his usual composure, his grey gaze blank, his tall, lean form motionless, his pale hair vivid in the dimly lit room.

"I would have liked to have come to the funeral." With nearly ten years separating them in age, Rupert had been Jamie's shadow growing up.

"There was no need. The boy was gone. Whiskey?" Abruptly turning away, Ernst moved toward the liquor table.

Picking up a decanter and glasses, he waved Jamie to two leather club chairs by the window and poured them drinks. Handing Jamie his, he switched on a table lamp and took his seat. "I didn't mean to be curt. I appreciate your sympathy. But Rupert was murdered. Out of pure greed," he bitterly added.

Jamie's shock was plain. "Are you sure? He didn't have an enemy in the world."

"He was garroted; the marks were plain."

"Jesus," Jamie whispered, trying to make sense of such gross violence. "Could it have been some heinous mistake?"

"No. Von Welden wants Dalmia," Ernst replied without a trace of emotion, his grief having given way to an icy vengeance.

"Did he say why?" Von Welden was not someone one wanted for an enemy.

"He said he liked the sea," Ernst said drily. "An obvious lie. But there's no question that he offered to buy the duchy."

"Fucking vulture. He couldn't even wait until your mourning was over?" Jamie pursed his lips in a grim line. "You're not selling, are you?"

"What do you think?" the prince acidly replied.

"I think you want an eye for an eye. We both do."

"I want him to suffer. Understood?"

"I'll find the Albanian to flay him alive." Jamie's voice was cold as ice. "Hajdu's the best. I'll see if I can track him down. If he's in hiding somewhere, I'll do it myself."

"I'll leave the details up to you."

It was approval and consent. "The planning will require some time. Our esteemed minister of police is guarded like a harem houri," Jamie noted. "Although, come to think of it," he added, "Von Welden's latest inamorata might be useful. Katia hates him. Von Welden exiled her rebel brother to that godforsaken prison monastery at Heiligenkreuz. She'll cooperate if we guarantee her and her brother's safety. I'll talk to her."

"Not just yet. More pressing matters brought me to London."

Jamie hoped like hell it wasn't some woman, although with Ernst's track record, he wouldn't be surprised. On the other hand, he was a bodyguard, not a priest. "What sort of matters?"

"I have to find someone."

"Male or female? Friendly or dangerous?"

"Female, and I'm hoping friendly," Ernst said with a smile.

Oh Christ, it is a woman.

Unaware of Jamie's misgivings, Ernst raised his glass as though to underscore the significance of his remark. "Do you believe in miracles?"

"No, and you don't either."

"You're right. I didn't." The prince leaned forward, a rare earnestness in his gaze. "But something unusual happened to me during my meeting with Von Welden. An idea came to me out of the blue—a vision, revelation, call it what you will. I may be able to secure the future of the duchy."

"An heir, you mean." The covenant was well-known to the Blackwood family. "Need I remind you that legitimacy is required?" Ernst was a libertine of wide and democratic scope.

"No, you needn't," Ernst replied with another startling smile.

Jamie's brows rose.

"My miracle concerns the magic of first love."

"Are you drunk?" Ernst and love were incompatible.

The prince smiled again, which was several more smiles than Jamie had seen in years.

"You don't think I could love?"

"Jesus," Jamie muttered. "What do you want me to say?"

"Have you ever been in love?"

"Hell no."

"Well, I was once." The prince looked away for a moment, overcome by nostalgia. "We spent a summer together in the Lake Country," Ernst went on in a conversational tone, having regained his composure. "It was sheer paradise. None were happier; we made glorious plans for the future: marriage, children, eternal bliss. Unfortunately, my family didn't agree. Amelia was unacceptable, British, a commoner; my parents were inflexible, Mother in particular—"

"And you married her anyway."

The prince met Jamie's quizzing gaze and nodded.

"Then you later divorced?"

"No." Ernst shrugged. "Amelia may have, but it doesn't alter the circumstances."

Jamie's eyes widened slightly. "Which means your marriage to the Princess of Bohemia—"

"Was bigamous." Another shrug. "No longer of any consequence, of course, with Marie dead these many years—and now Rupert. And frankly, money buys anything at the Vatican, so I knew if problems arose, they could be remedied."

"Are you sure your English marriage was legal?"

"We were married in the Austrian embassy—secretly, of course. The few people who were involved could be trusted."

Jamie softly whistled. "An unforseen obstacle for Von Welden. Not that he couldn't have you both killed."

"I'm sure he'll consider it, but we'll deal with him later. I'm about to meet my daughter."

"A daughter? You knew?" Jamie's voice held mild surprise and at the last a flatness.

"I heard about her birth shortly after my marriage to Marie. I attempted to write and send funds, but my letters and bank drafts were returned. I was distrait of course, angry, too, and resentful. Then life intervened, and I'm ashamed to say I eventually forgot." He blew out a small breath. "I don't have to tell you how irresponsible I am."

Jamie politely refrained from responding. "What if this long-lost daughter isn't interested in becoming your heir?" he asked instead. "What if she has a perfectly agreeable life? What if her mother taught her to hate you?"

"You know as well as I do that a princely title and a vast fortune will likely change anyone's mind," Ernst replied with assurance of considerable experience. "Or if she proves difficult, you can help me persuade her."

Jamie put up his hands. "Acquit me. You're her father."

"I could insist."

"You could try."

Ernst laughed. "You're as stubborn as your hardheaded father."

"I guard you. I'm not your keeper."

"Sometimes you are." Jamie was his voice of reason on occasion.

"Not in this."

"Very well, be obstinate," Ernst said with another of those surprising smiles Jamie was seeing frequently. "But consider, you'll be guarding me when I speak to her."

"No. I'll be outside the room."

Ernst grinned. "Sometimes I don't think you know your place."

"Most times. Remember, I don't need this job."

"As you often tell me, you impertinent cub. Come, we'll have another drink and I'll explain what the detectives know about my wife and daughter." He was beaming as he reached for the bottle. "As you can see, just thinking about my daughter puts me in an extremely good mood."

"I'm pleased for you," Jamie said with genuine affection. "Not that anyone can ever replace Rupert, but I admit, there's joy in fucking over Von Welden."

"I'll drink to that." Ernst refilled their glasses.

In the course of the next hour Jamie heard the entire

story of Ernst's early love affair and marriage, the current state of the search for Amelia and her daughter, and the prince's intentions to disclose to his daughter that she was heiress to the duchy of Dalmia.

As Ernst finished his explanation, the clock chimed as if on cue, and looking up, he said, "Christ, I'm late for dinner with Rutledge. We'll talk again in the morning. Say, eleven?"

Having gone without sleep since yesterday, Jamie readily agreed.

CHAPTER 7

ERNST'S GOOD CHEER was obvious when Jamie was shown into his study at eleven. An aberrant state with which Jamie was becoming familiar.

"Good news, I gather."

"Yes, yes, the best. Sit. I'll have Sims get you coffee." Walking over to the bellpull, he gave it a tug. "I've had too much already as you can no doubt see," he said, waving Jamie to a chair with an expansive gesture. "But the reports are excellent."

"In what way?" Jamie dropped into a sprawl in a club chair and contemplated Ernst as he nervously paced.

"They unearthed more information on Amelia. She's lived with an artist for years. They aren't married—which suggests, perhaps, she never divorced me. It could be lack of funds, although that's neither here nor there," Ernst added with a flick of his fingers as he swung back from his desk. "The point is—there's no question that my daughter is legitimate."

"Your men made contact with Amelia?"

"No, she's in the country somewhere, but a neighbor was talkative. Apparently, Amelia's an artist of some note—as is my daughter, Sofia, who, according to the neighbor, is quite a beauty."

Jamie slid upright in his chair, a sudden attentiveness in his gaze. "Your daughter doesn't use your surname, does she?"

"No, no—her mother's. Eastleigh."

"Small world."

Ernst came to an abrupt stop. "You know her?"

"I've met her." Now he knew why he'd responded to Sofia Eastleigh with such familiarity. "She has your color hair and Rupert's eyes—that cool shade of blue is distinctive."

"What did you think of her?" The prince dropped into a nearby chair and leaned forward in his excitement.

That she's extremely fuckable. "I met her at Countess Minton's—you remember Bella. Your daughter was painting her portrait. She's a superb artist, no question."

"And?" Ernst impatiently queried. "What does she look like? Does she speak well? How does she carry herself? Does she have Rupert's smile? Coffee for Blackwood, Sims," he said as the door opened. "Go on, tell me more," he briskly commanded once the door shut on the servant.

"She was working, so she didn't converse much, and Bella was chattering the whole while. She *is* very beautiful, delicate and slender. She seemed pleasant. And come to think of it, she smiled very like Rupert."

"With that mischievous quirk of the mouth, I'll wager. I can't tell you how excited I am to meet her. I'm hoping Thurgood can locate her soon. She didn't come home last night," he added, a note of unease in his voice. "You don't suppose Von Welden—"

"No—not yet," Jamie quickly interposed. "He's neither that clever nor efficient. I wouldn't be concerned about Miss Eastleigh's absence. She gave the impression of being independent—a modern woman as they say. A common enough quality in the sisterhood of the avant-garde art world."

"Yes, yes, no doubt you're right. Her mother had a streak of independence as well, although she was a complete darling in every way." Ernst sighed. "If not for family duty . . ."

"And the intervening females who served to divert your interests," Jamie sardonically interposed. "A convenient amnesia if you ask me."

Ernst surveyed his ADC with a jaundiced gaze. "May I remind you that a lecture from a libertine lacks credence. However, I understand your point. I intend to remedy my fatherly inattention forthwith."

"In that case, we're going to need more men to cover both you and Miss Eastleigh. It's only a matter of time before Von Welden picks up your scent."

"I'm afraid the principessa has stolen a march on Von Welden." Ernst lifted one shoulder in an expression of futility. "I'd forgotten that her lady-in-waiting is related to my secretary's wife. Antonella cabled this morning. I'm to meet her at the station tomorrow."

"I see." As a rule Ernst didn't respond to orders from his lovers.

"No, you don't," the prince observed, mindful of Jamie's insinuation. "It's nothing out of the ordinary. Antonella's simply more audacious than most."

Jamie dipped his head. "A charming quality in a woman."

"Indeed. Now how soon before the additional troopers arrive?"

"Two days."

"Then you must personally guard my daughter. She's in the most danger."

"Douglas is fully capable of protecting her." He preferred keeping his distance. Miss Eastleigh was forbidden fruit.

"I disagree." The prince's voice took on an edge. "Need I remind you of your promise to your father?"

Jamie drew in a small breath, exhaled, and reluctantly said, "No, you need not." The eldest male in Jamie's family had personally guarded the Princes of Battenberg for over a century.

Ernst smiled. "I knew I could count on you. Now you may stop scowling at me. I'm sure my daughter won't give you any trouble."

If I were a eunuch. "I'll do my best, sir," he said with more hope than certainty. Sofia Eastleigh was not only beautiful but also a flirt.

Ernst looked up as a servant entered the room. "Thank you, Sims. None for me."

The men waited while a tray was set down beside Jamie and the servant withdrew.

The prince leaned forward and patted Jamie's knee. "Come, my boy, no sulks. Humor me. My daughter's safety is of vital importance as you and I both know. I depend on you completely."

Jamie offered the prince a well-bred smile. "As you wish, sir." Chafing under his new orders, he picked up the cup of coffee that had been poured for him, drank it down, set the cup aside, and came to his feet. "I'll talk to the men and see that everyone understands the situation. How much do you want me to tell them?"

"Tell them that I've discovered my long-lost daughter and she'll require sufficient protection to guard her against those who murdered Rupert. As to the details, I'll leave them up to you. I intend to acknowledge her before the world as soon as possible and hopefully forestall Von Welden."

"A temporary deterrent at best," Jamie warned.

"I understand. If she agrees, I'd like to spirit her away to safety until we can deal with Von Welden."

"*If* she agrees."

The prince smiled. "I'm sure you can convince her."

"Jesus, Ernst, unlike you, I don't believe in miracles."

"Nevertheless, I have complete faith in you."

"Wildly misplaced," Jamie grumbled.

"My dear boy, every female in Vienna has thrown herself at your feet. And my understanding is that you've not turned any of them away." Ernst grinned. "I envy your stamina."

"This is different."

"I can't see how."

"She's your daughter."

"Didn't you say she was a woman of independence. Why don't we let her decide?"

"No, Ernst. You ask too much."

"To want my daughter safe?" Ernst blandly remarked. "I don't understand where moral scruples come into play when it's a matter of practicality. But I see you have your hackles up." His smile was benign. "I'll allow you your principles."

"Thank you," Jamie gruffly said, not sure what repulsed him more: Ernst's venal worldliness or his unbridled selfishness.

The prince softly laughed. "Off with you, my pious young man. When I have news of my daughter, I'll send for you."

Prince Ernst had not lived a licentious life for so long without having discovered that human frailty was most vulnerable when passion, desire, and willfulness coalesced. His handsome young ADC attracted women like the moon the tides, while his daughter apparently was predisposed to willfulness.

What better collaboration to insure her safety?

UNAWARE OF THE momentous events in the offing, Sofia spent another day in the country, finishing a landscape she'd begun the previous day. Engrossed in her work, she lost track of time, and only when the afternoon sun began to cool did she recall her dinner appointment at Rosalind's.

"Jessie! We have to go!" she shouted to the young boy who fetched and carried for her and drove her little cart. "I'm late, late, late!"

An hour later, Jessie dropped her off at her cottage in Chelsea and drove around to her studio in back to dispose of the canvas and painting supplies.

As Sofia approached her front door, a strange man appeared from around the cascade of pink roses climbing up her porch trellis.

"Miss Eastleigh?"

"Who are you?" Her voice was sharp. Men appeared on her doorstep with some frequency, none of whom she welcomed.

"I have a message from Prince Ernst of Dalmia. He would like to meet with you immediately." The man held out an official-looking envelope with seals.

"You must be mistaken." She ignored his outstretched hand. "I don't know any Prince Ernst. Now, if you'll excuse me, I'm late for a dinner," she crisply added, brushing past him. Opening her door, she slipped inside and slammed the door behind her.

What a bizarre approach, she reflected with a snort of disgust, quickly making her way to her bedroom. Even assuming this prince—or not—was attempting to court some woman, she rather doubted he'd have much success with such a crude proposal. Delivered by a retainer no less.

Really, there was no accounting for the arrogance of the nobility.

As if one had merely to reveal one's title—even a possibly fraudulent one—and a woman's acquiescence was assured. Insolent pricks.

Which frame of mind didn't bode well for the evening ahead. Lord Wharton was wealthy, titled, and feted far and wide for his athletic fame. She really wasn't in the mood for an aristocratic blue blood with the world at his feet. She should have remained firm in her refusals. Damn Rosalind's incessant harping.

Now, if only she could survive the evening without being rude.

A low bar, perhaps, but in her current temper not easily met.

Perhaps with enough champagne, she reflected, her mood might improve. Or more to the point, with enough champagne, she might become oblivious to her mood.

Swiftly undressing, she dropped her work clothes on the carpet. Pulling her Worth gown from the wardrobe, she laid it on the bed and shouted for the young maid of all work who helped her out on occasion. Knowing she'd need assistance with all the impossibly small hooks running down the back of her gown, she'd had the foresight to schedule Cassie. "Ah, there you are, darling. I need help with this gown, and if you could find my green silk shoes, I'd be grateful. They're not in the wardrobe."

"I seen them under the sofa in the parlor, miss."

"Really?"

"You brung that lovely bloke home from the theater last Thursday, miss. I recall cuz me mum helped me dress you that night. The shoes got left behind, I figure, when—"

"Be a dear and fetch them for me, will you?" Sofia interposed, preferring not to hear Cassie's suppositions apropos her behavior that night. Although Billy Orme was very sweet and gratifying in any number of ways. He'd stayed to entertain her for two full days—a testament to his talents beyond that of a championship jockey.

CHAPTER 8

JAMIE HAD SPENT a portion of the day with his troop, explaining their mission and arranging watch schedules before returning to his apartment in St. John's Wood. As eight o'clock approached and no summons from Ernst materialized, he decided that Miss Eastleigh must not have surfaced yet. The fact that she couldn't be found generated a mild apprehension until he reminded himself that Von Welden and his minions couldn't possibly be that competent.

Nonetheless, when a messenger from the prince arrived a short time later, he read the brief note with a sense of relief.

She's found. Dress for dinner.

Ernst's army of detectives had tracked down their quarry.

A half hour later, Jamie was ushered into the Battenberg town house by a harried butler. "Upstairs, sir. He's been asking for you." Directed to the prince's dressing room, Jamie found Ernst in a stew over what decorations to wear on his admiral's uniform.

"I can't decide. What do you think?" The prince waved his hand at a colorful array of various orders and decorations on his dressing table.

"If you're out to impress, the Order of the Golden Fleece will suffice." The medal was the oldest, most prestigious honor the Habsburg Empire bestowed, the recipients either from the royal families of Europe or from the ranks of exceptional military heroes.

"You're right. Less is more. It must be your Scots' blood."

"If we're discussing moderation, I'd dispense with a uniform. English society is more relaxed than the Austrian court. Military dress isn't de rigueur here. That much gold braid might frighten off your daughter." *Or offend her.* Jamie suspected the forthright Miss Eastleigh disliked martinets decked out in showy regimentals.

"Excellent suggestion. We'll restrict our accompanying guard as well. You're armed?"

Jamie nodded, his shoulder holster well concealed by his tailor, the dirk strapped to his ankle invisible as well.

The prince snapped his fingers at his valet. "Off with this uniform," he briskly ordered, and swearing all the while, he was quickly refitted into evening dress.

"Very nice," Jamie said with quiet amusement as the flurry of activity abated. "Now you owe Peters an apology."

The prince glared at Jamie. "I don't know why I put up with you."

Jamie smiled. "Because I keep you safe and tell you the truth when no one else dares."

"Hmpf. Impertinent brat." He turned to Peters and muttered, "Have Julius give you a raise."

"Very good, sir." No gentleman of consequence would do without an English valet and Peters knew it. "Have a pleasant evening, sir."

Ernst stalked away through the dressing room door, and Jamie winked at Peters as he rose from his chair. "He's lucky to have you."

"Thank you, sir. We do our best."

Which term would perhaps be useful as a catchphrase tonight, Jamie decided as he and Ernst entered the carriage waiting at the curb. Having met Miss Eastleigh, he rather doubted that she'd entirely welcome the news that she was heir to a duchy in Dalmia.

Her sardonic remarks about aristocratic ladies like Bella and the men who obliged them suggested a jaundiced view of the beau monde. Not that he necessarily disagreed with her assessment, but then his opinions were of no consequence tonight.

On the other hand, he sympathized with Ernst's joy in having saved his patrimony. After the loss of his only son to Von Welden's inhumanity and greed, Ernst had found reason to hope.

Ernst, however, was a dyed-in-the-wool autocrat, force majeure the norm for him.

Jamie softly sighed. This encounter between father and daughter could be confrontational. God knows what Miss Eastleigh had been told in the last twenty-some years. Or what Machiavellian coercion Ernst would employ.

Fortunately, he hadn't bet on the outcome.

CHAPTER 9

AFTER REACHING GROVELAND House and posting two troopers on guard outside, Ernst and Jamie were ushered in.

"Tell Groveland Prince Ernst is here," Ernst brusquely ordered, handing his hat and gloves to the butler who had come up to greet them. "Quickly, my good man!"

"His Grace has guests, Your Excellency," Mallory replied with cultivated sangfroid, smoothly disposing of the hat and gloves to a flunkey. "If you would care to wait in the green drawing room, I will inform His Grace of your presence." This was England. Not some foreign fiefdom.

"I have no intention of waiting any—" Ernst frowned at the light touch on his sleeve and turned his chill gaze on Jamie.

"We have time, sir."

At the unspoken warning in Jamie's eyes, Ernst drew in a breath of restraint. "Very well," he gruffly said. "Inform the Duke of Groveland I wish to speak with him at his convenience."

Mallory nodded to a footman before turning back to the prince. "Jeffers will see you to the green drawing room, Your Excellency." A model butler never lost his composure, although he saw no reason to make haste in delivering his message.

The prince and Jamie were shown into an Adams drawing room of well-preserved splendor and offered refreshments.

Ernst scowled at the servant while Jamie politely declined for them both.

"My God, you're civil," Ernst muttered, restlessly surveying the ornately Grecian room as the door closed on the flunkey. "And to a servant no less."

Ignoring Ernst's sputtering, Jamie said, "I suggest you observe the courtesies with Miss Eastleigh. She didn't appear to suffer fools any more than you. Perhaps less."

"You don't say." Ernst suddenly smiled. "Just like her mother."

"Then perhaps you understand the need for delicacy and tact."

"Stay and help me mind my manners. You have tact enough for both of us."

Jamie shook his head. "Sorry. This has nothing to do with me."

THE DUKE OF Groveland entered the room to find the prince pacing and Jamie propping up the fireplace surround, a magnificent bouquet of white lilac in the hearth scenting the room. "Good evening, Battenberg—Blackwood. A pleasant surprise. What can I do for you?"

Ernst came to a stop. "I apologize for intruding when you have guests." The prince was capable of politesse with those he considered his peers. "But I have a personal matter I'd like to discuss with Miss Eastleigh. I understand she's here tonight."

"You must be a fan of her painting," Fitz said, moving from the door toward the men. *Why have they chosen not to sit? Is there some urgency to this visit?*

"I expect I will be, but I'm here on other business."

A partial answer. "Join us for dinner. You know most everyone—Lennox, Wharton, Congreve, Egremont. Afterward, you and Sofia can chat."

"Thank you, perhaps some other time. I'm rather in a hurry tonight."

So I'm right. Fitz had initially assumed Battenberg was intent on a flirtation, as was usually the case when a pretty woman was involved, but apparently not. "Let me fetch Sofia," he offered. "I won't be long."

Returning to the dining room, Fitz met his wife's curious gaze and gave her a reassuring smile. Making his way across the large room, he stopped behind Sofia's chair. "If I might steal you away for a few minutes. Duveen is downstairs with news of some mysterious painting that's come on the market. I'd like your opinion." Without waiting for a reply, he eased her chair away from the candlelit table. "We'll be back directly," he said to those guests who were listening or staring. "You know Duveen," he mendaciously added for Dex, who was seated beside Sofia. "Everything's a crisis with him."

Rosalind signaled the footmen to serve more champagne as Fitz and Sofia moved away, and before they exited the room, the buzz of conversation had resumed.

Sofia gave Fitz a sidelong glance once they were alone in the hallway. "There's no Duveen, is there?"

Fitz smiled. "Was I that bad?" He nodded to his left.

"You sounded reasonable enough." She matched his pace as he moved down the carpeted hall. "I just happen to know Duveen's in Paris. So why this mysterious summons?"

"Prince Ernst of Dalmia is waiting to speak with you. I thought it best not to broadcast the news. He said it was a private matter."

"Good God, he's real then! I gave short shrift to a man who was waiting for me when I came home. He said he had a note from Prince Ernst. I thought it was a mistake or some clumsy attempt to woo me."

"Ernst is authentic enough and seems quite certain it's you he wishes to speak with. Here, take my arm," Fitz offered as they reached the top of the stairs. "You've been drinking champagne with a vengeance tonight."

She made a wry face. "I was trying to temper my foul mood. Rosalind practically forced me to come to dinner with Wharton tonight."

"Dex seems to be enjoying himself. I doubt he cares whether you're drunk or sober."

"Do tell," Sofia muttered, having been charmed throughout dinner by a very charming man who saw that her champagne glass was always full. "You, however, have to get me out of this quandary. No matter that Wharton's been entertaining and gallant, he's not my type."

"I didn't know you had a type," Fitz teased.

"Very amusing. Nor did you before your marriage."

"Touché. I'll say no more, and I'll see you home if you wish. Wharton will survive a set down."

"Thank you. You've instantly restored my good humor. Now, tell me about this Prince Ernst." She smoothly twitched her skirt out of the way before stepping off the last stair. "Do you know him?"

"We've often met over the years," Fitz replied, moving across the soaring entrance hall toward the west wing. "In Paris, at Ascot. The prince has a splendid string of thoroughbreds. Three years ago we were both racing in the Cowes regatta. And I've run into him here and there at the continental casinos. The Battenbergs are an old family with Adriatic properties as well as others in Bohemia, Hungary, and points east."

"I can't imagine what he has to say to me." She slipped off the white kid evening gloves she'd unbuttoned at the wrist to free her hands for dining and handed them to Fitz. "I always feel awkward with these things flapping."

Fitz smiled. "You never look awkward. Nervous?"

"I suppose I am a little. This is very bizarre."

"Here we are." Shoving the gloves into his pocket, the duke stopped before large double doors. "Don't worry, darling, you're dazzling tonight in that magnificent gown, and you're more than familiar with men who wish to make your acquaintance."

"Not princes."

"Since when have you been impressed with titles?"

"Never."

"There—you see? By the way, I forgot to mention, Jamie Blackwood is with Prince Ernst." He shot her a grin. "That should make everything slightly more tolerable."

"He's *here*?"

"In the flesh. Now mind your manners. You've had a great deal of champagne."

"Would you like to chaperon?" she teased, suddenly less fraught with angst. James Blackwood in the flesh was a delightful prospect regardless what this Prince Ernst had to say.

"Knowing you, it would be a useless endeavor. If you like, I could wait outside."

Sofia shook her head. "Go back to Rosalind and your guests." She winked. "Perhaps I can convince James Blackwood to entertain me for the rest of the evening."

Fitz grinned. "I wouldn't bet against it."

SOFIA'S CHEEKS WERE flushed when she entered the room, a small anticipatory smile on her face, and as the door closed behind her, her smile widened.

Ah—in the flesh—the magnificent James Blackwood, more gorgeous than she'd remembered. He seemed taller, if that were possible, although of course it wasn't. He was, however, as stunningly handsome as ever, his glittering green gaze guarded—pro forma perhaps in his occupation. His stark bone structure brought a twitch to her fingers, his harsh features a painter's dream. And his powerful body— honed to the inch beneath his fine tailoring—reminded her of that first meeting at Countess Minton's when the scent of sex was pungent in the air. Her gaze drifted downward at the explicit memory.

"Good evening, Miss Eastleigh," Jamie politely interposed as if she wasn't staring at his crotch. "May I introduce Prince Ernst of Dalmia. Ernst, Miss Sofia Eastleigh." He executed a graceful bow, intent on escape. Miss Eastleigh's graphic perusal had a predictable effect on his libido, as did her fetching appearance in the fashionable undress of evening. Her low décolletage was alluring. "If you'll excuse me, I'll leave you two alone."

"No, no! Stay! Oh, dear, forgive me," Sofia apologized with a rueful smile. "I've drunk a good deal of champagne tonight. What I meant to say was *please* stay. I feel as though I know *you* at least, Lord Blackwood."

Ernst directed a smug glance at Jamie. "I couldn't agree more, Jamie. You must stay. We wouldn't want Miss Eastleigh to be uncomfortable, would we?"

"No, of course not." Clipped, cool, and venomous.

"Excellent!" Ernst turned to Sofia with a smile. "Please, Miss Eastleigh, come in and make yourself comfortable. Would you like some refreshments?" he inquired as if he commanded the duke's household. "No? Then we'll talk. I've come from Vienna to speak with you. Sit anywhere. May I say your gown is lovely," he added as Sofia settled on an Empire sofa and smoothed her skirts. "Jamie, sit beside Miss Eastleigh."

Definitely not. "I need a drink. Anyone else?" Jamie inquired, ignoring Ernst's directive. The settee was very small, and monkish he was not.

"Perhaps just one." She shouldn't—a pot of coffee would

better serve. But why be rude when she was looking forward to his company tonight?

"A whiskey for me." Ernst took a seat in a sea green damask chair opposite the matching settee and gazed fondly at his daughter. He was delighted with the turn of events, her insistence that Jamie stay conducive to his plans. "You're not easy to find, Miss Eastleigh." His smile was affable, the warmth in his grey gaze genuine and rare. His daughter was exquisite, a glorious facsimile of Amelia who had won his heart so long ago.

"I've been in the country the last few days," she said, lacing her fingers in her lap in an effort to curb her excitement as she watched the baron walk away. His hair was longer, his skin more deeply bronzed, that beautiful, languid gait auspicious perhaps in terms of other motor skills as well.

"Were you painting with your mother? I understand she's in the country, too."

It took a second for the prince's question to register with her focus elsewhere. Swivelling back, she lifted her brows. "How did you know Mother's out of town?"

"My men learned of her absence when searching for you. But none of your neighbors knew where either of you had gone."

"You spoke to my neighbors?" This wasn't some casual quest by a gentleman looking to make a lady's acquaintance.

"I didn't but my people did. You quite live up to the descriptions they were given of a beautiful young woman."

That sounds like the beginnings of a flirtation. "Surely this could have waited until tomorrow," Sofia said, a touch of coolness in her voice. "I'm surprised Fitz agreed to this meeting."

"I told him it was important I speak with you. It's of *utmost* importance, my dear, or I wouldn't have intruded. Ah—here we are."

After handing whiskies around, Jamie remained standing.

Ernst raised his glass. "May I propose a toast to the future?"

After Von Welden's dead. But Jamie raised his glass in salute.

Sofia did as well.

Jamie tossed his drink down, disgruntled at being outmaneuvered, taut with restraint.

Sofia also tossed hers down. Restraint didn't figure in her life. Even less so tonight with James Blackwood, all brute force in elegant evening rig almost near enough to touch.

"Jamie, sit," Ernst ordered, oblivious to his ADC's moody gaze.

Short of making a scene, Jamie had no choice. Setting his glass aside, he sat as far from Sofia as the small sofa allowed. Unfortunately, she chose that moment to lean forward and place her empty glass on the table before them. Her lush breasts rose in soft mounds above her décolletage, a pale tress of hair loosened from her upswept coiffure fell over her bare shoulder, and the sweet scent of honeysuckle wafted his way. A sharp jolt of lust spiked through his senses. *Jesus.*

He beat back his cravings.

She was taboo.

Although her pale delicacy was powerfully erotic— female vulnerability an aphrodisiac, however indefensible the concept. Could she withstand a sizeable cock? Or how exactly would she—

He wrenched his gaze away.

"Let me explain why I came in search of you, Miss Eastleigh," Ernst fortuitously began, offering Jamie an opportunity to direct his attention to more pertinent issues. "Many years ago your mother and I met by chance. She was at the British Museum sketching the Parthenon marbles; I was incredibly bored in the midst of a group of cadets following a dull tour guide. I struck up a conversation with your mother and promised to take her to dinner anywhere she wished if she showed me the back way out."

Sofia smiled. "And Mama said the Café Royal."

"Yes. We spent the next three months together."

Sofia stifled a gasp.

"Your mother never told you of our association?"

"No, never." Sofia studied the man seated across from her with dawning understanding—his classic bone structure, pale hair, grey-blue eyes suddenly startlingly familiar. Still handsome, he must have been arresting in his youth. She could see how her mother had been captivated.

"We were very much in love. I want you to know that." Then the prince went on to explain the joy of that summer, his exasperation when his family rejected his request to marry Amelia, how they married anyway. "Then one morning on my way to fetch Amelia the special cakes she favored, I was spirited away by my father's troopers. I was brought back to Dalmia, imprisoned for months, and forced to marry a princess of Bohemia." His brows came together in a frown, and he looked away briefly before resuming his narrative. "As soon as I was free, I wrote to your mother and explained the circumstances that had taken me away from her, of what had been forced on me. She never replied. Shortly after, I learned of your birth and I sent a message and funds to her through the good offices of a friend. She refused to see him; she returned all my correspondence unopened. She cut me out of her life. I don't blame her," he said, the memory still surprisingly painful. "I don't blame her in the least."

Sofia looked down at her hands clasped in her lap, unable to ask the obvious question, unsure of how to respond to this man her mother had spurned.

"Look at me, my dear." Ernst hesitated, then very softly added, "I'm your father."

Sofia's nostrils flared, not in surprise any longer, but in consternation; she was unprepared to validate such shocking news. It was too sudden, too outrageous. "I must speak to Mother about this. I can't simply accept your word."

"By all means consult your mother, but the facts won't change."

For a moment Sofia searched the face of the man who called himself her father. "Tell me—why now . . . after all these years?"

A demonstrable despair flickered in Ernst's eyes, and when he spoke, a rare honesty marked his words. "I have no honorable answer. Painful circumstance has brought me here." A second passed before he gained mastery of his feelings. "My only son and heir was murdered recently," he said, his voice strained. "With his death, byzantine complexities came into play which put the Battenberg possessions at risk. An heir is required to retain our properties; otherwise they revert to the crown. The brutal truth is— please forgive me." He slowly exhaled. "I desperately need your help."

A small silence fell.

"You'd forgotten about me, hadn't you?" Sofia finally said.

It shocked Jamie to see Ernst so unsettled. He was not a man given to nerves.

"Yes, I'm afraid so. I have no excuse other than the most gross selfishness. I'd beg your forgiveness if it would be of any use after what I've done."

"I really do have to talk to Mother." Too much champagne along with this startling revelation had her brain in tumult. "Your disclosures require verification—I hope you understand."

"I do. Might we go in search of your mother?"

"Travel to Cumbria?" Her brows rose. "After all this time, why the urgency?"

"There's a possibility of—" Ernst looked to Jamie for assistance.

"Danger?" Sofia's pulse rate quickened as she spoke, the murder of the prince's son unhappily recalled.

"Perhaps *some* danger," Jamie quietly interposed in answer to the unspoken plea in Ernst's gaze. "There's a possibility—however slight."

"Are you serious? You're serious," she whispered, suddenly finding it difficult to catch her breath.

"Please, don't be alarmed." Jamie spoke with deliberate calm. "We'll have thirty more troopers in London within two days. Twenty are already here—two of them currently guarding the door of Groveland House. You're well protected." He shifted slightly to fully face her. "However, we'd prefer you leave London until we can deal with those who pose a threat."

"Deal with?" Her face was ashen.

"No harm will come to you. My word on it," he said, placing his hand over her white-knuckled fingers clenched in her lap.

The warmth of his large hand, the surety in his words served to nominally calm her fear. "What if I simply walk away tonight and forget I ever met either of you?" she asked in a near-normal tone of voice.

"The man who ordered Rupert's murder would learn of your existence regardless." Jamie saw the panic return to her eyes and wished it were possible to mitigate the uncompromising facts. "I'm sorry, Miss Eastleigh, but whether or not you or I wish it, the prince's enemies won't be deterred. Not now, not next week or next year."

Dropping her head against the back of the settee, Sofia shut her eyes and tried to come to terms with the looming disaster that *should* have nothing to do with her, she resentfully thought. Opening her eyes, she shook off the hand that she'd welcomed seconds ago and sat up. "I find it ironic that I'm embroiled in some dynastic struggle when I don't give a damn for the nobility, when as far as I'm concerned the concept of exalted birth is rubbish. Now, suddenly, I'm supposed to care that the Battenberg lands are in jeopardy?" Her temper rising, she pinned her newly announced father with a mutinous glance. "It's not fair to drag me into this. Why *can't* I disappear? You'd still have your required heir, just not a visible one."

"Prince Ernst will be hunted down whether you're visible or not," Jamie explained. "With his death and no apparent heir, his enemies will win."

"Why is that my problem?" she bitterly queried.

"Because you won't be able to hide either."

She turned to glare at Ernst. "I wish Mother had never met you!"

"I'm so very sorry," her father murmured. "I shouldn't have come."

Jamie stared at him. Surely some duplicity was in play. Ernst would no more give up his possessions than the pope would marry his mistress.

Sofia's expression instantly turned hopeful. "Then I may go?"

"You'll need protection of course. Jamie will see to it."

Her gaze narrowed. "For how long?"

"Until Von Welden is dead—he's the murderer," Ernst added.

"Von Welden?"

"Yes. He controls the Austrian secret police."

"Surely they have no influence in England."

"I'm afraid borders mean nothing to killers. Rupert was murdered in India."

Sofia groaned. "Oh, please God, let me go home, climb into bed, pull the covers over my head, and forget I ever had this conversation."

"I understand, my dear," Ernst gently replied. "But I'm afraid we're beyond such wishes. However, I promise you'll be safe."

Confronted with unavoidable circumstances, Sofia braced

herself to face the unwelcome prospect of having to flee for her life. "What of Mother? Is she also in peril?"

Ernst shook his head. "You and I, my dear, are Von Welden's targets."

"This Von Welden really intends to kill *me*? Are you sure?"

"He must in order to take possession of my duchy." Ernst smiled. "Our duchy."

"Then there's no possible way out for me, is there?" Her voice was taut with resentment.

Ernst had gently maneuvered Miss Eastleigh into agreement without resorting to force. Jamie admired his finesse. "Might I suggest we travel north tonight," Jamie suggested, taking advantage of the opening he'd been given. "My estate in the Highlands is remote and well guarded. Once there, further decisions can be made in safety." Miss Eastleigh's discontent and unease and whatever further negotiations were required to mollify them weren't his concern, nor were the vexing questions of inheritance. His duty was to see that everyone survived.

Except Von Welden.

Ernst put up a hand. "We have to wait until tomorrow when Antonella arrives."

"No we don't," Jamie curtly said.

"I do. You and Sofia leave tonight. Antonella and I will follow. Glower all you wish, Jamie. I won't go without the principessa."

"Even if you die because you delay?" Jamie said, his voice flinty.

"Antonella travels well guarded. And once the rest of the troopers arrive, we'll have more than enough men to protect us. You take the guard currently in London."

Sofia suddenly came to her feet, her thoughts separate from the men's conversation. "I have to tell Fitz and Rosalind what's happened." She needed counsel, a kindly voice of reason, help perhaps to escape the gathering threat.

Ernst looked at Jamie. "Go with Miss Eastleigh."

"That's not necessary. I'm perfectly safe in Groveland House at least," Sofia peevishly retorted. But when she opened the drawing room door and walked out into the corridor, Jamie Blackwood was at her shoulder. She shot him a sullen glance. "Are you my shadow now?"

"I'm afraid so." He spoke with painstaking politeness.

"Everywhere?" Furious at being snared in a trap not of her making, she was further rankled at his damnable civility.

"I'm afraid so," he repeated.

"That should be interesting. You can play lady's maid," she flippantly added. "I've never had one before. I hope you're good with buttons."

Jamie checked his stride, seized Sofia's arm, and wheeled her around. "We're going to need some ground rules."

"I don't like rules." She smiled. For the first time tonight, she was in control. She knew that covetous look in a man's eyes.

"Too damned bad." His voice dropped lower. "Just for the record, if I could refuse this responsibility, I would, so don't flatter yourself." He knew that smug look in a woman's eyes. "Now then, rule one: you must do as I say at all times or neither of us will survive. And two: if you even so much as *consider* evading my supervision, you'll regret it."

"Are you quite done?" she asked with a theatrical lift of her brows.

"Yes." Brusque warning in the single word.

"Excellent. Then let me apprise you of some relevant facts," she purred, undeterred by affronted males. She'd gained unprecedented success in the art world dominated by men because of her talent, nerve, and barefaced determination. "First, I don't take orders from anyone, so it appears we must survive willy-nilly. Second, I look forward to having you wash my back if I'm going to be under your constant supervision. And third, I don't like men who snore."

Her smile was cheeky. Releasing her arm, he quickly stepped away before he yielded to temptation, hauled her close, and made it clear who was in charge.

"That's better," she murmured, rubbing the marks his fingers had left on her upper arm. "I dislike being assaulted."

"I may retire from the service," he muttered.

"Really. It didn't look as though you had any more choice than I."

"It's complicated."

"Is he your father, too?"

He flicked a finger toward his face. "Do I look like he's my father?"

"No, I'm happy to say. I'd prefer not being related to you."

His gaze narrowed. "Just keep your distance."

"I didn't think I was allowed that option."

"You know what I mean."

"Are you afraid I'll seduce you?"

"No."

Her blue eyes widened, and a lazy smile lifted the corners of her mouth. "My, my, that sounds like a challenge. Would you care to make a wager? Two hundred says I can."

"I have no intention of betting with you."

"Coward."

He stiffened. "You've been drinking," he curtly said. "Otherwise I'd take issue with your remark. Now, weren't you on your way somewhere?" He disliked useless argument.

"I'm only mildly inebriated," she retorted, walking away. "Which under the circumstances is a blessing. Otherwise I might scream my frustration to the high heavens." She glanced up at him as he fell into step beside her. "I expect you dislike women who scream."

He refused to be baited. Hopefully in the morning she'd be rational.

"No answer?" She smiled. "Maybe I'll scream right now."

He shot her a look of disgust. "I don't like women who scream," he grudgingly affirmed.

"You're going to be *sooo* much fun." She ran her finger down his arm, intrigued by a man who refused her advances. More intrigued by a man who wasn't the usual docile suitor out to please her. "Are we truly leaving tonight?"

He silently groaned. It was going to be torture until Von Welden was dead. "Yes, tonight. Just as soon as you've taken leave of your friends."

"I have to pack."

"You can't return to your house. Von Welden's men might be waiting for you."

She shot him a playful look. "Am I confined to this gown for the duration?"

"Of course not. We'll buy you what you need," he said with patient tolerance.

"We?"

"Your father."

"Is he very rich?"

"Yes, very."

Mention of the prince brought her mother to mind. "We have to stop and see Mother on the way north. It won't be out of the way," she quickly added as Jamie began to frown. "She's practically on the rail line."

"We won't be traveling by train. The stations might be under surveillance. Do you ride?"

"All the way to the Highlands?" she asked with alarm.

"Relax. We'll take a carriage. But you may wish to ride on occasion. It's a long trip—more so since we can't travel by the post roads."

"This duchy must be very valuable."

"It is. And Von Welden's a sadistic thug."

"Did you know the prince's son?"

"He was like a younger brother."

"I'm sorry."

"Thank you."

It was the first time he'd spoken with kindness. She was surprised how the softness of his voice affected her. "You must miss him."

"Rupert followed me around since he learned to walk. Or at least he did until he turned eighteen and moved to Vienna. He was a good boy." A muscle twitched along Jamie's jaw. "Von Welden will be made to suffer."

The ruthlessness in his voice sent a shiver up her spine. Was she caught up in some wickedness beyond her powers to comprehend? Was she too gullible in accepting the tale she'd been told? Would James Blackwood turn on her with equal ruthlessness? "Promise me we'll see my mother before we reach the Highlands."

He'd spent a decade or more intimidating people. Men were afraid of him because he wished them to be. It was a useful attribute in his line of work. He recognized the apprehension in her voice, and for a moment he debated taking advantage of her fear. Perhaps she'd keep her distance if he terrified her. But as he turned to answer, he saw a beautiful woman half his size, her eyes wide with panic.

He didn't have the heart to frighten her.

In fact, in another life, he'd have taken her to bed tonight.

"I promise we'll see her," he gently said.

"Thank you."

It was his turn to be touched when he would have preferred indifference. She was so appreciative, her words so pathetically earnest, he had to remind himself that he was a soldier on duty. Reaching out, he circled her wrist with his fingers and gently drew her to a halt. Taking her by the shoulders, he shifted her slightly and looked down on her for a brief, contemplative moment, debating how best to deal with their awkward dilemma. "I don't want this to turn into a contest of wills or a silly game," he gently began. "I'm sorely tempted to take you up on your wager and, more to the point, let you win. You're enticing in every way known to man, and I would if I could but I can't." Releasing his grip on her shoulders, he dropped his hands. "My job is to protect you. Anything more will complicate things. I hope you understand."

"I'll try."

He took a short, calming breath. "You have to try very hard, Miss Eastleigh. I can't do this alone."

"Sofia, please."

"Very well, Sofia." This was going to be a real test of his willpower. "Now, first things first. We have to stay alive. Nothing else matters. Not what you want. Not what I want." *Definitely not.*

"Yes, yes, I'll really try to be good."

"I'd feel better," he drily said, waving her on, "if you were more certain."

"And I'd be more certain," she replied, moving down the hall, "if you weren't God's gift to women, if I hadn't seen you in your role of stud at the Countess Minton's, *and mostly*, if I wasn't in the habit of indulging my sexual desires." She gave him a sideways smile. "But barring those discrepancies, a platonic relationship isn't *completely* out of the question."

"It appears I'm on my own," he drawled.

"In truth, I don't understand your resistance. How can it possibly matter if we have sex? Particularly since we're going to be in close proximity for the foreseeable future."

"I don't mix business with pleasure."

"Never?"

"Never."

"In the event your principles are at all tractable, I want you to know that I have no intention of suddenly becoming Prince Ernst's daughter. Titles mean nothing to me, I have no need of money, I have a very comfortable life here in London, and wherever Dalmia might be, it's not London. So as soon as you can eliminate this Von Welden, I'll thank you both to leave me in peace. Not that I wouldn't enjoy an amorous interlude with you," she said with a grin, "in the interim."

"I can see you're going to be difficult," he grumbled.

"On the contrary, you're the difficult one. I've never had a man refuse my overtures"—she flashed him a playful smile—"until now. Ah, here we are." She stopped outside the dining room. "Why don't you wait here for me? I'm going in to finish dinner in order not to cause comment. Gossip is outrageous enough without this lunatic story becoming known." Without waiting for an answer, she pushed open the door and walked in.

Those guests facing the door surveyed her and her companion with such avid interest, the others turned in their seats to see what they were missing.

Sofia leisurely strolled across the brilliant Turkish carpet, a bland smile on her face.

"You don't take orders, I see," she whispered to the man at her side.

"No more than you do," Jamie said under his breath.

"Come then, meet my dinner partner. He's quite anxious to make love to me tonight."

Jamie smiled thinly. "We'll have to change his mind."

"Not we. I intend to be flirtatious."

"Don't fuck with me," Jamie warned, his voice hushed. "You'll lose."

Her gaze was sugar sweet. "If only I *could* fuck with you. As for who will lose, that's still a moot point. I'm sorry the countess isn't here tonight; you could fuck her."

"Now why would I do that when I have you to entertain me?"

"I'm afraid we won't be seated near each other."

"You don't know me very well," he silkily murmured.

CHAPTER 10

AFTER TAKING HER seat, Sofia was annoyed to see Jamie lean over and address Lord Airlie on her left.

Dex Champion was more than annoyed. He'd done as much himself in pursuit of a woman; he knew full well what Jamie was doing.

Speaking quietly so others couldn't hear, Jamie was appealing to the elderly man's benevolence. "Would you mind if I took your place and we found you another? My cousin Sofia wants to grill me on everything that's transpired in my life while I was abroad. You know women," he added in collective male lament. "She's already asked a dozen questions on the way upstairs."

Half-turned in his chair, Lord Airlie offered a commiserating smile. "Pesky ones, I don't doubt."

Jamie grimaced. "I'm planning on drinking my dinner." The man had the look of a country squire, stout and red-faced from drink and outdoor sport; he was sure to understand.

Airlie guffawed. "Can't live with 'em and can't live without 'em—eh?"

Dex couldn't help but hear that ringing declaration, the comment bringing knowing smiles to many of the male guests and alternately, pursed lips to the women.

Jamie didn't respond.

"Very diplomatic, my boy," Airlie jovially remarked, pushing his chair back and coming to his feet at the same time Jamie summoned his host with a lift of his hand. "But I'm thirty years' married with three daughters, bless their souls, and I know for a fact that womenfolk chatter like magpies. No offense, Miss Eastleigh," the squire bluffly added with a wink for Sofia, who was watching the proceedings with suppressed fury.

She could forgive Airlie; country gentlemen of his generation weren't likely to change their views on women. But Blackwood, damn him, should know better than to treat her like chattel. He had absolutely no jurisdiction over her life. None. *What's this?* Fitz was coming over and actually smiling. *Turncoat!*

After explaining the situation to the duke, Jamie watched Lord Airlie being led away before sliding into the vacated chair. Leaning forward, he reached past Sofia and put out his hand to the sandy-haired man on her right who was glaring at him. "Blackwood," he pleasantly said. "Cousin Sofia and I used to spend summers together as children," he added, perjuring himself without qualm.

Dex took Jamie's outstretched hand, his good humor instantly restored on learning he likely didn't have a rival. "Wharton. A pleasure."

"I'm off to Scotland tomorrow to do some fishing, so Cousin Sofia and I don't have much time to exchange family gossip." An explanation for his actions. As for his mention of fishing, he intended to engage Wharton's interest and in so doing, obstruct Sofia's flirtation.

"Salmon or saltwater?"

"Salmon. I might do some hunting, too. I've heard game birds are in good supply this year."

"According to my gamekeeper, the numbers are better than he's seen in years."

"My gamekeeper is in ecstasy," Jamie pleasantly said. "I'm getting telegrams every other day. Do you prefer hunting woodcock or grouse?"

At which point Sofia became largely invisible, with talk of coverts and gillies, of birds and shotguns, salmon and mountain streams capturing center stage. Midway through a discussion of Holland and Holland's custom-made guns, Jamie ordered whiskey from a footman.

Several drinks later, when the merits of each man's gun collection had been thoroughly dissected, Jamie smoothly shifted the topic of conversation. "Have you heard whether there's a date set for the polo match in Warsaw? Last word mentioned early July."

"The Uhlans are still waiting to hear from the Russians. You play?"

"A little. You?"

At which point, Sofia could have slid under the table and Dex wouldn't have noticed. Instant male rapport ensued, and using an idiom particular to the sport, the men analyzed every venue for polo from Argentina to India, comparing, contrasting, and evaluating the game with considerable laughter, congeniality, and several more glasses of whiskey. Occasionally an allusion to a woman they both knew gave rise to some incomprehensible reference that served to further irritate Sofia. The name Countess Minton in particular caught her ear—although she shouldn't care in the least.

And normally she wouldn't. But under the circumstances perhaps she was allowed a pettish tantrum or two. After all, her life had been thrown into complete turmoil—worse— imperiled. Furthermore, she was unaccustomed to being totally ignored, and needless to say, the baron's suave deceit was an *outrage*!

He was treating her as if she were a nonentity!

A favor she'd be more than willing to return, for she wanted no part of this grand conspiracy. She wanted her life back—a very satisfying life in every aspect—professionally, socially, personally. So while the two men went on about bloody polo as if it were the most glorious invention since the dawn of time, she began to apply herself to a scheme of her own—which entailed disappearing from Groveland House and London—alone.

Only when dessert had been cleared away and the ladies were beginning to rise from the table did Dex finally take notice of Sofia. "Darling, please forgive my inattention. But Blackwood's played polo in every corner of the globe," he cheerfully added as if that sterling fact exonerated his neglect. Taking her hand, he lifted it and kissed her fingertips. "I'll make it up to you after tea, I promise," he murmured, his smile warm and intimate.

"Unfortunately," Jamie interrupted, "I must steal Cousin Sofia away before tea. Uncle Douglas is expecting us tonight and it's getting late." Jamie's tone was apologetic. "You know how old men get crotchety when they're made to stay up past their bedtime. Why don't we meet for drinks at Brooks's tomorrow afternoon? I hear Tattersalls has some prime polo ponies coming on the block. I'd like your advice."

Recalling his sole purpose in coming to dinner tonight, Dex tardily redressed his role of suitor. "Darling, must you go?" he softly queried, his heavy-lidded gaze adoring. "I'm sure we can think of some reasonable excuse for your uncle."

Sofia hesitated; Wharton would be easier to evade.

"I'm afraid Cousin Sofia *does* have to go," Jamie crisply interposed, his goodwill stretched to the limit after an hour of worthless conversation with Wharton. "You don't want to arouse Uncle Douglas's ire, cousin dear," he said, his voice amiable, his gaze unblinkingly chilly. "Remember the last time you did, he threatened to cut you out of his will." Jamie turned to smile at Dex. "A perennial threat—still, who wants to risk losing a fortune?"

Dare she make a scene? Sofia wondered.

If so, what would Blackwood do?

What he did was come to his feet, pull out Sofia's chair, unceremoniously haul her to her feet, and nod at Wharton. "I'll see you at two tomorrow."

With a lesser capacity for alcohol than his companion, Dex was incapable of quick thinking. "Very well, at two," he said, for lack of a better answer.

Quickly propelling Sofia away with a hand at her waist, Jamie pushed her in the direction of their hosts. "That went rather well," he said, taking her hand out of prudence. "I didn't have to resort to a sparring match."

"You still might—with me," Sofia muttered, trying to jerk her hand away.

He shrugged. "They're your friends, not mine."

Christ, he didn't care if she kicked up a row, she realized, abandoning her futile exertions.

"Sensible girl," he murmured.

"Damn bastard," she hissed.

"Whatever you say."

His indifference was bloody *monumental*. Thoroughly piqued at his imperious calm, at her inability to retaliate against his physical strength, in time-honored female fashion, she resorted to verbal attack. "You certainly charmed and captivated Dex during dinner," she jibed. "I wasn't sure who he'd prefer tonight—you or me?"

Jamie smiled faintly. "Since polo's his addiction, I think I had an edge."

Did nothing prick his damnable composure? "You're a cold-blooded brute."

"So I've been told," he placidly said. "Now don't be trou-blesome, or any more troublesome than you've already been." He gave her a warning glance as they approached Fitz and Rosalind. "I'm more than willing to carry you out of here."

"Fitz might not let you."

"I doubt he's armed."

"Armed!"

"Always." He might have been saying, *I like sugar in my tea,* so innocuous was his tone. "Look," he said, a touch of exasperation in his voice, "I understand your frustration. I wish we had other choices, but we don't. As a matter of fact, I'd prefer being anywhere but here"—he shot her a glance—"with you. Now, let me do the explaining," he gruffly added as they reached their hosts.

Waiting on the margins of the group surrounding the Grovelands until he was able to catch the duke's eye, Ja-mie nodded in the direction of the door and said, "Could I have a moment of your time?"

A look passed between husband and wife before Rosa-lind turned to Sofia. "You're not going, are you?"

Jamie's grip tightened on Sofia's hand.

"I'm afraid so. I have an early appointment tomorrow."

Something in Sofia's voice signaled her unease, as did the fact that Blackwood hadn't released her hand. Turning to the guests clustered around her, the duchess offered them a polite smile. "Tea and sherry is being served next door, ladies. As for you gentlemen, I see the port and ci-gars are on the table. If you'll excuse Fitz and me for a few minutes."

The Grovelands, Jamie, and Sofia had almost reached the door to the hallway when Oz caught up with them. "Am I missing something?" he cheerfully asked and without wait-ing for an answer, strode past them, opened the door, and waved them through. Shutting the door behind him, he took note of Sofia's restive stance, of Blackwood's grip on her hand, and lightly touching the holster concealed beneath his evening jacket, he held Jamie's gaze. "Does anyone need my assistance?"

Jamie frowned. "And if I said no?"

"A gentleman would respect your wishes. However," Oz lazily replied, "I'm not a gentleman, I'm a nobleman."

As Jamie shifted in his stance, Fitz quickly held up his hand. "Please, not here. We can discuss this in the library."

The library at Groveland House was world renowned, much of the collection predating the Palladian mansion, and as the group entered the large chamber, the scent of history and old leather bindings pervaded the air. The jewel of the collection gleamed atop its carved pedestal in the center of the room, the eighth-century depiction of the Annunciation in the Lindisfarne Gospel lit from above. The gold leaf painstakingly applied by monks to the glory of God fairly glowed in the subdued light and gave everyone momentary pause.

"If the ladies would care to sit near the windows," Fitz said, breaking the silence, "I'll pour drinks for anyone who wishes."

With the circumstances anything but social, everyone demurred. Once the ladies were seated and the men were standing with the windows to their back, Fitz called on Jamie. "You have the floor, Blackwood. Don't scowl, Sofie. He'll be less—"

"Don't you dare say less emotional," Sofia muttered.

"I was going to say Blackwood will be less likely to overlook the details. Apparently there's some problem. You've not been yourself since you returned from your interview with Ernst. Obviously, something's wrong."

"If I may," Jamie said with time an issue. He briefly and emotionlessly explained the reasons that had brought him to London and Groveland House. "So you see, Prince Ernst and Miss Eastleigh must be protected until Von

Welden is no longer a threat. And the sooner we leave London the better."

His recital was greeted by a stunned silence.

"I'm not altogether sure I have to leave London," Sofia said into the hush. "I'd prefer not, although apparently"—she scowled at Jamie—"my wishes are irrelevant."

"Don't disregard the extent of your danger, Sofie," the duke counseled. "Von Welden has a very unpleasant reputation. Even here. It would be prudent to err on the side of caution." He turned to Jamie. "If you like, you could make use of my country homes on your way north. Several are close to your route. My staffs are discreet."

"Allow me to offer accommodations as well," Oz remarked. "The security on my estates is substantial should your troopers like to rest." Oz had been poisoned the previous year, barely survived, and as a result, was vigilant. "Fitz and I can telegraph ahead so you'll be assured of a warm welcome."

"Whether we stop overnight or not depends on Miss Eastleigh's stamina," Jamie politely replied, a measured contradiction, however, apparent in his tone.

"I'd prefer stopping overnight," Sofia said, taking satisfaction in the clenching of Jamie's jaw.

"Why don't I go along?" Oz volunteered. "I could use a little excitement." And a referee might be useful with the two principals at daggers drawn.

Sofia gave him a quelling look. "I doubt Isolde would agree."

Oz grinned. "She's persuadable."

"Not on this." Rosalind and Oz's wife had become good friends after his marriage, and while Isolde was indulgent to her volatile, devil-may-care husband—up to a point—Rosalind rather thought cutthroat killers would qualify as that limit. "Nor would I be persuadable on this issue," she firmly added, directing a sharp glance at her husband.

"My troopers are well trained," Jamie assured everyone. "We'll be in excellent hands. Now, if you'll excuse us, we've stayed much too long already."

"He means I insisted on finishing dinner," Sofia sardonically noted. "I didn't see any point in generating unnecessary gossip."

"I agree," Rosalind kindly observed. "Should anyone ask, we'll explain that you're in the country painting. You do often enough it won't cause comment."

"And tonight, we'll simply say that you ran off with Blackwood." Oz grinned. "That, too, is common enough to cause no comment."

Sofia sniffed. "Very amusing for a man with your past."

"I'm reformed."

"Perhaps I shall be someday as well."

Jamie broke into the conversation. "If you don't mind, Miss Eastleigh, we should be on our way." He moved toward her chair.

"I do mind of course, not that it matters in the least," she lightly said with a smile for her friends. "I'm at this man's mercy."

The cost of his restraint could be glimpsed in the slight flare of his nostrils, although Jamie chose not to reply to her flippancy. "I'll send word once Miss Eastleigh is safe in the Highlands." Offering his hand to Sofia, he helped her to her feet.

"In case I don't see you again, remember me fondly," Sofia airily proclaimed over her shoulder as she and Jamie walked away.

Checking his stride, Jamie turned back. "Miss Eastleigh is in no danger," he said. "You have my word."

Moments later, as the library door closed, Fitz blew out a breath. "I'm not sure who's at whose mercy," he said with a faint smile. "Sofia's damned uncooperative tonight."

Rosalind frowned. "She has reason."

"Under the circumstances, my dear, she'd do well to listen to Blackwood."

"I wouldn't worry about Blackwood," Oz drawled. "If he can handle Dex, he can deal with Sofie. You saw him at dinner. Wharton was fit to be tied at first, but before long the men were chums. And we all know how difficult Wharton can be when he's not wooing a lady." Dex had a reputation for being confrontational, particularly on the polo field.

"I suppose it helps that Blackwood's been dealing with a demanding patron for years," Fitz pointed out.

Rosalind smiled. "Like father, like daughter then. I wonder if the prince can actually convince Sofie to accept her title."

"More pressing is the question of whether she'll survive to accept it. I still think we should have gone with them, Fitz," Oz muttered.

"Sofie's in good hands. Blackwood's saved Ernst from assassination countless times."

Oz sighed. "You're right. Still."

"Don't even think it," Rosalind warned.

Oz grinned. "You can't stop me from doing that." He loved his wife and daughter, but that didn't mean he'd been tamed or that his wild nature was entirely subdued. "It won't hurt to put my men on alert for Von Welden or his crew. We'd be doing Sofie a good turn if we stopped them in London."

"Tell him no, Fitz. For heaven's sake, Oz," Rosalind protested, "don't even talk about entering this dangerous game."

"You're right, of course," Oz mildly replied. "I think I'll have some port and a cigar and contemplate the pleasures of life."

"Indeed. We should get back to our guests," Fitz concurred, but as the men were leaving the room, Rosalind in advance of them, he gave Oz a warning glance. "Don't take too many risks. But if you should need my help"—Fitz grinned—"just let me know."

CHAPTER 11

UNDERSTANDING THAT IT was now or never as they approached the entrance hall, Sofia initiated a makeshift plan. "If you don't mind, I'd like to run upstairs and find something of Rosalind's better suited for travel than this gown. I only need five minutes," she quickly added because Jamie was looking at her with suspicion. "I'd really like some pants and boots, but that's not likely, so I'll settle for a skirt and blouse I suppose, or perhaps a riding habit or bicycling pantaloons," she rattled on under his skeptical gaze. "It all depends on whether—"

"I'll go with you."

"I'm perfectly capable of finding my own clothes."

"Let's just say I'd miss your scintillating company."

"You're completely unreasonable," she muttered as they reached the main staircase.

"And you're not a very good actress," he said with amusement. "After you, Miss Eastleigh. Five minutes and counting."

"Oh devil take it," she grumbled. "Come along if you must." Picking up her skirts, she ran up the stairs.

Taking the stairs two at a time, he followed her, his pace less one of haste than a matter of matching his stride to her racing sprint. Two flights of stairs and one long corridor later, they arrived at the duchess's apartments.

Sofia breathless.

Blackwood on guard.

When Sofia burst into the duchess's bedroom, Rosalind's lady's maid, who'd been dozing in a chair, squealed in surprise.

"It's just me, Miss Tabby. Go back to sleep. I don't need your help. Rosalind said I could take some traveling clothes from her wardrobe, and this *gentleman*," she spleenfully rapped out, "insists on helping me."

"Oh dear." Miss Tabitha Purdie, who had been a member of the Groveland House staff long before the duchess was born, surveyed Jamie with a critical eye. "Perhaps, that is—I'm not sure this gentleman should be in my lady's chamber."

"We won't be long," Jamie replied with a bow and a smile for the frail old woman. "I'm a good friend of the duke. And since Miss Eastleigh is concerned with selecting something suitable for travel to Scotland, I said I might be able to help."

"Scotland?"

"We're traveling north of Inverness. Do you know the country?" Recognizing a hint of the Highlands in her voice, he'd deliberately broadened his accent and mentioned their destination.

"Aye, reet weel, up and doon and sideways, ye see," Miss Tabby said with a wide smile, lapsing into her childhood dialect.

With bitter resignation, Sofia watched Blackwood charm Rosalind's lady's maid. The two spoke in such a pure Highland dialect, she couldn't understand a word they were saying, but Miss Tabby's smile was obvious, and before long the elderly maid waved Sofia into Rosalind's dressing room. "Go on in, dearie. Jamie says ye're in a right hurry."

"What a coincidence," Jamie drawled as he followed Sofia into the dressing room and shut the door behind him. "She was born in the valley next to mine."

"And if she wasn't, I'm sure you would have told her she was."

Ignoring her snappish retort, he said, "She's a nice old lady. She knew my grandfather."

"If only I could elicit the same charming benevolence from you," Sofia sarcastically murmured, "the world would be perfection."

He hesitated fractionally, then put out his hand. "I'm willing to start over if you are, Miss Eastleigh. An armistice? What do you say?"

Did he mean it? Or was this more of the masterful manipulation she'd already viewed twice tonight. First with Wharton and now with Miss Tabby.

He glanced down at his outstretched hand, looked up, and smiled. "I'm serious. It's up to you."

"Very well. I accept your offer of detente." She shook his hand and told herself it wasn't really lying when one's life was at stake.

"Fair enough. Now, should we see if the duchess has some riding pants? A modern woman such as she might." The movement for women's independence extended beyond the right to vote; many women were choosing to abandon the encumbrances of feminine dress. His gaze quickly measured Sofia. "You're much smaller, though." He turned to the wall of built-in wardrobes. "We'll need a belt."

"You have an eye for female sizes, I see. But of course you—sorry," she quickly interjected as he shot her a jaundiced look. "I apologize. Although surely you understand why I'm not cheerful when my life has been completely disrupted."

Her lack of common sense was extraordinary. "If all goes well, Miss Eastleigh, our association will be brief and your life will return to normal," he politely said. "In the meantime we'd do well to concentrate on survival." He began opening wardrobe doors. "Despite your doubts in that regard."

"Allow me my doubts and I'll allow you your, shall we say, authoritarian inclinations."

"Gladly. Ah, here, this looks promising." He pulled out a pair of twill riding pants and bent to pick up a pair of low riding boots. "See if these fit or fit well enough." He tossed them on a chair. "I'll find you a shirt and jacket."

"I'm supposed to undress—here—with you?"

He swivelled around and gave her his widest smile. "I didn't think you'd mind. Didn't you say one of my duties would be washing your back?"

"Very funny."

"Change or travel in that gown. It's up to you." He turned back to his search.

His directive was uncompromisingly blunt. Furthermore, trailing skirts and a tight bodice would be a disadvantage to her escape. So she set aside issues of modesty. Kicking off her evening slippers, she pulled down her petticoats, stepped over the frothy pile of lace and tulle on the carpet, and swung around so her back was to Jamie. "Do you mind? I can't reach these hooks."

"Just a minute," he said, rifling through a shelf of blouses.

She clenched her teeth. Soon she'd no longer be subject to his will.

Moments later he carried over a linen shirt and leather jacket, dropped them on a nearby chair, and without a word, began unhooking her gown.

Studiously ignoring the scent of her perfume, the warmth of her skin, her closeness, he deftly unclasped the small, concealed hooks. He was familiar with the drill, but not, however, with the current hindrances that impeded what would normally be the next step after undressing a lady.

"There—finished," he murmured, trying not to inhale the scent of her skin or take note of her corsetless torso only millimeters from his fingertips. Save for the handful of fabric she held to her breasts, she was nude to the waist. And much too close. God help him.

Glancing over her shoulder, Sofia unknowingly offered him relief. "I'd appreciate it if you'd shut your eyes."

He instantly obliged her and felt the tension in his shoulders melt away. Even understanding the difficulty of this assignment, he was forced to acknowledge that he wasn't monkish enough to be in close proximity to Miss Eastleigh's ripe charms for any length of time. It might be wise to sleep outside her door. More than wise—a necessity.

Unless he suddenly found religion.

And he was years past such enthusiasms.

Fully intent on her plans, Sofia let her gown drop to the floor the moment Jamie shut his eyes. Kicking aside the voluminous yards of patterned silk, she quickly stripped off the drawers that wouldn't fit under riding pants, slid her arms through the shirtsleeves, closed the irritatingly small pearl buttons, and pulled on the twill trousers. Tucking in the shirttails, she buttoned and belted the pants. The leather jacket went on next, and with a glance at the mirrored doors of the wardrobes, she decided, *Good enough for what I have to do.* Everything was slightly large but not so much as to impede her actions.

She was grateful the boots were very near her size, and once she'd laced them up, she stood. "You may open your eyes."

Jamie surveyed her, careful to keep his breathing even. "Rough but practical. You'll be able to ride now if you wish." He held out his arm. "I expect we have a carriage waiting."

"A last request if you please." She looked up at him with what she hoped was a suitably shy expression. "I have to use the lavatory. I doubt we'll be stopping much and"—she lowered her lashes modestly—"a few moments surely won't matter."

He considered going with her. Trust was a worthless commodity in his business. But he decided to give her the benefit of a doubt. That they were on the third floor was a salient factor in his decision.

More fool he.

In a very few minutes, he knew he'd been gulled.

Swearing under his breath, he strode to the bathroom door and tried the knob. Locked—no surprise. Backing up a small distance in order to exert the most force, he kicked the lock with his heel, heard the satisfying crack of wood shattering, and with a second kick, the door swung open.

A sumptuous white marble bathroom lay before him.

With a window open wide to the starry night.

You have to give her points for courage, he decided, striding toward the open casement. They were three stories above the ground. Which meant she was either a circus performer or desperate—the latter most likely. Although it wouldn't hurt if she was the former as well, so he wouldn't have to report to Ernst that his daughter had been found dead on the drive at Groveland House.

Reaching the window, he quietly eased his head past the frame, careful not to frighten the devious little bitch and possibly contribute to her fall. *Judas Priest*. There she was—the intrepid vixen—inching along a narrow ledge thirty feet away. He guessed she was making for the roof of the porte cochere, from which she'd be able to descend any of several rose trellises to the ground.

He had two choices.

He could follow her out the window. But she might panic should he do so and be even more at risk.

His other option was to make haste to the drive and position himself to catch her should she fall. A better solution if he was swift enough.

In seconds he'd traversed the duchess's dressing room, slowing his step only as he passed through the duchess's bedroom in order to say to Miss Tabby, "I'll be right back. Miss Eastleigh forgot her reticule."

The moment he was outside in the hallway, he broke into a run, took the two flights of stairs in great flying leaps, and on reaching the ground floor, raced down the corridor opening onto the carriage entrance. He stepped out onto the drive in record time, looked up, and exhaled in relief.

Miss Eastleigh had reached the roof of the porte cochere and was agilely navigating the slippery slate shingles as if she routinely tread such treacherous surfaces. A moment later, he watched her slide her legs over the edge of the roof, momentarily search for a foothold on the rose trellis, and finding one, nimbly descend the rose trellis in a shower of white rose petals.

Just as her feet came to rest on the petal-strewn garden bed, Jamie stepped from the shadows. "I gather the armistice is over."

She spun around to find him towering over her, the devil in evening clothes. "Damn you! Go away—better yet, go to hell!"

"My feelings exactly. Now, may I escort you to the carriage." Meeting the blazing anger in her eyes, he brusquely said, "It's not a request."

"And if I scream?" She saw the rigidity in his stance, the harsh planes of his face, the grim set of his lips, and even then she chose to be rash and opened her mouth.

"Do it and I'll muffle you." He'd had enough nonsense for one night.

"I *hate* you!"

"I don't give a damn."

She swung her arm up.

"Don't," he said, his gaze as dense and unyielding as stone.

And even she didn't dare when she'd always dared anything.

She dropped her hand and stood there stubborn and contemptuous. "Very well, you win. I have no choice it seems. Either I'm threatened by you or some killer from Vienna."

"It's not about winning," he muttered, grabbing her hand and pulling her along. "It's about staying alive."

For a man who viewed women as pleasant diversions when the mood struck him, he was suddenly faced with a recalcitrant bitch instead of the usual willing-to-please female. In addition, he'd be closely sequestered with this temperamental artiste who didn't seem to understand that her life was in danger and who'd require constant guarding or she'd slip her leash.

Bloody hell!

But he curbed his temper because he knew he must, and after a taut moment of disciplining his emotions, he was able to speak with courteous forbearance. "I believe we've had this conversation before, but allow me to apologize again for the duress you're under. With luck, you won't be caught up in these adverse circumstances for long. We've cabled Vienna, and Von Welden and his men are being watched. The moment you're safe in the Highlands, my men and I will see that Von Welden's eliminated. Please bear with us for a few days. A week at the most." It was a lie, but perhaps not too much of a lie.

His voice was mild, his gaze benign, the warmth of his hand holding hers soothing in a bizarre way. With an inner sigh of resignation, Sofia yielded to his rationale or perhaps his apology, and while not entirely reconciled, she at least recognized his attempt to make amends. "I swear, Blackwood, you could charm a wild beast."

"At the moment, I'd be grateful if I could charm a

small wild thing in riding pants." His smile was practiced
and full of grace.

She lifted one brow at his suave rejoinder. "How very
sweet. Now, tell me—how many days will this require?
Lie if necessary."

"Honestly, as few as possible. Believe me, I want this
over as much as you. Perhaps more."

"Will you promise to be nice to me?" she drolly asked,
not entirely in jest.

"Of course." He would have promised her the moon at
the moment.

She smiled. "How nice?"

"Not that nice," he said with an answering smile.

"We'll have to see, won't we?" she lightly returned. "Perhaps I can change your mind." She found her good humor
marginally restored at the thought of a passionate interlude
with the splendid Jamie Blackwood. And at base, having no
choice in this misadventure, she might as well try to enjoy
herself.

Deep in thought as they made their way around the side
of the house to the front entrance, Sofia debated how best to
seduce a man. She'd never been faced with the necessity;
rather the opposite had always been the case. Although she
wasn't averse to the role of pursuer with the studly Jamie
Blackwood as prize.

The image of him that morning at the Countess Minton's
was etched in her memory—an athlete of the boudoir, a
great favorite of the ladies, all lean power, animal grace, and
flagrant sexuality. Hmm—she could picture him lying gloriously nude in her bed wherever that might be. A most gratifying prospect. She must see that she had painting supplies
with such a glorious subject at her disposal.

Unaware of his companion's amorous schemes, Jamie
was considering how to accomplish their departure from
London within the hour. Once they were on the road, he'd
deal with the other complexities.

Ernst's carriage was waiting at the door. Jamie knew it would be, just as he'd known the prince and his guard were long gone. Ernst wasn't one to cool his heels.

Assisting Sofia into the carriage, he followed her and out of prudence took the opposite seat. She looked tempting as hell in her men's attire, exotic, erotic, defiant of convention.

A major problem.

Unlike most women, she didn't wait to be asked.

As if on cue, Sofia patted the velvet upholstery near her thigh. "Come closer." Her voice was sweet, her gaze inviting.

"Not just yet." He chose evasion in lieu of discourtesy now that peace had been restored.

Leaning back against the green velvet squabs, she slowly smiled. "When?"

"We'll talk about it."

"I'd rather do something other than talk."

"We can talk about that, too," he said, his courtesy unimpaired.

"Under the circumstances, you can't avoid me for long."

"I know."

"Nor can you resist me forever."

"I don't have to forever."

"Let me reword that. I'm intent on seducing you. How do you feel about that?"

"No comment."

She grinned. "You don't *have* to talk. Just give me what I want."

He beat back the surge of lust spiking through his body, the thought of giving her what she wanted doing violence to his self-control. "We'll be traveling fast. There won't be time."

"I'll find time."

"Maybe I don't like assertive women."

She glanced at his crotch. "Tell *him* that."

His nostrils flared. "You're going to be a damned handful."

"I expect you're more than a handful." Her gaze drifted downward. "Actually, I can see that you are."

"Jesus Christ," he groaned. "Why me?"

"I couldn't agree more," she dulcetly replied. "But since we're both caught in this damnable trap, my dear Blackwood, why not take pleasure in our plight?"

"You don't understand." His voice, in contrast, was sharp. "None of this has anything to do with pleasure."

"Au contraire," she said, sultry and low. "I'm sure I'll enjoy sex with you."

Cursing under his breath, he slid into the far corner, shut his eyes, and tried to think about anything other than fucking Miss Eastleigh. Or whether she was equally audacious in bed. Which thought wasn't in the least helpful to his peace of mind.

By sheer will, he forced himself to focus on Von Welden, and for the remainder of their journey he occupied himself with various scenarios having to do with the manner of Von Welden's death. The image of Von Welden being flayed alive was particularly useful in curtailing his lust.

By the time the carriage came to a halt before Prince Ernst's house, Jamie's sensibilities were fixed on the mission ahead, and he was able to assist Miss Eastleigh to alight with relative equanimity.

CHAPTER 12

A CONDITION WAS sadly lacking as they stepped into the entrance hall—the scene one of total anarchy.

A swarm of terrorized servants were milling around while a slender black-haired beauty was seated on a pile of monogramed luggage screaming conflicting orders to both Ernst's minions and the many retainers who'd accompanied her to London.

A day ahead of schedule.

Which appeared to be the problem.

"I don't care whether you know where the prince is or not. *Find him!* Now, now, *now*! Don't tell me you don't know where to go. I don't *care*! And where's my *champagne*? I don't see it"—she waved her arm like a wild woman—"in my hand! What kind of household is this when a simple request requires hours, *hours*, to be discharged!" Another frenzied wave of her arm set afloat the swansdown trim on her silk cape. "Surely the prince has a bottle of '74 vintage! Or have the rabble in his staff drunk it all? *Why* is everyone still loitering about? Who are *you*?"

she snapped as Jamie approached her. "Have you brought my champagne?"

"Lord Blackwood at your service, ma'am. I'll see that the prince is fetched immediately."

Her expression brightened, her scowl disappeared, and she looked Jamie over with an appreciative eye. "I've heard of you, Blackwood."

"And I of you, Principessa," he said, his face neutral. "You weren't expected until tomorrow."

"I chartered a train. The French can be quite accommodating." She smiled. "One needs sufficient money of course. Now, you will find Ernst for me?"

"Certainly. Unaware of your change in plans, the prince accepted an invitation to dinner," Jamie lied, when Ernst was no doubt in his favorite London brothel with his favorite courtesan at this time of night. "I'll see that he's here within the hour. Allow me to introduce Miss Sofia Eastleigh," he added, politely drawing Sofia forward. "She's the prince's daughter—only recently discovered."

Principessa Antonella Gilamberti-Thun surveyed Sofia with the bold scrutiny given to those of exalted title and family. "Born on the wrong side of the blanket I'd warrant from the looks of you," she noted with a raking glance down Sofia's boyish garb. "But you have your father's coloring, I'll give you that."

"Miss Eastleigh is fully legitimate," Jamie asserted, knowing Ernst had no wish to conceal his daughter's identity. "I'm afraid Prince Ernst's marriage to the Princess of Bohemia was tainted."

"You don't say," Antonella cooed, her pink lips curving into a sunny smile. "So that ungodly bitch Marie wasn't Ernst's legitimate wife."

"I'm afraid not."

She laughed. "How utterly charming. Although," she added with a small frown, "darling Rupert would have suffered disgrace. Alas, poor boy, he suffers no more." She softly sighed, all her indignation and wrath suddenly gone like so much thistle down on the wind. "A comfortable chair if you please while I wait for Ernst," she decreed, holding out her hand to Jamie. "You'll see to my champagne?"

"Of course." He helped her down from her perch. "You'll find the library has the most comfortable chairs." He waved over Ernst's butler.

"Come, darling." The principessa shrugged off her sumptuous cape, and as a servant jumped to catch it before it landed on the floor, she crooked her finger at Sofia. "Come, you odd little thing—you must tell me how it feels to suddenly be a princess."

"Appalling."

Antonella glanced up at Jamie. "You have an unwilling princess on your hands?"

"So it seems. Excuse me." He turned to speak quietly to the butler hovering at his elbow, giving him instructions for fetching Ernst.

"Nevertheless we shall muddle along, won't we, Miss Eastleigh?" The principessa offered Sofia a dazzling smile.

"I'm not inclined to muddle along," Sofia replied tersely. "Nor do I wish to be here."

"Oh ho? Stubborn and unwilling. Ernst must find you charming. Ah, finally, the champagne. You'll join us, Blackwood?"

He nodded. "This way, Principessa." Turning, he took Sofia's hand with a faint bow. "Your servant, Miss Eastleigh."

"Like hell," she muttered under her breath.

Whether he did not hear her comment or he chose to ignore it, Sofia could not decipher. Dragging her along, Jamie followed the principessa, who was in turn following a servant bearing her '74 vintage on a silver tray.

Sofia scanned the hallway down which they passed with an eye to possible egress should the opportunity present itself. But all she saw were portraits of racehorses or racing yachts lining the walls—the decor wholly male, as was the faint scent of tobacco in the air. And with Black-wood's firm grip on her hand, even a door yawning wide to the outside would have been useless.

A flunkey opened the library door as they approached it, another carried in the champagne, and the small group—all with divergent ambitions—entered Ernst's inner sanctum.

"Ah—Ernst's cologne—it smells like home." Antonella inhaled the redolent scent of the sea. "Ernst should knight that perfumer. I don't know how Rampolla does it, but the man's a genius. You'll love our picturesque seacoast, my dear." The principessa reached out and patted Sofia's arm. "It's the most sublime scenery in the world."

The wealthy principessa clearly adored her home, and rather than be rude, Sofia politely said, "I'm sure it's lovely."

"An understatement, my dear. Tell her, Blackwood. You live on the coast as well. Is it not the most magnificent sea-scape?"

"Indeed, Principessa. Please, ladies, make yourselves comfortable."

Playing host in the prince's absence, Jamie saw that the ladies were seated, champagne was poured, and the ser-vants dismissed. After which, Sofia found herself left out of the conversation much as she'd been at dinner. The principessa and Jamie fell into a free and easy discussion of mutual acquaintances at the court in Vienna and in their duchies.

Not that she hadn't been initially included in the con-versation, particularly by the principessa, who had pep-pered her with questions. But tired after a long day and an oppressive evening, Sofia wasn't inclined to relate her life story for the entertainment of a stranger. Furthermore, the large leather chair she'd curled up in was so soft and cozy she found herself struggling to stay awake.

When she eventually dozed off, Antonella waggled a

finger in Sofia's direction. "Is she some child of the streets in those curious, outsized clothes?"

"No. Miss Eastleigh changed from a dinner gown into a friend's clothes—for travel and riding. We'll be leaving London tonight."

"We?"

"Miss Eastleigh and I, the prince as well."

"Leaving? What destination?"

"My estate in the Highlands." Jamie wasn't concerned with disclosing that information since the principessa didn't know the location of his property.

"Ernst knew I was coming and yet he's leaving?" Her gaze narrowed. "It has to do with Rupert, doesn't it? Rumors abound that he was murdered. All Vienna is abuzz. There's some danger?"

Jamie gave her a restrained smile. "Forgive me. I can't answer without the prince's approval." The less said the better. Any small rumor could lead Von Welden to them.

Antonella lifted her champagne glass in Sofia's direction. "She doesn't wish to go wherever you're going, does she?"

"No."

"But you're not giving her a choice."

He shook his head.

"She looks like him." Antonella smiled. "She's obstinate like him. And yet, Ernst needs an heir, doesn't he? You needn't look surprised. The fact is well-known in our part of the world. Other duchies, mine included, face the same threat, having been dragooned into the Habsburg Empire over the centuries on one pretext or another. Fortunately, I have three sons."

The principessa had been married very young to an elderly noble. But she was also rich and titled in her own right, her principality won long ago by an ancestor in the employ of Venice. At the height of its power, Venice controlled all the trade from the East, and many an Adriatic pirate gained his fortune and titles under the flag of the Venetian Republic.

"You're to be congratulated on your sons, ma'am."

"Indeed. I was fortunate as well that my husband died while I was still young."

There was no way to politely reply to such frankness. "Would you like more champagne?" Jamie inquired, leaning forward to pick up the bottle.

"How gallant, Blackwood. But surely you're no novice. You know how aristocratic marriages are arranged." A mischievous light appeared in her eyes. "Except for Ernst's, apparently. He married some pretty young thing, didn't he, and said fie to his parents."

"Not for long." He refilled the principessa's glass.

"Hence the Princess of Bohemia."

"Hence the princess," he agreed, setting the bottle down and leaning back in his chair.

"Marie was a self-righteous prig with a penchant for priests who dispensed sexual favors and doctors who dispensed laudanum. She was quite ugly, poor thing." Antonella shrugged. "But then anything can be bought for a price. Rome included."

Another comment impossible to answer.

A small silence fell.

"Do you know who murdered Rupert? You do, don't you?"

Merde. He should have spoken up, made some innocuous reference to current gossip, steered the conversation toward some harmless subjects. "I couldn't tell you if I knew," Jamie gently replied. "Again, a topic best left to Prince Ernst."

"You do your job well, Blackwood."

"Thank you, ma'am."

"So then," she brightly said, "I seem to be involved in some interesting contretemps."

"Not interesting, ma'am—dangerous." *She is a severe inconvenience.* "I suggest you return to the safety of your duchy."

"I'm sure you do." Her smile was playful. "But I'm no more likely to listen to your advice than is Ernst's lovely daughter."

"Then I'll refrain from further suggestions. If you'll excuse me," he added, rising to his feet, several more pressing matters than deflecting the principessa's questions on his mind. "I must see to a few things."

"Go, go . . . you've been more than gracious. I'll finish this champagne and wait for Ernst to answer my questions."

But the moment the door closed on Jamie, Antonella leaned over and prodded Sofia's hand lying on the arm of her chair. "Wake up, wake up. *Wake up!*"

Startled, Sofia jerked upright and, still partially dazed, tried to recall where she was and who the woman was staring at her.

"You must tell me everything you know about this whirl-wind trip north. *Vite, vite!* Blackwood might be back soon."

The name jolted Sofia fully awake and memory flooded back. "When did he leave?"

"A minute ago."

In a flash Sofia was on her feet and striding toward the door.

"Don't bother," Antonella advised. "He won't let you go."

"What he doesn't know won't hurt him."

"You naive child." The principessa had lived her entire life under the watchful eyes of bodyguards.

"I'm not in the least naive," Sofia brusquely retorted. Jerking the door open, she skidded to a halt.

Two very large, armed men stood on the threshold.

"I'm sorry, miss—orders," one of them politely said.

Slamming the door shut, Sofia stamped back, cursing Jamie with a bitter outpouring of profanity. After a last pithy defamation of his mother's character, she dropped into her chair, leaned her head back, shut her eyes, and silently decried her fate.

"Blackwood's excellent at what he does," the principessa unnecessarily pointed out. "Very efficient and capable. He's saved Ernst from assassination many times. From what I gather, you're in some danger. Surely you don't wish to be on your own at night in London with ruffians on the prowl."

"I'd manage," Sofia muttered without opening her eyes, feeling sulky and mad as a hornet.

"How very courageous you are."

Pushing herself up in the chair, Sofia opened her eyes and looked at the principessa with mild disdain. "I'm at home in the streets. I'm sure you wouldn't understand."

"Perhaps not entirely. But then you may not understand why I maintain a personal army."

"Touché. You have your life, I have mine, and never the twain shall meet."

"That may very well be. But our differences don't explain why you choose to spurn your father's interest in you."

"Recent interest," Sofia crisply corrected. "And he fails to recognize that I have a life of my own. A very good one."

"But in the streets, my dear. Surely not."

"I'm an artist." She wasn't sure why she said it. Perhaps it was the principessa's benighted ignorance of what Sofia conceived as the real world, or perhaps it was the principessa's faintly raised brows. "My work commands large sums. I live well. And a title means less than nothing to me."

"But your father needs you."

"*Now* he needs me. He didn't for twenty-three years."

"Ah—you're angry at him."

"Not in the least. I'm indifferent. Why shouldn't I be? I don't know him."

"Perhaps you two could come to some agreement. Without you, Ernst will lose the duchy that's been in the Battenberg family for over a thousand years."

"Certainly we'll come to an agreement, won't we, my dear?" Ernst amiably declared, walking into the library.

"Good evening, my darling Antonella. How was your trip?"

"Tedious of course. But now that I'm here, all is well. Blackwood tells me you're traveling to the Highlands with all speed."

"The destination is still under discussion," Ernst replied, bending to kiss his lover's cheek as he reached her chair. "We could go anywhere."

"Your hair's wet."

"It's raining a little," Ernst lied, when in fact he'd washed quickly before leaving Madame Declaire's brothel. "A sprinkling of rain—no more." Well aware of Antonella's impetuosity, he'd had one of his men at the station, watching for her arrival in the event—like now—that she arrived early. "Would you care for more champagne, ladies?" he inquired by way of a diversion, preferring not to dwell on the weather.

Antonella held out her glass, Sofia shook her head, and Ernst busied himself with pouring himself and the principessa a glass of champagne. Then taking the chair on the other side of his lover, he smiled at her. "Ask me what you wish about our little difficulties. I can see you're anxious to do so."

"All of Vienna is speculating about Rupert's death. Blackwood tells me that you and Miss Eastleigh are in some peril, but he'll say no more. He also suggested I return home." She smiled. "I won't, of course."

Ernst went on to explain Von Welden's part in Rupert's murder as well as his offer to buy the duchy of Dalmia. He had full trust in Antonella. She had enemies of her own—detractors who questioned her competence to rule and wished to oust her and her appointed ministers. Once those plotting her removal gained power, they thought to control the duchy through a regency since her sons were still minors. He finished by saying, "So we're all currently in transit. Sofia and I are to retreat to safety"—he smiled at Antonella—"and you, too, my darling, should you choose to join this dangerous game. At which point, Jamie and his men will track down Von Welden and see that he takes leave of this earthly coil."

"I wonder," the principessa said, a teasing note in her voice, "whether Blackwood might detour south and see to my enemies as well."

"I'm sure something can be arranged with Count Beventini." Ernst thought well of the young captain of Antonella's palace guard.

"No, no, darling," the principessa said, spurning the offer with a dismissive wave of her hand. "Perhaps later when all this messiness is resolved. The boys are with their tutors on a walking tour of Switzerland and won't be back until fall. They're in no danger, nor am I. Leave Jacopo to his little mistress for the summer. He deserves a holiday."

Sofia absorbed the conversation with disbelief, the prince and principessa talking of life-and-death issues with no more concern than they would discuss the latest court gossip. Bloody hell—what miserable wind of fate had landed her in this labyrinthine web? She simply *had* to find some way out.

As if she were doomed to failure, the door suddenly opened and Jamie walked in. He'd changed into riding clothes—his coat conspicuously well cut, his linen immaculate, his boots polished to a turn—which didn't bode well for her prospects of flight. His luggage was here. They must be leaving soon. *Think, think, I have to think!*

Jamie masked his surprise on seeing Ernst. The servant sent to fetch the prince had returned empty-handed. "You're back, I see," he mildly said. "How was dinner at Devonshire House?"

Taking his cue, Ernst replied, "Boring. Politics, politics, nothing but talk of politics over dinner. And yours?"

"Champion and I discussed polo. You remember him."

"Yes, of course. Ferguson informed me of Antonella's early arrival," Ernst offered, his underlying message conveyed with a bland smile. "It was a perfect excuse to take my leave. "

"I don't blame you. Politics can be dull fare. Does anyone besides me need something stronger to drink?" He glanced at Sofia.

"No thank you. I don't have your hard head."

Ernst laughed. "No one does. You need Scot's blood."

"Fortunately, I'm equipped," Jamie drawled, moving toward the liquor table. *So Ernst had Ferguson on the lookout for Antonella. Not his usual style. Alarming in fact.* The prince had never before concerned himself with the arrival of a lover—rather the opposite. *Damnation.* Was Ernst's interest in the principessa going to prejudice their plans?

A clairvoyant observation as it turned out.

Jamie had no more than relaxed in his chair with his drink than Ernst reached out to take the principessa's hand. Turning to Jamie, he restlessly cleared his throat before speaking. "Antonella and I were thinking we might sail for Madeira. Her cruiser could be in Portsmouth in a few days. I need not remind you that it's armored and carries twelve guns and a crew of a hundred. Also, as you know, her estate in the hills is guarded and secure. A safe enough venue, wouldn't you say?"

"Very safe. Take Miss Eastleigh with you, and the men and I will go to Vienna." *Perfect. Deliverance.*

Sofia sat bolt upright. "You're not taking me out of Britain!"

"Madeira is lovely, my dear." Ernst smiled at his daughter. "There's even a modicum of society for entertainment."

"I won't go! I *won't*!" Realizing she was sounding childish, Sofia took a calming breath. "I'm sorry," Sofia said in a more temperate tone, although the color was still high in her face. "I don't mean to be difficult, but I'm a Londoner born and bred, my friends are all here, my occupation is here, my dealers and clients. I don't want to go to some strange country," she firmly added. "I could even

hide in the city if necessary until this Von Welden is restrained. I know any number of cloistered haunts where
no one can find me."

"What a resourceful daughter you have, Ernst. She's
really quite charming. But my dear," Antonella went on,
turning to Sofia, "you don't understand a man like Von
Welden. He's a monster who'll stop at nothing to gain his
own ends. And for a duchy like Dalmia—really . . . I
shudder to think of what lengths he might go. Please, my
dear, do come with us."

Jamie recognized the phrase *Come with us* clearly signaled that Ernst and the principessa's plans were fixed. Or
Ernst, in his current extraordinary infatuation, didn't choose
to oppose Antonella's wishes.

Which put him back at square one.

Playing bodyguard to Ernst's uncooperative daughter.

Not completely insensible to the prince's dilemma, Sofia
suddenly recognized a way to accommodate Ernst and herself as well. "What if I were to present my case to the police or Scotland Yard? That way I'd be protected and could
stay in London until this Von Welden is dealt with."

Jamie frowned. "Von Welden speaks for the emperor," he
explained. "He would see that your story was discounted.
You'd be portrayed as an hysterical, irrational woman."

"Prince Ernst could validate my story."

"What story? Von Welden would deny everything. There's
no proof he had Rupert murdered," Jamie patiently refuted.
"There never is when others do his killing. And Queen Victoria's government isn't going to antagonize an important
official of a friendly monarchy without conclusive evidence.
I'm sorry. The system can be corrupt, justice for sale, et
cetera, but the police won't help," Jamie flatly said. "And
you'll be out in the open with a target on your back."

"Bear in mind that Von Welden had Rupert killed, my
dear," Ernst noted. "This isn't a police matter, nor a judicial one, nor even remotely concerned with ethics. I wish

you'd reconsider and sail with us. But if not," he said after a glance at Sofia's closed expression, "Jamie will see that no harm comes to you. You'll be in good hands. None better. Now if you'll excuse us," he added, a lifetime of self-indulgence exempting him from conventional courtesies, "Antonella has had a long journey."

As the door closed on the couple, Sofia murmured, "Once a libertine, always a libertine. I'd say we're on our own."

"I'd say you're right." The prince was seriously aristocratic and seriously rich; such men did as they pleased.

"It annoys you, too."

He shrugged. "I'm not paid to be annoyed."

"He must pay you very well."

"It's not about money. I have more than enough." He drained his glass and set it aside.

"Don't tell me you're bound by duty or loyalty— allegiance . . . all those antiquated virtues no longer of any account."

"Then you wouldn't understand," he said.

Uncurling from her lounging pose, she sat upright and looked at him with an unflinching gaze. "Try me. Make some sense out of this ungodly horror."

He looked at her, his expression unreadable. Then apparently coming to some decision, he spoke in a brief, detached way. "My family has served as guardsmen to the Battenbergs for almost a hundred fifty years. Loyalty and allegiance are core principles in our business."

"Your family must have emigrated after the defeat of the clans in '45?"

"At the time, the whole world was awash with Scottish mercenaries. It was that or the hangman." His voice was flat, the twice-told tale played out long ago.

"Yet you're still there, even after the restoration of Scottish lands and titles."

"I have an estate in Dalmia, men-at-arms, people who depend on me."

"Ernst who depends on you."

"It's not just that." His voice dropped in volume. "Rupert shouldn't have died."

"And you're Ernst's avenging angel."

"You're mistaken. It's a question of justice. Von Welden's doesn't deserve to live," Jamie said, brusque and curt.

"So you're doing the world a favor."

His smile was chill. "Something like that."

"What if he kills you first?"

"He won't."

A quiet certainty echoed in his words, the utter implacability of his conviction sending a small shiver down Sofia's spine. "But in the meantime I must go to Scotland."

He employed his comfortable voice. "I would naturally appreciate your cooperation."

"Or failing that, you'll use other means."

He didn't immediately reply, and when he did, he spoke so softly she had to strain to hear him. "Accept it or not, Miss Eastleigh, without my protection, your life is forfeit."

The blood drained from her face.

Finally, he thought.

She started shaking.

CHAPTER 13

HE HESITATED BRIEFLY, his charitable instincts tempered by his susceptibility to the lovely Miss Eastleigh. But she was pale and trembling, obviously stricken with fear, and common civility required he come to her aid. Rising from his chair, he reached her in two strides, sank down on one knee, and not trusting himself to touch her, said in carefully controlled accents, "You're safe. No one will hurt you. I promise."

She was shivering, her hands clenched in her lap; sweat had broken out on her brow. "I don't want to die," she whispered, as though he'd not spoken or she'd not heard. "I'm terrified. I don't know what to do!" With the words *your life is forfeit* ringing in her ears, she had finally grasped the enormity of her situation, and even *terror* was too tame a word for her unbridled fear. She looked up, her eyes bright with tears, a suffocating panic demoralizing her spirit. "Please hold me," she said, feeling desperately alone. "Hold me tight."

Dear God, he thought. It was an impossible situation.

He should refuse her. Directly or perhaps more kindly, indirectly. "There's no need for alarm, Miss Eastleigh. You're protected. My men and I won't fail you."

Her tears spilled over and a glistening trail of wetness ran down on her cheeks. "What if you can't protect me?" she said with a small gulping sob, wide-eyed and shuddering. "Antonella said that man was a monster. What if his thugs come and kill me in my sleep or torture me or—"

"They can't. I'll be with you—always." A promise he wouldn't have made if she wasn't becoming unstrung. "You're completely safe. Look at me. Look," he said sharply enough that she obeyed, although her blank, wild stare was worrying. "My troopers will be close at hand as well." He gave her a reassuring smile. "No one can come near you without our leave."

Drawing in an unsteady breath, she tried to return his smile but managed only a quivering twitch of her lips. "Forgive me. How trying this must be for you." He was a professional soldier, and she was being unnecessarily hysterical. "I shall strive to be more courageous. I promise— oh dear." She caught her breath as a fearsome image filled her brain, and swallowing hard, she whispered, "I'm sorry, but the image of—a brutish man with a knife . . . standing over me"—she paused, steeling herself against the ghastly specter—"keeps reoccurring. It's my overactive imagination I know, but—" She gasped. *The hideous, sunken eyes, the ghoulish face was drawing near.* "Hold me," she whimpered, lifting her hands in an imploring gesture. "Even just for a minute—*please.*"

She was the picture of woe with tears streaming down her face, her breath coming in little hiccuping sobs, her arms outstretched. A forlorn, frightened little waif in ill-fitting clothes—a far too beautiful waif. "I don't know if I can be responsible," he gently said, understanding that he had to be disciplined for them both.

"You don't—have . . . to be."

"Yes I do."

"I won't ask—for more. I promise."

He held her tearful gaze for a moment, then smiled. "Easy for you to say."

She laughed midsniffle, a small, silvery trill.

And he hoped the worst was over. Maybe he could oblige her and hold her for a few moments. The frightened waif was certainly easier to deal with than the reckless daredevil who'd climbed out the window at Groveland House or the headstrong coquette who'd threatened to seduce him. The lady was audacious like her father. Or had been until cold reality had tipped the scales.

So—a circumspect embrace seemed in order. He'd render Miss Eastleigh the consolation she needed—in a friendly yet impersonal way—and once she was reasonably calm again, they could proceed to the carriages waiting outside. His men were ready, his plans already afoot, and if all went well, they would be far from London by morning.

Like most intentions, it didn't fall out exactly as planned.

After lifting her from her chair, he gingerly set her on his lap, held her at a respectful distance, one arm at her back, his fingers slack at her waist, his other hand in limbo for a moment before bypassing her thighs to come to rest on his knee. Dipping his head slightly to meet her gaze, he smiled faintly. "Better now?"

The vivid green of his eyes was muted in the lamplight, but the sympathy in his voice was clear. "Much better, thank you. You're very kind." And with a soft exhalation, she relaxed against Jamie's hard, muscled body, surrendering to the sheltering warmth of his superior strength.

Curling the fingers of her left hand around the soft brown wool of his lapel, she rested her head on his chest with another sigh of misty-eyed relief. Any of Sofia's friends would have been startled; she was neither fragile nor clinging. In fact, she abhorred such females. But nothing was what it once was. In a world gone mad, Jamie Blackwood had become her bulwark against fear, her security, her island of calm.

Far from calm, Jamie was struggling hard to steady his nerves. Although there was little he could do to still the thudding of his heart or arrest his rising erection with Miss Eastleigh resting voluptuous and docile in his arms. Every libidinous impulse in his body was urging him on, every sensory receptor was responding instinctively to a familiar stimulus: a female in intimate contact.

Unfortunately, his normal response was inappropriate, although curbing his quickening lust was a Herculean task. Standing stud as he did for beautiful, importuning women the world over, the relative arguments apropos duty versus lust, conscience versus morality or the lack thereof had never been in dispute. And now they were—in spades.

Damn it—the lady was too close, too desirable, too available.

And abstinence had never been his strong suit.

He glanced at the clock, knowing there were limits to his self-control, knowing he must end this well-intentioned embrace—quickly.

But just as he was about to make some tactful excuse and rise, Sofia impetuously reached up, knotted her fingers in his hair, pulled his head down, and kissed her savior and protector—passionately, feverishly, with a complete lack of gentility. With the magnanimity of someone freed from fear.

No novice to female overtures, Jamie's body instantly responded to Sofia's brazen act, his erection swelling, surging higher, the rigid length pressing hard against her bottom in seconds flat.

How gratifying, Sofia pleasantly reflected, and no novice either, her uncommon fair-maiden-rescued-from-harm persona gave way to the more authentic, nonconformist female who lived by her own rules. Her kiss deepened, took on new urgency, shifted from ardent thankfulness to tantalizing provocation. Freeing her fingers from the tangle of his heavy hair, she moved her hands to hold his face lightly captive while she devoured his mouth in a wild, wet frenzy.

Such bruising kisses presaged well for her passions in bed, Jamie thought. When he shouldn't think anything of the kind, when he should force Miss Eastleigh to stop, toss her off his lap, and concentrate on leaving London.

But her flagrant assault undermined his devotion to duty or perhaps his contrariness, and he yielded to her beguiling play out of courtesy, possibly, or habit or idle pleasure. Kisses were harmless enough sport, he told himself.

Until what he perceived as innocent play abruptly ended moments later.

She shoved her tongue deep into his mouth, wanting more, willfully and explicitly goading him to respond.

He did.

He sucked in a breath, her forceful, probing tongue triggering every randy nerve and impulse. Violent, hot-spur lust savaged his self-control, his pleasant detachment underwent a perfidious transition, and rampaging passion rode roughshod over reason. He jerked his mouth away, the price too dear, the danger too great. For a heartbeat. Then, rejecting piety even as his inner voice screamed *No-o-o!* he picked Sofia up roughly by the waist, swung her around, and as her half-spread thighs settled on his legs, he flexed his hips and jammed his cock upward into the soft cushion of her sex.

He shut his eyes, restless, shaken, knowing what he *should* do and what he shouldn't.

Meanwhile, she was thinking, *How unspeakably lovely!*

The exemplary soldier had feelings after all.

While Jamie debated chair or sofa, and more crudely, timing—Sofia came up on her knees and settled more comfortably on his lap. Locking her hands around his neck, she leaned in close, her breasts crushed against his chest, her mouth brushing his. "It feels as though you really like me."

His reply was a soft grunt—whether affirmation or repudiation was unclear. But what was perfectly clear was his steely grip on her waist and his insurgent cock that was immune to conjecture, wielding authority, motivating him to kiss her again. For a long, heated interval, ignoring all but delirious sensation, the unorthodox couple fueled their respective libidos with kisses that were no longer kisses, but a prurient, gluttonous prelude to something more.

Until Sofia made the mistake of declaring with neither tact nor delicacy, "I need *more*. Hurry! Now, now, *now!*"

Jamie's spine went rigid.

Whether it was her imperative tone, the bracing air of morality suddenly cooling his brow, or her blunt command, he irritably said, "Fuck this," and rising with startling swiftness, set her on her feet.

"Damn you," Sofia exclaimed, her body strumming with sharp-set desire, her passions trembling on the brink, her frantic cravings left unsated, damn it—for no *good* reason. "You can't say you don't want it," she snapped, flushed and shaking.

"I sure as hell can," he snapped back.

She softly swore, tried to bring her twitching nerves under control, and shutting her eyes briefly, thought about revenge.

He didn't dare touch her, his own go-for-broke urges not yet completely leashed.

The silence lengthened.

Blighted hope and heavy breathing a miasma in the air.

Sofia opened her eyes and spoke first. "Forgive me for making demands," she said with a smile, having sensibly concluded that it was just a matter of time before Jamie Blackwood succumbed to his libido if not her allure—a belief based on personal experience. "I do thank you for your kind attention, though," she amiably added, dropping her gaze to the bulge in his riding pants that put the lie to his refusal. "As a matter of fact, I'm wonderfully tingly all over—inside and out—*inside* mostly and *very* much so, thanks to you."

Jamie was currently a universe beyond tingly and dubious of any apology with a codicil such as hers. In addition, hot-blooded lust was still hammering his senses with unprecedented force, the hard, pulsing spasms vibrating through his body with every beat of his heart. No novice to degrees of horniness, he recognized that Miss Eastleigh's fiery disposition might lead him to take undue risks.

And that he would not do. "We must go," he said. He didn't trust himself to say more.

"A final kiss?" She smiled, a small sweet smile. "For good luck?"

"No," he harshly said, then more graciously, "Don't ask. I can't."

But his erection had swelled and lengthened at her words, and before he could stop her, she'd reached out and touched it.

"Don't." He stepped out of range.

"I swear you must be a monk"—her gaze flicked downward—"to ignore that." Amiability forgotten, more prone to temper than reason, she could not conceal the frustration in her voice. "Or are you afraid of me or my father—of what people might say?" Still wanting what she wanted, she taunted, "I wouldn't have thought you so timid."

"This isn't a game," Jamie coolly replied, his brief madness overcome, saner counsel once again in command. "This is bloody serious. And I could give a damn what anyone thinks, you included. What I *am* afraid of is finding us in the crosshairs of Von Welden's killers if we don't leave quickly enough." Taking her by the shoulders, he spun her around and gave her a nudge in the direction of the door. "So while you're damned tempting"—he placed his hand in the small of her back—"you're not worth getting killed for. Now move or—"

A hard knock on the door cut him short.

"The horses are getting restless, sir."

He recognized the voice. "We'll be right there, Douglas." Only the twitch over his cheekbone gave evidence of his temper as he spoke. "They're high-spirited bloodstock, Miss Eastleigh. After you."

Good Lord, she had to give the man credit. He was cross as a bear yet astonishingly restrained, a virtual flesh-and-blood knight-errant while she was acting like a petulant child, she ruefully admitted. She turned back. "A last question," she said, taking pains to be equally civil, yet not entirely resigned to meekly submitting to prolonged abstinence. "Would you ever consider giving in to impulse—say of a sexual nature?"

"Even if I did, I wouldn't now. Survival trumps sex in my book, Miss Eastleigh. Although, I admit, under other circumstances," he added in the same cool tone, "you'd be lying on that sofa over there and I'd be fucking you. Is that a satisfactory answer?"

"Why not do it then?" Her voice was honey sweet. "It wouldn't take long."

"Maybe I don't like to rush." He unconsciously flexed his fingers against an almost overwhelming urge to pick her up and toss her on the sofa.

She contemplated his erection still evident beneath the tan twill of his jodhpurs, then looked up. "Why don't we find out whether you do or not?"

"Out." He indicated the door with a jab of his finger. "Now."

"Would it make any difference if I said no?"

He exhaled softly. "We're wasting time."

"Someday I'll get my way."

"I'm sure you will. But not on my watch."

Whether she was more galled by Jamie's intractability or her lack of control in the deteriorating chaos of her life, of one thing she was certain. Drawing herself up to her nominal height next to Jamie's strapping size, she said, "I insist we stop to see my mother. I'll brook no opposition in that regard. Do you hear?"

"Yes, of course. I said we would." He pushed her toward the door.

"And I suppose you always keep your word," she scoffed.

"Mostly."

She looked sideways, then up, and her sudden smile appeared bright as a rainbow after a storm.

Oh Christ, he thought.

"Do you mean to say," she softly queried, "that you might actually *consider* straying from the path of righteousness?"

"No."

"Now why don't I believe you?" she purred.

He inwardly groaned.

Bloody hell.

One evening with Miss Eastleigh and his defenses had damned near collapsed. It didn't prophesy well for the days ahead, or more to the point, the coming days were going to be a living hell.

Maybe he'd have to reconsider his scruples apropos sex with the prince's daughter.

Merde.

As if he needed any more problems.

CHAPTER 14

TWO TRAVELING CHAISES drawn by four-horse teams were waiting at the curb. After helping Sofia in, Jamie stood at the open door, his hand resting on the latch. "I'll be riding tonight." He looked away at a word from one of his troopers, nodded, then turned back to Sofia. "Sleep if you can."

He shut the door and walked away.

They traveled fast, but the well-sprung carriage softened the impact of any rough patches for the single passenger inside the lead chaise. At first Sofia watched the city streets race by, wondering when next she'd see them, wondering with a degree more apprehension whether they were being followed.

But once they reached the outskirts of London—the city lights distant now—the carriage came to a halt. The sound of jingling harness and men's voices was heard as the troopers dismounted, and then the quick tread of spurred boots was audible and drawing near.

The door opened and Jamie stood within the dim glow

of the carriage lamp, booted and spurred, the width of his shoulders filling the doorway, a quick smile flashing white in the gloom. "I thought you'd like to know that we're quite alone on the road. No one is following us."

"You must be clairvoyant. I was just worrying about pursuit."

"Leave the worries to me," he pleasantly said, as if he were in his element, as if fleeing from killers in the dark of night were exhilarating. "Are you comfortable?"

"Yes, very. Thank you."

"There's food if you wish, books"—he glanced at the inside carriage lamp. "You can turn up the wick if you like. We'll be stopping toward morning for breakfast. We'll find a hotel with, er—washing facilities unless you require them sooner."

"No, no, I'm fine."

He dipped his head and smiled again. "Sweet dreams, Miss Eastleigh."

The door closed on his stark beauty, professional competence, and unexpected cheer, and with a disgruntled sigh, Sofia lamented his unfortunate sense of duty. But wishes weren't horses, as everyone knew, so she busied herself inspecting her sumptuous prison.

A very luxurious prison indeed, it turned out with numerous amenities tucked away in compartments under the seat: a fur carriage robe, several silk-covered down pillows, a hamper of exquisite picnic fare, one of chilled wine, a small stock of books, a brush, comb, and silver-backed mirror, a toothbrush and toothpowder, and a change of clothes, underwear included, that appeared to have been purloined from a maidservant.

Blackwood was indeed efficient as the principessa had noted. He'd thought of most everything, Sofia marveled. Opening another small cupboard under the seat, she stared wide-eyed at the stack of clean, white flannel. Not just *most* everything, she thought, smiling despite herself—

everything . . . the indispensable necessities for her monthly courses conveniently on hand.

Did he have a checklist? she wondered.

Or was he just supremely efficient?

Or did he travel with women so often such mundane matters were second nature to him? Which last thought she found irritating for no good reason. Really, none at all, she decided, shutting the cabinet door and dropping into a sprawl on the seat. The women in his life were no concern of hers.

Yet—the thought was annoying. As if she had some claim on him. When she didn't. When she clearly didn't. When she'd never in her life even wished to make a claim on a man.

Nevertheless . . . she found herself reflecting on his many perfections—from a purely artistic point of view, she spuriously told herself. Like an artist considering a potential subject. She had no personal interest—other than one of a purely sexual and transitory nature.

In fact, had she not first seen Jamie Blackwood half dozing after a night of obvious sexual excess at the Countess Minton's several weeks ago, she might not have perceived him with such fascination. But he'd been so patently the countess's personal stud in residence, the erotic implications had been searing. Additionally, if he hadn't so casually ignored Bella's possessiveness, if his indifference hadn't been so undisguised, she wouldn't have found him so intriguing.

His attitude was very similar to hers.

She, too, preferred casual attachments.

And having met her male counterpart, why wouldn't she fancy him?

Furthermore, caught as she was in the amber of Blackwood's authority, an amorous liaison would not only test her ingenuity apropos his canons of behavior, but it would also dispel the boredom of a tedious journey.

Didn't someone once say, *The will to do, the soul to dare*?

A small lustful ripple slid up her vagina at the salacious possibilities occasioned by long days with Jamie Blackwood on their travels north. She pictured him with her in the privacy of the carriage and pleasantly recalled the feel of him, the taste of him, the phenomenal size of his cock. He was really quite extraordinary, and she should know with sex one of her favorite amusements. The graphic memory of his finely tuned body and physical endowments whetted her appetite, titillated her consciousness, warmed her blood, escalated her breathing.

With considerable effort she managed to calm her breathing; she disliked being so affected by the baffling man. She begrudged his scruples and her aberrant, practically giddy response to him when her love life had always been free of this bedeviling neediness. "Hell and damnation," she grumbled. Why couldn't he be like every other man she knew and fall at her feet?

Since he obviously wouldn't, however, she must curtail her impetuousness and plan her campaign with levelheaded subtlety. Yielding to reckless desire would be counterproductive if she wished to play the seductress; the role required clear thinking and guile.

Particularly when her warder had rebuffed her at every turn.

Unfortunately she was by nature neither cool nor pragmatic, her life to date one of unhindered freedom. Consequently, planning a campaign of seduction soon gave way to more enthralling contemplation of Jamie Blackwood, his image in her mind vivid, sexually graphic, and despite rare attempts, impossible to dislodge. That she was cursed with an artist's infinite capacity for visualization was a distinct liability. Or not, she decided, the sudden vision of Jamie au naturel lying above her, his dark hair framing his face, his gaze heated, close, his erection—oh, damn, here she was, panting and eager and *alone*!

A dilemma that never arose in London.

One she wouldn't be experiencing here either if not for his stupidity!

Overwrought, skittish, her body glowing, she could practically *feel* the hard, rigid length of his cock as if she were still sitting on his lap; she could almost *taste* the peaty Highland whiskey on his breath as she'd plundered his mouth, *see* his broad shoulders filling the doorway of her carriage moments ago.

In the name of God—why does he have to be so pious? She trembled as a soft, stirring desire coiled deep inside her, the rising heat curling upward, spiraling like flickering flame through her senses, warming her skin, drenching her vaginal tissue in readiness. A swamping wave of orgasmic urgency overwhelmed her, and she squirmed on the soft, cushioned seat.

She ached, quivered, throbbed, the need for satisfaction no longer a wish but a requirement. Her mind racing, she debated the means: the hairbrush or mirror handle; the neck of a wine bottle; some appropriate vegetable from the picnic basket? Or, or, or—a small excitement gripped her. Was it possible her warder's efficient packing included a dildo? Considering the miscellany of items she'd already discovered—*please God!*

If he'd been so considerate, she'd forgive his brusque authority and senseless rebuffs, his complete unconcern for her feelings. In fact, in her current mindless frenzy, she was indifferent to all his slights if only she attained orgasm *now, now, now*, and with that goal in mind, she dropped to her knees and rummaged madly through the storage cabinets under the seats. Seconds later, she opened a carved wooden box, cried, "Eureka," came up off her knees in a flash, stripped off her riding pants, and speedily put the exquisite ivory dildo to good use.

Racing headlong toward climax, wallowing in a lavish, transcendent ecstasy, she forgave him *everything—every little thing!* Having been tantalized all evening by a man who pleasured other women but not her, a man who'd *almost* succumbed to her blandishments, her climax was almost instant. And so violent she couldn't find the breath to scream.

Fortunately.

Nor time to pull down the shades, she noticed afterward with horror. *Oh God.* Hastily jerking down the silk shades, she briefly anguished over possible witnesses while her heartbeat subsided and the last orgasmic flutter died away. In the end, though, she concluded that no one would dare mention it to her face.

With any possible awkwardness dismissed and her initial frantic urges assuaged, she began to more leisurely explore her revived passions. To that purpose, she occupied herself with her tried-and-true substitute for reality—her imagination. She conjured up her handsome protector: that large body, those huge hands, his weight, the way he moved, with a grace rare in big men. She recalled his stark beauty, his cool, dangerous gaze; he was a man of substance among lesser men, she pleasantly decided as she plied the ivory dildo with deliberate languor. In and out slowly, slowly—a small helpless gasp as breathy punctuation each time she pressed it home. But wanting him instead, wishing all the while that it was Jamie between her legs, his cock gliding in, penetrating her slick warmth—gently, gently.

Or would he be rough and forceful instead? Would he indulge himself rather than her? Was he a brute with that prizefighter body? Not likely, she decided a second later, not with Countess Minton one of his harem. She was a connoisseur of men and their talents.

As the miles rolled by, Sofia continued her solitary, voluptuous game, varying the scene, the rhythm, the picture of Jamie in her mind. And pleasure took on new meaning, an exalted delight, a heightened degree of arousal that could only be attributed to her charismatic, imaginary partner.

She experienced a series of ravishing climaxes—all thanks to the baron's stunning face and form, his stirring virility, his careless indifference—that last quality triggering her fiercest orgasms.

Sofia recalled his cool insouciance and suave courtesy on display that morning at the countess's, the measured neutrality in his attitude as he waited to service the countess again. It had been clear that he was available as stud so long as he was humored.

Sofia had never had to humor a man.

How exactly did one do so?

A most provocative focus of her attention that proved to be highly stimulating, abundantly orgasmic, and ultimately, sweet prelude to sleep.

The sun was a faint golden glow on the horizon when the troop and carriages came to a halt.

The men dismounted, the drivers climbed down, and everyone stretched their muscles after a long night on the road. As conversation broke out amongst the men, Jamie made for the lead carriage. He was tired, desperate for a cup of coffee, and not in the mood to face the troublesome Miss Eastleigh. Silently rehearsing a polite good morning, he approached the carriage and on reaching it, braced himself, forced a smile, and opened the door.

His smile faded.

Sofia was sleeping on the forward seat, half-clothed, one arm trailing on the floor, the dildo fallen from her fingers. But it was her lower body that occupied his attention. She was nude save for the fur robe draped over one leg, her pale pubic hair gleaming in the faint shadows of the interior, her sex sleek and wet from masturbation, a light tincture of residue on her upper thighs.

He had to forcibly restrain himself from climbing into the carriage and waking her with a more substantial substitute for the engraved ivory device. One booted foot was already off the ground before he caught himself. Dropping his foot, he quietly shut the door and took a moment to tamp down his mindless resentment and bring his breathing under control. *Christ, this is all so bloody impossible.* With a muttered curse, he strode away.

But his men took note of his scowl and the small tic near his eye, and when he curtly said, "Miss Eastleigh's sleeping. We'll stop in the next town unless someone objects," no one dared do so.

On the next leg of the journey, he rode far ahead of the troop at a hard, steady pace, putting distance between himself and temptation. Douglas and his brother exchanged glances as they rode side by side, leading the cavalcade. "The bonny lad wants that bit o' fluff, I ken," Douglas said with a grin.

Robbie lifted his chin in the direction of their leader far in the distance. "He canna last long the mood he's in."

"I dinna doubt ye're right."

"Tonight?"

"Aye, if not before."

Both men nodded.

In the next village, Jamie was waiting for them outside a modest hotel that proclaimed its attraction as the holiday residence of some poet long forgotten. The name was unfamiliar except to the locals, although Jamie had been apprised of the man's life story in brief as he'd bespoken a parlor for Miss Eastleigh and breakfast for them all.

He waited for Douglas and Robbie to dismount before coming up and speaking to them, his face absent of expression. "I want you two to guard Miss Eastleigh. The facilities are rather primitive here. No surprise in this rural outland. Escort her to the outdoor facilities and wait for her. Breakfast will be waiting for Miss Eastleigh and both of you in the parlor. She might try to run. She's done it before. So take care. If you lose her," he said, "I'll cut off your balls."

"Ye can try," Douglas said with a grin. "But dinna worry, my bonny boy. We'll be savin' the lassie fer ye."

"Screw you."

"Suit yerself. But she wouldna mind bein' more friendly, I ken." He'd seen how Sofia looked at Jamie when they'd walked out to the carriage, how Jamie had tried to keep his distance. "Nor would ye mind a wee flirtation come ta that."

"It won't come to that," Jamie said, his voice a deep rumble. "And knock on the carriage door before you open it. She might not be dressed."

The brothers exchanged a quick look. *She'd found it then.* They'd overseen the loading of the carriage. "We'll be reet polite to the lass," Robbie noted, trying not to smile. "Losh man, we're a' discreet a' o' priest."

Jamie gave them a gimlet-eyed look. "Just keep it to yourself." Then he turned, took the stairs in a leap, crossed the porch, and entered the hotel. He ate alone, well distant from the troop and the parlor where Sofia and his cousins were breakfasting. He didn't want to see her; he didn't want to think about her. He wished he'd never opened that carriage door.

After he'd quickly eaten, he left orders with one of his men to meet that evening in Kenilworth. "We'll stay there the night," he said. "The lady might be tired of the carriage by evening."

Sofia had been surprised Jamie wasn't at the carriage door when she'd responded to the knock. But she soon understood she was being closely guarded; neither of the two men were more than ten feet away from the privy door when she walked out. Jamie was still absent when they returned to the hotel, and as she entered a private parlor, Douglas pointed. "Yon a washstand for yer convenience, me lady." And he shut the door behind her.

She was grateful for an opportunity to wash, grateful as well for the tasty breakfast that had been laid out on a table set for three. So once she'd finished her ablutions, she opened the parlor door and as expected found her guards waiting outside.

She smiled. "Please join me for breakfast. I gather you are my warders today. I'm Sofia Eastleigh."

"Douglas Blackwood and me brither, Robbie. Pleased to meet ye."

The men looked slightly older than Jamie. Douglas was dark like him; Robbie's hair was a mass of blond-red curls. They were polite, talkative in a reserved way that gave away little of a personal nature, and obviously hungry. As they ate, Sofia asked questions about Jamie's estate in the Highlands, curious about her future hideaway. They answered everything except questions about the location. She understood.

When breakfast was over, she was escorted back to the carriage and the small troop continued their journey. They traveled on back roads, the scenery picturesque under the risen sun: fields of unripe grain; small villages, each with a parish church of divers antiquity; bucolic pastures, herdsmen minding their flocks, sheep and cows and horses; a long stretch of dense forest that cut out the sun for an hour or so. All lovely, green England in May, but a slow, slow, tediously slow journey.

She would have liked to ride, but she hadn't seen Jamie since last night, and when she'd rolled down the window and asked Douglas, who was riding alongside, about him, he'd only said, "Jamie be ridin' ahead," with a reticence that discouraged further questions.

So she read a bit and slept a little and drank some wine after a struggle with a troublesome cork. But it was an unremittingly boring day; she didn't look forward to another as monotonous. She would have to accost Jamie when next they stopped and see that he gave her leave to ride for at least part of the time. She wished to ask him as well if they were approaching the Lake Country where her mother was on holiday.

To her surprise, though, they didn't stop again, other

than for a brief halt where she was offered the opportunity
to relieve herself behind a screen of bushes. Douglas and
Robbie kept a discreet distance but clearly were on guard.

When she returned to the carriage, she was offered a wet
towel. "For ye, my lady," Douglas said with a small bow.

"Thank you," she said, taking the towel from him. "You
think of everything."

He grinned. "Orders, miss."

Her surprise showed for a moment. "I shall have to
thank him then," she said. "The baron is most hospitable."

"The bonny boy could put an army in the field, miss."

"Indeed."

"Yes, miss. Like his father afore him. Now, we won't
be stoppin' again unless ye call out."

Sofia marveled at the horses' stamina as the day wore
on. Prime bloodstock indeed; the teams must have been
bred for endurance. Left with nothing to do, she resorted
to another book. A shame no one had thought to include a
French romance or two. Julius Caesar's *Conquest of Gaul*
turned out to be sufficiently engrossing, however, and
when the cavalcade finally stopped, she took note of the
time on the carriage clock with surprise.

Half past seven, the sun still high in the sky with mid-
summer only weeks away.

Stretching languorously, she turned to look out the window and her spirits brightened. Jamie was directly in her
line of vision, handing his reins to an ostler and apparently
saying something amusing, for the man threw his head back
and laughed. The baron stripped off his gloves as he talked,
and he must have been issuing instructions, for the ostler was
intermittently nodding. A few moments later, the nodding
stopped, Jamie clapped the man on the shoulder, said something more that made the ostler smile, then he turned and
spoke to one of his troopers.

He wore his hair longer than fashion dictated, Sofia

noted. A light breeze was ruffling his dark curls, already disheveled after a night and day on the road.

As if responding to her thoughts, Jamie swept his fingers through his hair in a quick, cursory gesture, and she sucked in her breath, the intimate gesture conjuring up roseate hopes. How would those strong hands feel on her body? How gentle or ungentle was his touch? How calloused were his hands? *Oh God, stop*, she chided herself. Such foolishness was adolescent.

This was simply a job for Blackwood—*she* was simply a matter of business for him.

He'd made that perfectly clear.

But *perfectly clear* aside, was she not at least allowed a purely artistic assessment since he was standing within yards of her—big as life? *Of course*, a selfish little voice whispered in her ear. *You're an artist, after all. A professional artist.*

How easy it was to be convinced when Blackwood presented such a handsome subject. He was standing, large and magnificent, beside his sleek black thoroughbred under a cloudless sky, a bustling village street in the background, his troopers surrounding him. A perfectly lovely narrative painting. She'd title it *The End of the Hunt* with everyone dismounting and milling about. Hunting scenes were much in demand.

Naturally, a central focal point was required in any composition.

In this case, the tall, handsome ADC to Prince Ernst would do. He stood just left of center in the scene, looking splendidly male as usual, tautly muscled beneath his expensive tailoring: his coat was open as if he were relaxing after a long day in the hunting field, his shirt collar unbuttoned, the tanned column of his throat meeting his dark chest hair in the vee of his open shirt.

She let her gaze drift downward, surveying his lean torso

and flat stomach, coming to rest for a moment on the faint swell evident beneath the placket of his snug riding pants. Even inert his virility was unmistakable, although it wasn't possible to realistically portray his sizeable cock unless the painting was for private viewing. Not exactly a rarity in the art world; erotic paintings had always been commissioned by collectors.

Then again, perhaps she might have a private viewing of her own should Blackwood have a change of heart. She grinned. Never say never.

Although he certainly was proving a difficult quarry. At which point he walked away, moving out of view as though to underscore the fact.

Sofia was escorted into the travelers' hotel by her two guards, the large structure typical of many that had sprung up in England with the advent of good roads and in some cases, the railroad. A bustling lobby, numerous palms in large pots, a haze of cigar smoke, portly men in suits reading the papers or conversing in boisterous voices greeted the eye as they entered the lobby.

Apparently, Douglas and Robbie knew their destination, for they walked through the large columned room without stopping, although her garb drew a few sharp glances. From there, she was led upstairs and into a commodious suite situated at the end of a short stairway and narrow hall in the rear of the hotel. "Jamie thought ye'd be likin' the peace a' quiet," Douglas said. *Jamie also thought the isolated entrance would assure that the two guards at my door draw no attention.* "Yer dinner is ordered, a' if ye need ought"—he jerked a thumb toward the door—"we're outside."

After he and Robbie left, Sofia surveyed her lodgings. A large sitting room, a bedroom through the door to her right, even a bathroom, she discovered after walking into the bedroom. A tub, a loo, running water. All the amenities.

A bath would be lovely. Even more lovely would be a change of clothes. She would have to ask about purchasing some tomorrow. Flopping down on the large four-poster bed, she stared up at the pleated canopy and wondered what her elusive protector was doing.

Hiding, apparently, she decided, which in itself *might* be a small triumph. On the other hand, she reminded herself, he was playing the ascetic. Why would he put himself in her way?

She was no nearer an answer when her dinner was carried in by a servant who gave no indication that a woman dressed in male clothes was unusual. He said, with a deference prompted by Jamie's brief directive and lavish tip, "Dinner, miss. Where would you like me to put it?"

Sofia waved him over to the table near the window, and the slim, middle-aged man in the ubiquitous black of the serving class set out her meal, opened the bottle of champagne, lifted the covers on several dishes, and with the grave formality granted royalty, asked her if she required anything more.

She smiled, said, "Thank you, no," and surmised that the man's fulsome courtesy was attributable to the evasive Lord Blackwood. She knew very well her manner of dress was unconventional. *Like everything else in my life at the moment*, she lamented as the door closed on the servant.

Alone again, she pensively mused. A social creature at heart and much in demand in the fashionable world, she half smiled and wondered what Blackwood would have said if she'd asked to bring a lover along for company. Her smile broadened at the dramatic possibilities. What would he have said to Dex, for instance?

With a soft chuckle, she turned to her dinner. The delicacies in the picnic basket aside, she was hungry again. Sitting down at the table, she spread a crisp white linen napkin in her lap and surveyed her small feast. The food was simple but excellent: beefsteak, lamb cutlets, creamed asparagus, fresh peas, two puddings—one treacle, the other a strawberry cream. And, of course, the champagne.

CHAPTER 15

JAMIE AND HIS men ate dinner in a private parlor. The troop was ostensibly a group of friends traveling north for hunting. Everyone wore civilian dress, their weapons were concealed, their native Scot's accent useful for their masquerade. A German accent would have turned heads.

Not that Jamie had explained any more than required to the desk clerk; offering too much information only raised suspicion. But in the privacy of their parlor, the business of the day was discussed in a glib polyglot of languages— their linguistic fluency necessary when the prince traveled so extensively.

Since everyone would be standing guard duty at some point that night, no one drank to excess. But the men were Scots by blood if not circumstance, so even with the restrictions on intake, a good deal of liquor was consumed. With the exception of Jamie. Coffee was his beverage of choice, although even that went largely untouched.

Such curious behavior raised figurative eyebrows among his colleagues. Aqua vitae, *uisge beatha*—whiskey was the water of life to a Scot, and Jamie had never been an abstainer. But after his moody withdrawal earlier in the day and his solitary ride in advance of the troop, not to mention his unusual reticence at dinner, no one put voice to their thoughts. Until a young trooper who'd indulged his taste for whiskey more than most blurted out the question on everyone's mind. "It ain't like ye, Jamie." He jabbed his finger at the coffee cup. "Have ye taken the temperance pledge?"

Jamie looked up and smiled slightly. "I'm just tired."

Archie McDougal grinned. "That niver stopped ye afore."

"It has tonight," Jamie said precisely.

And everyone knew the subject was closed. Although the men had their own ideas why he wasn't drinking, and it had nothing to do with fatigue.

Jamie continued lounging in his chair at the head of the table while his men's conversation eddied around him, the sounds of their voices muted at times by the white noise of an idea whose time had come. An idea he was unwilling to consider. At other times, he'd participate in the conversation and banter, adding a comment or quip, a judgment on some matter at hand, but by and large, his mind was elsewhere. He'd pick up his coffee cup and set it down again without drinking, idly twirl the signet ring on his finger, trace the carving on his chair arm, and if someone asked him a direct question, he'd look up as though he'd come awake from a dead sleep.

And so he remained—challenged by that idea whose time had come, trying hard not to offend his sense of duty.

Or bring on disaster.

Until the case clock in the corner suddenly chimed the hour.

He looked up at the sound, drew in a small breath, and came to his feet. He stood perfectly still for a moment, immune to the numerous glances trained on him, to the hush in the room. Then his green gaze focused. "I'm going to turn in early," he mildly said, surveying his men. "I'll see you all at seven."

As the door shut behind him, Archie smirked. "Damn. I dinna think he'd last this long."

"Nor go withoot ev' a wee dram to drink."

"Dinna want to disappoint the leddy, I ken," another trooper said with a grin.

Someone down the end of the table said, "He can drink all night an' still be right brisk with the leddies."

"Not this one, though, eh?"

Every eye swivelled to Duncan Scott. The concept of personal feelings for a female was quite outside the pale when it came to Jamie's love life.

"Ye're drunk," Archie hotly accused.

"Aye, but he hasna looked her way since mornin'. Ain't like 'im. More like a grass green striplin' it be."

"Stupid twit. As if himself ain't long past stripling games." Archie pelted Duncan with the bread in his hand. "Half-wit muttonhead."

His playful barrage was taken up with gusto by every man at the table, escalating ridicule and adding to the raucous pastime until Duncan, laughing, finally threw up his hands in surrender. His hair was crumb splattered, his grin a flash of his strong white teeth. "Fook ye all. I'm right, ye'll see. Now hand over the bottle. I've a mighty thirst."

The entertainment was over as quickly as it had begun, and conversation turned to other matters.

WHILE HIS MEN had turned to other matters, Jamie was in his suite stripping off his clothes, running water in the bathtub, and telling himself to find another woman if that's what he needed. But he didn't need a woman in general but one in particular, and try as he might to evict that lunatic thought from his brain, try as he did to persuade himself to be reasonable, before long he was bathed, dressed, and making his way to the suite of rooms at the back of the hotel.

Douglas and Robbie were resting comfortably on the floor flanking Sofia's door, their backs against the wall, their legs crossed at the ankles. At Jamie's approach, they came to their feet. "Evenin, sair," they said in unison.

Jamie came to a stop at the door. "No activity I hope."

Douglas shook his head. "Quiet as the grave, sair."

"Good. Archie and Ian will spell you soon. It's been a long day so we're keeping the shifts to three hours. And don't even think of saying what you're about to say."

Robbie looked at his brother, his grin breaking free. "Ye won."

"Told ye."

"Very amusing," Jamie grumbled.

"Dinna forget to sleep a wee bit, my bonny boy." Douglas lifted one brow. "Von Welden plays o' wicked game."

"She might throw 'im out," Robbie teased. "Ye niver know."

"We leave at seven." Jamie wasn't about to discuss the night ahead. "And I'd appreciate no more betting."

Douglas's grin widened. "Would ye now."

"Too late," Robbie said.

Jamie groaned. "At least she's not to know. Are we clear?"

"Yes, sair, yer lordship," Douglas replied, trying mightily not to break out into a guffaw. An unspoken democracy in the Scottish mercenary tradition played the devil with rank and authority.

"Oh Christ, I give up." Whenever his men called him *your lordship*, there was no point in carrying on a serious discussion.

Jamie grabbed the doorknob and gave it a turn.

CHAPTER 16

WHEN HE WALKED in and shut the door behind him, Sofia glanced at the clock on the mantel as if it mattered.

As if the time would be a clue.

"Do you have an appointment?" he said, watching her, not moving from the door.

"It seems I do now. Or do I?" She set her napkin on the table, leaned back in her chair, and looked him over with a speculative gaze. "Why are you here?" It was a woman's question, wanting to know everything.

"I thought you might like me to wash your back." A man's nonanswer.

She smiled faintly. "You've changed your mind."

He shrugged. "Some things are possible and some aren't. I'm not going to agonize over it. Did you like the dildo?"

She lost a modicum of her sangfroid. "You saw that?"

He nodded. "I almost woke you."

A small lascivious jolt. A pause. Then she said, "I wish you had."

"There were too many people around."

"Where do they think you are now?"

"Here—fucking you."

A infinitesimal moment passed; she wasn't being wooed. But how did it matter when she wanted the same? "Will they snicker tomorrow"—she lifted her hand in a small gesture—"about this?"

He shook his head.

"They're afraid of you?"

"Respectful in their fashion. I outrank them."

"Who outranks whom here?"

He smiled. "You, naturally."

"I'm not sure I believe you. In fact, I know I don't."

"Don't worry. It won't come up."

"You know that, do you?"

He could have said, *It never has before*, but he knew better. "Would you like a bath?" he said instead.

"Not yet. Or would you like me to? You've bathed, I see." His hair was wet, slicked back behind his ears. "And you've changed clothes." He was casually dressed in a soft chamois jacket, an open-necked linen shirt that looked as though a valet had just ironed it, black wool trousers, and soft leather half boots with decorative tracery on the toes and braided trim down the sides. "I like your boots. Hungarian?"

"Croatian."

"Close."

"Only in a geographical sense." He smiled faintly. "I won't give the lecture on their many long-standing disagreements."

"I'm afraid I was unable to change." She felt as though she needed an excuse when faced with such sartorial splendor—simple and unaffected as it was.

He smiled again. "You'd look good in sackcloth, Miss Eastleigh, or if I might persuade you—in nothing at all."

"You persuasive?" Her brows rose delicately. "An obvious challenge for a man of your authority."

"But not impossible, I think you'll discover."

She held his amused gaze for a moment, wondering how many times he'd stood before a woman, confident and assured, knowing he was wanted. "At the risk of breaching this new rapport," she crisply said, instinctively reasserting her position, "I *will* need clothes tomorrow."

"Then we'll get you some tomorrow."

"Just like that?"

"Just like that."

His will was like a physical force, the impact on her body swift and explosive. "Your air of command is a potent aphrodisiac." She forcibly restrained the tremor in her voice. "You know that, I suppose."

He supposed he did. "Your brazenness is an aphrodisiac, Miss Eastleigh."

"Sofia. Since we're going to be friends," she added, knowing how to play the game as well as he, dismissing her niggling reservations. Had she not been wanting this for some time?

"Yes, of course." He pushed away from the door, slowly crossed the room, came to a stop beside her chair, and bowed faintly. An elegant, effortless bow. But then he'd been trained by a Spanish princess one summer at Biarritz in his youth. "Might I interest you in furthering our friendship now?" he softly inquired. "I feel sure we have much in common."

She met his cool, insolent gaze and smiled. "You'll certainly be an improvement over the dildo."

"Indeed I will."

"So immodest, Blackwood."

"Jamie. And I selected that dildo, so it's fact, not lack of modesty."

"I thought of you the whole time I was using it," she said, capable of dégagé conversation once again, her raging desire under control. "You were my inspiration."

"You've inspired me as well," he smoothly replied.

She looked up at him from under the lacy fringe of her lashes. "Enough to give up your scruples, I see."

"Or ignore them."

She laughed. "I don't have many scruples."

"I noticed."

"Hmpf," she said, looking up at him with a frown.

"Come," he said, pulling her chair out, taking her hands, and lifting her to her feet. "I don't want to argue. I don't even want to talk unless you do." His brows arched faintly. "I recall you mentioning you don't require conversation. A commendable quality in a woman."

"Or man."

He smiled. "We really will get along," he said, drawing her toward the bedroom.

"Did you ever doubt it?"

"Honestly, no. I just preferred avoiding it."

"But lust intervened."

"Yes." He stopped in the bedroom doorway and met her gaze. "Unfortunately."

"Why did you change your mind?"

"I have no idea. You're too enticing, I suppose. I tried to stay away."

"Will you be angry afterward?"

He smiled. "Hell no."

"No guilt about loyalty or duty?"

His mood was suddenly sober. "This doesn't impinge on my duties," he said. "As for the rest, it was more bloody-mindedness than high principles." He'd disliked Ernst pimping his daughter, disliked being drawn into some family dynamic that was none of his concern.

"To think I could have had you rather than a dildo." She grinned. "Where did I go wrong?"

"You have me now," he said. "All night in case I didn't mention it. Don't expect to sleep."

"In that case, did I mention that you're riding in the

carriage with me tomorrow? At least for a time."

"Hmm," he said. Then his expression cleared and his smile warmed his eyes this time. "It would be my pleasure." He touched her on the cheek, very lightly, with just the tip of his index finger. "Ready?"

"First, I have a shopping list."

Nothing moved in his large body. "You do?"

She looked up and scrutinized his narrowed green gaze. "Am I not allowed?"

"Yes, of course you are." The warmth returned to his eyes.

"I'm sorry. Does every woman say that?"

The answer was yes if he'd been willing to give it. "Not in exactly that way," he said instead.

"Did you think I was different?"

"I suppose not. Maybe it's the country air. It reminds one of simpler times."

"And less-demanding women."

He shrugged. "I'm guilty as well of making demands."

"Dare I say, oh good?"

He laughed. "Say anything, darling. This is all so stupid anyway. If not for your father I would have had you in bed long ago." He pulled her fully into the bedroom and shut the door. "Now, what's at the top of your list?"

"You."

His gaze rested on her for just a second. "Besides that."

"No, I mean I want to watch you undress. Don't look at me like that. It's perfectly reasonable. I want to paint you, not here, but later—so I want to look at you. I'm going to get paints and canvas from Mother when we see her."

She wouldn't be painting him anywhere. Once they reached Blackwood Glen, he was dropping her off and returning to Vienna. "Sit over there." He pointed to a chair. "Or on the bed." He began unbuttoning his shirt, willing to please her. Later he'd please himself. "I've never posed for a painting," he said pleasantly.

She sat across the room and watched his confident hands slide the buttons free, the long, slender fingers working quickly, and she suddenly thought when she shouldn't: *Has he killed anyone with those hands?* Or more to the point tonight, how many women had been caressed with those hands, brought to climax, stroked, and petted? She shivered slightly, wanting to feel those fingers on her, in her, everywhere—on her skin, face, hair, deep inside.

He saw her shiver and understood. Women were peculiar; they liked brute force even while they pretended they didn't. Not that he cared about the subtleties or the reasons why. He'd just learned long ago how to share their excitement. "Would you like to help?"

She shook her head, anticipation tightening the back of her throat. "I don't think I can move without shattering into a thousand pieces."

"I'm sorry you had to wait so long. Do you still want me to do this? I could keep you from shattering, and we could finish this later."

Her smile was a wince. She shook her head.

He moved more swiftly. She might think she could wait, but he wasn't so sure, and for reasons he chose not to scrutinize, he didn't want her to go on without him. Like some tenderhearted cub, he grimly thought. Now that *was* stupid. His jacket, shirt, and shoulder holster came off in concert, and he dropped the lot on a chair. He pulled off his boots and socks next, and as he began to slide his trousers down his hips, he heard a small little squeak. "Wait!" he said fiercely, stripping off his pants. His tone changed abruptly, softened. "Think of something else, of your first teacher, a pet you liked. Did you have a dog, a cat? I had a dog," he said, quickly covering the distance to the chair.

A second later, he had her in his arms and was carrying her to the bed. "His name was Aramis for one of the Three Musketeers." He placed her on the blue silk counterpane, swiftly unlaced her boots enough to jerk them off, and speedily stripped off her pants, which shifted the focus of her thoughts more than any conversation about a dog. My God he was forceful, a professional who knew what he was doing, his hands moving skillfully, deftly. All her former lovers shrank to insignificance—all the men who'd flattered and cajoled and asked her for what they wanted.

Not him, she feverishly thought, hastily spreading her legs as he lowered his body over hers and guided his erection to her throbbing sex. *Not him*, she reflected with a little muted cry as he pressed forward and her warm, pulsing flesh yielded by slow degrees to the swollen crest of his cock.

Jesus. How the hell is he going to fit?

While Jamie was wondering if he should go on, every nerve and cell in Sofia's body was melting in a welcoming frenzy. This is what she'd been wanting from the first sight of Jamie Blackwood weeks ago—this dissolving rush of pleasure at the feel of him inside her. "More," she whispered, stretching her thighs wider to accommodate his sizeable body, lifting her hips in a flagrant act of seduction. Or perhaps it was an act of submission. Not that motive mattered when she was feverishly conscious of the hard, solid feel of him stretching her taut, when she was currently in the grip of the most blissful delirium vibrating outward from the pulsating, exquisitely tenuous merger of their bodies. "Oh God, please, more, more, more!" A flash of a sulky look. "Do you hear?"

Good God, she needed manners. But that was surely permission. Although the question still remained whether permission translated into feasibility. Not that he was in the mood to question anything at the moment with his senses seriously focused on orgasm. He eased forward with caution. That she was lusciously wet was a blessing.

"Please, I really need you," she breathed, reaching up to reverentially touch his face.

"You have me." The lady's capricious moods didn't alter

the fact that he was sunk only crest deep in her sleek, hot flesh. He was more than willing to ignore her previous sulkiness so long as her satiny tissue continued to give way—like that; he forced his erection in another small measure. A pulse beat later he penetrated deeper still with a cautious forbearance that brought a fine sweat to his brow.

"You needn't be so careful," she whispered, her hands at the small of his back urging him on. "I won't break."

"I'm not taking any chances." She was incredibly tight. Sliding his hands under her bottom, controlling his forward motion like a tightrope walker working without a net, he invaded her with painstaking deliberation, using all his considerable finesse to slowly drive his rigid cock deeper.

Unfortunately, his witless attempt at abstinence the past day was playing havoc with his normal control. Dragging in a breath through his teeth, calling on all his willpower, he curbed his rampaging libido. *Slowly, slowly, you can do it. There, like that.* And he glided into the tightest little pussy he'd ever encountered a deft fraction more with a tenderness that acknowledged Miss Eastleigh's—he'd have to get used to calling her Sofia—fragility. He couldn't banish the unnerving thought that she might suffer if he treated her too roughly. He'd noticed that first day—how small she was beside Bella, how slender.

She gasped.

Oh Christ. He froze.

"No, no . . . it's wonderful," she acknowledged with a blissful sigh.

Every muscle in his body rebounded from its seizure; he exhaled the breath he hadn't realized he'd been holding. "You must tell me when I've gone too far. Tell me and I'll stop." *Somehow.*

"Don't you *dare* stop!"

He was consoled by her imperious tone. "Is that an order?" But he was smiling.

"Yes, and for your information, I'm getting frustrated."

That makes two of us. "You're almost too small," he said, instead of being rude.

"Or you're too big."

"In any case, we have a problem." Although in his present state of arousal, he was seriously considering alternatives to intercourse.

"We do not!" she said in a deeply aggrieved tone.

"You know that, do you?" He wasn't so sure. His erection was only half submerged.

"What if I said I knew because of Dex? Would that irritate you enough to forget your damned caution?"

He looked down on her and frowned. "You said you didn't know him."

"I didn't say I didn't know him. I just said he wanted to have sex with me that night. I didn't say it was the first time. There now, that's better." His cock had instantly swelled inside her.

"Bitch." But his voice was velvet soft.

"A very hot, eager, impatient bitch," she purred.

She was opening like a flower. He should have known. Some women liked discord with their sex. Dropping his head, he whispered in her ear, "I don't want to hear any complaints afterward."

"And I don't want to hear any more caviling from you," she replied, flippant and pert. "You'd think I was a virgin."

He grinned. "I'd never think that. But I also didn't want to have to call in a doctor."

"Are we done with this conversation? I have other things I'd rather do."

Christ, she could be a brat, as if it were his fault she was half his size. "You're damned annoying."

Her eyes flared wide. "*I'm* annoying? I've never had to wait so long for an orgasm."

An inexplicable resentment flooded his senses. "How long do you usually wait?" he asked, thin-skinned and edgy.

"Certainly not this long. I should find that dildo."

"First you'd have to be able to move," he drawled.

"Are you threatening me?"

"I suppose I am." Her vaginal tissue was softly pliant now, her drenched cunt unfurling with gratuitous spontaneity.

"Do you often threaten women?"

"I've never had to before." There—in a few inches more. The audacious little wanton liked confrontation.

"They all fall into your arms, I suppose."

"More or less." Almost there.

"And you pick and choose."

"Sometimes. Sometimes I accommodate them all." Ah, finally. He was buried to the hilt. Apparently, she liked men who talked after all. "But you can be first tonight," he added, driving in that infinitesimal distance more where the true essence of lurid pleasure is revealed.

"Oh God, oh God, oh *God*!" Her voice was no longer contentious but wispy, breathless, devoid of friction.

He smiled; the doors to paradise were open wide. "I can make it even better," he whispered, having honed his skills to perfection, knowing a modicum more pressure incited an even more feverish response. "Like this."

It took a moment before she found the breath to speak with a blissful soul-stirring glow pervading her senses, her body, the known universe. "I—can't . . . *thank* you enough."

"Nor I you." A strange thought, but then he'd never gone so long without fucking a woman he wanted, he told himself. His cock was aching, his heart pounding against his ribs, the small lady impaled on his erection challenging previous notions of sexual nirvana. "Try a little more now," he softly urged, withdrawing slightly before gliding in again with considerably more ease—what was tight, supple now, what was hot, hotter, what seemed impossible before, now indescribably sweet, heady, spine-tingling, and any number of other illusions he'd always considered sentimental nonsense.

When he came to rest again, buried deep inside her, held fast in her sleek, warm flesh, he no longer questioned the concept of bewitchment. Then her fingernails dug into his back, her climax suddenly commenced, and his thoughts turned to more prosaic matters like *Thank God*—he wasn't sure how much longer he could have lasted.

He chivalrously waited, though, until her orgasm stilled, until her fingers unflexed, until she opened her eyes and complained, "That was too fast."

He knew what she meant. "Better than climaxing without me," he said.

"I suppose," she grumbled.

"We have all night."

Her expression brightened. "Forgive me. I can be selfish. About everything," she added with a rueful smile.

"I'll forgive you if you'll do the same. I usually can wait, but I've been thinking of you, of this, for a very long time. Or what seemed like a long time. I can't wait anymore."

She laughed, and he felt it down to his toes.

He grinned. "At least we'll have the introductions out of the way."

"And very pleasantly. You must be invited everywhere." Her gratified nerve endings were still humming with his glorious cock lodged inside her.

"This is the only invitation that interests me *now*."

"Oh sorry, you're waiting, aren't you? You can't come in me, though," she added, a sudden seriousness in her voice.

"God no."

Before she could decide whether his vehemence was an insult or a courtesy, he abruptly moved, slowly withdrawing, or almost withdrawing before plunging back into the deepest depths, and she gasped instead as an unspeakable ecstasy bombarded her senses. "Do that again," she whispered, feeling as though she were blissfully dissolving in a golden cloud of rapture.

He understood that a degree of gentlemanly behavior was required, although he wasn't quite sure he was capable of it. But he tried because he wasn't a novice and he wished to please her. A startling thought at this point in his arousal. But there it was, so he *did it again* and then again, and several more times, drawing on his considerable experience to delay his orgasm and allow the lady to climax once more.

But it was a damn close call.

His eyes were shut tight in deterrent, his powerful back arched against the urgency of the rushing torrent about to explode, and a certain tension in the rhythm of his breathing was audible as he politely waited for the lady's orgasmic ripples to wane. When *at last* he gauged her reasonably satisfied, he uttered a low guttural growl, set his teeth, and by sheer determination jerked out her enticing little cunt a mille-second before a pent-up flood of semen exploded in a shuddering ejaculation that laid waste every preconceived notion of sexual gratification in his canon of erotic sensation.

Already personally aware of the rule changes in terms of sexual gratification, Sofia lay docile beneath him, basking in the afterglow while the splendid man who'd radically altered her notions of pleasure climaxed. His broad shoulders were taut under the convulsive strain, his muscles starkly defined in extremis, his hands hard on her hips, restraining her, exerting his power.

That unequivocal display of authority was also tempering Sofia's views on male domination—at least in the bedroom. And why not, she decided, when she was being serviced by the most sublime, blatantly virile lover she'd ever had.

She understood more fully as well why Jamie Blackwood was such a favorite of the countess. Not only was he hung like a bull, but he was both skilled and magnanimous in managing that valuable asset. A little flurry of anticipatory ferment raced up her spine at the prospect of enjoying his attentions again; he'd promised to keep her up all night.

How nice.

She'd have to be polite; she wasn't always.

She must take pains to be agreeable, even though his seminal discharge currently pouring over her stomach was—she smiled—leaving a mess.

Seconds later, his green eyes flicked open, and pushing the counterpane aside with one hand, he smiled sideways at her. "That was very nice," he said, well-mannered and flattering as he grabbed a corner of the sheet and, dropping back on his heels, wiped himself off. "Thank you."

"I hope you're not done!"

His hand froze for a moment, a fresh portion of sheet crumbled in his fist. "I'll need a minute or two," he said, his face devoid of expression, and dropping the crushed linen on her stomach, he began sopping up his semen.

"I'm sorry," she said into the sudden oppressive silence. "My manners are atrocious."

"It doesn't matter. Manners aren't high on my list of priorities right now." He tossed the sheet aside, skidded her over on the silk counterpane with a shove of his hand, dropped onto his back beside her, and exhaled a long, unhurried breath.

His bluntness was provocative, a refreshing change after so many fawning men. More pertinent, his dismissive tone was flagrantly arousing, as if he viewed her as no more than an object of his lust. Ummmmm . . . pleasant thought. She could almost *feel* his huge cock gorging her full.

Tantalized by recent memory, she came up on one elbow to view the handsome, hard-bodied man who excited and provoked her desires, who made her greedy for sex when she'd never felt such urgency—when sex had never been about compulsion . . . until now.

Have two minutes passed? Is it too soon to ask for more?

His eyes were half-closed, his long lashes shadowing his gaze, his strong, lithe form motionless.

Dare I intrude? Restive and uncertain when she never was, when she prided herself on a life of spontaneity, she softly sighed.

His head didn't move, but his eyes swivelled her way. "Two minutes more and I'll be with you."

She flushed under his gaze and thought about offering demur.

He smiled. "I didn't know you could blush."

"I'm not blushing," she said like a child caught in some obvious mischief. But treacherous longing carried her gaze downward to his upthrust penis, only marginally diminished with his orgasm.

He followed her gaze and, lazily lifting his hand, ran his finger up the length of his turgid cock. "He likes you."

A wild impatience warmed her blood as his erection swelled larger before her eyes. "The feeling's mutual," she said on a caught breath, the veins of his penis prominent and pulsing, the prodigious increase in size breathtaking. "And I beg your pardon in advance," she added with future gratification tantamount in her mind. "I can be outspoken at times."

His lashes lifted marginally as though such understatement was enough to gain his attention. "You're absolved in advance," he smoothly replied, future gratification on his agenda as well. "Feel free to say what you like."

She took exception to his careless drawl. "Because it doesn't really matter what I say, does it?"

He finally opened his eyes fully, turned his head, and rather than respond to her tart comment, smiled faintly. "What I meant was—*nothing* matters when I'm focused on *this*," he said, turning smoothly on his right hip, slipping his left hand between her legs, and shoving two of his fingers palm deep into her hot flesh. "But talk if you like," he added, gently stroking her dew-wet tissue. "I'm listening."

Suddenly she didn't have enough air in her lungs to talk, to breathe, to bring a coherent thought to utterance. Resentment and umbrage vanished in a blaze of white-hot desire, and shutting her eyes, she fell on her back with a soft melting sigh.

Such ripe vulnerability, Jamie pleasantly thought. The lady had an enticing proclivity for arousal, almost a frightening receptivity if he was inclined to question his sexual prowess. He wasn't, though; in fact, he was debating whether to use his cock or his fingers this time. He supposed he knew the answer before he even asked the question, and climbing on top of her, he entered her slippery warmth without preliminaries or foreplay, without so much as a kiss.

They mated that time with a wild, reckless savagery—their frantic coupling an act of blind desire, of fiery, self-centered lust, of a reluctance to give credence to their calamitous feelings—but feeling them nonetheless in every raw, exposed nerve and throbbing bit of flesh. Feet braced, he pounded into her, and she met his hard driving rhythm with equal fearlessness, crying out in an openmouthed frenzy at every violent downstroke, clutching at his arms each time to restrain his withdrawal, their bodies sleek with sweat, both selfishly taking, not giving, as if they might never have another chance to rut like beasts, as if the world might end in the next few seconds, as if there should be a bronze marker to commemorate the occasion.

He collapsed afterward, drained, utterly sapped, conscious thought in abeyance.

Panting to catch her breath, Sofia reveled in the feel of his weight pressing her into the mattress, the vibrations of his heart hammering against her breast; paradise was no longer a land of mystery.

Rarely neglectful of courtesy in the boudoir, a moment later, Jamie raised his face from the mattress near her shoulder, levered his body up a fraction so he wasn't crushing her, and meeting Sofia's warm gaze, ruefully said, "Now it's my turn to apologize. I hope you're not hurt."

"What do *you* think?" A grin in every syllable.

I think you're the hottest little puss on God's green earth. "Good," he said. "I wouldn't want to make you angry."

"Considering the night's young."

He smiled. "Yes. And I'm sorry I've ruined your shirt." He'd had the presence of mind the first time to push up her shirt before coming on her stomach. Not so, this time.

They were both sticky.

She shrugged. "I don't care about my shirt. However"—she shut her eyes briefly before opening them again—"the thing is"—she stopped again, then blew out a breath, clearly reluctant to voice her thoughts—"oh hell, here goes."

He repressed his smile; she was a wild, fey spirit. He expected no less.

"Anyway, I have the strangest feeling, about you, us—no, mostly about me . . . that I'm somehow losing myself, my independence, my will." The fear had come over her suddenly, like a dangerous undertow in an otherwise calm sea, that the outrageous happiness she was feeling was in violation of all her rules against entanglement. Amorous play was a game after all—or had been. Now, damn it, some unwanted magic was in play. "Sex is never like this for me," she grumbled, her face pinked with emotion. "Men ask and I decide if I want them or not. But I never do for long, and now"—her nostrils flared—"I don't like feeling so out of control, so dependent on"—she pointed at his penis resting against her thigh—"that."

"Don't worry. There's nothing wrong with feeling good." His mind was moving quite coldly and calmly now. He could manage this. "It's not a personal crisis. It's one night or—"

"Don't forget about tomorrow. You promised you'd ride with me, damn it. Blackwood?" Her brief moment of uncertainty was effaced.

"I heard," he said. He was trained to deal with crises—or noncrises, as it were in this case. "I'll ride with you. I said I would and I will," he added in a reasonable voice. "And you needn't be concerned about losing your independence. This is simply about pleasure—yours and mine. We'll stop to visit your mother, we'll stop overnight once or twice more, you can give me all the orders you want." He smiled. "And I won't complain. We'll find you some clothes tomorrow, too. I'll take you shopping." It never failed, promising to take a woman shopping.

She grimaced. "You're way too smooth."

"No. This feels different to me, too."

She snorted. "See? You'll say anything."

He shook his head rather than explain that he'd never felt this way before. But mostly he didn't want to lie because he knew he wouldn't feel this way next week or next month. He'd fucked a lot of women; he understood time limits. But he spoke with genuine affection when he said, "I'm more than willing to be accommodating when it comes to your pleasure, until such a time as you make that decision you always make with men." He smiled. "Although I'm willing to bet I can keep you interested longer than most."

She reached up to touch the fine straight bridge of his nose. "Arrogant man. Although I'm not about to take issue with you," she said with a sudden smile. "I'd rather think about what we should do next?"

Crisis averted. "I'd suggest we start by taking off your wet shirt."

And after quickly wiping himself off, he did just that with fastidiousness and dispatch.

There was nothing clumsy about him, Sofia pleasantly thought, as he eased her back on the pillows after disposing of her shirt. She was reminded of that first fateful morning at Countess Minton's when Jamie had navigated the perilous currents between Bella and Lily Chester with ease. He knew how to handle women.

"I'll be right back. Don't move." Jamie slid from the bed with her shirt and riding pants in hand.

"What if I did?" she said to his back.

He shot a grin over his shoulder. "You couldn't go far." He stopped in the doorway to the bathroom, turned, and held up her clothes.

A small unsettled feeling gripped her. "Am I your prisoner?"

"Of course," he said. "You have been from the first."

When he returned from the bathroom, he carried towels, one of them wet. "Should I or would you like to?" He offered her a wet and dry towel.

She scowled at him. "I don't wish to be your prisoner."

"I'll be very kind. You won't notice." Ignoring her scowl, he started wiping away the residue of their lovemaking from her stomach.

"Don't talk to me like I'm a child."

"Then stop acting like one." He shoved her legs apart and shot her a look from under his lashes as he began wiping away the stickiness.

"Does the Countess Minton like you to do this?" Sulky and fretful, she swept her hand downward to indicate his swabbing.

"I wouldn't know."

"What the hell does that mean?"

"It means it's none of your business."

She slapped his head—hard, and he jerked upright, frowning.

"Do I have to tie you up to do this?" he muttered.

"Does the countess like to be tied up?" She was green-eyed with jealousy when she had no right, when she should be worrying about the duration of her imprisonment.

"I couldn't say. Do you?"

"It depends," she replied, oversweet and provocative.

He didn't like her answer. There was no godly reason why her answer should matter one way or another, but it did. "What does it depend on?" he asked in a tone of voice that would have put anyone who knew him on guard.

"On the mood I'm in, I suppose," she flippantly declared.

"Do you like whips, too?"

This time she recognized the extent of her danger in his low, carefully controlled tone. "What are you going to do?" she quickly inquired, conscious once again of his size and power, of the temper in his eyes. And if it had been possible to take a step back, she would have.

The fear in her voice stopped him, although it took another second before he was able to speak composedly with the graphic image of other men making love to her roiling in his brain. "I apologize. I didn't mean to frighten you." He bent his head to kiss her but stopped midway when she shivered. "Here, you finish," he said, tossing her the towel. "I'll sit over there"—he pointed—"so you needn't be alarmed. I'm sorry, I've been in the wrong job too long."

There was something in his voice, an underlying weariness that touched her, that instantly eclipsed her resentment and fear. She watched him walk away, drop into a chair halfway across the room, slide down on his spine, and shut his eyes. He looked afflicted, if a body that strong could display suffering. But he did at least appear to be bearing a heavy cross.

A moment later when she slid off the bed, he opened his eyes.

"You look unhappy," she said, moving toward him.

"I'm just tired. I haven't slept much lately."

"Would you prefer sleeping now?" Coming to rest before his bare outstretched feet, she met his gaze. "I know how to be obliging, although I haven't acquitted myself well with you. I'm sorry for that."

"You needn't apologize." But he spoke the words automatically, as if his mind was elsewhere.

"Would you like to sleep? I won't bother you if you do." She wanted his attention, though. She wanted him to say no; she selfishly wanted him to fix his priorities on her.

He looked up at her, his green eyes somber as if pondering his answer, as if wanting to respond honestly.

"I'd understand whatever your answer," she said.

His gaze traveled up her body, slowly, leisurely, stopping for a moment on her breasts. Her breathing was disordered, agitated, and her breasts were quivering slightly. He could have driven a bargain with her when she was in that state. He could have asked for anything. But he wasn't that sort of man—or at least not with her, or at least not tonight.

Hauling himself upright in the chair, he put aside his fatigue and held out his hand. "Come here, brat. You can try to be obliging, and I'll try not to frighten you."

She promptly launched herself at him with unbridled delight, and his reflexes supple, he caught her in midair, set her on his lap, and held her close. Tomorrow he'd worry about the pointlessness of all this.

Snuggling against his warmth and power, his strong, muscular neck, Sofia exhaled a blissful sigh. "I adore feeling this way," she murmured. "Head-over-heels joyful. You've bewitched me." Lifting her head slightly, she met his amused gaze. "Don't laugh. I'm serious. You don't know how I normally deal with men."

He grinned. "I can guess. You tell them jump and they jump."

"And you refuse to," she said with a playful pout.

He dipped his head and touched her forehead with his lips. "You're just not used to taking orders. You'll get used to it," he roguishly said.

"What if I don't?" She wasn't entirely teasing.

"You forget that I'm large and you're small," he said,

smiling. "And," he added, a jaded note suddenly evident in his voice, "I've been giving orders for a very long time."

"You sound as though you're tired of it. Are you?" She paused a moment. "I expect taking care of my father can be trying."

"Yes," he said realistically. "And you're like him in more ways than you'd care to acknowledge," he gently added.

"I am *not*!" she bristled.

"Tell me about your mother." He didn't want to fight again. At least not tonight. "Will she be surprised to see us?"

She had to admire how deftly he changed the subject. "Mama and Ben always have a great many guests." She, too, was more than willing to shift the topic to one less fraught with contention. "We'll be welcomed along with all the rest."

"They won't think it strange when we suddenly arrive?"

She shook her head. "The farmhouse in the summer is a favorite destination for all their friends. Artists come and go, some are invited, some aren't, but no one seems to care. The house is big, and everyone's familiar with unusual living arrangements since finances are uncertain in the art world. My parents are well-off, though. Mama sells anything she paints, and Ben was a successful artist before he met Mother."

"So you've not lived a life of deprivation."

"I suppose in Ernst's terms we have. But not compared to others."

"Have you always wanted to be a painter?"

"Not seriously at first. I began as a model—yes, yes, I know," she said with a grin. "How could I do something so scandalous? But it wasn't scandalous to me or my family. I knew lots of men and women who posed for paintings or for drawing classes. It was perfectly normal."

"Do you still pose?" A gently put query.

"Heaven's no. Not since my work began to sell. I only modeled because I didn't want to be dependent on my parents. I wanted to succeed on my own; it was my rebellious phase, you see."

He understood perfectly, but he knew better than to say so.

"You're very polite." His reticence was commendable. She knew how the conventional world viewed women who posed nude and rebellious women in general.

A faint smile lifted the corners of his mouth. "I'm trying. You feel good—warm and soft—a notable object of joy, I might add. Like you, I don't normally feel this way or give voice to such outré emotions. So I have no intention of taking issue with anything you do in your life— including this."

She grinned. "I may harangue you with impunity then?"

"Preferably not. But if you must, I've probably heard worse."

"I hope you're not referring to the women in your life," she said with a petulant sniff.

"Of course not," he lied, but he liked her jealousy. It made his own rash impulses less bizarre.

"Good," she pithily said. Then she giggled. "This is totally outrageous, isn't it?"

"Totally." He didn't have to ask her what she meant.

She slipped her hand between them and gently touched the crest of his erection that lay hard against his flat belly. "Were you going to ask, or would you have let this go to waste?"

"I probably wouldn't have asked, since every other man you know does, but," he said with a lift of his brows, "it wouldn't have gone to waste either."

"Because you're large and I'm small."

"Yes, but I would have been polite."

"How polite?"

"Polite enough that you asked me."

A small silence ensued.

Then he turned her slightly and kissed her gently, a

gallant's kiss, a poet's kiss, eloquent, lyrical, sweet as sugared violets. And she waited, breath held, when he lifted his mouth and met her wide blue gaze. "Is that polite enough?" he softly queried.

A smile lit her eyes. "*Too* polite."

He laughed. "More boldness is in order then."

His lips touched hers again, less gently this time, but still marked by neither impatience nor urgency—as if he were inured to sexual fervor, immune to the heat coursing through her body, indifferent to the increasingly slippery sensation of her sex rubbing against his thigh.

As if he could wait indefinitely.

His kisses probed, tantalized, skillfully asserted his physical dominance with a shameless assurance that whetted her appetite for more than kisses, and soon she was trembling like some blushing tyro at her master's knee. Although perhaps she *was* a tyro, those familiar with Jamie might conclude.

Unaware of his sexual history, however, and indifferent to it in any case with vaulting desire at fever pitch, she leaned into him and opened her mouth to him, wanting him to know he could have anything he wanted, even her heart, although she suspected she must be insane for even thinking so. But insatiable need was coloring her every thought, corrupting reason, giving new meaning to the word *desperation*. Abruptly pulling back, she looked up, revealing the heat in her eyes, the unwise affection that he wouldn't care to see, and whispered, "I'm asking now."

It was almost anticlimactic. With anyone else it would have been. But there was nothing normal about this night, this woman, his gut-wrenching lust. Sliding his hands through her pale, silken hair, he gathered it gently in his fists, and quietly said, "I'm obsessed with you, dangerously so. You must stop me if I become too violent." He knew even as he spoke that he should never have said what he said, and he wondered if it was too late to retrieve it.

Whether he might utter some glib, flirtatious phrase that would paper over his monstrous mistake.

"Do anything you please." She looked him straight in the eye with the boldness he'd come to recognize. "I'm not your voice of reason." Her eyes were midnight blue and fevered. "You've made another conquest. Now hurry."

"Are you sure?" A sop to his conscience; the sense of victory infusing his soul something else entirely.

She smiled. "It's either you or one of your troopers."

He was laughing when he lifted her by the waist, swung her around to face him, and holding her up on her knees with one hand under her bottom, guided the head of his penis into an advantageous position. "By the way, my troopers are off-limits to you," he quietly said, his gaze steady and suddenly humorless as he relinquished his hold and leaned back in the armchair. "Now show me what you can do."

Damn his cool arrogance and bloody insolence! How dare he treat her like some woman in a brothel! For a prolonged moment, Sofia hovered, willful and angry, torn between carnal need and rage. But reason and intellect were defenseless against powerful craving and feeling; as if she were drowning in a whirlpool of insatiable longing, she capitulated. She held his gaze, though, as she slowly lowered herself down his erection, her eyes blazing with an incendiary light that scorched him, challenged him, dared him to reach out and touch her.

He didn't. He wouldn't.

Arresting her descent with his massive cock only half absorbed, Sofia offered him a cheeky, getting-even kind of smile. "Now what?" she murmured.

A second passed, two, three—four, the silence strained and viperous.

Jamie drew in a breath—the small sound barely audible. Exhaling as quietly, he deliberately placed his hands, fingers splayed, on either side of her waist and gradually tightened his grip—as though he were indecisive or reluctant, perhaps for less virtuous reasons. His face was a mask, his gaze shuttered, his intent and motives unclear.

A second passed, belligerence in the air—the issue joined as it were.

Then with a twitch of his lips and brute force, Jamie pushed Sofia downward with ruthless dispatch.

"I'm sorry," he said as she shuddered under his hands, impaled on his massive cock. "That lacked finesse."

"I hate you," she hissed.

"That's too bad," he said in a distracted way, adjusting his fingers at her waist. "How much more can you take? This much?" He flexed his hips and drove upward. "Or this much?" He pressed deeper and stopped only when she cried out. "Sorry, I'll be more careful," he said. But his lazy drawl was without a hint of penitence. Nor did his cool gaze suggest benevolence.

He disliked his craving for this quarrelsome woman, disliked more his lack of restraint, regarded his inability to walk away before or now as lamentable at best and more likely ruinous. But knowing his antipathies didn't dispel a scintilla of his lust, and when Sofia didn't answer, moody and edgy, he said, "Answer me, because I want to know. Am I too deep or not deep enough? Does this feel like Dex? Or one of your other lovers? Are you ready for more?"

His rancorous queries went unheard.

Sofia's entire consciousness was focused on the agonizing pressure, the sweet, agonizing, ripe, consummate, up to the ears, up to the brim, lock, stock, and barrel, prodigal, without restraint glory that was almost, *almost* too much of a good thing.

Recognizing that the woman transfixed on his cock was insensible to all but prurient sensation, that she was trembling on the brink of excess because of him, because she wanted him the same way he wanted her, he was chastened and appeased, deeply gratified as well. Taking pity on her or perhaps only raising the stakes, he hoisted her body upward ever so slightly to ease her seething, overwrought nerve endings. Then leaning close—no longer vengeful but giving her warning even as he fought to subdue the baffling savagery impelling him—he put his mouth to her ear and whispered, "You must help me."

She struggled to open her eyes. His voice was tautly drawn, his hands at her waist biting into her flesh, his broad shoulders rigid under her palms. "I'll do anything for you," she whispered, volunteering her answer without restraint. Then opening her eyes fully—an act of considerable will—she reached up, framed his face in her hands, drew his mouth to hers, and kissed him greedily.

Her impetuous response wasn't exactly the temperance he sought. On the other hand, Miss Eastleigh was who she was—headstrong, impatient, provocative, and provoking. Whatever restraint was required would be his responsibility.

He smiled faintly under her frenzied kisses, reminded of her remarkable zest for fucking, of their very agreeable sexual rapport, of the lush heat of her body snugly enveloping his cock. Controlling his brutish impulses would be a tolerable quid pro quo for the notable pleasure she delivered. At which point he mustered the necessary gallantry; he was after all proficient at this game.

"You decide when too much is too much," he gently said. "It's entirely up to you." Loosening his grip, he watched her closely as she descended that small distance more and came to rest on his thighs once again.

Glancing up through the fringe of her lashes, Sofia whispered, "*Almost* when."

"Your most obedient servant, ma'am," he whispered in return, penetrating her tight little cunt an exquisite modicum more. Then they both shut their eyes to absorb the shimmering rapture, the balmy, fragrant glory that beggared description, dazzled the imagination, measured joy in degrees of exaltation.

"Can one die of pleasure?" Sofia whispered moments later, the concept of breathless wonder no longer an abstract concept.

"As many times as you want, darling." A practical man at base, he'd found his bearings, his fit of madness overcome.

"You're offering me carte blanche?"

"I am."

She wrinkled her nose in a charming little bunny twitch. "I'm jealous of such casual largesse, or I would be if I wasn't more interested in my own selfish pleasures."

"Sensible girl." He grinned. "Although you're not the only one intrigued by selfish pleasures. I seem to have a perpetual hard-on with you."

She gave him a saucy smile. "Only with me, of course."

"Only with you," he replied, prevarication a responsibility and obligation in the bedchamber. "See how this feels." And he proceeded to indulge Sofia gladly and often, no longer chafing at her presumption or assertiveness, no longer concerned with who did what to whom, only conscious that she touched him in strange and countless ways. Although she impressed him most with her wild, unbridled passion, her insurgent spirit attuned to his predacious impulse to take her by storm more often than not.

Until a good time later, having moved to the bed, they were both still heedless of all but the continuing fierce, hysterical delirium. Sofia was frantically, breathlessly, wildly begging for more, and Jamie almost forgot the primary rule in the game of love. He almost forgot to withdraw.

At the very last second, he wrenched himself free from her arms and legs that were holding him in a death grip and twisted away. Falling on his back, he lay spread-eagle beside her, his semen spewing everywhere, his heart pounding, and gasped, "That was fucking close."

"Once wouldn't—really . . . matter—would it?"

His head snapped around.

Her fair skin was pinked from her exertions, her blue gaze still heated, her brows raised faintly in query. "What?"

"Nothing." He blew out a breath. It was true. Your life *did* flash before your eyes.

"Oh Christ," she said, suddenly conscious of his distrustful gaze. "Do you think—I'm trying to . . . trap you?"

It took a moment too long before he said, "No," and reached for a towel.

Her downy brows came together. "Do they *all* want to—trap you?" she incredulously inquired.

He didn't answer as he wiped himself dry.

"My, my, and even then you can't keep your randy cock from obliging all of them," she playfully noted, her breathing restored. Rolling closer, she reached out to stroke his glorious, indefatigable erection.

He flinched.

She laughed, her hand arrested short of its target. "I suppose it won't help to say I'm not like all the rest."

He abruptly sat up, the conversation not one he cared to prolong. "I need a drink." He dropped the towel on the floor. "Would you like one?"

She glanced at the clock.

His dark brows arched. "Am I keeping you from something?"

"I'm not sure you'd like my answer." He might be prickly, but so was she. It boggled the mind that every woman he knew wanted to snare him. Did the silly fools have no identity of their own?

"Fine. Let me know if you want a drink." He slid off the bed and walked away. He objected to women who wanted to discuss their feelings or his. It was a subject he always avoided.

He was standing before the liquor table in the sitting room, pouring himself a healthy bumper of whiskey, debating whether it was time to bring the entertainment to an end, when Sofia called out, "Bring the champagne from dinner."

As if his cock was trained to the sound of her voice, it instantly rose to attention, and he sensibly decided that quarreling was counterproductive when there were hours yet until morning. He was here, she was here, and apparently his cock was calling the shots.

As if he could have walked away from the audacious little bitch in any case, he understood. Nor could any man in possession of his faculties.

A sentiment similar to the one Sofia had adopted after only a few moments of selfish contemplation. How could it possibly matter what his other lovers thought, she decided. It would be an act of great foolishness to deprive herself of several more orgasms simply out of spite. "I apologize for teasing you," she offered as he returned with his whiskey and the half-drunk bottle of champagne. "It makes no difference to me what other women do." She smiled. "I've decided to concentrate on my own pleasure. If you don't mind being of assistance?"

He laughed. "Does any man ever say he does to a question like that?"

"I really couldn't say."

"Forgive me. We shall avoid the personal."

"With the exception of our particular intimacy."

"Yes." He handed her the bottle. "Would you like a glass?"

"No, I'd like something else," she bluntly replied.

Taking a seat beside her on the bed, Jamie raised his whiskey. "As soon as I finish this."

She took a sip of champagne, found it too warm, and set the bottle aside. "How long will it take to finish your drink?" she sweetly inquired.

An irresistible spur to fucking his brains out, he decided.

Draining the liquor in one gulp, he dropped the glass on the carpet and smoothly settled between her legs in a graceful flow of coordinated muscle and athletic agility. "You have my full attention, sweetheart." His smile was very close and boyishly sweet. "The timing's up to you. You know the drill; you first, I follow."

But he was very much less willing to tempt fate now, less willing as well to accept Sofia's avowal that she had no interest in trapping him when most women he knew did.

From that point on, he made love with his intellect fully engaged.

Not that Sofia noticed. Jamie's sexual talents were versatile enough to afford her pleasure so tempestuous and stunning that cerebral concerns were entirely deferred. And for the next few hours the suspension of clear-eyed judgment continued while the lovely prisoner and her rutting warder played at love and dazzled their nerve endings in an unremitting celebration of orgasmic fervor.

Much later that night when passion had been explored in all its many manifestations—first accommodating her wishes, then his, then theirs—Sofia lay replete in Jamie's arms, half asleep, her head cushioned on his chest, her small form warm against his body. "Why aren't you married?" she drowsily queried.

Jamie's blood turned to ice in his veins. But his voice when he replied was deliberately mild. "Marriage isn't practical in my line of work. A wife might soon become a widow."

"Have you ever been tempted to marry?"

She was almost asleep so his panic was manageable; at least this wasn't a discussion over the breakfast table. "Not really," he said. "I suppose I haven't met the right woman." Women believed in the romantic possibilities. Personally, he preferred to put his trust in the caliber of his handgun.

"You'll know it when you do." Her voice was barely audible, spellbound as she was by gratification so stupifying she wasn't aware how abnormal her comment. She'd always been averse to romantic sentiment, quick to ridicule the lovesick, spoony muck that passed for polite flirtation.

"I'm sure I will," he tactfully replied, recognizing that her breathing had slowed, that she was about to nod off.

A moment later when she finally fell asleep and his inquisition ended, he relaxed. Not that he was likely to dwell on freakish notions like marriage in any event when serious life-and-death issues confronted him.

In the quiet of the room his thoughts turned to such issues, and he took the opportunity to systematically review their plans for tomorrow, verifying once again the necessary details to see them safely to their next night's lodging. With assassins on their trail, every exigency had to be examined and reexamined. Their choices were few and all of them harsh. They couldn't afford mistakes.

As the clock struck four, he considered getting up and leaving to sleep in his own bed. If he was sensible, he would. But he didn't for reasons he chose not to acknowledge. He was damned tired, he rationalized. The lady had exhausted him. He'd have to come back and wake her soon anyway. He might as well stay where he was.

So having disposed of irksome doubts and reservations, he immediately slept, waking an hour later by his internal clock—a skill acquired long ago as a subaltern in the field. Quietly slipping from Sofia's embrace, he quickly dressed and ignored his men's smirks when he walked out into the hall and shut the door behind him.

"Good mornin', sair."

"Morning. I'll be back soon. No one's to leave."

"Right nice mornin', sair," the other trooper brightly noted.

"Yes, it is." Jamie exhaled softly, knowing what both his men wished to ask. "I'll send someone up so you two can breakfast before we leave." And he walked away, wondering how the hell he was going to deal with Miss Eastleigh. His pattern with women didn't included being sociable much beyond the morning after. Occasionally he shared breakfast with some inamorata, and on rare occasions the morning after included a visit to a dressmaker or jeweler; he might tarry longer with Flora, but they were friends.

He blew out a disgruntled breath.

And now it would be five days or more before they reached his Scottish estate and his precedents of a lifetime were under assault.

Merde and every other bloody expletive known to man.

Out of temper though he was, he sensibly dismissed future unknowns and on reaching his room, concentrated on the present. He swiftly bathed, dressed, breakfasted alone, and tracked down a dressmaker before returning to Sofia's suite.

Two new guards greeted him, although their expressions were as droll as the previous troopers'.

"You find this entertaining?" Jamie grumbled, coming to a stop at the door.

"No, sair," one guard replied, his lips twitching.

"Been shoppin', sair?" the other man queried, nodding at the wrapped package Jamie carried.

"Would you like to know what I bought?" Jamie asked in a dangerous voice.

"No, sair," the young man crisply replied. "Not on yer life, sair."

"I need not remind you that the lady is to be treated with respect, do I?" Jamie's warning glance shifted from man to man.

Both men shook their heads, their expressions somber.

But after the door shut on Jamie, they looked at each other and grinned.

"Himself's different. Protective, I ken."

"Might be nothin'."

"Could be, though."

"Nah—ye'll see. 'Tis no more than sport."

* * *

BUT IT WAS at least noticeably *different*, for Jamie was standing motionless in the doorway to the bedroom as his men discussed him, enthralled by the enticing image before his eyes. Sofia was sleeping curled up like a kitten, the counterpane tucked under her chin, a tumbled mass of flaxen hair falling over her cheek. He was surprised at the raw emotion she provoked, for she was neither kittenlike nor docile as she was now in sleep, and her lush form, which could conceivably trigger a powerful response, was completely concealed. There was no logical reason why he should feel this fierce, raging desire to mount her.

He softly swore at the same time his fingers closed on the package in his hands.

Sofia came awake at the sounds, quickly scanned the room, and smiled as she caught sight of Jamie. "You're dressed."

"It's half past six. I'll draw your bath."

She stretched lazily. "Will you join me?"

He shook his head.

"Have you come to wash my back?" Her question was playful.

He shook his head again. "We have to leave in half an hour." He swiftly strode across the room and entered the bathroom, his self-discipline sorely taxed. He was fighting the impulse to chuck everything for a quick fuck. Christ—as if he should be thinking of sex now, with Von Welden's dogs on their heels.

A dash of proverbial cold water—that reminder.

His composure restored, he turned on the water in the tub, left the package on the dressing table, and returned to the bedroom, his libido in check.

"I have to talk to my men. You have"—he glanced at his wristwatch—"twenty-five minutes. There's a dress of sorts in that package in the bathroom. We'll stop this afternoon and find something better. This village is too small for fashionable shops. I apologize for the unstylish garment, although the dressmaker was kind enough to open her door at this early hour, so." He shrugged. "I tried."

"I'm sure it's perfectly fine." He was restless, but then she didn't live a soldier's life. Apparently timetables mattered. "I'll hurry."

He'd been expecting dissent; he was relieved. "Thank you," he said, with a small courtly bow. "Now if you'll excuse me, I have matters to attend to. I'll have breakfast sent up. The guards outside your door will see you to the carriage once you're ready." He smiled suddenly. "I appreciate your cooperation."

She laughed. "Were you worried?"

"A little."

"I appreciated *your* cooperation last night," she said with a teasing grin. "Surely I'd be remiss to refuse your simple requests this morning."

"Thank you again," he urbanely replied. "And please keep an eye on the time. My men will be mounting up soon."

"Then I must rush." She threw back the covers and leaped from the bed.

It was all well and good to intellectually overrule the notion of fucking Miss Eastleigh with time so limited. But her voluptuous body manifest in all its glory as she bounded from the bed was something else entirely.

Her plump breasts bounced provocatively.

Her pale pubic hair glistened even more provocatively.

Torrid memory flooded his brain, the feel and scent and smell of her drumming through his senses, his erection rising to conspicuous attention.

Softly swearing, Jamie beat a quick retreat.

CHAPTER 17

SOFIA WAS LATE coming down.

Jamie sent most of the troop ahead. He didn't wish attention drawn to such a large a group of mounted men. They could wait outside the village where their presence would be less noticeable.

Meanwhile, the carriage was at the door and Jamie was leaning against a porch pillar, checking his watch from time to time and becoming increasingly annoyed. *Why can't women be on time?*

He was just about to go and fetch Sofia when she exited the hotel, flanked by two troopers dressed in casual sporting garb.

When Jamie's men saw him push away from the pillar, one of them grasped Sofia's elbow and brought her to a halt.

On his approach, Jamie politely dismissed his men. "Duncan has your mounts. We'll be right with you." He turned to Sofia. "I'll take that." He nodded at the package in her hand.

Conscious of the slight curtness in his voice, Sofia quickly handed over the package with her clothes from the previous day rewrapped in the paper from the dress shop. "I'm so sorry I'm late. I hurried, I really did—and thank you for the dress, the brush and comb, et cetera." She wasn't about to mention the lingerie. "You're ever efficient."

Jamie smiled politely, not about to argue over thirty minutes that couldn't be recalled in any event. "That color becomes you."

"Thank you. I rather think I look like a schoolmistress." The tailored frock in cerulean blue messaline was primly cut; she'd pinned her damp hair in a coil at her nape.

"It fits," Jamie said, his smile warming. "The dress, not the schoolmistress role."

"It does fit rather well, doesn't it? I commend your eye."

"Did you enjoy your breakfast?"

Such extreme urbanity; he must be every hostess's dream. "Yes, it was delicious. Even fresh strawberries. You think of everything."

"The cook was pleased to accommodate you."

She flashed him a smile. "Was he indeed?"

"As we all are," he said with well-mannered grace. He held out his arm. "We stop again in Bolton. We'll find you a wardrobe there."

She placed her hand on his forearm. "Are you riding with me?"

"I will later," he said as they moved toward the stairs.

In a splendid mood after Jamie's exemplary attentions last night, Sofia didn't press him. Not only had he given her enormous pleasure the past many hours, but he'd also left her eagerly anticipating further gratification tonight and in the future. "I want to thank you again for everything," she said in a voice that didn't carry.

"You're very welcome. It was my pleasure."

He could have been giving thanks for a pleasant afternoon tea so impersonal was his tone. A mildly vexing phenomenon for a young woman familiar with male adulation.

On reaching the base of the stairs, he handed her up into the carriage, set the package on the seat, and tapped the small compartment nearest the door. "I washed the dildo myself." He smiled. "In the event you can't wait."

How sweet, how thoughtful. "I'd much rather wait," she said with an answering smile, her vexation instantly dispelled.

"Until later then." With a graceful bow, he shut the door, slapped his gloved palm on the lacquered carriage wall, and signaled the driver to set off.

As the carriage drew away from the hotel, Sofia leaned back against the cushions and basked in a delicious content. James Blackwood had been irresistible last night—part rogue, part diplomat, wholly male, and obscenely sexual. He'd been alternately autocratic and gallant, sweetly considerate—as in the washed dildo—and at times forcibly selfish.

That last quality she'd found most pruriently aphrodisiac.

But then she was intimately acquainted with men she could manipulate; Jamie Blackwood was different. And that difference, she'd discovered, was deeply arousing.

While Sofia pleasantly reflected on the events of the previous night, Jamie moodily watched the carriage drive away.

There went heaven and hell and everything in between, he grudgingly thought. And damn it all—he didn't have time to deal with a seductive temptress *or* his outrageously primal response to her. They were two days out of London, which meant pursuit was in full cry. Even Von Welden, inefficient or not, had men in England by now.

With a muttered expletive, Jamie spun around and strode to his waiting mount. Vaulting into the saddle, he nudged the powerful black stallion into a trot, then a canter, and as soon as the village was left behind, he loosed the reins and let the sleek thoroughbred stretch his legs.

Once everyone was reunited several miles beyond the village, the troopers fell into place, before and after the carriage. Two scouts rode ahead, reconnoitering, while a small rear guard served as deterrent against pursuit.

Riding with Douglas in the vanguard of the convoy, Jamie contemplated an uneventful journey to Bolton. While everyone was on alert, realistically, they should still be ahead of whomever Von Welden had sent over. Several hours of peaceful riding lay before them. Time enough, Jamie decided, to resolve the unresolvable or at least rationalize away his unwanted feelings—that a more likely possibility.

He'd also have the opportunity to catch some much needed sleep. As an experienced campaigner, dozing in the saddle was as natural to him as breathing.

He glanced at Douglas, who rode beside him. "I'm going to sleep for a few minutes. Wake me—"

"Dinna worry, sair. Take yer time. Nither hide nor hair o' foreigners are in sight."

Jamie smiled. Six generations of Blackwoods had lived abroad and yet Douglas still referred to Austrians as foreigners. Then again, the clan had always fostered their Scottish heritage, generally married other Scots, and perceived their role as mercenaries for hire. "Wake me in twenty minutes anyway."

"Yes, sair," Douglas crisply replied.

But a Scot rarely took orders with good grace; it was an inborn conceit. Douglas didn't argue with Jamie. He just didn't wake him. The bonny lad needed his rest after last night.

CHAPTER 18

WHILE JAMIE, SOFIA, and the rest were traveling north at a brisk pace, Von Welden was sitting at his desk in the ministry building in Vienna with a cable in his hand and a scowl on his face. The cryptic cable message read, *Tom and Ned missed breakfast. Advise.*

No Tom or Ned existed, of course, although the men using those names did, or had. They'd both failed to arrange their morning rendezvous in London.

Tapping his fingers on his desktop, Von Welden softly swore, knowing full well neither man had chosen to neglect the meeting. He turned toward the open door leading to his outer office. "Krauss!" he bellowed.

His secretary appeared at the run, his epaulettes glittering in the morning sunlight, regimental uniform de rigueur for the police ministry staff.

Von Welden waved his hand. "Shut the door." Shoving the cable aside, he leaned back in his chair. "As you saw, we have a problem." His ADC handled all his correspondence.

"Not entirely unexpected," Ludwig Krauss drily said. "Blackwood's resourceful."

Von Welden grunted. "More's the pity. You know I tried recruiting him right out of Theresienstadt Military Academy, he was so clearly more gifted than all the rest of the aristocratic sprigs and scholarship wunderkinder. But the bastard refused me. He wasn't interested in working for a decaying institution, he said," Von Welden bitterly noted. "I should have imprisoned him on the spot for treason."

"His father might have taken exception to his imprisonment," Krauss sardonically observed. "The Blackwood troops are talented professionals and, more importantly, ruthless." Krauss was stout, bald, red faced, entirely loyal to the minister, and privy to Von Welden's various machinations. He had leave to speak bluntly. He was also a meticulous manager, preferred his mistress to his wife, and was consequently more available when Von Welden required his services. The secret police wasn't a bureaucracy that observed normal business hours. "It seems to me that the question is not whether Blackwood is competent—he is— but rather how many more men you need in England to accomplish your mission."

Von Welden shut his eyes for a moment. Then, raising his lashes, he spoke, slowly and deliberately. "Since we've lost two in as many days, I'd say six more at least. Eight perhaps if you think we'd be better served. Arrange for the new recruits as quickly as possible. Then send Latour a cable informing him that additional teams will soon arrive." An acid note entered the minister's voice. "Fucking Blackwood."

"You knew it wouldn't be easy, sir," his secretary observed in a commiserating tone. "Battenberg's men are first-rate. A bloodthirsty lot, most say."

"Plainly. I wonder they missed Latour."

"Perhaps they didn't dare murder a nobleman."

"I doubt it." Von Welden briefly stared into space. "I

expect they're playing some game with him. Perhaps," the
minister said in a musing tone, "we should treat Latour's
mission separately."

"An excellent idea, sir. In the event he's being watched."

Von Welden suddenly sat up and placed his palms on
his desktop. "Very well. Send out the crews. The best you
can find. Cable Latour to continue as previously ordered.
He'll be advised later to any change in plans. That's all."
Von Welden waved his hand in a dismissive gesture but
then a thought struck him. "Wait."

Krauss turned back.

"Have we any word of where Battenberg or this mysterious daughter of his might have gone?" They'd received
news last night that the prince had disappeared from his
London home, along with the unwelcome information that
he may have an heir after all.

Krauss shook his head.

"They both have to be eliminated—understood? No
excuses," Von Welden growled. "Heads will roll if they're
not dispatched," he warned.

"Yes, sir."

"Make sure everyone understands."

"Yes, sir." Although Krauss knew better than to relay
such information to the assassins he was sending to England. Warning killers that failure meant death would be
witless. Anyone whose loyalties were for sale to the high-
est bidder was by definition corruptible. If threatened,
they'd either sell out to the opposition or disappear.

After the door closed on his ADC, Von Welden leaned
back in his chair with a weary sigh. The degree of profes-
sionalism required—particularly when sending men to a
foreign land—was difficult to muster these days, even
with adequate funds. In many respects Latour von Metis
was eminently more suitable than common killers. As a
nobleman he was well-known and accepted in fashionable

circles; he'd have access to any gossip pertaining to Prince Ernst or his recently acknowledged daughter.

Which pertinent thought suddenly brought Von Welden upright in his chair. He shouted for Krauss.

When his secretary appeared in the doorway, Von Welden briskly commanded, "Send additional funds to Latour. He's the best resource we have at the moment, and knowing him, he's probably already gambled away what we've furnished him. I want to make certain he's welcome in the best clubs where gossip abounds, and if he owes gambling debts, he won't be able to show his face. I want him to have enough money to assure his acceptance in society."

"How much, sir?"

"Five thousand English pounds."

Krauss's eyebrows rose into his nonexistent hairline.

"Just do it, Krauss," Von Welden snapped. "If he finds Ernst and whatever her name is, it'll be worth every shilling."

LATER THAT MORNING, Count Johan Latour von Metis was pleasantly surprised by the cable he received in his suite at the Ritz: *Continue as before with your visit to Auntie May. Additional funds are available at Lloyds Bank. Love, Uncle George.*

A very *welcome* surprise indeed. He'd lost heavily at White's last night. He also preferred working alone. The two men sent over with him were contemptibly common, their accents were terrible, and he rather thought their shoes gave them away at first sight. Not that he was about to tell Von Welden how to conduct his business. But it was clear something had happened to his two colleagues. They were to have contacted him this morning by phone at eight to set up a meet. He suspected they were lying on the bottom of the Thames—a convenient graveyard for the world's largest metropolis.

Tucking the cable into his pocket, the count rose from his breakfast table and shouted for his valet. He'd bathe, dress, pick up his new funds, then stroll to White's. He looked forward to an afternoon of gaming before the evening soirees commenced.

WHILE COUNT VON Metis was contemplating his new prosperity, Oz and Fitz were having a late breakfast in an Indian restaurant tucked away on a narrow back street in the East End.

"Ernst and Antonella should be in Portsmouth by now, I'm happy to say," Fitz noted with a smile. His staff knew many of Ernst's staff; gossip traveled quickly below stairs. "The principessa seems to have a remarkable influence over Ernst."

Oz grinned. "Who would have thought? The man's been an arch libertine for most of his life."

"Maybe he's slowing down."

"Maybe she came into his life at the perfect time."

"Whatever the case, it was fortunate that she arrived in London with such fanfare. A private railcar from the coast, for instance."

"And a very large, flamboyant entourage complete with luggage enough for a trip around the world."

"She might as well have left a trail of breadcrumbs to Ernst's door."

"Indeed. It was almost too easy, Sam said. They picked up Von Welden's two men the instant they arrived at Ernst's town house." Sam commanded Oz's small private army. As owner of the largest bank in India and others globally, Oz had enemies who coveted his holdings; the last attempt on his life had almost been fatal.

"There's no question they were working for Von Welden?"

"None," Oz softly replied.

Fitz nodded. Sam was a competent interrogator; those who'd made the attempt on Oz's life last year were dead.

"I've sent telegrams to our country homes in the event Blackwood chooses to stop overnight. I informed him that two of Von Welden's killers are gone. I also warned him that Latour is involved." Oz had sent Jamie a note before he left London, listing their properties and locations. "I expect Von Welden will send additional men." Oz shrugged. "We'll have to see how many."

"It might be useful to send a telegram to Sofia's mother at her farm. Considering the shocking news about having a new father, Sofia may stop to see Amelia and Ben." As a major collector, Fitz was well acquainted with the London art world. Prior to his marriage he'd also been well acquainted with many of the models, and one of his lovers had invited him to accompany her up to the farm.

"Good idea. Hopefully Blackwood will receive one of our messages, although I didn't get the impression he wished to stop anywhere overnight."

"Don't forget Sofie's willfulness. She usually gets her way."

"True." Oz grinned. "He doesn't stand a chance, does he?"

"Not a chance in hell."

"So then," Oz cheerfully asserted, "care to make odds on when the next batch of assassins arrives? Von Welden won't mind spending the emperor's money to feather his own nest. I say tomorrow night at the earliest."

"I'll lay you ten to one they're here on the morning train."

Oz grinned. "You're on. That's damned fast."

"Someone's watching Latour?"

"Round the clock. By the way, he lost a good deal at White's last night. Franz Joseph's going to have to ante up more cash."

"I know the governor of the London Clearing House. The funds transfer will have to go through that institution. If you're finished eating, we could swing by and talk to Freddy." Fitz tossed his napkin on the table. "We'll find out how much Latour is worth to Von Welden."

An inveterate gambler, Oz smoothly inquired, "Would you care to bet on Latour's worth to Von Welden?"

"Of course. Would you care to make a wager on whether Blackwood has eluded Sofie's seductive snare?" Fitz countered, grinning.

"Christ no. Sofie's impossible to turn down. An observation only. The art world was beyond my purview in my rakish days."

Fitz laughed. "You might not have had a chance anyway. Sofie's taste in men has always been capricious. And," Fitz added with a small smile, "the art world was within my purview for many years."

"According to gossip, Blackwood's had no practice at all turning down women," Oz drawled. "So acquit me on that particular wager. I'd be losing money."

"Very well. Five hundred says Latour receives three thousand in new funds."

Oz shook his head. "Too paltry. The man's a rank amateur at cards. Von Welden has to know that. I'll raise you five hundred and say ten thousand for Latour."

With a quick handshake, the men confirmed their wagers and rose from the table. Oz shouted something in Hindi to the proprietor, who grinned and replied in a cheerful free-flowing burst of words.

With a wave, Oz walked toward the door, laughing.

CHAPTER 19

AT THE SAME time Oz and Fitz were seeing to it that the train stations were watched, Latour continued under surveillance, and Freddy at the London Clearing House had been paid a friendly visit, Sofia and Jamie arrived in Bolton and were currently ensconced in a private room at the best dressmaker in town.

"I don't see why you need me here," Jamie said. Not that he'd leave Sofia alone, since he didn't entirely trust her, but he didn't have to sit in this inner sanctum. The outside reception room would have served as well. Much better, in fact. He didn't relish having to watch her undress and dress; it would strain his self-control. "I should think it would be less embarrassing for you if I waited outside."

"Really?" She turned from examining one of the many framed fashion prints on the walls. "You mean you've never escorted a lady to a dressmaker before?" What she really meant was *Do you want to chat up the dressmaker in private?* Mrs. Lynne had been beyond fawning. Not that it should matter, but stupidly it did.

"This is hardly the same."

"In what way is it different?"

It isn't of course. "Could we change the subject?"

"Surely *you're* not embarrassed?" He appeared at ease even though his powerful frame looked incongruously out of place lounging in a pink satin chair with frippery fringe and tassels.

"I don't get embarrassed."

"Then I don't see what the argument is," she shamelessly replied, ignoring the fact that they'd been disputing the logistics of clothes buying for some time. Jamie preferred a department store and ready-made clothes in the interest of speed. And of course, left unsaid, was her irritation with the dressmaker.

Jamie softly exhaled. "There's no argument," he wearily said. "So long as your shopping is accomplished expeditiously."

Sofia moved toward a table stacked with pattern books. "I'm sure it will be. Since you're in a rush, though, and you have to pay the bill, you might just as well be handy here," she airily concluded.

"Handy?" Incredulity sharpened his voice. He wasn't John the footman who paid my lady's tick and carried her packages. "I should tell you to go fuck yourself," he growled. "But knowing you, you might—and I'm in a hurry." He shot a surly glance at the door. "Where the *hell* is that dressmaker?"

"Assembling what she has in my size, I expect." Sofia flipped open an embossed leather cover and glanced at the first fashion plate—a walking dress in rose silk.

"Whatever she has, she can wrap them up and we'll leave."

Sofia bristled at his peremptory tone. "I should at least try on the clothes. There's no point in buying something that's unwearable."

"I don't know about that," Jamie lazily drawled.

"Very funny."

"An opening like that? Who could resist?"

"I suppose you prefer women be nude all the time."

He shrugged. "In certain circumstances."

"Libertine."

"Did you think I wasn't?"

"I didn't think of you at all," she huffily replied.

"You could have fooled me. As I recall, you promised to seduce me shortly after we met."

"We'd met before."

"You're right. I shouldn't have been surprised then."

This time she was the one who said, "Could we change the subject?"

"Gladly. Where the *hell* is the dressmaker?" Hauling himself out of the low slipper chair, Jamie strode purposefully toward the door.

"You needn't make a scene."

"How can it matter?" he said without looking back. "We'll never see her again."

But just as he reached for the latch, the door swung open to admit Mrs. Lynne, the tall, willowy, blonde dressmaker who'd greeted Jamie so warmly on their arrival. She'd obviously taken the time to add a bit of rouge to her cheeks, color to her lips, and fresh perfume if the cloud of fragrance invading the room was any indication.

"I do beg your pardon for the delay," the pretty young woman silkily purred, standing indecently close to Jamie and gazing up at him with a seductive smile. "My girls are bringing in some frocks. Might I offer you and the lady some chilled champagne?" she inquired without once looking at Sofia.

"No, thank you."

"Yes, please," Sofia replied, her words overlapping Jamie's refusal.

Jamie turned a gelid gaze on Sofia. "Our time is limited."

"Not that limited, *darling*," Sofia cooed, taking umbrage

at the dressmaker's blatant coquetry when she really should know better. When the concept of jealousy was completely unjustified.

"Very well, *sweetheart*," Jamie murmured, bestowing a heated glance on Sofia. Two could play that game; if he played it well, they might leave sooner rather than later. "Champagne would be much appreciated," he said with an intimate smile for the dressmaker.

The woman blushed.

Sofia seethed.

"Consider it my pleasure, my lord," the dressmaker murmured. "I'll order our best champagne." Swinging around, she called out through the open door, and a young girl appeared so quickly she must have been waiting in the corridor. The champagne was ordered. Turning back, Mrs. Lynne held Jamie's gaze for another lingering moment. "Please be seated, Lord and Lady—" The dressmaker paused, waiting expectantly for a surname.

"We're not married," Jamie bluntly said. Perhaps putting Sofia to the blush would spur their departure.

"He refuses to marry me," Sofia bemoaned with a doleful expression. "No matter what I say or do. And after all your promises," she said, turning to Jamie with a melancholy smile.

Christ, she was shameless. "Perhaps after Mama dies, my dear. You know how she feels about your family."

"If you *really* loved me," Sofia lamented like an actress in a bad farce, "you wouldn't allow your malicious mother to malign me or my—"

"Would you excuse us for a minute?" Jamie took the dressmaker's elbow and guided her out the door. "I'll come to fetch you," he said, his face blank, and abruptly shut the door on Mrs. Lynne's astonishment.

Swinging back, he took one look at Sofia's smug smile and snapped, "Don't push me. You'll regret it."

The sharp edge to his voice gave her warning. Or should

have given her warning. Or would have given her warning if she responded to such things. "Did you see how that woman *looked* at you?" Sofia inquired, her amusement giving way to petulance.

"Jesus, who cares? Or better yet, what the hell did you want me to do? We need some clothes for you. She *has* those clothes. Whether she smiles at me or not is inconsequential."

"So you did notice?"

"Of course. I'm not blind." He chose not to say he'd seen that look a thousand times before. "You're being childish. Von Welden's men are closing in even as we stand here and argue." He took a small breath to tamp down his anger, a dressmaker the least of his problems. "Please," he softly said, holding her gaze, "could we finish this business quickly? I'd be very grateful."

He looked so earnest and grave, Sofia instantly felt contrite. "I'm so sorry. I don't know what came over me."

He smiled faintly. "Your temper, darling."

She made a small moue, knowing her behavior had defied every principle of female independence she esteemed. "I know," she ruefully admitted. "I shall try to restrain my temper in future, and you must remind me more often of our danger."

"Consider it done. Apropos that danger, could we now begin to expedite this little shopping trip?"

"Of course." Sofia waved in the direction of the door. "Go and get the obsequious woman. I promise to behave. Don't give me that look—I will. You'll see."

Jamie had few illusions when it came to Sofia behaving, so he took the precaution of taking Mrs. Lynne aside when he found her and giving her a sizeable sum to *not* look at him. "My darling Sofia's jealous," he explained, "and honestly Mama *is* the worst kind of shrew." He bestowed a sympathetic smile on the dressmaker. "I expect you see that type of overbearing matron often enough in your business. Also," he added in a kindly tone, "if we could accelerate this little transaction, I'd be willing to add five hundred pounds to your bill."

"Five hundred?" the dressmaker breathlessly echoed.

"Over and above our purchases," Jamie noted in clarification. He was in a damned hurry.

With such largesse as lure, Mrs. Lynne didn't so much as glance at Jamie when she returned to the dressing room. Her assistants carried in a dozen frocks in rapid succession, and Sofia allowed herself to be convinced that the dresses would fit; she needn't try them on.

Jamie didn't care if they fit or not.

In short order, their selections made, the dresses were wrapped, money was exchanged, and the packages were carried out to the second carriage waiting at the curb behind Sofia's chaise.

With the bottle of champagne in hand, Jamie escorted Sofia back to her carriage. "Thank you for hurrying. I appreciate your understanding," he said, handing her up into the vehicle.

"You must have said something to her; the dressmaker was completely indifferent to you when she returned." Sofia grinned. "Did you threaten her?"

Jamie laughed as he climbed in and dropped onto the seat opposite her. "I didn't have to. I think she feared the onset of some vulgar scene. You shocked the hell out of her."

"You started it."

He hadn't, but he wasn't about to prolong what would only be a useless argument. "The point is, my pet," he mildly said, "most inamoratas are more discreet." He placed his booted feet on Sofia's seat and slid into a comfortable sprawl. "They don't berate their lovers at the same time they're accepting their gifts."

"Perhaps more of them should speak their mind."

He smiled. "And perhaps the sun will set in the east."

"Hmpf. The world would be a better place with fewer smug, condescending men in positions of power."

He didn't necessarily disagree. But he also understood that the day women gained those positions of power was in the distant future—if ever. "I'm sure you're right, dear. Champagne?" He held out the bottle.

"God I hate it when a man agrees with such gross insincerity."

"It's survival, darling. Men learn early on. Here, have a drink. Relax."

She flung her hand up. "Maybe I don't want to relax," she muttered, taking issue with his calm dismissal of what she considered a grave injustice. "Maybe women's rights matter a great deal to me."

He arrested the bottle partway to his mouth and paused an infinitesimal moment, recognizing diplomacy was required. "Acquit me, darling, of indifference to women's plight. I understand the inequalities are irksome. I also agree that there shouldn't be gender bias and discrimination."

"Why do I hear the inevitable *but* in your words?"

He drained half the bottle before he replied. "Because, darling, someday female equality may be the law of the land, but at the moment it mostly certainly is not." He shrugged. "I'm sorry. I don't wish to offend you, but I only deal in realities. If I didn't, none of us would be safe. Your father included."

"And now you have me to protect as well," Sofia softly said, the plain, unvarnished truth obliterating less pertinent philosophical debate.

"Yes. I wish it weren't so, but Von Welden is infinitely more troublesome than issues of gender inequalities. He has to be my sole focus."

"Do you really think they're getting close?" It was the kind of question a child would ask, hoping for an agreeable answer.

He knew what she wanted to hear and debated lying.

But in the end what good would it do to offer false assurance when the danger was all too real? "They could be," he said. "But we're more than ready for them. And if it's any consolation," he added as the color drained from her face, "it's difficult to find both skill and intellect in hired killers. My men are much more capable, better trained, and utterly loyal."

She'd slid into the corner of the seat as he'd spoken and was huddled now, eyes shut and silent. She looked smaller in the muted light with the shades half drawn. The flickering shadows dramatized her fragility, heightened her pallor, gilded her hair with saffron. He felt an unexpected affection quite separate from lust, although carnal thoughts were never far from his mind with Miss Eastleigh—a breach of discipline that continued to disturb him.

Soft, pale tendrils framed her face, the coil of hair at the nape of her neck having come partially undone; she looked sweetly tousled and incredibly sexy. He would have preferred a less provocative image. She needed reassurance and kindness, not masculine lechery. Dropping his feet on the floor, he sat up and leaning forward, gently touching her arm. "Don't be afraid, sweetheart," he said softly. "I'll protect you against the world."

At his tender declaration, she opened her eyes and saw before her a man of striking beauty who simultaneously disturbed, defended, and enchanted her. His bronzed skin was darker in the shadowed interior, the stark planes and angles of his face accented in the refracted light, his features a veritable masterpiece of perfection.

Her perusal paused as their eyes met—his steady, confident gaze a promise and warranty of boundless comfort and support. He was both savior and hardened warrior, serving her in martial and also more pleasurable ways, and she was infinitely grateful. Having summoned her courage, she spoke in as near to a normal tone of voice as she could muster. "Thank you. I appreciate all you're doing for me." She smiled. "I know you would have preferred another assignment."

He smiled back. "As to that—you've rather dramatically changed my mind."

Any lingering fear, however small, disappeared as if by magic at his candor, and tantalizing delight flared through her senses. "You flatter me, my lord," she whispered, lying back in an indolent pose reminiscent of a languishing odalisque, gazing at him from under her half-lowered lashes.

He laughed. "Minx. How quickly you turn temptress." But he was pleased to see the fear gone from her eyes and her saucy impudence returned.

She looked him over slowly from head to toe, her survey coming to rest at last on his crotch. "I can't help it, my lord. There's something about you that excites and inspires a burning eagerness of a particularly carnal nature."

He smiled. "You looked at me in exactly that fashion at Groveland House. I just about carried you out on the spot that night, devil be damned."

"You should have."

"Your father wouldn't have understood."

"I'm sure he would have," she said, softly ironic.

Jamie didn't reply. How could he? She was right.

She laughed. "You needn't be tactful. I have no illusions about a man who forgot me for twenty-three years. Now then, apropos the here and now, I'm much in need of comfort and consoling."

"Is that what you call it?" he said with amusement.

"Call it what you will, darling," Sofia replied, beginning to draw her skirt upward. "You supply it most excellently."

He glanced out the window.

"Don't you dare say no," she crisply said.

"I was just checking our location." In all likelihood, they'd reach Sofia's mother's tonight. He pulled down the shades completely. "And I couldn't possibly say no," he added with a grin. "So tell me what you want. There, here?" He pointed to his lap. "Or we could throw the fur robe on the floor and see if we could get comfortable. Carriages are a little small for my size, but"—he indicated the bulge in his trousers with a languid wave—"my cock is willing to work out just about anything right now."

"Right now sounds wonderful," Sofia murmured, wiggling out of her drawers. Tossing them aside, she smiled sweetly and spread her thighs. "Come and console me, darling."

He grinned. "How could any man refuse?" Her pink, pouty flesh glistened in readiness, framed by her pale pubic hair. Temptation incarnate, primed and ready and within reach.

"I have only to look at you and I melt inside," she whispered. "It's terrifying and mystifying, but delicious all the same. How do you do it?"

"I don't know," he pleasantly said. "But if it pleases you, I'm content." While he didn't understand the inner workings of the female mind, women often had said as much to him, so he understood his essential part in what came next. "I suggest we take off your dress. Your mother might wonder what you've been doing if it's wrinkled beyond recognition."

"So coolly practical, darling. Do you always plan ahead?"

"Mostly."

She smiled. "You said that once before."

"I remember."

"We should have wagered. I would have won."

"We both won," he said with a roguish grin. "Now you're going to have to move; we're not going to fit on that seat." Rising, he bent his head under the low ceiling, picked her up, sat back down, settled her on his lap, and began unbuttoning the bodice of her gown.

She liked his quiet management skills. He removed her gown with deft proficiency, folded it neatly, and placed it on the opposite seat. "You must do this a lot," she said, her voice heated and low. "It's very arousing . . . your competence at undressing a lady."

"You find everything arousing," he replied, his gaze amused.

"Only with you. Normally, I don't—"

"Talk so much," he brusquely interjected, oddly conflicted by her amorous past. He slid his finger down the warm valley between her breasts, cupped the soft flesh, and bending, kissed her cheek. "This is all mine," he whispered, quickly disposing of her chemise, delicately squeezing one pink, rosy nipple.

Sofia softly moaned, the streaking rush of pleasure terminating in the pulsing core of her body, and she pressed against his lightly manipulating fingers, covetous, yearning, wanting more.

"I like that you're always ready for me," he gently said, testing that readiness with a light, drifting finger up her slippery cleft.

"I'd like to hate you for making me this needy," she murmured, "but the rewards are so sensational I'd be a fool to do so. This"—she cupped her palm over the bulge in his trousers—"is magnificent and gratifying in every way." She grinned. "I thank you in advance."

"Do we have time for kisses or foreplay or either?" he teased, unbuttoning his trousers and turning her so she was straddling his thighs, "or should I know better than to ask?"

Leaning forward, she quickly kissed his cheek. "There. Now onto more delectable sensations." Coming up on her knees, she slid her hand into his opened trousers, gripped his rampant erection, and eased it away from his belly.

He chuckled. "What if I said I was in the mood for romance?"

She looked up from positioning the head of his penis in the sleek folds of her sex. "You'd be lying."

A flashing grin lit his green gaze. "You could be wrong,

Miss Hot and Bothered." Although, in truth, her eagerness was one of her most charming qualities.

"Umm, stop talking now—ummm—oh . . . my . . . God," she softly exhaled, coming to rest on his thighs, his huge, rock-hard cock buried to the hilt, her eyes shut tight against the gluttonous pleasure rippling out in waves from her taut, stretched vaginal tissue.

A small silence fell while two bodies and brains registered the shocking intensity of raw sensation—while nerve endings trembled in time to their heartbeats and empirical perception took on a new, explosive prodigality.

Jamie drew in a breath first because flights of fancy were a breach of custom for him. With Sofia still motionless in his arms, concerned she might be hurt, he whispered, "Are you all right?"

As if his voice was trigger to reality, Sofia inhaled a great whoosh of air, opened her eyes, and softly said, "I'm never, *never* letting you go."

"How nice," he said. "We'll live on moonbeams and passion fruit and make love in the daisy-strewn meadows of Xanadu."

She giggled. "Glib-tongued Lothario."

He smiled. "At least we can make love until we reach your mother's. How would that be?"

"That would be"—she rotated her hips slowly—"*fantastic*."

When his spiking pulse rate diminished marginally, he readjusted his hands on her waist and murmured, "Let's try that again." He did, they did, and the ensuing lascivious sensations required another several hushed moments to fully enjoy and assimilate. He kissed her with tenderness, prompted by a rare gratitude, and lifting his mouth a moment later, he murmured, "You please me." And as a seasoned hedonist and connoisseur of dalliance, he understood better than most the diverse shades of pleasure.

"In the lap of the gods," Sofia murmured.

He didn't have to ask her what she meant. "Yes," he said. "That."

And when he kissed her again, she kissed him back, acknowledging their rare affinity, the unrivaled pleasure they felt, the simpatico that didn't require explanation. And then she said, "Give me more," because she was always more greedy than he.

"You can have it all," he simply said. "As often as you wish."

Perhaps the closed, shadowed world within the carriage gave them license to be defiant of reality, to play in a wonderland of their senses, to indulge their whimsy. Or perhaps it was something more mystifying and profound.

Whatever it was, no matter how unlikely or contrary to their normal lives, these two people who normally looked at the world with clarity and engaged in seduction as a game surrendered to some fated imperative and rashly pressed the boundaries of emotion.

Not that Jamie forgot his manners or failed to give the lady all the pleasure she craved. He did in full measure, servicing his hot little companion, keeping her gorged full and orgasmic until she was half-delirious from overwrought sensation.

"Should we rest?" he gently asked some time later as she shuddered in his arms.

Her eyes drifted shut, a soft little vexatious moan her only answer.

His smile was affectionate. "Very well." He was capable of interpreting her unspoken wishes by now, and forcing her slick cunt down his erection again, he held her momentarily captive as she squirmed and panted and wallowed in a seething ecstasy. Then he set a deft, practiced, tantalizing pace that quickly brought her to another feverish, violent orgasm.

And so it went, the lady lost to all reason, Jamie doing what he did so well, pleasure ramping up to new blissful levels, a mutual enchantment charming body and brain alike.

Until in the course of time, they were making love on the floor of the carriage, both hot with lust, Jamie still partially dressed with Sofia's demands having taking precedence. His hair hung in damp curls, his skin was sheened with sweat, his cock thrust hilt deep in her succulent cunt.

She was screaming as another climax savagely assailed her overdrawn senses, then whimpering softly, she clung to him as it began to wane.

Cramped within the constricted space, Jamie's movements were hindered, his legs numbed after so long, his shoulders wedged between the seats. But in the passionate pursuit of pleasure he'd been more than willing to overlook any discomfort, his libido if not as insatiable as Sofia's, more than amenable.

And since she'd just climaxed again, it was his turn.

A decision based mostly on the fact that his orgasm was fast approaching the point of no return. He flexed his legs as his climax began—the act of withdrawal so instinctive no rational thought was involved. It took a flashing second before he realized he was stuck fast, his right foot pinioned and immovable. The braided trim on his boot was firmly caught on the latch of one of the underseat compartments, and another perilous second more elapsed before the threat fully registered in his brain.

Another second passed before he frantically tore his boot free and then another before he finally jerked his cock from Sofia's honeyed passage.

Moments too late—an eternity too late.

His seed was ruinously drenching Sofia's vagina.

He swore, then swore some more, at his stupidity, his ineptitude, the fact that he didn't have enough sense to take off his boots. When at last his tirade was over, he said, grimly, "Forgive me. Is there something here we could wash you out with?"

"You drank all the champagne," she said. "Don't glare at me," she added with arched brows. "I didn't drink it."

"This isn't funny." Unfolding himself from the floor, he hauled himself up on the seat.

"I'm not laughing. Have the carriage stop somewhere if you like, and we can buy another bottle of champagne."

"You're taking this rather calmly," he muttered, buttoning his trousers as if it mattered now.

"I doubt hysterics would do any good." She pushed herself into a seated position against the door. "I'm not in the market for a husband," she succinctly said. "Just so we're clear."

He didn't immediately reply, his gaze as direct as hers. "We'll stop in the next town," he said in cold, flat tones. Was she sincere or designing like so many women? Irrelevant at this point, he bitterly lamented, and softly exhaling, he handed her one of the table napkins they'd been using for mopping up. "Look, it's entirely my fault," he said with a reluctant civility. "Please accept my apology."

"Accepted," she crisply replied, "because it *is* your fault. Although," she said more temperately, "the risk can't be great—only once like that."

"I'm sure you're right." It was timing, not odds, however, when it came to a pregnancy.

Sofia reached for her drawers. "You're under no obligation."

"How very kind of you. I would naturally be willing to lend you any financial assistance should it come to that."

"Thank you, but I don't need your money."

"As you wish." Concealing his relief, he held out his hand and helped her off the floor and onto the seat. "May I say, up to this point, it's been a most enjoyable journey."

"And so it will continue," Sofia replied with equal civility, reaching for her folded dress. "I'm truly not interested in marriage. You're completely safe. Don't give this little gaucherie another thought."

"Very well, I won't. Would you like some help with those buttons?"

She liked his urbanity. He overcame crises with equanimity. What she liked best of course was something quite apart from his equanimity. She hoped he wouldn't spurn further sex because of this little lapse. "You could buy some condoms," she said, looking up at him as he buttoned her gown. "If you're worried."

"I could," he said.

"As insurance," she pointed out.

"It's a possibility."

"You don't like them."

"Not much. Normally, I'm very dependable."

"Lots of practice, I suppose."

"I suppose so," he placidly said. "There now." He patted the last button. "You need a comb for your hair."

"I hate all the women who came before me. Don't give me that sardonic look. I don't have to be reasonable. I wish there weren't any, so there."

"Then why don't we say there weren't any," he pleasantly replied.

"I'd dearly like that." Rash and impetuous as ever, she threw her arms around his neck and smiled up at him. "You always know how to please me."

"I live to please you," he softly murmured.

"Good," she said, and resting her head on his shoulder, she nestled close, reveling in the feel of him, bewitched and infatuated. "You're ever, ever so nice," she purred.

Nice, perhaps, he thought, *apprehensive, certainly.*

He'd blundered rather badly.

With luck, hopefully not irreversibly.

CHAPTER 20

IT WAS DARK when the carriage rolled up the long driveway leading to a sprawling medieval structure that had once been farmhouse, barn, and outbuildings combined, and was now a luxurious country house with eighteen bedrooms, three receptions rooms, and numerous studios for artists.

Jamie sat braced against the outside carriage wall, one leg on the seat, the other on the floor, Sofia asleep in his arms. As the lighted facade of the house drew near, he bent his head and lightly kissed her forehead. "We're here, darling."

"So soon?" she drowsily murmured.

He smiled. He hadn't dared move for the last two hours. "We made good time," he politely said. "There was hardly any traffic on the roads."

Slowly coming awake, Sofia stretched lazily. "You make a very comfortable bed in addition to all your other charming assets," she murmured, smiling up at him. "I have a great deal to thank you for."

"And I, you, darling. You please and delight me in

countless ways." The fact that he actually meant it he sensibly dismissed.

"I know I shouldn't ask, but—"

"Don't you always?" he noted with a grin.

She grinned back. "Then you won't be surprised. Do you think we might stay here for a day or so? Surely we're far enough off the beaten path for safety."

"I'd rather we didn't. Safety's a relative term at the moment."

She sighed. "I suppose I must be agreeable since you were so *very* agreeable to my desires. And so *very* many times."

"The pleasure was all mine," he silkily replied.

"Allow me to disagree." Her voice was a low, sultry contralto. "In fact, I've become quite enamored of your, shall we say, virtuoso artistry."

He laughed. "And I of your insatiable desire for cock."

"*Your* cock."

"Better yet." When he'd never aspired to exclusivity. Never even contemplated it. He glanced out the window as the carriage came to a stop. "Now mind your tongue," he cautioned. "There's nothing your parents can do to help us, so there's no point in alarming them." Lifting Sofia off his lap, he deposited her on the opposite seat with expeditious ease. "You're sure now—your mother won't find it odd that you're accompanying me to my Scottish estate?"

Sofia grinned. "After one look at you, believe me, she'll understand."

"A servant's about to open the door," he warned, grateful not to have to respond. "Remember, the less your parents know, the better."

The door was opened, Sofia cried, "Billy!" jumped out, and hugged the footman as Jamie stepped out behind her. Within moments they were literally welcomed with open arms by her parents, Amelia and Ben, and a great number of people who poured out of the house onto the drive. Sofia knew them all; Jamie didn't even try to remember all their names since their visit would be brief. He planned on leaving early in the morning.

As Sofia had predicted, neither her mother nor anyone else took issue with the fact that they were traveling together, although an explanation *was* required for the size of their entourage. The fiction of a hunting and fishing holiday in the Highlands served to satisfy the curious. The horses were led off to the stables along with the carriages, and Sofia and her traveling companions were made comfortable in the great hall that served as drawing room, communal dining room, and gallery space.

One wall of the lofty timber-framed space was given over to a fireplace large enough to roast an ox. A long monastery table capable of seating forty fronted the hearth. An area adjacent to a lengthy window wall facing an inner courtyard displayed artworks in various stages of development, while the remainder of the commodious hall was occupied with an array of comfortable chairs and sofas distributed over an ancient oak floor covered with colorful Oriental rugs.

Several more bottles of wine were brought in and set out on the monastery table, Jamie's men added a number of whiskey bottles, servants carried in additional platters of hearty fare for the male guests, delicacies for the ladies, and an evening of conviviality ensued.

Guards had been quietly posted outside. Jamie had spoken sotto voce to Douglas on the drive. Douglas in turn had indicated those men who'd take first watch with a nod or a look or a cryptic hand signal, and the chosen had drifted off into the darkness during the milling bustle of their welcome.

The next several hours were occupied in companionable drinking and conversation. The farmhouse hospitality was free and easy, the guests and lodgers mingling in friendly bonhomie, considerable liquor bridging the gap between artists and soldiers-cum-sportsmen with much merry laughter underscoring that rapport.

Chairs had been pulled up surrounding the sofa and chairs where Sofia, Jamie, Amelia, and Ben sat. Others found places on the floor or perched on chair arms or sofa backs in close enough proximity to join in the conversation— centered largely, once the polite courtesies had been exchanged, on the happenings in the art world: who was showing where, who was selling what, the particular projects various artists were engaged on, and the usual complaints about the lack of discriminating taste in those who styled themselves art critics.

With the crowd essentially composed of bohemian artists, eventually the inevitable question was breathlessly posed to Jamie by an inebriated young woman: how had he met their darling Sofia?

"You tell them, darling," he said with a smile, diverting the question to Sofia; he was unsure what she wished them to know.

Sofia's answer was a neutral, edited version. "I met Jamie at Countess Minton's. I was painting her portrait, he was visiting, and we found we both liked . . ." She impudently paused and, catching his eye, gave him her sweetest smile.

"Art," he smoothly interposed, thinking he'd like to wring her neck. "We both liked art. My mother was an artist, you see. Quite a good one," he shamelessly prevaricated.

"Portraits, wasn't it?" Sofia blandly noted.

"Watercolor landscapes, darling. You don't listen," Jamie replied, equally blandly. "I even showed you one."

"Sorry, dear. Perhaps I had too much to drink."

"I believe you did."

It was impossible to shake him, she disgruntledly thought. The man was nerveless.

"As I recall," Jamie went on in silken tones, "our impromptu trip to Scotland was based in part on your avid wish to taste my prized estate whiskey." He surveyed the attentive throng, most of whom were waiting for Sofia to pitch into him for his slur. "A more than compelling reason from my point of view," he added with a smile for the assembly. "And I did coax you as well, didn't I, dear?" he acknowledged, turning a much more personal smile on Sofia, whose chair flanked his.

She held his gaze for a lingering moment, not sure whether she should be angry or not, but certain of one thing at least. She was thoroughly enchanted by this chameleon-like man who was never disconcerted or embarrassed, always calm—or *almost* always, she pleasantly thought, recalling the violence of his passions. "Indeed you did. You can be *most* persuasive," she purred.

"In what way?" a female voice jocularly inquired. "Details, details, darling."

"Hush, Cynthia. You're drunk."

"Well so are you."

"And so are many of us," a male voice interposed. "But not so drunk as to completely forget our manners."

"Here, here," a tipsy guest agreed. "Now pass the bottle."

As glasses were refilled, the conversation turned to less personal topics, and before long, several guests were spontaneously inspired to perform. Some sang: music hall tunes, opera arias, original music of every stamp. Others recited poetry, from classic or original works. A diatribe or two was delivered on the question of women's rights or the state of contemporary politics, and a beautiful young man expounded in the most flattering way on Ruskin's worldview.

It was an impressive array of talent.

Such a cultured environment had nurtured and fashioned the expectations, judgment, and unbridled individualism of the woman at his side, Jamie reflected. It explained her indifference to the aristocratic world where titles often dis-

tinguished only mediocrity. It explained as well, he more
luridly thought, her creative imagination; she had a true
genius for sexual play.

Not a thought he could reasonably pursue with so many
eyes on him.

He refocused his attention on the pretty woman performing the latest music hall ditty instead. But he kept one
eye on the clock. He wanted to leave as soon as dawn
broke, because, by now, there were men in England looking
for them.

As midnight approached, Ben and Amelia's friends began wandering off to bed amidst talk of rising early to
paint—morning light of particular freshness and purity, apparently. Jamie's men made no mention of retiring, although
they politely withdrew to the monastery table after the other
guests departed.

Douglas knew that Sofia hadn't yet had the opportunity
to speak privately with her mother.

Sofia's parents occupied a small sofa upholstered in Ti-
tian red linen. Jamie and Sofia sat opposite them in comfortable club chairs of buff leather.

Amelia Eastleigh was still a recognized beauty at forty-
two, slight and fair like her daughter, slender and supple in
a Grecian-style gown of Nile green charmeuse. Ben bore a
striking resemblance to a Viking of old—blond, tall, sturdy
as a tree, the elder of the pair by a dozen years, Jamie
guessed. He was clearly patrician despite his casual dress, a
kind of quiet dignity distinguishing his manner; a younger
son no doubt with money but no title.

"Ben, pour more whiskey for Lord Blackwood."

"I'm fine, thank you," Jamie said, his drink largely untouched. "It's getting late." He directed a glance ripe with
significance at Sofia. "We do have to leave early, dear."

Sofia smiled at her mother. "I'm being prodded." But she
didn't immediately broach the subject for which she'd

come. Instead she said, "It was so wonderful to see everyone again. Avery is gloriously funny as usual, and Henrietta missed her calling. She should be on the stage. Not to mention Georgie. Her description of Bertie in pursuit was hilarious. And Janie—I've never seen her sing so well, in fact . . ." Her voice trailed off. She carefully placed her wineglass on a small table, then turned to her parents. "I'm afraid there's no tactful or delicate way to say what I have to say."

"Really, dear, you've been nervous all night." Her mother's smile was benevolent. "Go on, darling. You know you can tell us anything."

"I met someone you once knew, Mother."

Amelia and Ben exchanged quick glances, and Ben reached out to take Amelia's small hand.

They know, Jamie thought. *They've been waiting years for this moment.*

"Whom did you meet, dear?" Amelia's voice was controlled with some effort, her fair skin slightly flushed.

"Prince Ernst."

Amelia stifled a small gasp.

Ben put his arm around Amelia's shoulder, drew her close, and bending low, whispered something in her ear. When he raised his head, he met Sofia's gaze with a calm directness. "We were hoping to avoid this. Incorrectly, perhaps, but I assure you, not out of any animus."

Sofia looked from one to the other. "Would you *ever* have told me?"

"No," Amelia blurted out before Ben could speak. "I didn't see the point." She smiled up at Ben before turning back to Sofia. "We argued about it, but I always insisted the decision was mine and no one else's."

Incomprehension numbed Sofia's mind for a flashing moment, quickly replaced by a flood of muddled emotions: chagrin, regret, reproach—a sense of injustice prevalent.

"I didn't want the scandal to touch you," her mother softly said, interrupting Sofia's tumultuous thoughts. "I didn't want my misdeeds to become yours."

"But you were married," Sofia said. "Surely that's not scandalous."

Amelia gently sighed. "It wasn't that simple. I wasn't sure of anything after Ernst disappeared. For all I knew I could have been the object of a grand hoax and nothing more than a fleeting amusement. When word of Ernst's marriage appeared in the London papers, I didn't know what to believe."

"Your father was from a much different world, Sofie," Ben submitted, his voice subdued. "Nobles of his rank don't play by the same rules as ordinary people—or more aptly, by any rules."

Sofia smiled ruefully. "Having met him, I have to agree."

"It wasn't as though your mother could openly dispute his marriage to the Princess of Bohemia. Or rather that she wished to under the circumstances," he finished, directing a loving glance at Amelia.

"I understand," Sofia said, realizing how her mother must have felt at the time, abandoned, bewildered, perhaps lovesick as well. "It must have been very difficult, Mama." Her emotions were still in turmoil, though, for she faced the consequences of that long-ago passion. "The reason I stopped by was not only to let you know that I'd met Prince Ernst," Sofia said, exchanging a quick glance with Jamie, "but also to tell you why he came and sought me out." She went on to explain in a severely edited account the reason the prince had come to London looking for her, explaining only that Rupert's death had prompted his search. "So," she finished, "I was face-to-face for the first time with a man who called himself my father."

"I'm so sorry, darling. It must have been a shock." Her mother's voice was contrite. "But I was never quite sure what to say to you even if I'd chosen to tell you; it all happened so long ago it hardly seemed real anymore." Amelia gazed at her daughter with affection. "Although I never regretted for a second that you were born of that whirlwind affaire. But in all honesty, dear, I always felt that Ernst's world wouldn't be to your liking. I hope I wasn't wrong."

"No, you weren't," Sofia assured her. "Nor would Ernst have welcomed me had I confronted him . . . until now," she realistically added. "I did tell him rather clearly that I wasn't interested in becoming a princess. Much as I sympathize with the loss of his son, I told him that I have a comfortable life of my own." Sofia nervously scanned the room at the sudden reminder of the monster who'd murdered Rupert, and her voice quivered slightly as she continued. "The truth is, however, I'm not quite sure . . . what to do. Without an heir, Ernst's principality reverts to the crown."

"He has an heir in you," Ben pointed out. "Isn't that sufficient?"

"Yes, yes, certainly—you're right," Sofia quickly replied, unable to reveal Von Welden's continuing malevolence.

"It's really just a matter of instituting some legal procedures," Jamie interposed, his voice deliberately mild. "The Austrian judicial system is fearfully antiquated, unfortunately, so a certain amount of political influence and money is necessary to oil the bureaucratic wheels. There's no question that Prince Ernst's sovereignty will be upheld; it's just a matter of time." *And one man's demise.* Jamie made a show of looking at the tall case clock in the corner. "It really is getting late," he said, wishing to put an end to the conversation before too much was said. "If you'll excuse us." He stretched out his arm and touched Sofia's hand resting on her chair. "Morning comes early, dear." He came to his feet.

Sofia didn't move. "Are you sure we can't stay for a few days?"

Amelia took note of the entreaty in her daughter's gaze. "We'd love to have you extend your visit," she pleasantly said. "Please consider staying, Lord Blackwood."

Jamie smiled politely. "My gillies are expecting us. Perhaps some other time when we're not traveling with so many friends. I feel we're imposing."

"Nonsense," Ben gruffly remarked. "You're not imposing in the least." He glanced at Sofia. "Perhaps *you'd* like to stay on, Sofie dear, and travel to Scotland later." He wasn't entirely sure of the relationship between his stepdaughter and this man who traveled with a small army. A hunter himself, he'd taken note of their weaponry; it wasn't for hunting. "Amelia, do coax Sofie into staying on with us. We haven't seen her for so long."

"Really, dear, I wish you would," Amelia said warmly, smiling at her daughter. "The landscape is gorgeous this time of year, and the spring light is simply stupendous. Ben and I hardly come in to eat we're so eager to capture the colors on canvas. We can send you along to Scotland in a week or so."

"Why don't I return later this summer instead," Sofia tactfully suggested, knowing it was impossible for her to stay. "I promised Jamie I'd come to see his estate; he's described it in such glowing terms I'm quite looking forward to our holiday. Which reminds me, I need some canvas and paints. I was too lazy to pack much."

While Ben didn't dispute Sofia's laziness, what bothered him was that Sofie was wearing someone else's frock, the dress clearly not her style. Why was she traveling without her own clothes or her usual green leather trunk?

Additional factors fueling his unease about this Scottish holiday.

Jamie turned to Sofia, his brows lifted faintly. "Are you coming, darling?"

"You go. I'll be up shortly. I haven't had a chance to

quiz Mother on all the latest news and scandals in the art world," she added with a playful grin.

Dare he insist? If Sofia kept drinking. who knew what she'd say?

"Speaking of news!" Amelia exclaimed. "I'd quite forgotten! A telegram arrived yesterday for Lord Blackwood. We thought it was some mistake. Ben, where did we put that envelope?"

"I'll get it." Ben rose from his chair.

Instantly on alert, Jamie said, "I'll come with you." Who the hell knew he was here? More aptly, did the wrong people know he was here? "Don't stay up too late, darling," he said, the fiat in his voice only thinly veiled. "I'm going to wake you early." *Perhaps extremely early depending on who sent the telegram.* With the merest lift of his chin, he summoned Douglas to his side, and together the two men followed Ben from the room.

"He's stunning," Amelia murmured as Jamie disappeared from sight. "You're going to paint him no doubt. He's utterly lovely in a brute sort of way, much different from your other beaux. Almost *indifferent* I'd say, except the way he looks at you quite discourages that notion. I suspect you're enjoying yourself," her mother added with a small smile.

"Very much so, Mother. He can be very attentive."

"Always an attractive feature in a man, isn't it? He's nicely dressed as well; European tailoring has a certain flair. I almost took out my sketchbook as he lounged in his chair, nursing his whiskey and watching you. I can't decide, though—is his tailor Venetian or Viennese? The lapels suggest the Venetians. They like a bit more drama, not to mention the complementary color of the stitching on his pockets. I particularly like his elegant waistcoat, such a glorious pongee silk. And his coat of angora wool is very suggestive of Venice—any enormously expensive fabric delights the Venetian eye."

Sofia grinned. "Only you would notice a man's clothing. Would you like me to ask him the name of his tailor?"

"No, no—actually yes," Amelia amended with a piquant twinkle in her eye. "There's an elderly lady who sews for all the old, moneyed Venetian families." She pursed her lips in musing thought. "I forget her name, but I believe that colored stitching is her trademark. And while we're on the subject of clothes," she added with a disapproving glance, "where in the world did you find that horrid dress?"

"It was a gift."

Her mother lifted her brows. "Obviously from someone without taste." Amelia's wardrobe was in the avant-garde of fashion, as was her daughter's.

"I'm sure he wouldn't care to hear that."

"Surely, you don't mean—"

"No, Mother. A barrister friend," Sofia lied.

Amelia snorted. "That explains it. Such a weary lot, barristers."

"Some are pleasant enough, Mother. You entertain Lord Parker from time to time."

"Only because he's Ben's cousin."

"And also because he's your best bridge partner."

Her mother's lashes drifted downward. "Very well, I stand corrected. Martin has some fine qualities. Now tell me the truth," she said, curtailing their current topic, using the stringent tone mothers used to command honesty in their children. "Why exactly are you going to Scotland? I can't imagine Ernst allowing his ADC to go on holiday when he's in London. As I recall, your father was rather a selfish man."

Sofia looked her mother straight in the eye, having learned as a child that an evasive glance tainted one's credulity. "The prince seems not to have changed in that regard, but he and Jamie must have come to some agreement. I only spoke to Ernst briefly, so I wouldn't know what they arranged," she lied. "Ernst was entertaining other guests at the time."

"A woman, you mean," her mother said.

Sofia shot her a quick look. "Does it bother you?" *Good. A change of subject.*

Amelia shook her head. "Too many years have passed. I'm sure if we met again neither of us would find each other as charming as we once did. And I dearly love Ben—I have for ages."

"He was a very good father to me—is a very good father," Sofia quickly corrected, Ben the most kindhearted of men.

"He *is* an absolute darling, isn't he?" Amelia paused for a moment, choosing her words. "As to this title you've been offered, you must do as you wish. Ben would agree." She took a small breath. "But bear in mind, sweetheart, Ernst isn't known for his loyalty. I wouldn't want you hurt."

"Like you were."

"Perhaps I was for a time." Amelia smiled faintly. "But not for long. Ben was with me even before you were born, and I've had a very good life. I have you, a husband who loves me, and a career anyone would envy. I hold no grudge against Ernst. Poor man—his parents completely controlled his life, and word had it his marriage proved unhappy. Naturally, I'm sorry for the loss of his son. But don't feel you have to provide your life in compensation. You don't."

"I know. Don't worry, Mother, I'm not the sacrificial type. I more or less told Ernst as much. Not that he believed me, but I expect he will eventually."

"Now there's my darling girl," Amelia said with obvious relief. "Ever practical." Amelia bestowed a doting smile on her daughter. "Not that I'm advocating you relinquish either the title or wealth if you don't wish to. You know whatever you choose to do is fine with us. We've always allowed you your independence."

"For which I'm grateful. One last question," Sofia said, leaning forward slightly in her curiosity. "Why did you never consider divorce?"

Amelia shrugged. "I had no assurance that I was married. The ceremony was performed in the Austrian embassy, Ernst took possession of the papers, and once he was gone, I had no proof that the ceremony was legitimate. Then when Ernst was married soon after to the Princess of Bohemia, naturally I questioned the authenticity of *my* marriage." She softly sighed. "So beyond the obvious doubt . . . I didn't have the means to sue for divorce without proper documentation. And had I asked the Austrian embassy for those papers, I assume they would have been withheld to protect Ernst's new marriage."

"Meanwhile, Ernst couldn't divorce or he'd risk some bureaucrat disclosing the proceedings and Rupert's legitimacy would have come into question." Sofia grinned. "Your impetuous love affaire posed some serious problems."

"Or perhaps fate took a hand that long-ago summer." Amelia offered her daughter a good-natured smile. "You *are* a princess after all."

"If only I *wished* to be a princess," Sofia ruefully noted. "Which I most certainly do not. Oh hell," she muttered, vexed and moody, "enough about this ungodly mess. I need some distraction—some new and scandalous gossip. How goes Burke and Mona's affaire, for instance? Have they decided to marry, or has Mona flitted on to some other lover?"

CHAPTER 21

"DOUGLAS IS MY lieutenant," Jamie said as he and his aide entered Ben's study, shut the door behind them, and approached the desk where Ben was pawing through a pile of papers. "He's privy to Ernst's business."

Ben looked up. "Which is?"

"Nothing untoward," Jamie calmly replied.

"I saw your weapons. They're not for hunting."

"We happen to like them for hunting."

"You have guards outside." Ben waved his hand at the windows.

"Force of habit."

"You're wearing a shoulder holster. I felt it when I welcomed you."

"Again—force of habit."

"Sofie's traveling without her luggage. She never does."

Jamie smiled. "You can blame me for that. I was in a hurry to reach Scotland."

"So she bought clothes in Bolton." He'd seen the packages unloaded.

"Is that a problem?"

"It could be," Ben growled. "She normally shops in Paris."

"She seemed willing to compromise."

"Bloody hell!" Ben exploded. "Enough evasion, damn it! Look," he said, tamping down his temper with effort, his nostrils flaring slightly with the attempt, "I hunt. I don't own guns like yours."

"My friends are particular."

"They're not your friends. They're your army."

"Allow me to disagree."

"Stop fucking with me."

"If I might have my telegram," Jamie gently said, trying not to show his anger.

"*This* telegram?" Ben spoke as gently. He held the found item aloft and out of reach.

"Yes, please." A small edge had entered Jamie's voice.

"I want some answers first. I don't like Ernst. I never have, not in the beginning nor any time since."

"I don't see what that has to do with my message."

"It has to do with my daughter."

Jamie's brows rose infinitesimally.

"She's my daughter a thousand times more than Ernst's," Ben curtly said.

"Again, an issue that has nothing to do with my telegram." Jamie scanned the room with a soldier's eye, debating his options, deterrents, whether Ben had weapons on hand. His gaze at the last fell on the cluttered desktop and his heart skipped a beat. "Perhaps we could come to some agreement," he said, his voice carefully modulated. He indicated with a flick of his fingers an envelope of fine quality paper lying amidst Ben's documents. A family crest embellished the envelope, the device familiar to Jamie: double eagles, crossed swords, and lions couchant supporting a cartouche. "Might I ask when you received that?"

"Why?"

"It interests me."

"My only interest is Sofie. Her safety particularly."

"Then it might be useful for you to turn over my telegram and that letter," Jamie quietly said, although he could have whispered and still have been heard in the taut silence of the room.

"She *is* in danger. I knew it."

"I'm not at liberty to betray the prince's confidences, but we both want Sofia protected."

"From whom?"

"I can't say."

"I'll ask Sofie."

"No you won't."

"You'll stop me?"

"I could," Jamie said with impatient economy.

The two men faced each other over the untidy desktop in the untidy room that smelled of paint and turpentine and linseed oil—both large, powerful men, separated, however, by significant differences. Like any English gentleman, Ben knew how to handle a gun; his collection of custom-made hunting guns was extensive. Like any soldier, Jamie didn't restrict his hunting to four-legged prey. Therein lay the novelty of their positions.

The precarious silence crackled with resentment.

Jamie glanced at the clock, wondering where Von Metis was sleeping tonight, wondering how foolish Ben Miller intended to be, wishing like hell they were already into Scotland. At Ben's small indrawn breath, he refocused his gaze.

"If I were to give you this telegram and letter," Ben offered, simmering reluctance in every syllable, a tangible spleen as well, "you'd assure me of Sofie's safety?"

"Yes."

"Do I have a choice?" Ben glanced at Douglas. "Two against one, probably not."

"Probably not," Jamie said. "I'm sorry." He held out his hand.

After ripping open the telegram, he ran his glance over it. Two points for their side, he thought, softly exhaling. He hadn't discounted a taunting message from Von Welden.

TWO OF YOUR DOGS HAD TO BE PUT DOWN, the telegram read. ONE ESCAPED. AN ALSATIAN SHEPHERD BREED. WE'RE HOPING TO KEEP THE DISEASE FROM SPREADING OUTSIDE YOUR KENNEL.

LENNOX AND GROVELAND

Two assassins had been eliminated, his friends were on watch for more, and they'd signaled an Alsatian—Von Metis—had disappeared.

And was now found, Jamie grimly reflected.

Everyone knew Von Metis worked for Von Welden as embassy envoy of one kind or another; it was also common knowledge that he flaunted his family antecedents— hence the allusion to Alsace.

Jamie drew out Von Metis's note, dropped the envelope on the desk, and unfolded the single sheet. The count's flowing script swept over the fine, hand-pressed paper, his message couched in the most fulsome flattery. He began by addressing Ben as the preeminent portraitist in the world and went on in unctuous phrases that extolled the artist's masterful talents. He humbly hoped for an audience as soon as may be—in the morning if possible since he was traveling with friends who weren't inclined to tarry. He aspired, however presumptuously, it went on, to have his portrait painted by Ben. *With kind regards, your most obedient and respectful servant, et cetera, et cetera.*

Jamie looked up from the letter and met Ben's eyes. "Do many write to you like this? Obsequious and genuflecting?"

"Quite a lot."

"Interesting," Jamie marveled. "How do you stand it?"

"I ignore it."

Jamie nodded, then looked away and handed the two messages to Douglas. "We'll need men at that hotel on the envelope. Don't let him out of your sight." He turned back to Ben. "Have you replied to the Von Metis letter yet?"

"I did, although I see I shouldn't have."

"When is he coming?"

"At ten. Who is he?"

"A dangerous man."

"Should we call in the local constabulary?"

"God no. Here's what I'd like you to do."

Ben listened to Jamie's unemotional account of potential disaster and their plans to nullify the impact—Douglas adding a comment or two from time to time. Jamie spoke in general terms, not naming Von Welden, referring to him only as an enemy of Ernst's who'd apparently learned of Sofia's relationship to the prince, had included her in his vendetta, and had sent Von Metis to do her harm.

Ben was red faced with anger by the time Jamie finished. "I hope you're going to kill him," he said.

"Yes, of course. We have to."

"That's all I need to know. Damn Ernst, he's been nothing but trouble from the first. I almost called him out that summer Amelia became involved with him. If not for her feelings at the time," he said with a grimace, "I would have. But she would never have forgiven me for shooting him."

Jamie smiled. "He might have shot you."

"Hell no, he wouldn't have!"

Jamie rather thought Ernst had escaped an early grave; the man was sure of himself. "Well then, I thank you for your cooperation. I'll talk to Sofia once she comes to bed and explain to her that you convinced me to indulge her request and stay another day."

Ben gave him a dry look. "Not likely she'll believe that. I suggest you play the affectionate swain and give in to her out of fondness."

Jamie hesitated long enough for Ben to break out laughing.

"You don't relish giving in to her, I gather," he said, still chuckling. "She's rather a handful, isn't she?"

Jamie grinned. "I blame you."

Ben dipped his head. "You're probably right about that. She's always been able to wrap me around her little finger."

"In truth, I think Sofia was very fortunate in her childhood." Jamie had watched Ernst in the role of father; he was remote and distant, his natural charm saved for his paramours.

"Just keep her safe," Ben ordered. "By whatever means," he grimly added.

"You have my word."

"Remember, Amelia's not to know any of this. I don't want her frightened."

"Agreed. And if you'll see that she and Sofia stay in tomorrow. They can't be outside for any reason. Lock them in their rooms if necessary."

Ben chuckled. "You couldn't stand the din. I'll think of something."

Jamie nodded. "Until morning then."

CHAPTER 22

VON METIS SLEPT the peaceful sleep of a man without a conscience, content in his plans. He anticipated a
productive visit, the information gleaned sure to please
Von Welden. It would also allow him to set a new course
in pursuit of his quarry.

The count was relatively certain that Miss Eastleigh
would have informed her mother of her life-changing news.
Women, after all, were loquacious as a gender. Which meant
his mission would be to exert a double helping of charm—
a familiar enough tactic used countless times in similar
situations—and gain from this man, Miller, the necessary
details of Miss Eastleigh's flight.

The astonishing tale of Sofia's new status had spread
like wildfire through the ton. Von Metis had heard the news
at White's immediately upon arriving at the club. In the
course of the next hour while he'd won some hands and
lost some—not that it mattered with his newly replenished
funds—he'd tactfully grilled his acquaintances for the
particulars of the scandal. The who, what, when, where—

mostly where in his case. By the time he'd taken his leave, he'd discovered that Prince Ernst's recently acknowledged daughter was a beautiful enchantress of marked independence, an artist of some renown, and offspring of parents well placed in society and the avant-garde.

On the cab ride back to his hotel, he'd separated the wheat from the chaff in terms of useful intelligence—a habitual methodology for him. To all appearances, Sofia Eastleigh, along with her father and the principessa, had departed London and were most likely beyond reach at the moment. Although based on experience—Latour's handsome charm found favor with the ladies—he was optimistic with regard to Sofia having contacted her mother. He only hoped that her farewell message had included an address where she could be reached.

Hence, his flying trip north.

Also not to be discounted, inveterate gambler that he was, he'd been seized by a sharp sense of inevitability—like knowing the odds of winning with a royal flush in hand.

He'd felt damned lucky.

As if in confirmation, when he'd retired to the club car on the train and joined a table of fellow travelers playing cards, he'd won.

Consistently.

A portent of success, he'd pleasantly concluded.

WHILE JAMIE WAITED for Sofia in their bedroom that night, he reviewed the morning's affairs with a clinical specificity; semper paratus (always ready) was his motto.

Latour wasn't an amateur—except perhaps at cards; he'd come fully armed with the Roth Steyr handguns he preferred. The count was an expert marksman; even years ago at the military academy where they'd first met, Von Metis had been a crack shot.

He was a professional, deadly opponent—the fact that

he'd tracked them down a demonstration of his competence. Von Metis had always been clever and quick-witted with more than his share of self-esteem. Completely indifferent to the military ideals of honor and devotion to duty, he possessed instead a Machiavellian guile that had brought him to Von Welden's notice—and an addiction to gambling that continued to bind him to his devilish master. In addition, Von Metis had a propensity for savagery—rumors of torture were persistent. Where better to exploit that depravity than in the dark underbelly of society where thuggery was sanctioned as political expediency?

As for Von Metis's self-assured swagger, Jamie considered it his greatest weakness.

On balance, Johan was manageable. If he escaped Jamie's retribution, he'd never get out of the farmyard alive. Whether he knew they were here or not, or whether he was only reconnoitering Sofia's family, the answer would be the same.

Jamie glanced up as the bedroom door opened, smiled, and transferred his attention to more pleasant affairs.

"You're still awake." Sofia shut the door behind her and moved toward the bed where Jamie lay, propped against the pillows, nude and waiting. "I was hoping you would be."

His intimate green gaze was smiling, too. "I need not ask why."

"I should hope not after—what . . . two days?"

"Three, two of them spent servicing you."

"For which I'm eternally grateful."

"And yet?"

She wrinkled her nose, not entirely sure she liked being so dependent on his services. "Don't be so smug."

"I believe *bewitched* is the word," he softly said.

"Oh good!" She offered him a dazzling smile and kicked off her slippers. "I thought you might not want to make love after—well . . . you know."

"You thought wrong." He wouldn't be making love in

cramped circumstances tonight. "Come, darling," he said, patting the bed. "I've missed you. Did you have a nice coze with your mother?"

"I did—sharply curtailed, however, by my need for you."

"We seem to be in accord. I was thinking about coming downstairs, picking you up, and carrying you back upstairs, and if not for your parents, I might have."

She smiled. "Because you're as obsessed as I."

He hesitated briefly at the word *obsessed*. Then he smiled and said, "Yes." It was perfectly reasonable to be obsessed about sex.

"Was the telegram anything of importance?" She was swiftly unfastening the bodice of her gown, selfish in her desires as usual—intent, impatient.

"Some good news actually." Her complete lack of affectation always charmed him; most women required the pretense of seduction. "Oz and Fitz eliminated two of Von Welden's men."

Her fingers paused for a moment and she looked up. "You don't say?"

"I do. We're much safer now, and if you'd care to stay for another day," he said at his most sincere and disarming, "I'm amenable."

Her gaze widened. "Are you serious?"

"I am. It's up to you."

"Then, yes, yes, yes, and thank you!" Sofia exuberantly proclaimed, resuming her unbuttoning with less frenzy now that the threat of departure had been warded off. "Fitz and Oz are darlings, aren't they, along with Oz's personal militia, which I assume was instrumental in the operation."

"No doubt. The telegram didn't go into detail. Come here; let me do that. I'm in the mood to rip off your clothes." An impulse partly attributable to the hazardous events confronting him. The violent urge for sex was inextricably linked with the chance of dying—as any soldier knew. "In the case of that dress," he added with a roguish smile, "it's no great loss."

"My mother would agree. I had to tell her it was a gift from a barrister friend in order to protect your reputation," Sofia explained, coming to a stop beside the bed. "She knew I'd never have bought it."

"Barrister friend?" The faintest rebuke echoed through the words, unintentional, unwanted, and quickly ignored. Sliding up into a sitting position, he plucked her off the floor and deposited her on his lap, intent on dismissing Von Metis from his thoughts and focusing on pleasure instead.

"Much like your female friends in Vienna," she silkily replied, lightly kissing his cheek. "I heard you and Antonella discussing them."

He caught himself before he said something he'd regret, something that would characterize their relationship as different from those in Vienna. "I apologize," he smoothly remarked. "I'm sure your barrister friend is very agreeable."

She grinned, a playful gleam in her eyes. "Such aplomb, Blackwood. How do you do it?"

"Habit, courtesy, my tutor's tendency to beat me when I was rude. And why start a fight?" he said with an amused half smile, his errant emotions contained. "Especially when you tend to scream."

"You're afraid I might scream?" The impertinence in the lift of her brows wouldn't have disgraced an actress on the London stage.

"Actually, no," he replied with a maddening calm, and rolling her under him with daunting speed, he shoved her skirt up in a flash, nimbly settled between her legs, and covered her mouth in seconds flat.

"Mmmmm."

He smiled against her mouth, shoved her skirt out of the way, guided his erection into place through the convenient opening in her drawers, and felt her body's usual wanton

welcome. Driven by the exquisite feel of her slippery liquid
heat, by wild, selfish impulse, by his prolonged wait, by the
ever real specter of death, he made a point of seeing that
Sofia came to orgasm quickly—always easily managed with
the untrammeled libido of the lady currently shattering his
eardrums.

In his ramped-up, hot-spur mood tonight, she couldn't
have come too soon.

And now he was restlessly awaiting his turn.

The same orgasmic rapture rippling through her cunt
pulsated up his stiff cock with such gut-wrenching, excru-
ciatingly raw sensation that even after the alarmist events
of the afternoon, he was considering coitus interruptus a
burden.

Only briefly of course.

He wasn't so foolish, although his discretion was being
seriously put to the test with his seething, high-pressure
orgasm about to explode. Calling on every shred of willpower, he managed to discipline his frenzied nerves, although the instant her heated cries faded away, he pulled
out of her silken warmth, and with a muzzled grunt of
satisfaction, poured a gushing deluge of semen over her
stomach. Afterward, braced on his hands, he hung over
her for some moments, his hair in his face, his breathing
labored. Then he blew out a small breath, raised his head,
and said, "Christ, that was incredible . . ."

She didn't hear him, or if she did, it didn't seem to matter, for at the moment, she was suspended in a sybaritic
limbo—seemingly lit from within, a residual strumming
delicately palpitating her vagina, immeasurable bliss in-
undating her senses. Eyes shut and aglow, she whispered,
"Could we just do this forever?"

"Whatever you want," he said, thinking, *Til morning at
least.* "And I apologize. I usually can wait longer." He
rolled off her with a sigh and lazily stretched.

Opening her eyes, she turned her head and smiled. "You waited just long enough."

"I heard." *Hopefully the rest of the house didn't.*

"Should I apologize?"

"To me—God no," he answered mildly.

"I don't *always* scream, you know." She reached for a towel on the bedside table. "Take it as a compliment."

"I'd prefer not discussing whether you always scream or not. Take *that* as a word of advice."

She paused in stripping off her semen-soaked drawers, her gaze theatrically wide-eyed. "Oh *my*—should I be frightened?"

"Damn right." Coming up on one elbow, he smiled. "Because I'm going to rip off your dress, and then I'm going to fuck you until you swoon."

"What if that doesn't happen—the swooning, I mean?" Sliding her legs free of the drawers, she tossed them on the floor and wiped her stomach with the towel.

His green eyes glittered. "Believe me, it will." Taking the towel from her, he rubbed his cock dry.

"Umm," she purred. "I'm getting hot just thinking about it, and of course looking at your large, lovely, indefatigable erection."

He glanced down, then up again. "You're the one keeping me in full rut, little wanton."

"I prefer *emancipated female.*"

"I prefer naked female." Dropping the towel, he slid his fingers under the open neckline of her gown, closed his grip, and with a sharp jerk, tore the fine silk bodice agape to the waist. "Now then, how do you feel about being ravished?"

He was smiling, and whether he truly meant it or not, her body responded with undisguised eagerness. A hard pulsing commenced deep inside her, a rising flush colored her cheeks, and ravenous desire drenched her vagina. "I'm not sure I'd like to be ravished," she said, suddenly moody. He was too bloody assured, his smile shameless, knowing.

"Really." His gaze met hers, and a teasing light stirred in the shimmering green. "Finish undressing. We'll find out."

"I don't feel like taking orders," she muttered.

This wasn't the time to point out that she'd already given in to him on numerous occasions since leaving Ernst's—actually leaving, the first instance. "Come, darling, you may not like to take orders, but we both know that you take cock rather well. Undress and I'll give you all you want."

"Arrogant man." And his bloody seductive smile he wielded so well. "Perhaps I don't need you."

"Suit yourself," he politely said. "If you'll excuse me, I'll take care of this hard-on myself."

"No!" An explosive cry immune to logic, prodigal desire carrying all before it—intellect, restraint, chafing resentment—everything.

"Then undress," he brusquely said, buffeted by restive, incomprehensible feelings of his own. Drawing in a conciliatory breath, he reminded himself that this was about fucking, nothing else, and he more gently added, "If you would, please, I'd appreciate it." The lady had distinct views on women's rights; this wasn't the time to press her when he didn't want to think or fight, he only wanted to fuck the night away. "And if you don't like ravishment, we can call it something else."

"Love, perhaps?" She grinned. "How would that be?" In command of herself again, she understood as well as he that this was exclusively about sex.

"If you like." Women always did. "We'll call it love."

"Lovemaking."

"Lovemaking it is," he drawled.

His gaze flicked downward again to his erection lying hard against his stomach, then back to her. "Whenever you're ready, darling." Her breathing had changed. He could see the hard tips of her nipples through her chemise. She was her usual hot-blooded self. As if he didn't know.

But it took a moment for him to steady himself as she sat up, slipped her chemise down her arms, and bared her large, plump breasts, the crests rosy pink, jewel hard, and very close.

"Touch me. Here," she said, brushing a fingertip over one nipple.

"Finish undressing." He tapped the crumpled silk of her skirt. "Then I will."

"That's not very loving."

He smiled faintly. "Why so combative tonight?"

"Because it shouldn't always be a man's world, I suppose." More personal inclinations didn't bear scrutiny in this world of casual sex.

"In our case, though, I can masturbate more easily than you. So I might have the advantage."

"How do you know?"

The lewd image in his brain took a moment to beat down. Then he sportively said, "I suppose we could find out."

"Damn your impudence." Tears sprang to her eyes. "Are you ever even remotely serious about anything?"

Living, he thought, pragmatic as ever. *For all of us.* "Darling, please, don't cry," he said instead, gathering her into his arms. "I'm so sorry," he murmured as she sniffled into his shoulder. "I don't want to fight. I want to make love to you all night and for the next decade or more. Don't ask me why. I don't know, I just do."

She lifted her head and gave him a teary smile. "I don't know either. It's really stupid."

"We're obsessed, darling. We don't have to be rational. We probably couldn't be if we wanted to."

She exhaled a long, quiet breath. "Thank you. A reason at least for this insatiable fever of mine."

"Ours," he quietly corrected, his glance for a moment

proprietorial. Then, because he wouldn't allow himself such startling sincerity for long, he grinned and said, "And now I'm going to ravish you with copious and prodigal *love*."

He eased her onto her back and set out to please her, kissing her rosy nipples as he stripped away the remnants of her gown, gently suckling and nibbling each taut peak as she softly writhed and moaned and lost all sense of perspective. Then he slid his fingers into her sleek, silken cunt and explored the hot, moist interior until she was squirming with impatience and softly pleading for him to enter her *Now, now, now!*

"Show me where," he gently said. "Look at me, darling. Where would you like my cock?"

It took her a moment to fully open her eyes and a moment more to distinguish the speaker.

"Look." He ran his fingers up the full length of his erection and circled the swollen crest with a fingertip. "Now where would you like this?"

Her impatient blue gaze locked on his, she spread her thighs, placed her fingers in the lush folds of her sex, and opened herself. "Here," she said on a little caught breath, overwhelmed with a seemingly unquenchable desire that overlooked all but the burning need for surcease. "I want you here—please, Jamie, for the love of God, please."

For some monstrous reason he neither understood nor acknowledged, he required her submission—the perverse impulse lost in some labyrinthine obscurity. Perhaps the violence facing him tomorrow or the violence in his past was cause; perhaps it was nothing more than a dogged resistence to this enticing woman who inspired emotions he didn't want to admit.

Couldn't and wouldn't admit.

Categorically refused to allow.

But now with her capitulation achieved, his mastery absolute, he became the quintessential soul of benevolence.

He indulged her in all things sensory and perceptive, fervent and earnest, his experience wide, varied, and vetted by grateful lovers the world over.

He willingly gave her orgasm after orgasm. He wooed her with sweet caresses and tender kisses, with dulcet words and honeyed promises. He willingly accorded her the entirety of his much vaunted sexual repertoire, gifted her with his impressive and cultivated sensibilities, gave her unrivaled pleasure.

Touched by her joy and gratitude, he rendered her stud service with an unparalleled solicitude that in the end enchanted them both.

When finally, sated and content, Sofia fell asleep in his arms, Jamie lay awake, pleasantly exhausted and replete. He consciously ignored the clock ticking in his head, ignored the dangers confronting him tomorrow, ignored all the mortal uncertainties in the future, because he was gratified beyond his memories of gratification—and happy.

CHAPTER 23

Count JOHAN LATOUR von Metis was greeted at the door by a footman who, on hearing his name, took his hat and gloves and said, "This way, sir. Mr. Miller is expecting you."

As the count followed the young footman, he automatically studied his surroundings, taking particular note of points of egress. The house was quiet at that hour with some guests still abed, although most were in the studios or outside, painting. Von Metis had noticed several artists in the distance as he'd ridden up, all busily at work at their easels, a sunshade perched over their heads. Drawing his horse to a halt, he'd taken out his field glass from his saddlebag and studied the distant figures on the chance that one met Miss Eastleigh's description.

Alas, no.

He unbuttoned his hacking jacket as he was being led toward the back of one wing of the house, twitched his shoulders to settle his twin handguns comfortably under his arms, and rehearsed the sequence of his questions. First, of course, were the requisite compliments to the artist. Then he'd allow a casual remark about the gossip in London concerning Miss Eastleigh. Had Mr. Miller heard, he'd ask. He must have of course, how startling it was, although perhaps not to the family. He'd offer a tolerant smile at that point, a mild comment about the ways of the world, a respectful query as to whether congratulations were in order—and gauge his response before going on. Then, if politesse failed to elicit the information he required, he'd resort to other means.

He automatically shifted his shoulders again to verify the solid weight of the weapons in his holsters as he strode forward, his gait easy in his custom-made riding boots, his mind unencumbered, confident and assured.

He was good at the cloak-and-dagger nasty stuff.

On reaching the end of the hallway, the footman threw open a door, and walking past him, Von Metis entered Ben's office. After quickly scanning his surroundings like a wolf on the scent, he greeted his host with a well-mannered smile. "An honor, sir," he said, putting out his hand as he approached the desk where Ben sat, dressed in black like a funeral director, his expression unreadable. "Count Von Metis at your service."

Ben came to his feet, but he didn't extend his hand.

Strange. The count almost heard the phrase *fix bayonets* in his ear, and a moment later he knew why.

A familiar voice said, "You're a long way from home, Johan."

He slowly turned. James Blackwood had come in silently and was shutting the door behind him. "I might say the same of you," Von Metis said in an affected drawl, a fleeting smile on his handsome face.

"I'm on holiday. Ben's my relative," Jamie lied, hoping the fabrication might put Von Metis off the scent. He preferred the count think Sofia was with Ernst, although at base, it was an unnecessary precaution. The man wouldn't be leaving the farm alive.

"Ah, I see. Are you just nursemaiding then, or planning on marrying into the family? Or should I say both families." Miss Eastleigh's various lovers had been discussed at White's with admiration and unconcealed longing, while Blackwood was a legend in the boudoir. He'd bet a fortune the couple had found common interests. And Blackwood was no more Miller's relative than he was unarmed.

"I'm just doing my job," Jamie said, dismissing any false hope that Von Metis thought Sofia elsewhere.

"In any case, Wharton's going to be pissed. He's out for your blood."

"He'll have to get in line."

Von Metis laughed.

Jamie glanced at Ben; he was supposed to have left when Jamie came in. "I can handle this from here."

"I'm not in a hurry," Ben replied, unmoving and plainly unmovable.

Oh Christ. Someone else in the line of fire. "You didn't actually come here for a portrait, did you, Johan? Tell Ben you didn't so he can get on with his day."

Von Metis grinned sardonically. "Actually I did. I came into some funds recently and decided to indulge my vanity."

"I wouldn't waste your money."

"Is that so?"

"It is."

For all his composure, Von Metis was balanced like a cat, ready to move, and it was clear to everyone that something ugly was about to happen.

"I'm going to have to ask you to come with me," Jamie quietly said.

"Not likely that." A grin creased the count's handsome face, a nonchalance resonated in his voice, his swagger

emerging in the tilt of his shoulders and the wicked gleam
in his eyes.

A toe-curling silence fell.

Then the door suddenly opened and Sofia said, walking
in, "I'd like to—"

Jamie glared. "Get out."

"Go," Ben added without Jamie's snarl.

She'd stopped on the threshold. "First, tell me what—"

"Jesus Christ," Jamie growled. "Do what you're told once
in your life."

"Why not let the lady stay?" Von Metis pleasantly suggested, his voice soft as velvet.

Sofia looked at the visitor for the first time, met his sin-
ister gaze, felt a cold chill of fear, and realized she'd
stumbled into danger.

She turned to leave.

Too late.

Von Metis's hands flew up to his weapons.

Faster than thought, driven by instinct, Jamie hurled
his body toward the door, wrenched his Mauser from its
holster, and threw himself between Sofia and Von Metis's
eight-millimeter rounds.

A volley of shots rang out, Sofia screamed, Jamie grunted
as two rounds tore into his shoulder, and Von Metis fell
dead, shot multiple times in the head and once in the heart.

Jamie preferred head shots.

Ben's forty-five round had blown out half Von Metis's
chest.

Sofia's hysterical screams pierced the air in an unremitting, shrill, earsplitting cacophony of terror—her gaze
riveted on the bloody gore that had once been a man.

Shoving his Mauser back into its holster, Jamie came
upright out of his dive, pushed the shrieking Sofia aside,
slammed the door shut, and locked it. There was blood
and shredded flesh everywhere, Ben's large-caliber round
having made mincemeat of Von Metis's torso, Jamie's

nine-millimeter rounds leaving a cleaner albeit just as deadly path of destruction. What was left of the count lay facedown in a widening pool of blood. Dragging Sofia to a chair, Jamie put his hand over her mouth. "Stop!" He pushed her into the chair. "We don't need witnesses."

Whether it was his curt tone or her abrupt descent, she was shocked into silence or sanity or both. Gulping hard, she drew in a breath and looked up at Jamie. "Oh God, you're shot," she whispered, wide-eyed.

"It's nothing—a flesh wound," Jamie muttered, ignoring the fact that he was bleeding all over the carpet. "Ben, could you let Douglas in?" He nodded toward the window where Douglas was about to break the glass with his rifle butt. He'd been outside, far enough away not to be seen, his rifle scope trained on the room, serving as backup should things go wrong.

His men would be in the hallway by now, standing guard at the door. Jamie had talked to everyone last night after Sofia had fallen asleep. They knew what to say or do to keep people out.

Sofia pointed a shaky finger toward the dead man. "Who is that?"

"One of Von Welden's men. We're fine now, you're fine, don't worry. Stay there, I'll be right back," Jamie added, moving toward the door and letting in two of his men.

Douglas was already rolling the carpet around Von Metis's body, and the two troopers bent to help him, one of them uncoiling a looped rope he'd carried in. Douglas had stripped the body of weapons, wallet, and passport, placed them on Ben's desk, and in short order the count was wrapped, tied up in the carpet, and carried out the door. Turning back from shutting the door behind the two men, Douglas looked at Jamie. "We're ready whenever you are."

In the process of searching through Von Metis's wallet, Jamie held up one hand, fingers splayed.

"That shoulder needs looking at," Douglas observed.

"In a minute."

"I'll leave two men outside."

Jamie nodded and, moving from the desk, tugged off his cravat, pulled up a chair near Sofia, and sat. "I'm afraid we have to leave now," he said, looping his neck cloth tightly over his shoulder and around his arm to stop the bleeding. "There's no telling if Von Metis was operating alone or not." He knotted the makeshift bandage with his teeth and looked up. "He usually works alone, but we can't be sure."

Sofia was trembling faintly. Ben was perched on the arm of her chair holding her hand. "Why can't we protect Sofia here?" he asked.

"If full-scale hostilities break out, some of your friends could get hurt. There's no point in jeopardizing others when my Highland estate is impenetrable. Also, the constabulary might want to become involved if reports of gunfire reach them." His brows lifted slightly. "Not a good idea."

"I'll go with you," Ben said.

"That's not necessary. I've twenty troopers with me and two score more in the Highlands. In fact, I'll leave some of my men to protect you and your friends."

"He's right," Sofia said. "Stay with Mother. The sooner we leave, the sooner everyone here will be safe."

Jamie didn't have time to explain all the ramifications and possibilities of Von Welden's mad pursuit, all that could go wrong and might. "I'm sorry, Ben. You'd just be in the way. And," he more kindly added, "Amelia needs you. You know she does."

Ben softly exhaled, well aware that Jamie's troopers were thoroughly professional. "I don't suppose it would do any good to argue."

Jamie shook his head. "Give Amelia my regards. I don't want her to see me like this." He came to his feet and held out his good hand to Sofia. "We have to go. You have fifteen minutes to talk to your mother. Don't mention any of this. Tell her I'm being difficult"—he smiled—"like men are. I'll wait for you in the stables." He pushed her toward the door and turned back to Ben as she left. "The men I'm leaving behind will clean up this mess. They know what to do. If you don't want Amelia to know they're staying behind, they can bivouac outside. They're used to it. They won't mind."

Ben nodded. "Keep Sofia safe."

"I will."

"If possible, let us know when you've reached safety."

"I'll send word." Jamie walked to the desk, picked up Von Metis's belongings, and turned to the window. "I'll go out this way so I don't leave bloody footprints all the way down the hall." He smiled, an automatic civility, a quick flash of white teeth. "Ciao."

CHAPTER 24

VON METIS'S BODY was buried where it would never be found, Sofia performed her part well and lied to her mother like the worst Judas, Jamie's shoulder wound was hastily cleaned and bandaged, and the troop minus eight men were on the road within the half hour.

Jamie sat beside Sofia, holding her with his uninjured arm. His booted feet were braced against the drift and sway of the carriage; Sofia's slippered toes just brushed the floor.

"It fits."

She shot him a puzzled look.

"Your dress. Puffy sleeves and all," he added, flicking the ruched organza on the fashionable leg-of-mutton sleeve. "I like it." She was wearing one of Mrs. Lynne's dresses.

"Thank you."

Her reply was automatic and detached. "Are you tired?"

She nodded, rather than try and explain that she couldn't so easily turn to idle chatter after all she'd seen.

"Sleep if you like. We won't be stopping for several hours."

And then, like intimate strangers thrown together by circumstance, they both fell into a ruminating reverie.

Sofia was struggling to reconcile the violence of the scene she'd just witnessed against the normalcy of her former life. An impossible task with the image of the ravaged man haunting her. The savage finality of death was etched on her retinas; the expanding pool of blood on the carpet replayed endlessly in her mind, what had once been a living man lying there spiritless and still.

She understood how narrow her escape. Jamie had thrown himself into the path of the gunshots meant for her; she owed him her life. Yet, she wondered how he could live in such a bestial world, how he remained human himself when he did what he did. And she wondered most how she could care for a man who so easily took another life. He'd shown no remorse, nor a scintilla of concern for the dead man, his attention focused instead on the disposal of the body and the speed of their departure.

How many people had he killed to be so hardened and inured to the act?

How skilled in the murderous arts did one have to be to discharge one's weapon in a tight, methodical pattern while hurtling through the air? Such clinical expertise took practice.

She shuddered, assailed by doubt and fear.

Jamie drew her closer. "I'm sorry you had to see that," he said, as if reading her thoughts. "If it helps, he was a cutthroat many times over; he deserved it."

"There'll be more like him, won't there?" Despite her ethical reservations, she understood the life-and-death issues facing them.

"I'm afraid so, although once we reach Blackwood Glen, we'll be safe." He rested his head against the padded seat, the morphine he'd taken for pain beginning to tranquilize his senses.

"You'll stay there with me, won't you?"

"Of course." A necessary lie.

"Good." Shifting slightly, she turned into the warmth of his body, and setting aside her misgivings, yielded to his strength and power. He was her port in a storm, her unshakeable protector, the man who stood implacably between her and death. In a life less fraught with danger, perhaps she could afford a conscience.

But not now.

Not until their enemies were vanquished.

Shutting her eyes, she abandoned issues of right and wrong and concentrated instead on the peaceful life awaiting them at Blackwood Glen.

Surrendering to the palliative morphine, relieved of his pain, Sofia consoled for the moment, Jamie turned to the knotty, unresolved perplexities troubling him.

He was unsure whether definable limits to personal loyalty existed, but if they did, he'd reached that extremity. Ernst was sailing south on Antonella's gunboat, out of danger and probably fucking his brains out—not that he gave a damn one way or the other. But what he did care about was Sofia's safety, and ultimately, with her future assured, he found himself harboring a novel impulse to consider his own future.

Something he'd never consciously regarded before.

Something that had always been inevitable and beyond dispute, the orthodoxy long established that the eldest Blackwood son follow in his father's footsteps. Five generations of Blackwoods before him had served the Battenberg princes; his destiny was foreordained.

Or was it? he wondered for the first time in his life.

Certainly, he'd long been conscious of the changing world and increasingly edgy about the obsolete monarchy currently wielding power in Austria. He'd been conscious as well that the myth of aristocratic exceptionalism was rotten to the core. Trained as a soldier, though, he'd resisted debating philosophical issues, giving his allegiance instead as his family always had to the princes of Battenberg.

And now, resist or suppress as he might, circumstances had brought him to this point of personal decision.

Unfortunately, he didn't have the leisure to debate his options at the moment. Von Welden would continue sending out killers because that's what he did—like some goddamned demented Caligula with grandiose plans and no fucking soul.

So, the only question was: should he wait to be attacked or take the offensive? And the answers were all unpleasing.

Their party wouldn't reach Blackwood Glen for three more days; another four or five would be required to return to Vienna—provided luck was on their side and they met no interference. The determining factor, however, was the increasing pain in his shoulder that suggested he didn't have time to wait. If the wound festered, it could incapacitate him, possibly kill him, although he could probably last a week before collapsing. If he wanted to see Von Welden on his way to hell, he could hope for the best in terms of healing, but it would be better to prepare for the worst.

That worst-case scenario allowed only a narrow window of opportunity.

So then, first things first: a good supply of morphine and coca leaves from their traveling pharmacology was in order—morphine for the pain, cocaine to counteract the opium sleep. He needed all his mental faculties operating at full capacity in order to slip into Vienna undetected, contact Katia, find the Albanian, and see Von Welden dead.

Christ—a daunting task even under the best of conditions with the city crawling with secret police. And his arm semiuseless.

Fortunately, he was ambidextrous.

He'd flay Von Welden with his left hand if he had to.

And afterward, if he lived, he could afford to be human. Perhaps even consider a future.

THAT EVENING, THE troop stopped in a forest clearing invisible from the road and set up camp. After a tasty meal was prepared and eaten, a night guard was posted and everyone retired to their tents. Jamie and Sofia's accommodations were simple but comfortable; the ground was covered with a carpet, and a large camp bed held center stage, flanked by a folding washstand and two chairs. Dropping into a chair, Jamie visibly winced as he bent over to pull off his boots.

"Oh dear," Sofia cried, moving toward him. "Let me help you."

"Be a good girl and bring me another draught of morphine," he said, nodding toward the washstand.

He was white-faced and resting against the chair back, his boots off, when Sofia returned with the uncorked bottle. Taking it, he poured a large dose down his throat, handed it back, murmured, "Thank you," and, shutting his eyes, sat very still as the harrowing pain washed over him in waves. Hours of jostling in the carriage had been hell on his shoulder.

"Could I help you into bed?" Sofia whispered, terrified to see him in such agony.

His eyes opened marginally. "Give me a minute." He smiled faintly. "If you'll excuse me tonight. I'm afraid I won't be much good to you."

"Heavens, I'm not so unfeeling. Your dressing really should be changed." It was wet and bloodstained, the bleeding having resumed whenever he moved too much. "Let me do that for you."

He shook his head. "Douglas will. He's better than any surgeon. But thank you. It should be much improved by morning. I heal quickly."

"Oh, good," she said with such obvious relief he would have chuckled if he'd dared. "It looks ever so painful."

"The first day's always the worst. Don't worry, darling, I'll be fine soon."

"I never did properly thank you for saving my life. Thank you a thousand times. You were enormously brave."

"My thanks as well, darling." He grinned. "I appreciate all you've done for me."

"Don't tease. I'm serious. You saved my life."

"Allow me to say in all sincerity then, you've brought me great joy."

"As soon as you're mended, I'll see that I bring you additional joy," she brightly said, charmed and smitten, her heart filled with tenderness.

Jamie smiled. "Now there's incentive."

BUT WHEN MORNING came, she woke up alone and immediately knew Jamie was gone. Quickly dressing, she flew out of the tent and tore into Robbie, who'd been left in charge and was calmly waiting for her.

He faced her furious displeasure with unvarying courtesy, meeting her angry barrage of questions with polite evasion, deflecting her insistence on following Jamie with a mild, repetitive refrain. "Sorry, miss, I have me orders."

Finally, after ten minutes of overwrought female rage and affront while her tent was being disassembled behind her, Robbie quietly said, "If ye'd be so kind, miss, as to climb into the carriage, we'll be off."

"And if I don't!" Frustrated and cross, choleric at having been left behind, her scream rose into the trees.

"I have me orders, miss." Those orders clearly defined by Jamie last night before he and Douglas had ridden cross-country to catch the night train to London.

Her temper at fever pitch when faced with such obstinacy, Sofia swore like a fishwife while Robbie stood motionless, his face a mask. "Jamie's going to pay . . . for this outrage . . . damn him!" Sofia finally gasped, bringing her tirade to an end out of sheer necessity, like a child who'd screamed too long.

"Yes, miss." Robbie glanced at the open door of the carriage, drew in a breath of restraint, and said, "If ye please, miss."

She flounced toward the carriage, knowing she was being childish and pettish, well aware that Jamie was only doing what he considered his duty. But the sad, awful truth was she already missed him terribly for no good reason and a thousand innocuous reasons. It suddenly felt as though the sun had gone out of her life, her world was utterly cheerless, and what was worse, she had to worry about Jamie dying not just at the hands of some murderer but possibly from his wound. It had taken a terrifying amount of morphine last night to bring him relief.

The moment Sofia entered the carriage, Robbie slammed the door shut as if having lured a wild beast into its cage.

Quickly shoving down the window, Sofia said, "I know Jamie's gone after Von Welden. You don't have to tell me, just nod your head. He can't chastise you for that."

Robbie didn't answer for a moment, then he nodded and immediately signaled the driver to move off. He didn't want to chance it that the rash young lady might take it in her head to bolt. He had his orders and he'd discharge them if it meant tying her hand and foot until they reached Blackwood Glen.

But he breathed more freely as he threw himself into the saddle; the carriage was bowling away at a good clip.

Huddled in the corner of the seat, Sofia could feel her heart beating wildly against her ribs. She was terrified for Jamie's safety—although she'd probably known all along or suspected at least that he'd turn and fight. Pray God he had sense enough to summon his men from Dalmia before he faced Von Welden with only Douglas at his side—or better yet, he should rouse an army to face the evil fiend.

She silently bewailed her fate, trapped in a carriage, surrounded by armed men, being hied off to Scotland like so much baggage. It was grossly unfair, completely unjust, and flagrantly discriminating. Why should men make all the rules and expect women to simply comply? Why couldn't she have gone, too? She could ride, she could shoot—well maybe not very well, despite Ben's tutelage when she was a child—but certainly, she could be plucky and brave.

Although, in all honesty, she had to admit that she'd rather fallen apart that first night at Ernst's in London; she hadn't been particularly valiant screaming her head off in Ben's office yesterday either. Faced with the unflattering truth, she made a wry face. Perhaps, she conceded with a sigh, there were some things men could do better than women. Or at least men like Jamie Blackwood who were resolute and bold and about to fearlessly walk into the cannon's mouth.

Her tears spilled over in dribbling drips and drops at first, sliding down her heated cheeks, splashing onto the printed linen fabric of her gown, unbidden and unwanted. *Just like a woman*, she thought, quietly sobbing. Like a stupid woman, fearful of losing the man she loved. At the word *love*, the floodgates inexplicably opened and the drizzle turned into a veritable deluge.

Could it be? Is this love?

Sniffling and sniveling, she soon decided it really couldn't be. She'd known Jamie so few days and so slightly—sex aside, of course. Furthermore, she wasn't inclined to fall in love. In fact, she didn't actually believe in love beyond those commonplace endearments men were likely to utter in the midst of passion.

And sex surely wasn't love.

There, that was better—reason was restored.

She drew in a calming breath.

But emotions weren't so easily repressed or dismissed, she discovered, and as the advancing miles separated her from Jamie, her fondness and affection, her lovesick longing only intensified.

Dear Lord, keep him safe, she prayed when she hadn't prayed since childhood. *Heal his wounds, merciful God, bring him back to me—don't let him die.* That she prayed for most.

And she couldn't stop crying despite her disgust of weeping females.

By the time they stopped to make camp that night, red faced and bleary-eyed, she realized that whatever constituted love, however love was defined, by word or deed or aspiration, she had the ill fortune to love a man who not only didn't love her, but also might never return.

CHAPTER 25

THREE DAYS LATER, traveling under forged documents collected from Ernst's house in London, Jamie and Douglas arrived in Vienna. They'd entered Europe at Ostend rather than Calais to avoid Von Welden's sentinels, traveled to Munich, then south by local trains since Von Welden's spies would more likely monitor the express trains. Outfitted as farmworkers, the two men melted into the crowd of peasants from the countryside who were bringing their produce to market and slipped away down a narrow alley before reaching the market square.

Making their way across the city with the streaming influx of laborers on their way to their daily toil, they reached a tree-lined street in a bourgeois neighborhood. Maintaining a reasonable distance, they followed a group of chattering seamstresses down a private drive leading to the back of a dress shop that served only the crème de la crème of Viennese society.

Midway down the drive, one young girl who was a few steps behind the others glanced back and nervously quickened her pace. Two very large workmen shouldn't be making their way to Madame Szogyenyi's establishment at this time of day or perhaps ever. Her employer retained her own laborers and craftsmen, and none of them wore garb more customarily seen on the farm.

But as the group of women were entering the shop, Jamie called out in a voice pitched only for the ears of the pretty laggard, "Mitzi, wake Flora for me, will you?"

The girl spun around at the familiar voice and saw Jamie with his finger to his lips. She nodded, acknowledging his warning, and with a quick smile she turned and followed her companions into the shop.

Jamie led Douglas to an inconspicuous black door in the corner of the three-story Baroque-style mansion. They waited perhaps five minutes in the shade of a large ivy-covered topiary before the door opened and a female voice murmured, "Come in. Quickly now."

Both men silently followed the slender woman in a violet silk dressing gown up a narrow staircase to the main floor where she hurriedly conducted them down a short hallway and waved them into a small, elegant sitting room.

"Are you *mad*?" Madame Szogyenyi exclaimed as she closed the door and collapsed against it. "Clearly you are," she said, answering her own question. "You must know Von Welden has every spy in Vienna looking for you."

"We noticed. The two across the street in particular."

"Odious creatures," Flora said with hearty contempt. "It's your fault of course that I'm being harassed. Were they busy with their morning coffee?"

He nodded. "They didn't even see us."

"Herr Reuss serves them their breakfast with my compliments. Although the poor man has lost customers since they took up their posts outside his café. The blackguards are really too obvious."

"I do apologize for bothering you," Jamie said, taking a small breath against the excruciating pain gripping his senses. "I thought perhaps you might not mind if we use your attic for a few days."

"Of course I mind, you callous rogue. Anyone with half a brain would."

"The question is," he politely said, "how much do you mind?"

Her eyes rested a second on the cool, self-contained man who stood very still by dint of his considerable will, she suspected. She softly sighed. "How can I refuse you anything, you darling man."

"As ever, I thank you." Jamie smiled faintly. "I'm more than happy to pay you a fortune for the accommodations."

"Pshaw. As if I need money." The dressmaker tut-tutted softly. "You look terrible."

"I look better than I feel." His face was marked with stresses, his eyes dark shadows.

Straightening, she briskly said, "You need a doctor. I'll have Kasper come over. Someone shot you, I presume."

"Von Metis."

She quickly shuttered her startled look. "Did he survive?"

"No."

"Good riddance," she said, wishing she could kill Von Metis again for what he'd done to Jamie.

"Do you mind if I sit down?" His pallor was marked, his hands suddenly clenched to deter their trembling. "We've been traveling for three days."

"Tut. And you in that state," she murmured, moving toward him with outstretched hands. "Sit anywhere, darling. Here, lie on the sofa," she said, gently touching his arm. "Help the poor boy, Douglas. He's practically ready to topple over. And you needn't use the attic, Jamie dear, when my apartment is perfectly safe. Von Welden wouldn't dare accost me or invade my premises. His wife would cut off his balls if he offended me."

Jamie grinned. "I was hoping that was the case." He

sank heavily onto the malachite green moire sofa and shut his eyes.

Madame Szogyenyi shot a worried look at Douglas. "I'll summon the doctor."

"No," Jamie muttered without opening his eyes.

"Don't be silly. Kasper's a friend. Now, don't argue. I expect you've come for Von Welden. You might as well live to see him die." She went to a small desk and scribbled a quick note. Calling in a servant, she handed it over with murmured instructions before turning back to Douglas. "Help the dear boy into my bedroom. We'll get him into bed. He can sleep until the doctor arrives."

A short time later, after having put an only faintly protesting Jamie to bed, Douglas and Flora sat across from each other at a table in an adjoining room that had been set with a substantial breakfast in their absence.

"Please, eat." She waved a slender, ringed hand over the table. "Coffee or tea?"

"Coffee, thank ye."

After she poured Douglas coffee and he began to eat, Flora rested back in her chair, ran her fingers through her disheveled auburn curls, and said after a short, considering silence, "How bad is he?" Jamie was her favorite lover, her only one when she tired of the vulgar world, which was more and more often of late.

Douglas looked up from his plate. "He'll manage."

"For how long?" Her eyes were bright with unshed tears, regret soft in her voice.

"Ye know him," Douglas replied, unblinking and direct. "For however long it takes."

She gathered herself, understanding a cold-blooded expediency was required to see the personal vendetta through. "What's Jamie using to counter the morphine?"

"Coca leaves. They're mild but do the job."

"I'm not foolish enough to think he'll go home and recuperate first."

"Nor foolish enough to think Von Welden would allow the bonny boy that respite."

She shrugged, perfunctory issues dismissed. "Agreed. What can I do?"

"We have to talk to Katia Karolyi. Can ye get a message to her?"

"Of course." They were fellow Hungarians. "She hates him, you know. She'll be perfect."

"That's what we were thinking. She also might like to see her brother freed."

Flora laughed softly. "She might kill Von Welden herself for that incentive. She loves her brother above all things. I'll have a servant carry over a note directly." She raised her brows. "Couched in suitably veiled terms. Von Welden monitors Katia's activities as if he were charged with guarding an heiress's maidenhead. Fortunately," she added with a faint smile, "he daren't come here with his mistress."

Douglas held her gaze over a forkful of ham. "Because his wife is rich?"

"And concerned with maintaining the proprieties." Flora's violet gaze was sardonic. "Aren't we lucky."

Douglas grunted. "We're going to need all the luck we can get."

HAVING STAYED THE night as he often did, Von Welden was breakfasting with Katia when Madame Szogyenyi's message was delivered.

After reading it, Katia handed it across the table. Von Welden was suspicious of all her correspondence as he was about everything in her life.

"Cloth of gold?" His brows rose over an inquisitor's gaze.

"I thought you might like me in something flamboyant," Katia murmured with a charming smile, ever the actress for Von Welden. "Madame Szogyenyi promised to design something dramatic for me—for your enjoyment of course," she softly added.

He smiled at the beautiful young woman with strawberry blonde hair and the most voluptuous body in the empire. "Flamboyant—I like the sound of that. Is it ready then?"

"No, dear. Just another fitting. Come if you like." An artful bluff.

"And run into my wife? I think not."

"Suit yourself," Katia casually replied, well versed at masking her feelings with Von Welden. "But surely she must know. Everyone else does."

"Knowing and admitting one knows are two different matters. Ignorance is bliss, my dear. She's the mother of my children after all."

"How are the darlings?"

"You'd have to ask their governesses and nannies. They look well enough when I see them, although I fear Hans has his mother's features. Poor boy. The Wittelbachs are not a comely family."

"But a wealthy one," she said, passionless and cool.

He looked up at her tone, wondering if a gift of jewelry was required to assuage that unpleasant glimpse of temperament. Straightening the cuff on his uniform, one of several he kept at his mistress's apartment, he took another moment to debate his response. "It's a business arrangement, my dear. Like so many marriages. Now then," he said with a lazy smile, "why not find yourself a bit of jewelry to complement this new gown. I'll send word to Lawry that you're coming in. Tell me, when will this gown be ready so you can show it off for me?"

"I'll let you know after my fitting. Madame Szogyenyi's an artiste who refuses to be harried. More coffee?"

No mention of his offer of jewelry. If the bitch wasn't so lush and succulent, he'd have her flogged for her damned impertinence. "Alas, duty calls," he said, low pitched and pleasant. Rising from his chair, he bowed with a click of his heels. "Until tonight, my dear."

The moment the door closed on him, Katia summoned a servant to carry her answer to Madame Szogyenyi, then ordered her lady's maid to draw her bath. She wished to scrub away any trace of Von Welden—a customary ritual on his departure.

CHAPTER 26

JAMIE WAS UP and waiting for Katia by ten. His wound had been seen to; he'd been dosed with drugs and bathed and dressed in his own clothes from a minimum selection he kept at Flora's for just such occasions. There were times when he came into Vienna and wished to avoid his own apartment; the secret police could damn well watch someone else.

Austria was a reactionary state: the press censored, the mail read by the police before delivery; telegrams might as well have been published in the papers; every person of note—and those of lesser stature, too, if they had the bad sense to attend the wrong lecture—were watched day and night. Even the imperial family wasn't immune from the scrutiny of the secret police.

At the moment, however, beyond their reach, Jamie was feeling in the pink of health thanks to the doctor's injections. Nothing hurt, he could move without wincing, his mind was alert; no one but those with a practiced eye would have noticed his dilated irises. Flora had drawn the shades.

Jamie appreciated the doctor's professional attention. Jamie had been monitoring the delicate balance between the morphine and coca leaves himself all the way to Vienna, fully aware that he couldn't sustain the morphine regime for long or a train of alarming symptoms would ultimately lead to his collapse. The ingestion of coca leaves also required stringent control; excess use could lead to bodily and mental failure. He'd felt like a damned apothecary, measuring out his doses, maintaining a credible interval between, trying to consume as little as possible to mitigate his pain.

He was truly grateful to Flora; he was relaxed, better able to face any contingency. Not that the circumstances had changed, nor had the doctor done more than clean and redress the wound with pursed lips and grim-faced censure.

"You could lose this arm," Kasper had muttered, "or your life. You know that, I suppose."

"Not, I hope, in the next day or so," Jamie had pleasantly replied, in harmony with the young Hungarian doctor since he'd injected a painkiller directly into his wound before beginning his task.

"You might last that long; as for this infected shoulder . . ." The doctor paused in his gentle swabbing of the wound and held Jamie's gaze. "It's turning putrid."

"I know. Just clean it up for now. I'll deal with it later."

"How many days have you been on the drugs?" Kasper asked then, assessing damage and future damage, the speed at which the infection could possibly kill him.

"Three."

He quickly surveyed Jamie's body, his gaze exacting. "Any vomiting or nausea?"

"Not yet."

"Hallucinations?"

"A few. Nothing major."

The doctor set down his swab and lifted Jamie's wrist, checking his pulse. "Still relatively steady," he said, setting Jamie's hand down. "When it weakens, you won't have much time before you lapse into unconsciousness."

"I only need another day, two at the most," he said without expression.

This man was obviously marshaling his strength for some urgent matter. "Whatever you're doing must be important or Flora wouldn't have called me. We're all at risk, though, over this."

"I appreciate your coming. If it helps, my mission will eliminate one of Hungary's enemies. He's a new major landowner in your country with grand designs to build another Versailles."

"Filthy Austrians," the doctor muttered. "They have no right to our land." There was no love lost between cultures, no matter an ostensible partnership existed in the Austro-Hungarian Empire. It was a partnership in name only, the government firmly in Austrian hands.

"This Austrian in particular," Jamie said with a soft and frightening venom. "By the way, if you could leave me some syringes, I'd be grateful," he added in a voice pitched to such a degree of politesse the doctor thought for a moment he'd misheard the previous comment.

"I'll see what I have." Once Jamie's wound was rebandaged, the doctor rummaged through his bag. "There now," Kasper said, placing some syringes on the bedside table along with additional drugs. "Enough for three, possibly four days." Although Jamie would require greater and greater doses to produce less and less effect.

"Thank you. You're most kind." Jamie's voice was easy, his green gaze clear and unwavering. He might have been expressing gratitude for a spring tonic.

The doctor was shrugging into his coat. "Will I see headlines in the papers with regard to this mission?"

"I'm sure you will," Jamie casually replied, although there was nothing casual about the look in his unsmiling eyes. "However, the gentleman in question will have suffered a heart attack or some such thing; like the spurious reports that were put out on the crown prince's death. The event will come to pass very shortly." Jamie smiled faintly. "For obvious reasons. Although, at the moment I feel quite restored."

"Only until the drugs wear off," the doctor reminded him.

Jamie's smile widened. "I don't expect they'll be wearing off anytime soon."

DRESSED IN GREY flannel slacks, a white linen shirt, and soft elk-skin slippers, Jamie was resting now in the large, high-backed chair Flora had purchased for him shortly after they'd met. She'd already been well established in her career, married with a young daughter (who was currently away at boarding school in Switzerland), and saddled with a harassing, aristocratic husband who spent all her money at the gaming tables.

One night outside the casino at Baden, or so gossip had it, Jamie had taken the opportunity to speak to Flora's husband. Whatever was said—and neither man had ever commented on the incident—the harassment as well as the drain on Flora's funds had come to an end.

Her husband had never approached her again.

Even if their affaire hadn't already begun, Flora would have thanked Jamie exactly the same way, for he'd given her back her life. He was nineteen at the time, she was twenty-six, and a decade later, their friendship still endured.

"You *should* eat something," Flora insisted once again, watching Jamie from her vantage point on the divan.

"Ye should," Douglas urged, Jamie's loss of appetite a characteristic of the drugs.

"I feel too good right now. Let me rest." His smile was angelic. "I promise, my dears, to eat as soon as Katia leaves."

"You're not allowed to drink," Flora directed. "Don't forget."

"Why would I want to? As you see, I'm quite content. Kasper is a prince among men. My compliments, darling, on your good sense to call him in."

"Just remember my good sense later when I bring you food. If you don't eat, you'll become weak."

Jamie shut his eyes as though to arrest the continuous barrage of orders, and Flora and Douglas exchanged worried glances.

Then everyone sat in silence.

Jamie made plans behind his closed eyelids. Under the high intake of drugs, he was keyed up to an intense level of imaginative activity.

Douglas made plans of his own; his had to do with keeping Jamie safe if the drugs made him careless.

Flora worried; how was it possible to get to a well-guarded man like Von Welden and live to tell the tale?

When the door opened and Katia was announced, Flora quickly came to her feet. "Thank you for coming, my dear." She spoke in Hungarian. "Since I know how you hate cloth of gold, I knew you'd understand my little subterfuge."

"A perfect contrivance, I agree. Von Welden was there." She shrugged. "He's quite unaware."

"Good. Please excuse the dim light. I have a headache," Flora dissembled in the way of an explanation. "Come see who's in town."

The men had risen on Katia's entry.

"Jamie!" Katia softly exclaimed, moving across the shaded room to take his outstretched hands. "How nice to see you again, no matter the circumstances." She turned to

Douglas as she clasped Jamie's hands, both men friends through Flora's acquaintance. "Douglas, hello. You're both still safe, I see."

"And you?" Holding her hands lightly, Jamie bent and, avoiding the brim on her bonnet, kissed her on both cheeks. "How goes your durance vile?" His Hungarian was pure and unaccented.

She stepped back and her gaze turned hard. "I count the days until it ends."

"Would tonight do?"

"No, no," she cried, clearly distrait. "Please don't. He'll have Andor killed. My brother's hostage to my compliance."

"Don't worry, we'll see your brother safe first," Jamie said, briefly. "Come, sit." He offered her a chair. "Let me explain." And he did with all the patience and skill at his command. When he finished, he waited, smiling faintly, his gaze steady on Katia, who sat head bowed and breathing fast. "We can have men on the way to the monastery at Heiligenkreuz by afternoon. Enough men to kill every monk and every Von Welden guard if necessary. Make no mistake, we will if we have to. I want Von Welden dead, and a few monks one way or another matters little to me."

Katia looked up at his cold, chill tone. The Jamie she knew was charming and smooth and infinitely amiable. Confused and fearful, her thoughts in tumult, she could feel her heart thumping in her breast. "What if things go wrong? What then? He'd kill us all; you know he would."

"I have sixty men in Vienna. Everything will go smoothly, I guarantee. Help us, and you and your brother will be free by morning," Jamie said, controlling his voice when so much was at stake, when he had to convince her that she'd come to no harm. *When nothing was certain.*

Taking a deep breath, Katia sat up and squared her shoulders under her stylish walking costume of petunia silk. "Explain it all again. Tell me the plan from start to finish." And when he did, she said, "Once more so I have it clear in my mind. Guarantee or not, my role is pivotal."

"You're required to do no more than you have all these many months," Jamie softly noted. "Surely, for this reward, you can play your part one last time. You said you have dinner waiting for him at nine? We'll be there at nine fifteen. Someone will escort you out immediately—under protest of course," he mockingly added. "You won't be involved in any other way."

She didn't speak for a moment.

Jamie's lashes lay at half-mast, his gaze beneath watchful.

"Very well, I'll do it," Katia said in a strong, firm voice.

"Excellent," he said charmingly, and his pulses leaped. The plan was in motion. Commanding his mind to more prosaic matters, he offered Katia a benign smile. "Flora tells me she brought you here with some fabricated story. Do you need some particular item to show that you were here? I'm sure it can be arranged."

"No, I told Von Welden I was coming only for a fitting. Although I'll stop at Lawry's on the way home and pick out a bibelot I was promised. A final one," she cheerfully said, "to allay suspicion."

"It might be wise for you and your brother to leave Vienna afterward. At least until the furor dies down."

"I thought as much. Paris would be nice. We have an aunt there who's well connected. Her husband's with the Hungarian embassy."

"Perfect. Pack your valuables and what else you wish to take. We'll have a carriage waiting for you at the back of the building. We'll see you and Andor safely to the German border. There're places enough to cross without exposure, and once you're both in Munich, you can travel to Paris by train. Any questions?"

"Just don't be late. I'm afraid my agitation will show."

"We won't be. We'll be there minutes after he arrives. And you'll be fine. Think of it as your last performance."

"I'm grateful, don't think I'm not," she softly said.

Jamie smiled. "We'll visit again in Paris. You can introduce me to your aunt. How would that be?" He glanced at Flora.

Taking his cue, she rose in a swish of heliotrope silk muslin. "Perhaps a cup of tea before you go, Katia," she suggested with a small flutter of her ringed hand. "A fitting would normally take a half hour at least. Why don't we adjourn to my conservatory. My orchids are quite lovely, and I have some wonderful plum eau-de-vie if you'd like."

CHAPTER 27

JAMIE'S MEN HAD been arriving in Vienna in small groups over the course of the last three days, having been sent instructions by telegram prior to Jamie and Douglas's departure from London. Sixty men were assembled and waiting in a town house owned by the Swedish embassy. Jamie had personal friendships at the embassy; favors were occasionally exchanged. Although, he'd called in a great number of markers in this instance because he needed this particular location from which to operate.

Gustav was kind enough to send an embassy carriage to Flora's, his wife inside. When Lady Magnus exited Flora's mansion after ordering several new gowns—gifts from Jamie—she was accompanied by two Swedish guards.

It was three o'clock when Jamie and Douglas entered the town house. After warm greetings, a war council was held, and Jamie, speaking with even-voiced speed, detailed the two simultaneous plans and assigned everyone their duties. Then, shortly after, several groups of men in mufti left the town house at intervals and made their way by carriage, horse, or train to the village of Heiligenkreuz twenty miles outside the city.

As the troopers arrived over the course of the next few hours, they collected at a local inn. They were ostensibly a group of wealthy men come to the vicinity for sport. Their fishing gear was carried in custom cases, and the dinner they ordered from the innkeeper was of the finest quality. As they ate well and drank little, they quietly went over their strategy.

The timing of the operation was by necessity precise.

Andor would be taken out first—fifteen minutes before Jamie and his men entered Katia's apartment. They couldn't risk a telegram being sent from the train station informing Von Welden of Andor's liberation. With the monastery up in the hills outside the village, their time frame should be sufficiently safe.

Jamie would go with the bulk of his men to Katia's apartment, although some troopers were on the streets already, keeping track of Von Welden's watchers. As evening fell, they'd also monitor the additional guards that would appear prior to Von Welden's arrival.

The Albanian had been found and sat beside Jamie, silent, finely tuned and alert, waiting like everyone else. He wasn't Albanian, although he had no more knowledge of his ancestry than anyone else. Orphaned young, he'd grown up on the streets of Durazzo and lived hand to mouth until he'd been taken under the wing of a Turkish assassin from whom he'd learned his trade. His mentor, the story went, had died in Trieste some years ago after a drunken brawl in a seaport tavern.

The young, slender, dark-haired Albanian had received his instructions from Jamie. Then the two men had retired to a small study at the back of the house where Jamie had paid him in advance from a small Gladstone bag stuffed with bills. He'd also offered him the name of an honest banker.

Hajdu had smiled for the first time at that point and said, "I thank you, effendi, for your kindness. A safe home for my money is most welcome." The men in the underworld who called themselves bankers were highly unreliable.

"What you offer me is also most welcome," Jamie acknowledged. "This man who dies tonight has caused me much suffering."

"Was he the cause of your affliction, too, effendi?" the Albanian gently asked. "It is a great illness thou hast."

"In a way I suppose he was." Jamie shrugged. "It's not important." He'd increased his injections so he'd be capable of quick action, able to bear pain; it was one of the great virtues of the drugs to be able to perform intolerable feats without difficulty, without halting or slackening pace. But enhanced physical power and the capacity to ignore pain lasted only so long. And he knew if not when, that eventually his body would fail.

But after tonight it didn't matter.

The two men returned to the large hall where everyone waited, where the sound of the clock on the wall could be heard for the silence. Weapons were looked to, the weapons of choice that night the blade and garrote—both mute. The sound of a gunshot would pose innumerable difficulties.

The planning was over now, all the meticulous arrangements made, the talk and listening past. There was nothing more to say. Only the deed remained to be done.

At nine, Jamie came to his feet, feeling no pain, although his finely tuned body was under strain, his mind racing faster than it should. "I wish you all luck, gentlemen," he said with simplicity. "Shall we?"

He turned and strode toward the door, just as the first guard at the monastery was killed quietly and Jamie's troopers moved on to the next.

* * *

A short block from the Swedish town house, mid-way down a quiet street, lay the apartment building with Von Welden inside. The night sky was overcast, a hint of rain in the air, the evening shadows grey on grey as Jamie, Douglas, and the Albanian made their way toward the building. Other troopers moved off in diverse directions to make certain that the entire block was cordoned off. A dozen more followed Jamie in twos and threes, giving every appearance of gentlemen out for an evening stroll.

The street was deserted. Everyone who was going out for the evening had already left. The others were ensconced in their luxury apartments, hidden from the world behind drawn draperies.

Two carriages followed the men at a discreet distance, although the eventual occupants wouldn't be going to dine at one of Vienna's many fine restaurants, nor would they be attending any of the numerous theaters that were the monarchy's equivalent of Roman bread and circuses. As in Rome, the government subsidized the price of grain in order to curtail laboring class unrest. And for those citizens whose daily existence went beyond mere survival, the government-financed theaters served as a distraction from the police state circumscribing their lives.

As planned, at nine ten, all of Von Welden's men within sight of the apartment were taken out with a quick knife thrust to the heart or a swift garroting—professional noiseless, bloodless deaths. The carriages drove up, the bodies were tossed in, the coachmen set their horses to a smarter pace, and in minutes the street was tranquil once again.

The concierge smiled at Jamie through the open door of her parlor as he walked into the foyer at nine twelve. "Good evening, sir. The lady has company." It was both warning and greeting. Jamie had visited Katia before; he always made a point of chatting with the old lady and leaving her a few florins.

"We won't be staying long. How goes your granddaughter's violin lessons?"

"The sweet girl has a rare talent," the plump matriarch replied, beaming.

"Good for her. You might like to shut your door," Jamie said with a small smile. "There's a draft in the hall." Then he moved toward the stairway.

The concierge took note of the dozen men following in the wake of the young baron. Quickly rising from her chair, she stood in the doorway for a moment watching the men swarm up the stairs at a run before shutting and locking her door.

She knew full well who Von Welden was. Who in Vienna didn't? She knew as well that Katia was obliged to entertain him for her brother's sake. That too was no secret. But then a man like Von Welden cared nothing for rumor or scandal; he was beyond society's censure.

As Jamie and his compatriots reached the third floor—chosen by Von Welden for security reasons—the Albanian separated himself from the others. While the rest remained out of sight near the elevator shaft, Hajdu walked down the hall toward the two guards posted outside Katia's door. Dressed in the loose robes of his Muslim culture, he carried a small gold-chased coffer with a jeweled clasp. He held it out from his body so it was clearly visible as he approached.

Stopping before the two guards who viewed him with suspicion, he murmured with unctuous servility, "A gift for the lady—by order of your master." Glancing up, he smiled slyly. "His Excellency wishes to especially please his lady this evening."

"We know nothing of a gift," one guard gruffly retorted, scowling.

"Here, see for yourself. It's a most magnificent gift." The Albanian advanced closer and offered up the box with a graceful gesture. "His Excellency has engraved the pretty toy with the words of a devoted lover." He began lifting the lid on the coffer.

Intrigued by the sexual innuendo in the remark, both guards leaned in more closely to examine the contents.

Hajdu dropped the box, and naked steel flashed from under his robes. Two long-bladed yataghans drove upward expertly and so fast they were propelled by instinct alone. The swift, slashing steel sliced both men's throats clean through to the spinal column.

The guards died with blank surprise on their faces.

Jamie and his men rushed in, the two guards were carried away, and with a glance at his watch, Jamie murmured, "Andor should be out now." He spoke over his shoulder to the men behind. "Make sure Katia knows when she's taken away." Then with a glance up and down the hallway, Jamie gave a nod to Douglas and the Albanian at his side. "Ready?" Or more to the point, *At last.*

His slender fingers closed on the door latch and he quietly opened the door.

The foyer was empty. As expected.

Katia had said Von Welden insisted on privacy.

But one never knew when the game rules might change, and Jamie crossed the small space with soft-footed caution. The subdued resonance of conversation was audible as they reached a short corridor, and he moved down the carpeted hall toward the sound. Arriving noiselessly, the men paused outside a door that separated them from the muted voices and automatically checked their weapons.

Jamie stood utterly still for a moment, resisting with steely resolve the exhaustion that suddenly threatened to swamp him. The moment passed. Once again under control, he opened the door into a well-appointed, candlelit dining room with two occupants.

Von Welden was facing the door, and he half rose from

his chair when Jamie walked in only to sit back down and turn ashen when he saw the Albanian.

"No need to get up," Jamie said in a soft, almost disinterested tone. Without turning, he said to the men who'd appeared on the threshold behind him, "Take away the lady, although I warn you, my dear, if you scream, we'll kill you."

"You're mad, Blackwood. You won't get away with this," Von Welden threatened, flicking a glance at Katia as she was being dragged from her chair by two of Jamie's troopers.

"Of course I will."

"I have men everywhere," the minister of police said with unassailable arrogance, his nerve restored after the initial shock. "And believe me I'll take great pleasure in seeing you die."

"Perhaps not," Jamie said briefly. "You *had* men everywhere. How many were there, Douglas?" Jamie asked without taking his gaze from Von Welden.

"Eighteen."

"Did we miss any?" Jamie lightly inquired.

Von Welden blanched again, his skin chalky against the black of his military tunic.

"Ah—apparently not," Jamie murmured. "Now then, you presumably know why we're here," he said, his voice unhurried, his face calm. "You shouldn't have killed Rupert. He was like a brother to me. There was no need to murder the young boy when he had his whole life ahead of him." Jamie drew in a small breath and his expression changed, a cold-blooded look entering his eyes. "So I am come to deal out justice, retribution, and I'm afraid," he gently added, "some personal vengeance."

"Wait," Von Welden quickly said, his eyes wild with fear. "Surely we can come to some agreement." His voice was shaking, his frightened glance flicking back and forth

between Jamie and the Albanian, who stood motionless
and expressionless at Jamie's side. "I have money, land,
power. The emperor and I are on friendly, friendly terms."
He was half-breathless with fear, his words tumbling over
themselves in his panic. "You have only to name your
price, Blackwood. Anything, anything at all!" His voice
had risen at the end, his panic escalating at the total indifference of his audience.

"Unfortunately," Jamie said, his unforgiving stare resting
on Von Welden, "I promised myself I'd send you to hell."
He caught his breath as a spasm of pain tore through his gut
and a moment of helplessness threatened to topple him. But
he marshaled his strength by will alone and said with a
serenity won at grievous cost, "Now, where was I? Oh, yes.
Take off his clothes."

"No, no! God, please no!" Von Welden shrieked. He'd
hired the Albanian himself on more than one occasion—
and watched. "Please, I beg of you! I'll give you everything I own!" he screamed. "I'll sign everything I have
over to you, I swear! Bring me some paper and pen! Listen to me! *God in heaven, please!"*

"Muffle him." A whisper of sound, taut and strained.

Jamie's men cast a quick glance at their leader, saw his
bloodless face, and leaped to the task.

"We dinna have to do this, Jamie," Douglas quietly said
as the men manhandled Von Welden from his chair. "It
doesna matter how he dies so long as he dies."

"No." The snarl from deep in Jamie's throat was more
animal than human, a pure bestial rage. Focused solely on
seeing this through so far as was humanly possible and
running with sweat, Jamie held himself upright by sheer
force of will. "Goddamn it, do it."

But by the time Von Welden was strapped to the table,
his mouth stuffed with an embroidered table napkin, his
splayed body the open palette for the Albanian's art form,
Jamie was shivering violently. As Hajdu made the first

sweeping cut up Von Welden's inner thigh so he could peel the skin from his leg in one piece, Jamie's mind slipped briefly from its shackles and he swayed unsteadily. Catching himself, he braced his feet like a sailor on a storm-tossed vessel and dragged himself erect.

Willing to discharge his duty up to a point—one that didn't include watching his pigheaded commander die—Douglas grabbed Jamie, shoved him into a chair, jammed his face up to Jamie's, nose to nose, and growled, "Open your eyes, damn it, if ye can."

The struggle was enough to put fear in everyone's heart.

Jamie finally managed to open his eyes the merest slits, although his face was sweat sheened, his hands twitching, and he was gasping for air.

"There's no goddamn point in having Von Welden die if ye die with him," Douglas said flatly. "I'm finishing this. Stop me if ye have the strength."

His breathing was very fast, and dark head bent, Jamie put his hands on the chair arms and tried to rise.

"It's over now, leave it," Douglas said, curtly.

"It's not over." Jamie's voice was even and low. He'd managed to manhandle himself steady for a moment, his whole consciousness reduced to a single focus, a single thought—Von Welden's splayed body in the narrow lens of his vision. His eyes blazing, driven by pride and temper, he commanded his body one last time and hauled himself to his feet. But dogged will alone no longer sufficed to force his body to move, and he gasped and doubled over as great waves of cramping pain nearly brought him down.

Breathing hard himself, Douglas said grimly, "You damned fool. Enough," and walked straight for Von Welden.

Jamie's head came up as though struck, and with stark fury in his eyes, he watched Douglas stride to the table where Von Welden had fainted away and with one powerful stroke of his saber sever the head from the body. Jerking his blade out of the table, Douglas grabbed the flamboyant, overlong hair, swung the cleaved head up, and flung it at Jamie's feet. "He's in hell now. Are ye satisfied?"

"Damn you," Jamie said so faintly only those closest to him heard.

Then his eyes misted over, nausea rose in his throat, and he collapsed, his body wasted, his intellect exhausted, his tenacious strength of will played out.

CHAPTER 28

THE TELEGRAM REACHED Blackwood Glen a week later.

No one in Vienna had had time to consider anything more than seeing Jamie back to Dalmia where he'd said he wished to die. He'd been conscious only once briefly when they'd carried him into his palazzo—perhaps the familiar scent roused him—and he'd whispered, "Let Sofia know she's safe."

A servant had seen to the message.

No one else had time for such mundane matters with Jamie battling for his life.

Sofia's telegram had merely stated, uncoded and plain, *Von Welden dead. Safe to go home.* She asked Robbie afterward whether he knew anything more, and most important, whether Jamie had recovered from his gunshot wounds.

"As far as I know," Robbie evasively replied, "he's home in Dalmia." If Jamie had wished her to know more, he would have had the information relayed to her. His message from Douglas had been more explicit; Jamie was barely alive.

Two days later, Sofia was home in London.

She should have been more cheerful, more satisfied and content. Her ordeal was over, she was once again in the city she loved, and she could plunge wholeheartedly into her busy career and convivial social life. As for the uncommunicative Jamie Blackwood, she'd always known that their amorous liaison was of the most transient nature. Why had she expected anything more from him? It was over. And that was that.

Which was exactly what she said her first day back when Rosalind asked her the obvious question. "Jamie was quite lovely in every way," Sofia urbanely said, smiling at her friend as they sat in a shaded pavilion in the rose garden at Groveland House. "I enjoyed myself immensely. But all good things must come to an end," she airily noted. "Especially with men like Jamie, who are always on some intrepid mission." She smiled. "Although he heroically threw himself in the way of a bullet meant for me before he left."

"My goodness!" Rosalind exclaimed. "Was he badly hurt?"

"He was in a deal of pain at first, but he said he healed quickly. He left soon after so I'm not entirely sure. But I assume he's fine. He's back in Dalmia."

Sofia's replies were a trifle brittle, Rosalind thought, or perhaps only less dégagé than usual. "Do you miss him?" Her gaze on Sofia, she was startled to see a blush color her cheeks. "Or are you still tired from your adventure?" she tactfully added, not wishing to embarrass her friend.

"To be perfectly honest—both," Sofia replied, surprising herself with her answer; she didn't as a rule miss men. Shrugging away the anomaly, she sensibly added, "He's an exceedingly charming man. Why wouldn't I miss him?"

"You've known any number of charming men and never

given them another thought once they were gone." Rosalind's gaze was amused.

Sofia sighed. "Perhaps I'm a little infatuated with the man. He's quite extraordinary." Another sigh, a grimace, and the shocking words, "Not that it'll do any good if I'm infatuated or not. He's clearly moved on."

The women had been friends a long time; Rosalind had never seen Sofia sigh like some smitten young maid. "Could it be you've finally been struck by cupid's arrow?" she gently observed.

Sofia snorted. "Don't be ridiculous. Who falls in love in a few days?" She'd had time in the ensuing interval to come to her senses apropos the distinctions between love and sex.

Rosalind leaned back against her cushioned chair, her smile amiable. "I was enamored of Fitz from the first."

"If only I was a wild-eyed romantic like you," Sofia dulcetly said.

"Maybe you've become one."

"I *most* certainly have not. I am a rational female, no offense, darling," she added with a grin. "Now pass that cake plate. I do so adore coconut and pineapple together. And hand over the champagne bottle, too." Leaning over, she plucked the two items from Rosalind's hands. "Now then, my dear, could life be any better? I'm back in London having champagne with my best friend, the scent of roses is in the air, and all's right with the world."

"You should go and visit him."

Sofia sloshed champagne over the edge of her glass. "Are you mad?" she said, setting the bottle down. "Can you imagine what he'd say if some woman came uninvited to his house? Especially all the way from England?"

"He might say, *How nice to see you. Come in.*"

"Or he might say, *What the hell do you want?*" Sofia retorted.

"And you who prides herself on her nerve," Rosalind mockingly observed.

"Be serious." Sofia directed a hard, pointed look at her friend. "It's all well and good to be nervy in fashionable circles where everyone expects flirtatious repartee and a fleeting night of pleasure is nothing out of the ordinary. But it's something else entirely to hie oneself all the way across Europe for a romp in the hay."

"I'm just saying you should think about it."

"And I'm just saying you're completely demented," Sofia pithily replied.

Rosalind grinned. "There's always Dex, I suppose."

"Very funny. He's not my style."

"Then you'll have to find someone who is, won't you?"

"I suppose I must," Sofia murmured with an air of feigned docility. "Do you have any candidates in mind?"

"I have a couple," Fitz cheerfully said, appearing around the side of the pavilion. "Hello, darling. Hello, Sofie." Bending low, he kissed his wife's cheek. "How are you feeling?" he whispered.

"Better." Reaching up, she touched his arm. "Monty was asking for Papa."

"I'm on my way up to the nursery. I just wanted to see how you were first."

"Fine, fine. Sofia is entertaining me. But we must find her some entertainment now that she's back in London."

"The line is long, darling, for the lovely Sofie." He grinned at her. "Dark or blonde, sportsman or intellectual. You have but to name your choice, my dear."

She smiled back. "Surprise me."

Fitz laughed. "Now there's an order. You know everyone." He glanced at his watch. "Monty will be up from his nap." He lifted his hand. "Ladies, enjoy your afternoon."

Rosalind watched her husband walk away with such love in her eyes, it cast a further pall over Sofia's pesky megrims. Not that she actually admitted Jamie's absence was of any real consequence. But she couldn't muster her usual cheerful spirits either. And as if she weren't disconsolate enough, Rosalind's next words only added to her lowered mood.

"In case you're wondering what that was all about, I'm pregnant again," Rosalind said, her smile euphoric. "I'm so blessed; I never thought I could have children. And Fitz is such a dear," she added, with the besotted look of a wife truly in love. "He stopped by because I was nauseous this morning when he left."

"Congratulations," Sofia managed to say in a normal tone, when the news only aggravated an issue of her own. "I should have known. You're fairly blooming, as the saying goes."

Rosalind put her hands to her cheeks and smiled. "I'm so *very* happy. We both are. Fitz is a devoted father. He adores Monty, and Monty's first word was *papa*. They're practically inseparable."

Two years ago, no one would have bet a shilling that the Duke of Groveland would give up his bachelor ways, fall head over heels in love, and completely dote on his wife and child. In fact, several members at Brooks's had lost a considerable sum on the shocking events that transpired.

"We must find someone equally wonderful for you," Rosalind cheerfully said. "Really, dear, I shall set my mind to it forthwith."

Out of sincere regard for her friend's happiness, in the course of the next fortnight, Rosalind engaged herself in supplying eligible dinner partners for Sofia. Sofia, in turn, obliged her friend and occupied her evenings with a number of handsome men. The Season was in full swing, dinners and dances abounded, and in an effort to rid herself of the glorious, beguiling memories of Jamie, Sofia did her best to enjoy herself. And forget she'd ever met Jamie Blackwood.

To no avail.

No matter how delightful, handsome, or attentive her

companion, she always made some excuse at the end of the evening and slept alone.

It was truly shocking and unsettling to a woman who prided herself on living in a man's world with equal boldness. Sexually and otherwise. She was beginning to fear for her sanity.

She began painting with a frenzy, working long hours, slashing paint on her canvases with abandon, never quite satisfied with the outcome, always beginning again on a fresh canvas. And so it went, frantically socializing at night, wildly painting every day, fretful and brooding throughout.

Until Oz finally took her in hand.

They were out on the moonlit terrace of Groveland House, the heady scent of roses in the air, the ballroom behind them awash with dancers and music and hilarity. Oz was drinking as usual, though more judiciously now since his marriage; he lifted the glass in his hand and jabbed it in Sofia's direction. "You're pining, my dear. I never thought to see you so blue deviled. I fear you're falling into a decline," he said with a grin.

"Perhaps if I was some lily-livered, faint-of-heart damsel from another century I might fall into a decline," she snapped.

"My, my, and snappish, too. Would you like my drink? It calms the nerves."

"I'm perfectly calm," she snapped again.

"Perhaps you really shouldn't go to see him," he sweetly said, "if you're going to be nasty to him. He's only just crawled out of the grave, I'm told."

She swung around, skewered him with her gaze, and whispered, "Grave?"

"I thought you knew. Jamie's been at death's door."

"I didn't know." She was finding it hard to breathe.

He set his drink down on the marble balustrade and took her hands. "Forgive me," he softly said. "I didn't mean to frighten you."

"Rosalind never said anything."

"She must not have known."

"Did Fitz know?"

"I'm not sure. I thought it was common knowledge."

"How did you hear?"

With a banking business that spanned the globe, Oz had a hundred sources of information. "A business associate in Athens, I think, but surely others in London have heard. His cousin no doubt and his uncle, too."

"No one told me."

"Ah—and you wish they had."

She didn't reply for so long, he bent and kissed her gently on the cheek. "If it's any consolation, darling," he said, looking down on her in the silvery night, "I had the same struggle with love or the meaning of love, with personal freedom or the lack thereof. It isn't easy to accept change in your life. But if you'd like my advice, I'd say go to him."

"He may not want to see me."

"Don't be foolish. There's no man alive who wouldn't want to see you."

"There might be one."

He smiled. "You won't know unless you try. At least you'll find out one way or the other. As a betting man, I'd lay odds you get what you want."

"If I want it."

He shrugged. "That's a different matter."

She softly sighed. "You're happy now, aren't you?"

"Over the moon, darling. And I abhor such rubbishy expressions, but it's true."

"So then."

"So then," he softly echoed. "Nothing ventured—et cetera, et cetera. Would you like me to see you through the hopeless train schedules in southern Europe? It's not really safe for a woman alone."

"Isolde wouldn't appreciate you going."

"She's so busy with her fields this time of year I doubt she'll notice I'm gone. She's a farmer."

"And you're not?"

He smiled. "I'm a banker who's learning to farm in England. A novice at the moment. Let me talk to her. Stay here. This won't take long."

Sofia lifted one brow. "So sure Isolde will oblige you?"

"We always accommodate each other in every way." He grinned. "It seems to be working."

Oz found his wife in a salon adjoining the ballroom where she and a small group of men were deep in a discussion of the price of corn, and he felt as he always did on seeing her. As if he were the most fortunate of men. "If I might speak with you for a moment, my dear," he said, with a gracious smile for the gentleman surrounding her. Taking her hand, he drew her away.

"Lucky fellow, Lennox," one of the men grumbled. "Don't find women like the countess every day. A damned good farmer and a stunning beauty, too."

Everyone nodded, and a few *hear, hears* were uttered along with one wistful sigh. Not everyone was there to discuss the price of corn.

"He's a demned lucky dog if you ask me," a middle-aged squire muttered, watching them walk away. "Cocky young buck."

"So how is the price of corn?" Oz cheerfully inquired as he threaded his way through the clusters of conversing guests to a quiet corner of the room.

"Better. How's Sofia doing?"

Oz's glance drifted right. "Are you a mind reader?"

"I am of yours."

He grinned and came to a stop. "What am I thinking now?"

Isolde slapped his arm lightly with her folded fan. "Behave, darling. People are looking."

"I always worry about that," he softly mocked. "But very

well, I'll behave," he added in deference to his wife's quelling gaze. "I have a favor to ask."

"And I as well. When you see Blackwood, will you give him a good tongue-lashing for me? Poor Sofie's been brooding over him ever since she returned to London."

"I tremble before your prophetic vision," Oz said with mock alarm.

"Pshaw. How could I not know? She's been steeped in melancholy since her return like some tragic opera heroine. More to the point, she's been celibate despite any number of men who've tried to tempt her otherwise. One doesn't have to be intuitive with such blinding evidence. And," Isolde said with a benevolent smile, "I know how you like adventure."

"Thank you, darling. I'll make it up to you when I return."

"Just don't stay long."

He grinned. "Yes, dear, whatever you say, dear."

"Very funny," she murmured. "Now give me a kiss, then go and tell Sofie the good news."

SOFIA AND OZ left the next morning and traveled through Europe by private railcar staffed with a full retinue of Lennox servants. Oz was by turns consoling and bracing, supporting Sofia when she wavered, giving her the confidence that she'd made the right decision.

"We'll rent a yacht in Trieste and continue by sea. The roads in the Balkans are atrocious, and the railway doesn't come within fifty miles of Jamie's home. There now, give me a smile."

She'd invariably laugh; he in turn would flash her a grin, refill his glass, and lift it to her in salute. "I'm betting on you, darling. Don't let me down."

When they arrived at the small port near Jamie's estate, Oz tactfully chose to remain on the yacht and send her ahead in a rented carriage with an escort from his staff.

"My people will wait for you in his drive," he said after handing her into the carriage. He didn't say, *In case Jamie kicks you out*, but that's what he meant.

She felt like some shy, tremulous maiden on the journey, the narrow road skirting the Adriatic seemingly endless. Her nerves were all aflutter, her heart was beating in double time, and she kept smoothing the silk muslin of her skirt as if it mattered that she look her best.

When, at last, the carriage came to rest before an apricot-hued palazzo that could have graced the Grand Canal in Venice, she alighted and gazed up a long, wide marble staircase leading to huge doors bracketed with polished brass fittings. The splendor was off-putting, as was the sprawling Roman palace behind the pastel palazzo that soared like a monstrous, ancient monument up the ragged escarpment.

She almost turned around and reentered the carriage. In fact, she was about to do so when a familiar voice called her name and she turned to see Douglas hurrying down the stairs.

"I'm so pleased to see ye," he said, smiling broadly as he came to a stop before her. "Ye came alone?"

"Oz is waiting in port. In case I'm thrown out."

He grinned. "I might have a wee something to say about that."

"How is he?"

"Difficult and quarrelsome, with a tongue like an asp. But himself's on the mend, and he misses you."

"Did he say that?"

"No, but he does."

"If only I could believe you. Although," Sofia said with a smile, plucking up her courage, feeling a measure of her old assurance, telling herself she'd already once brought the mighty Blackwood to heel, "I might like to see if my womanly wiles still work." Untying the ribbon on her straw bonnet, she took it off and shook out her pale curls. "There, I'm ready."

Douglas laughed. "Aye and ye have my blessing. He's like a man with an itch. Come, I'll take ye to the monster in his lair."

CHAPTER 29

DOUGLAS ESCORTED HER to Jamie's bedroom and quietly said, "He's awake. I'll leave ye here. Much luck to ye, lass."

She watched him walk away, waited until he disappeared, and nervously ran her palms over the peach silk of her skirt. Douglas's last words weren't exactly encouraging. Then she reminded herself that she'd come a very long way for this and discretion had never been her strong suit anyway, nor the sensibilities that passed for virtue in the timid. So fie on useless apprehension.

She opened the door without knocking.

Standing in the doorway, she gazed at the dark-haired, handsome man lying in a magnificent rococo bed of bleached wood. "I came to see you," she said.

"I see that." She could have been at a picnic outing, he thought, in her bright summer gown, a straw hat dangling from its ribbons in her hand.

"I'm thinking of staying."

He didn't answer.

"Let me reword that. I *am* staying."

He still didn't speak, although his gaze traveled slowly down her form.

"Even if you refuse to talk to me."

He finally spoke. "I'm not sure I have anything to say."

"You needn't talk." She shrugged. "I don't care."

He smiled faintly. "I recall you said that once before."

"And I recall things worked out rather well that night despite the lack of conversation. You're too polite to throw me out anyway."

"I'm not polite at all."

He was clearly only recently returned to health, but he spoke as he always did, his voice clear and strong. "You've been polite in the past," she said with a lift of her chin.

"And you think I might be again." He regarded her thoughtfully, as though having come to a fork in the road, he was deciding which path to take, or whether he'd turn back instead. He pursed his lips as though to speak, then apparently changed his mind. He let a pause develop, his expression unreadable, until at last a smile slowly unfurled. "Welcome to Dalmia."

She smiled back. "Thank you." Her world was sun filled once again, the birds were singing, the air perfumed. She hadn't known until then whether he'd let her stay.

"I'd get up if I could." He crooked a finger. "Come. Tell me what you've been doing."

She'd remained in the doorway until then and now she came in. "I haven't done anything out of the ordinary," she said, crossing the room. "The usual round of receptions during the Season. Was it awful?" she softly inquired as she reached the bed, taking in the changes in his powerful body. He was leaner, rawboned, his shoulder still swathed in bandages, a new austerity in his facial structure.

"I've felt better," he said wryly. "Although if ever I had reason to heal, I do now." He extended his left hand across his body. "Let me touch you."

Letting her hat drop to the floor, she took his hand and felt her heart constrict as his fingers closed hard on hers. His strength was still formidable, his smile as seductive, his dark beauty intact.

"Kiss me," he said. "I'm still pretty useless in terms of moving."

She sat carefully on the embroidered silk coverlet, cautious not to jar the bed or its occupant. Leaning over, she kissed him, softly, lightly, barely exerting pressure while sweet joy infused her soul and her loneliness disappeared as if by a magician's hand. When she lifted her head, she met his roguish grin.

"I'm not fourteen," he playfully said. "You can do better than that."

And she did then, but prudent still, knowing how very close to death he'd been; even now he could barely move.

"Jesus," he whispered when she finally raised her head. "I'm going to have to get better real soon. That's not nearly enough."

"It'll just have to be enough for now," she firmly said, sitting back. "I don't want to chance hurting you."

He would have laughed if he dared, the thought of kissing as dangerous in a life such as his ludicrous. "I'll talk to the doctor. We'll see what he says."

"No you won't. We can wait."

"Maybe you can wait. I can't." And if he hadn't nearly died from a drug overdose in addition to his infected shoulder, he would have seriously considered having an injection. Just enough to alleviate his pain so he could have a sex with the woman who'd been in his thoughts from the moment he'd regained consciousness. Before that, too, Douglas had told him.

"Nevertheless, you have to wait," Sofia insisted. "And I brought along a chaperon for protection, so you'd best behave."

"It better be an old woman," he muttered.

"Oz came."

"He's fucking undependable," Jamie growled. They'd spent too many wild nights together over the years.

"He's happily married I'll have you know."

Jamie's expression brightened. "Ah, his wife came, too."

"No, apparently it's a busy season for farming."

His scowl was back in place. "He'd better not have touched you."

She smiled. "I adore your jealously, but it's wildly misplaced with Oz. He's deeply in love with his wife, cherishes his daughter, and sends them telegrams three times a day. He'd be shocked if I flirted with him."

Jamie blew out a breath. "Very well. I could be wrong."

She grinned. "I love it when men apologize."

"I don't care to hear about men, plural, in your life."

"That reminds me," she said, recalling all the tedious evenings she'd recently spent in London. "Why didn't you send me a message, a note—anything?"

"Reminds me?" Another glowering look. "What the hell does that mean?"

"It means that I was moping over you to such an extent that Rosalind was throwing men at me to distract me from my misery." She raised her brows in mild reproof. "You should have written."

"I did."

"I don't mean that seven-word telegram."

"I was thinking about writing."

"Liar."

"I didn't know your address."

"You could have sent a note via Fitz, you know, Lord Groveland, Groveland House." She grinned. "Back in your court, darling."

It took him a moment to answer, and when he did, he struggled to find suitable words. "You figured rather largely in my hallucinations," he slowly began. "Ask Douglas, he'll tell you. But"—he started to shrug and thought better of it—"we hadn't known each other very long . . . only a few days—and I wasn't sure"—a rueful grimace—"what it all meant. It just didn't make sense . . ." His voice trailed off. "For any number of practical reasons."

Sofia nodded. "I said as much to Rosalind at first. Not that I didn't miss you. But I thought it was probably the sex I missed, and there were any number of men who—well, you know what I mean."

He was scowling again, so she said, "Your ego doesn't need further bolstering, but the truth is—no one appealed after you. So there—your reputation is unsullied. You're quite extraordinary," she ended with a little sniff.

"You are, too." An unsimple, difficult truth.

She contemplated a space over his head, not sure she dared broach the subject. "You know, Rosalind actually believes in love at first sight," she said, being the most likely woman in the world to dare anything. "I never have."

"Me either."

"There, you see how much we have in common?"

"What we have in common, darling," he softly drawled, "is something else entirely. Although"—his smile was dazzling—"I'm more than willing to call it love if you wish."

She grinned. "Or lust."

"Yes. Hot, blissful, earthmoving lust. Christ, I really have to talk to the doctor," he muttered. "Maybe he can give me a shot or something," he recklessly asserted.

"There's no rush. I'm not going anywhere."

"Allow me to disagree on the matter of urgency." His voice was crisp. "I happen to be in a damnable rush."

"Speaking of, say, issues of urgency, I have a small matter to discuss with you."

He looked up, instantly alert, prompted by a sixth sense perhaps or something in her tone. "I'm listening," he carefully said.

"What if I were to say I was pregnant?"

His brows rose. "I'd say congratulations to you and whomever the father is or else I'd kill my boot maker."

"And I'd point out that you're the father. There was no whomever, and we never did stop for champagne or any other useful remedy that day."

"You fell asleep."

"You could have wakened me."

He should have; he had no excuse. "Is that why you came?"

"No. But I thought you might like to know. I'm not absolutely sure yet, but mildly sure. My menses are two weeks late." She was full of joy over it, but she didn't mention that.

"And your courses have never been late before?"

She shook her head.

"I thought you said I didn't have to worry about this. I thought you said I was safe."

"You were—from this." She touched her stomach.

A jolt went through him at her small gesture. Not *this*. A child.

"Babies and issues of paternity don't matter all that much in my unconventional world. I wouldn't have come for that," she said, feeling a need to explain when he was looking so *displeased*, she supposed was the word. "But a baby together with love," she softly added, forging ahead because she couldn't help herself after coming so far. "That made all the difference. And I found I couldn't live without you or I felt as though I couldn't, particularly after being courted by any number of dull and dreary men through any number of boring evenings. Oz noticed my melancholy—*pining away*, he called it. He talked me into coming here. I'm not altogether sure I would have otherwise."

Another jolt—this one familiar in his profession. Fear. What if she hadn't come? What then? "Hmm," he said, the soft sound conjecture and uncertainty—benign possibility infusing the resonance at the end. "So have you thought about getting married?" So might he approach a wall of artillery—with wary vigilance.

"No, I haven't. What about you?"

"It's never crossed my mind."

He is direct. "You know I wouldn't lie about something like this."

He didn't say anything for a moment, because of course it was the oldest ploy in the world. The sound of voices outside his windows could be clearly heard as the silence lengthened.

Sofia thought it was Italian being spoken, but then Jamie lived in a Venetian palace. Why wouldn't his staff speak Italian?

Her calm demeanor exhibited neither artifice nor guile. Reassuring, he supposed, if he needed reassurance. But Sofia was the least likely female to resort to artifice or guile. Outspoken and blunt was more her style. "Did you hear about Antonella?"

"I did," she said, as if he'd not changed the subject. "They stopped by in London. I'm glad for them. Ernst seems genuinely excited about Antonella's pregnancy and their coming marriage."

"I didn't know how you'd feel about being usurped."

"You didn't?"

His brows arched faintly. "Money can be alluring."

She lifted her hand in a small sweeping gesture that encompassed the costly, sumptuous room. "You know that from personal experience, I suppose."

"Don't be a bitch." But he was smiling.

"Be nice to me or I might jump on you."

"Promise?" A low, husky rasp.

"All in due time, dear. Do you have your own priest or minister? You look as though you're rich enough to furnish a clergyman's living. We could be married here."

He grinned, some decision made, or if not, deliberately overlooked. "You never wait to be asked, do you?"

"As if you're interested in demure maids."

"True."

"I would naturally insist on fidelity."

"As would I. Should I call in my solicitor?"

Her gaze widened. "Do you keep one on the premises?"

"I do."

"Whatever for?"

"I suppose for ladies who drop by and wish to marry me. Solicitors know how to drive a hard bargain."

"If you say I'm not the first I'll turn sulky."

He smiled. "What do you think?"

"I think you waited for me."

"And I think you waited for me."

"We're very lucky, aren't we?" she said, mischievous and playful, her eyes alight.

"Very lucky." That they'd met, that he'd survived, that she'd had the good sense to track him down, that he might be a father. "Now go and shut the door and lock it. Douglas is like a mother hen, and if I faint, you can revive me with kisses. We'll have our honeymoon first and we can be married tonight. I don't want any arguments." His smile was perfumed with good humor. "If you're good I'll let Oz be best man."

"Are you sure? I wouldn't want to hurt you."

"Be a dear, lock the door, then undress for me," he said, ignoring her demur.

"I mean it, Jamie. I don't want to cause you harm."

"I could shout for a servant and *he* could lock the door."

She held his gaze for a moment and saw the familiar determination in his eyes. "You would, wouldn't you?"

"In a minute. I don't get married every day."

Slipping off the bed, she walked to the door, shut and

locked it. "I could still refuse you," she said, crossing the large sun-filled room, stopping just short of the bed.

"Why would you want to?" Softly put, but willful beneath the gentle tone. He was not a man tolerant of resistance.

"I don't get married every day either," she said with matching willfulness. "And I'd like a living, breathing husband in the end."

"I promise to keep breathing. Now, hurry, will you?" He smiled. "As I recall, that's usually your demand."

"Not today," she steadfastly declared. "I intend to make no demands whatsoever."

"How unselfish of you, darling, but you needn't be noble minded. Look." He twitched his hand downward and flicked the coverlet aside. "He's more than happy to accommodate you."

She sucked in her breath, his enormous erection as vigorous and virile as ever.

Aware of her interest, aware as well of her gratifying eagerness for cock, he blew out a small breath. "I think you're going to have to undress later or I'm going to embarrass myself. Do you know how many wet dreams I've had because of you?"

"Do you know how many times I've used my dildo because of you?" Her gaze was riveted on his memorable physical presence: the graceful, athletic, long-limbed body she'd dreamed of so often, leaner but dynamic still, his bronzed skin dark against the white linen sheets, his rampant cock inflaming her desires, recklessly subverting issues of prudence.

Ignoring her largely rhetorical question, he drew in a harsh, steadying breath. "I changed my mind," he tautly said. "Undress first. I can wait." His dreams and sleepless nights were over. He wanted more.

"Maybe I can't wait," she shakily replied.

"Try." He smiled, a brilliant, mischievous smile. "It can be your wedding gift to me."

Her hands were trembling so violently as she unbuttoned her bodice that he began speaking to her of his vineyard, describing how it had been planted by the Romans, telling her he'd show it to her when he was better, when he could walk again—quietly distracting her, calming her. It was not unexpected that his stratagem worked. He was skilled at comforting women, at charming and beguiling them, and he selfishly wanted this for himself.

Her gown came off, then her chemise, at which point he almost changed his mind about waiting. "Your breasts are bigger," he murmured, his erection surging at the sight. "So soon?"

She looked up, her fingers on the tie at the waistband of her drawers. "I don't know. Is it soon?"

"I'd think so, but perhaps not." He had no experience with enceinte women.

"My breasts are more sensitive, but then my whole body is more susceptible to touch, sensation"—she met his heated gaze and shivered—"everything."

"Come, let me feel them." He'd disciplined his voice to a mild equanimity. "We'll see how sensitive they are."

She let her drawers slip to the floor, and the sight of her lush and voluptuous and nude was almost too much for his self-control. But his voice was pleasant and undisturbed a second later when he said, "Sit here by me," and indicated his left side where he had the use of his arm.

He watched her walk around the foot of the bed, contemplating the subtle changes in her body: the new ripeness in her breasts, the slight lengthening of her nipples evident only to a discriminating eye, the deepening rosy hue of her aureoles. He wasn't a doctor or a midwife, but perhaps she was right.

"Don't make me wait too long," she whispered as she

climbed up beside him. "You know I can't—here . . . like this."

He smiled. "Otherwise you could."

"Dressed and halfway across the room I might be able to."

"I won't make you wait long." But he didn't immediately touch her breasts; he lifted a pale coil of her hair lying on her shoulder, rubbed it gently between his fingers, and quietly inhaling, said, "You smell the same. I would have known you in the dark. What's that scent?"

"Honeysuckle." Her throat closed at the low timbre of his voice, at the warmth she could feel radiating from his body; the smoldering green of his eyes beneath his long lashes touched her to the quick. "Please, Jamie." She went still, then shuddered. "I'm more ravenous—with the changes in my body," she whispered. "Desire's like an out of control wildfire at times . . ."

"And no one's helped you put out those fires?" He tried to keep the growl from his voice but didn't quite succeed.

"Don't you *dare*," she said, frowning. "When I turned down countless men because of you. When you didn't so much as write. When I've been miserable since you left."

His mistrust assuaged by her bluntness, having missed her as much if not more, he gently said, "I most humbly beg your pardon. I deeply regret my comment."

"A favor perhaps will restore your credit," she softly said.

He grinned, her abrupt volte-face charmingly predictable. "I need not ask what."

"I should hope not. But I warn you, once you're well, I shall expect you to perform your husbandly duties assiduously. I've become quite insatiable."

"Is that new?" he teased.

"It is."

"Then I consider myself extremely fortunate. Come now, I won't keep you waiting any longer. And nothing hurts, I guarantee, so don't be shy."

Everything hurt of course; he wasn't at his best. But strong willed and capable of withstanding considerable pain, he didn't even wince as Sofia straddled his thighs and lowered herself down his erection. Nor did he cry out when she accidently grabbed his injured arm to steady herself.

"Oh God," she whispered. "I'm sorry, I'm sorry."

"No, no, I'm fine," he said, ignoring the racking pain, the explicitly carnal sensations convulsing his cock more than adequate compensation. "But go slowly, darling. I wouldn't want to faint midway." He didn't wish to faint at all. But a moment later, he said, "Stop for a second," and once his dizziness cleared and he could see her again, he smiled. "There. I'm good."

"We shouldn't be doing this." It was the most charitable statement she'd ever uttered, with his magnificent erection gorging her, with her burning desires trembling on the brink, with nirvana almost within reach.

"Yes, we should." He drew in a small breath. "Just don't move too quickly."

Eminently grateful and obliging, Sofia rode him languorously and gently, with the vigilance and care accorded those walking on thin ice. His eyes half-shut, Jamie delicately fondled the billowing fullness of her breasts—his fingertips passing and repassing over her soft flesh. Over and across, up and down in a lazy, soothing rhythm, as she slowly ascended and as slowly descended, the sleek skin to skin friction overpowering his pain, glorious reality obliterating former dream fantasies, lust advancing by predacious, triumphant degrees.

Despite Sofia's unfrenzied pace, the physical act itself, the trembling need and exquisite pleasure, was profoundly alien to two novices in the tender passions. A kind of lunatic joy infused their souls, love took on a corporeal form, and they breathed in scented magic. The woman who'd traveled so far on hope and the damaged man restored by her coming discovered that day new degrees of rapture, a glowing celebration of life, and at her first breathy cry he recognized so well, he said, "I'm always with you now . . ."

And glorious ecstasy engulfed their senses.

And the earth moved as it always did for them.

Afterward, Jamie said, panting, "Stay, stay—don't move. You're not hurting me." Everything ached, his limbs belonged to someone else, his strength was ravaged.

"If I'm not pregnant, I might be now," Sofia said with a happy sigh.

He smiled. "I'd like that."

His heartbreaking smile brought tears to her eyes. "I'm sorry, I seem extremely vulnerable to tears lately. But thank you. Some men wouldn't wish to hear such news."

His eyelids lowered faintly, and he gazed up at her from under his lashes. "No more talk of some men or other men if you please. Ever."

"Yes, sir," she demurely said, looking every inch the docile maid.

"Oh, God, don't make me laugh."

At his comment, she quickly glanced at his bandaged shoulder. "Heavens, you're bleeding!" she cried. "I'll get help!"

"Hush, it's nothing." He had every intention of climaxing again; his cock at least still worked.

"I wouldn't want to make you worse."

"Not likely that. I feel very much better." At some expense in terms of pain, he shifted his hips to better feel her slick, encompassing warmth. "How about you?"

She smiled. "I am cocooned in bliss and contentment."

"I'm sorry I didn't write." He paused. "I suppose it was because I'd always dealt with things differently."

"With women you mean."

"No, everything." His business was managing people, and making plans and more plans to keep everyone alive; women had never been part of his plans.

"But I'm different from"—she grinned—"your every-things." She was at base a confident woman.

"Yes, unmistakably." His smile was warm with affection. "I would have come for you. I know that now."

"I'm just more impatient."

He grinned. "A blessing in more ways than one—your impatience."

"Speaking of which"—she wiggled her bottom faintly, cautiously—"you seem to be fully revived."

"I think he's happy about getting married."

"But only to me."

"Of course. That goes without saying." He glanced at the clock. "I think we might have another hour before Douglas begins to worry."

"And?"

"I'm afraid he'll take the door down."

"Then I'd better do my wifely duty quickly."

"We're well matched," he said, his gaze amused. "We were from the beginning. I don't know why I didn't notice."

She smiled. "You had a few other things on your mind."

"True. Unlike now when I have but one thing on my mind," he said, stealing her breath away with his beautiful, lazy smile. "My sweet darling."

And with no sign of effort, because there were things more important than pain, in the next hour, he dispensed with seeming ease that boundless comfort and joy so familiar to his sweet darling.

EPILOGUE

THEY WERE MARRIED that evening with Oz as best man and a young girl from Jamie's staff as Sofia's maid of honor. The brief ceremony took place in Jamie's drawing room, the bridegroom having been carried down on a litter, a new warmth and color to his skin. Afterward, a celebration took place with Oz, the entire staff, Douglas and company in attendance and the bride and groom beaming at one and all.

Jamie's recovery continued apace, although he had every incentive to regain his strength with carnal desire a constant in his life. When his convalescence was complete in September, the young couple returned to London where they received a warm reception from family and friends. Heartfelt congratulations were extended not only on their marriage but also for their coming child.

Sofia and Rosalind happily compared the various physical changes of blossoming motherhood while their husbands agreed that pregnancy put increasing and gratifying demands on their libidos. Both marriages were the stuff of dreams—affectionate, loving, passion filled.

After a busy week of socializing, Sofia and Jamie left London and traveled to Blackwood Glen where they planned to spend a month or so before returning to Dalmia when the weather turned cold.

But the night before they were to leave, Sofia woke to find herself alone in bed. She immediately experienced a strange, incipient fear—needless perhaps, but vivid nonetheless. Perhaps it was because Jamie had been subdued of late, thinking about things he wouldn't talk about, setting up small boundaries again that she couldn't cross. Worried about his recent moodiness, she climbed out of bed and pulled on a robe.

She found him downstairs, standing before a window in his study, watching the sun begin to color the horizon. He'd pulled on his trousers but was otherwise unclothed, his tall, broad form silhouetted against the dim light of predawn. Even from the doorway, she could see the tension in his body.

"I missed you," she said.

Startled, he swung around, and for a second, under his right shoulder, the two white star-shaped scars of his bullet wounds glinted in the half light. "I was coming back up."

She caught her breath as she often did at the sight of his scars; she knew how close she'd come to losing him. "Have you been here long?" she asked, forcing herself to speak calmly, reminding herself he was alive and safe.

"A while."

She noticed the half-empty bottle on the sill and wasn't sure what to say. "Would you like breakfast?"

He smiled. "You're turning into a dutiful wife."

"As you are a husband," she replied, her own smile tantalizing.

His smile widened. "Is that why you came down?" His duties as stud were persistent and unfailingly delightful.

She shook her head. "I was worried. You've been more quiet lately."

"I don't think I'm going back," he abruptly said.

"To Dalmia, you mean?"

He nodded. "I've been weary of it all for a long time— the oppression and knavery of the government, the evil that men do, the senselessness of it all. Ernst has others who can guard him, Antonella's troops for one. I thought I'd write to Douglas and the men and tell them to stay if they wish or come here. It's their choice."

"I'd love for us to stay here of course, but are you sure?"

"I think I'd like to see my child grow up. I'd like to live with you in peace and"—he shrugged—"there's no guarantee of that if we go back." Or any guarantee that he could protect them from the coming violence in the empire. "I'm being selfish."

"There's no crime in that. You don't have to take care of everyone all the time. You've served Ernst loyally. And speaking of selfish, no one's more selfish than Ernst."

He grinned. "So we're agreed?" Although, he'd been sure since yesterday when the baby first kicked.

"Aren't we always?"

"So long as I let you have your way."

"That's what I meant. Now, if you have the time, I could use your services in bed."

"Why else am I here?"

Her smile was playful. "Why else indeed?"

She held out her hand, and he came to her with that easy stride that always reminded her of latent male power and animal grace. Reaching her, he placed his palms lightly on the rising curve of her stomach. "You bring me great joy—you and this gift of a child you give me," he whispered, his green gaze full of love, and he held his hands on her stomach one moment longer before he raised them and slid his slender, bronzed fingers through the pale froth of her hair. Bending his head, he sought her mouth like a man too long alone seeks comfort and attachment. He kissed her slowly, deeply, with disarming affection and passion, with pleasure and delight and in the end with a mounting faith in the future. Lifting his mouth from hers at last, he whispered, "You've carried me out of the darkness and into the light. I thank you."

"And you've given me love beyond measure," she said on a light breath, her heart in her eyes. "My dear, my dearest."

Bending with lithe grace, he slipped one arm under her legs, lifted her in his arms, and strode from the room. "I might be able to amplify that uncalibrated love if I put my mind to it," he said, smiling. It was still new, confiding in someone, and he elected to be playful instead. "What do you think?"

"I think I made an excellent choice that night at Ernst's when I agreed to come with you to Scotland."

He laughed. "You *agreed*?"

"Well, in a way. The point is," she brightly added, "I took a real fancy to you when I saw you at Bella's. I'm so very glad I did."

"I couldn't agree more, darling." And dismissing all the Herculean trials in between—the killings and near killings, the close calls and rivers of blood—he was in accord with his wife.

He'd spent a dozen years at war and years more before that learning the art of war.

And now it was finally over.

As he mounted the stairs in his manor house at Blackwood Glen, his sweet, adored wife in his arms, he understood that at last he was truly home. The evil and self-seeking ambition of the world was distant from his glen. He'd earned this—his retreat from the world, with senses on permanent alert, with slaughter and carnage, with feats of courage few men faced. And now released at last from the hazards and ambiguities of his past, he looked to his future with delight. He would take joy in his wife, beget children, till his fields, and sleep easy at night.

Love had given him all that and he rejoiced.

Keep reading for a preview of the next
historical romance by Susan Johnson

SEDUCTIVE AS FLAME

Coming soon from Berkley Sensation!

Groveland Chase, November 1894

THE DUKE AND Duchess of Groveland were entertaining at their hunting box in the West Riding of Yorkshire. The original party had been small, although more guests had arrived yesterday and tomorrow the local squires and farmers would come out for the day's hunt. As was often the case with country house parties, those invited arrived with unexpected companions. Charlie Bonner, for instance, had come with his wife, who neither rode to hounds nor liked the country. *"Sorry Fitz,"* *Charlie had murmured with a grin for his host. "I couldn't shake off Bella."* And surprisingly, Lord Dalgliesh had brought *his* wife. They barely spoke. But her young son had wanted to see a hunt someone said, and Lord Dalgliesh doted on the boy.

Not that all aristocratic marriages were as ill-conceived and regrettable, although love matches *were* a rarity in the haute monde. Long-held custom in the fashionable world had always viewed matrimony as a business transaction and marriage settlements as a means of enhancing family wealth, prestige, or bloodlines. Should anyone be looking for love, that was available elsewhere.

Naturally, there were exceptions to prevailing custom. Three of those exceptions were currently having coffee and brandy in a sitting room off the terrace. The Duke of Groveland and his friends, Lords Lennox and Blackwood, were having an early morning eye-opener while waiting for their beloved wives to come down for breakfast.

"To family." With a smile, the duke raised his cup. "May our tribes increase."

"A pleasant endeavor," Oz Lennox murmured. "I'll drink to that."

Jamie Blackwood lifted his cup. "We're fortunate, all of us."

"Indeed. To kind Fate," Oz said softly and drained his drink.

A small silence fell, each man fully conscious that life was uncertain, a gamble at best. They all understood how impossibly long the odds had been against meeting the women they loved in the great vastness of the world. How bereft their lives would have been had they not.

Into this contemplative moment a striding figure intruded, sweeping past the long span of French doors. The woman was tall with magnificent flame-red hair, the spectacular lynx coat she wore equally resplendent.

Fitz smiled as she disappeared from sight. "Rumor has it she's a witch."

"In more ways than one," Oz drawled, pushing himself upright in his chair in sudden interest. "What?" He shot his friends a grin. "I love my wife, but I'm not dead. Did you see those flashy spurs? I'll bet she's a wildcat in bed."

"And you should know," Fitz waggishly noted.

Oz cast a sardonic glance at his friend. "Please—as if either of you were puritans before you married. Hell, Fitz, you had Willery's bountiful daughter sizing you up under Rosalind's eye last night at dinner. I thought she might lean over just a little more and let her plump, quivering breasts spill over on your plate. And Bella practically ate Jamie alive while we were having drinks in the drawing room." He shot a look at James Blackwood, who'd spent years standing stud to not only Bella but a great many other ladies. "Did you have to make amends to Sofie afterward? She didn't look happy."

"Bella's always been difficult," Jamie coolly replied. "Sofie understands."

"I beg to differ," Oz drolly said. "I know Sofie. She doesn't understand at all."

"Let's just say I was able to atone for Bella's sins. Satisfied? And the enticing Zelda happens to be my cousin so mind your manners."

Oz grinned. "You're kidding. Zelda? What a perfect name for a bodacious lady witch."

"Her name's Griselda, so relax," Jamie muttered. "And the gossip about witches arose because she's recently returned from the jungles of Brazil with some native artifacts that she chooses to wear. She's no more a witch than you or I."

"Isn't she the one who raised all her younger siblings when her mother died?" Fitz asked.

Jamie nodded. "All five of them."

"So witch and earth mother," Oz waggishly noted. "Every male fantasy."

Jamie gave his friend a warning glance. "Fucking behave."

"Or?" Oz's grin was brilliant.

"Or I'll tell Isolde you're lusting after my cousin," Jamie silkily returned.

"And I'll tell her I'm not."

"Screw you," Jamie grumbled.

"I'm afraid I'm no longer available," Oz sweetly replied. "My wife doesn't approve."

The stunning apparition suddenly hovered back into

view, arresting the raillery. Coming to a stop at one of the doors, the flame-haired woman opened it and stood for a moment on the threshold, her tall form limned in golden sunshine.

The extravagant lynx coat fell to her feet, her flamboyant hair was untamed and wind-tossed, her long, slender legs were buckskin clad, and her booted and spurred feet firmly planted. While a faint smile graced her lovely mouth, mild query arched her dark brows. "Am I intruding?"

"No, not at all. Do come in, Zelda," Jamie quickly offered, rising from his chair along with the other men. "You're up early."

"It's not that early. Hello, everyone." Shutting the door, she stripped off her gloves. "Father and I've been out riding since dawn, although I seem to have lost him somewhere between here and the stables."

"No doubt he stopped to talk to someone." Sir Gavin was everyone's friend. "You know Fitz," Jamie observed. "And this is Lord Lennox. Oz, my cousin Zelda MacKenzie."

"A pleasure," Oz said, moving forward and putting out his hand. "You must tell my wife where you found your coat. It's magnificent."

"Thank you." *He has a very lucky wife*, Zelda thought, shaking his hand, *and he must care for her or he wouldn't have mentioned her in his first breath.* "A wonderful tailor in Edinburgh made this for me. I can give you his name if you like."

"I would." Oz's smile was boyishly warm. "You weren't here last night."

"We came in very late."

"Would you like a drink?" Fitz interjected, because Oz charmed without even trying, and Jamie had warned him off. "We're drinking our breakfast."

"Fitz has smuggled brandy so it tastes much better," Oz said, shifting slightly to include his friends in the conversation. "I recommend it."

"Perfect. Just what I need. And may I compliment you on your jumps, Lord Groveland," she added, turning to her host. "They're wicked. I'm looking forward to the chase."

"I can't take credit for the hedges. They were planted long ago. But I've added an obstacle or two over the years to make the run more interesting. Please, have a chair. I'll get your drink."

Zelda was shoving her gloves into her coat pocket and Fitz had turned to the drinks tray when the door to the hallway suddenly opened and a large, dark-haired man walked in. "Morning, gentlemen." The Earl of Dalgliesh advanced into the room. "It's a perfect day for hunting—frost, crisp, cold. You couldn't have ordered any better weath"—his cool blue gaze suddenly fell on Zelda and a warmth entered his eyes. "Good morning, ma'am." A connoisseur of beautiful women, he automatically surveyed her as he strode toward her—taking in her glorious face and form, the exotic garb—particularly the tight buckskins that left nothing to the imagination. He'd never seen a woman dress like that in public. "I don't believe we've met," he said, bowing slightly as he reached her, looking down at her with a beguiling smile. "Dalgliesh at your service."

"Alec, allow me to introduce my cousin." Jamie moved closer to Zelda, Dalgliesh's interest apparent and his reputation such that female relatives required protection. "Alec Munro, may I present Griselda MacKenzie, Sir Gavin's daughter."

"A pleasure, sir." Zelda smiled and put out her hand.

Grasping her fingers lightly, Alec brought them to his mouth and brushed her knuckles with his lips. For a lingering moment, he held her fingers in his warm, cupped palm before releasing her hand. "I haven't seen you before." His voice was velvet soft, lazy with provocation.

But his gaze wasn't lazy; it was predatory, like an animal on the scent. "My father and I are down from Scotland," Zelda replied, half breathless under the unmistakable lust in his eyes, the warmth of his hand still tingling on her skin; her heart was suddenly pounding.

Their eyes held for a moment—pale blue and amethyst—and a flurry of ripe, unguarded expectation shimmered in the air. Hotspur and graphic.

Alec recovered first because he wasn't given to blind impetuosity. "You've been out riding, I see," he smoothly said.

"Yes, I was just telling Lord Groveland what lovely acres he has." Zelda, too, had regained her composure. "Have you hunted here before?"

"He has several times," Fitz said, stepping in to diffuse what was clearly a volatile encounter. "Alec has a hunting box in the neighborhood. Come, both of you, please have a seat. I'll see to the brandies and coffee."

"*There* you are, Alec!" a female voice vexatiously exclaimed, the high, sharp cry shattering the faint hush of carnal ambivalence. "I've been searching for you everywhere!"

Five pairs of eyes swivelled toward the open doorway.

A fashionably gowned, diminutive blonde woman dressed in crimson cashmere stood dwarfed by the lofty door frame, her frown marked. "Christopher was wondering when you were coming back?"

"I'll be up in ten minutes."

"Would you like coffee, Violetta?" Fitz politely inquired. He couldn't very well not ask. Although her husband offered her no welcome.

"No thank you. I have to go back and calm dear Christopher." Lady Dalgliesh's smile held a hint of melancholy. "He's such a high-strung little boy. You won't make him wait long, will you, Alec?"

"No." Soft and dismissive.

"You shouldn't have run off like that," she scolded, either not noticing her husband's dismissal or not caring.

"Chris was upset to find you gone when he woke. But I'll do my best to console him until you return."

The earl's jaw clenched. "Mrs. Creighton is more than capable of consoling him."

"Really, Alec," Lady Dalgliesh said with a sniff of disapproval. "I don't know why you insist on that woman. She's so common."

"Chris likes her. Now, if you'll excuse me," the earl said, a dangerous edge to his voice.

The small woman hesitated fractionally, then with a little toss of her blonde curls, she crisply said, "Very well, don't be late," and flounced off.

Dalgliesh exhaled quietly before turning to the others. "Please forgive the drama. Violetta always enjoys making a scene. A double brandy for me, Fitz. No coffee."

"There's nothing to forgive," Fitz calmly said. "Please, everyone, sit. One double brandy coming up. How about you, Zelda?"

"A single, please, with coffee." She took the chair Jamie offered her.

Once everyone was seated and their drinks were in hand, the talk turned to hunting, the discussion focused initially on Fitz's hunting pack. Ten generations of Moncktons had succeeded in breeding the fastest pack of hounds in England with the nose, voice, and stamina to handle the coverts and bogs natural to the area. Yorkshire was the most sporting part of Her Majesty's dominions, the county where fox hunting first had been established.

The subject of thrusters came up next—riders ready to jump anything in sight with no care for the hounds. It was agreed that the men would all do what they could to restrain the louts. Riders of that ilk could raise havoc with the dogs by throwing them off the scent or worse: a pack worth thousands of pounds could be seriously damaged if ridden over.

Everyone in the room was experienced in the field. Oz had first hunted in India with leopards as coursers, Jamie had ridden to hounds in Hungary and on the Continent, particularly with the Empress Elisabeth, who liked to surround herself with handsome, world-class horsemen. Fitz and Zelda had hunted since childhood here and abroad.

Consumed with her own thoughts, Zelda only half listened to the conversation. Comfortably ensconced in a large, down-cushioned chair, she sipped her drink and tried not to stare at Dalgliesh. But he was murderously handsome, dark as a gypsy with sleepy, bedroom eyes, his hunter's gaze shuttered now that he was lounging relaxed in his chair, his brandy glass resting on his chest. His legs were stretched out before him, his hard, muscled body of unusual height—that height particularly attractive to a woman as tall as she. He didn't wear correct hunting dress—nor did anyone in the room; she was among men who shared her disdain for conformity. Or perhaps like she, they rode for pleasure, not to parade their pretensions or wealth.

Dalgliesh's coat was black, not red, his riding pants buff, not white, his boots devoid of the pink or brown tops of the fashion-conscious hunter. But his broad expanse of shoulder was shown to advantage under his elegant tailoring, and his green foulard waistcoat was buttoned over a hard, flat stomach. The powerful thighs of a superb horseman were evident under his tight buckskins, as was his virility, impressive even in repose.

A sudden suffusion of heat she didn't in the least wish to feel stirred deep inside her. Wrenching her gaze from his crotch she upbraided herself for such recklessness. Good Lord . . . Dalgliesh was married, with a child—and a difficult wife. Nor did she usually respond with such madcap indiscretion to a man. In fact, never. Not that she was some virginal miss. She lived her life with considerable freedom, her independence nurtured, she supposed, by the casualness of her upbringing.

Although no question—Dalgliesh had been offering her more than cultivated pleasantries a few minutes ago. He'd been offering her an invitation to unbridled sex.

She'd couldn't accept, of course. It would be the greatest foolishness to antagonize a spiteful woman like Lady Dalgliesh. Particularly in the midst of a country house party with so many people in attendance.

Good God! Meaning what?

If there weren't so many people about... might she *consider* being foolish? *Of course not*, a little voice inside her head sternly asserted. Her father was here for heaven's sake, and while Papa probably wouldn't notice with his mind rather narrowly on sport and drinking, this was hardly the venue for such rash behavior.

Get a grip, she told herself. And with that pragmatic injunction, she turned her attention to the men's conversation.

She hadn't known, but her scrutiny hadn't gone unnoticed by the object of her attention. More practiced, however, Alec's surveillance of the splendid Miss MacKenzie was well disguised. But he was having second thoughts about a carnal flirtation. Apparently the lady's father was here for the hunt. He'd met Sir Gavin before, the hard-drinking Scottish baronet typical of his class: bluff and friendly, physically large in the hardy Norse tradition, his life entirely devoted to sport and drink.

And at base, Dalgliesh reflected, he *had* come for the sport. Fitz's gamekeepers were superb, his lands extensive, his hunt master the best in England.

As for amorous amusement, there was plenty enough of that in London, he reminded himself. And had not the sudden, unexpected vision of the exotic Miss MacKenzie captivated every libertine nerve in his body, he might have more sensibly controlled his initial reaction to her.

Furthermore, both Violetta and Chris were in residence; surely that was reason enough for restraint. Starting now,

Alec decided after a glance at the clock. His ten minutes were up. Draining his glass and setting it aside, he came to his feet. "If you'll excuse me," he said. "We'll see you all outside. Chris is looking forward to his first hunt." He turned to Zelda, his smile urbane. "A pleasure to meet you, Miss MacKenzie." There, that wasn't so hard. It was just a matter of self-discipline.

"Indeed, a pleasure," Zelda replied, smiling back, ignoring the inconvenient little flutter coiling in the pit of her stomach.

After the door closed on the earl, Fitz gruffly said, "I've never understood why he doesn't divorce her."

"Rumors are rife in that regard." Oz had heard the stories from Marguerite when he had been spending a great deal of time in her luxurious brothel and bed. "Margo says it's something more than the boy that keeps Dalgliesh fettered." Oz shrugged. "I'd divorce the bitch, pardon my language, Zelda, scandal be damned."

"Perhaps he doesn't wish to hurt the boy," Jamie remarked. "The lad's still quite young isn't he?"

"About six I think," Fitz answered. "He was two when they married. The same age as Monty is now." Fully aware of the attachment between a parent and child, the duke quietly said, "I suspect the boy has come to depend on Alec. They're very close."

Zelda looked up, her brows lifted. "The boy's not his then?"

"No, Violetta was a widow when they met. Or rather I should say when they became reacquainted. She'd grown up near Alec and returned after her husband died. They married rather quickly soon after Alec came back from South Africa to visit his ailing mother."

"Marry in haste, repent at leisure," Oz murmured. "Although not in my case," he added with a grin. Oz had married Isolde after having known her only a few hours. "I'm happy to say, I'm the exception."

"None of us had a long courtship," Jamie pointed out with a smile for his cousin.

Zelda shrugged. "Hardly a requirement if you find someone compatible."

"You didn't meet anyone in the Brazilian jungle, I gather," Jamie teased.

"They were all rather short. The native tribes," she added. "And while the local landowners were charming enough, I'm afraid I towered over most of them as well. Not that I was actually interested in a permanent stay in Brazil. I'd miss the children."

"Zelda was on an orchid hunting expedition in Brazil," Jamie recounted to his friends. "You came back with some precious specimens I hear."

"Yes." Zelda smiled. "I won't bore you with the catalogue, but suffice it to say, the conservatory is now awash with colorful blooms." Then she said for no good reason or perhaps for entirely reprehensible reasons, "Why South Africa?"

None of the men so much as blinked an eyelash; they'd all spent considerable time in dalliance prior to marriage. In fact, the three men together held the distinction of having serviced a record number of women here and abroad.

Jamie glanced at Fitz. "You know more about Dalgliesh than we do. Explain South Africa."

"It was an accident as I understand," Fitz began. "Having left after a pitched battle with his father—they had a long history of strife—Alec was on his way to India and decided to stop in Cape Town. The Orange River diamond discoveries were first coming to light, and he invested in a small mining venture that made everyone a fortune. He returned to England when his mother took ill. Happily, she recovered, although his father died soon after. Alec and his father were in a heated argument apparently when the old earl collapsed. He lingered on for a few days, unable to speak or move." Fitz shrugged. "Alec's father was a brute. No one mourned his loss."

"Is Dalgliesh's mother alive?"

"Yes, although she's in uncertain health. Alec remains in England because of her, I suspect, and of course for Chris. He and the dowager countess both adore the boy."

"Why did he marry?" Zelda asked, her gaze searching. "He and his wife seem incompatible—although many aristocratic couples are, I suppose."

"No one knows why they married," Fitz replied. "There were rumors of a stillbirth, but he's never spoken of it, nor has she. A word of advice, dear, and I mean it most kindly. I saw how he looked at you. He has a reputation for profligacy."

Zelda smiled. "I'm warned. And coming from profligate men such as yourselves"—she scanned the handsome group—"I'll take your advice to heart."

"Formerly profligate," Oz corrected with a flashing grin.

"Just take care, my dear," Jamie gently said. "Dalgliesh is known to break hearts."

"I was mostly curious about him, that's all," Zelda casually replied. "Thank you for the abridged biography, Fitz. His wife was so bloody unpleasant I just wondered what sort of man would marry a woman like her."

"The entire world wonders," Oz drawled.

"Should you find out why," Jamie pointedly said, knowing Zelda for a purposeful woman, "you might wish you didn't know." His cynical view of the world had been tempered by a loving wife, but not entirely suppressed. He knew better than most that men were imperfect at best and occasionally reprehensible.

"I don't expect to find out. I'm generally more sensible than impulsive. Had I not been," she said with a flash of a smile, "I would have married Johnnie Armstrong when I was fifteen and let Da raise the children himself."

"I'm sure your father appreciates what you did."

"I'm sure he doesn't. He didn't even notice."

A fact impossible to refute. "Is this where I say you'll get your reward in heaven?" Jamie facetiously noted.

"I'll be getting it long before that," Zelda sportively replied as she came to her feet in a ripple of glossy fur. "I've enjoyed this chat, gentlemen. I'll see you all in the field."

After she was gone, Oz raised his glass in homage. "There goes a dazzling and engagingly candid woman. If I didn't adore my wife, I'd envy Dalgliesh."

"Perhaps there won't be anything to envy," Jamie retorted with exacting precision.

Oz looked at him from under his lashes, his dark gaze amused. "Such cousinly anxiety. If she wasn't related to you, I'd bet a thousand Dalgliesh doesn't last the weekend."

"I agree," Fitz said. "Which means we'll have to shield Zelda from Violetta's sharp claws. We'll take turns holding the bitch at bay."

"Ah, what delightful entertainment is in store," Oz murmured. "A quixotic seduction, a snarling wife, a possible pursuit and retreat." He looked up. "Will Dalgliesh actually refuse her?"

"I doubt it," Fitz said.

"Fuck no, he won't," Jamie muttered. "Who would with a wife like that?"

FROM *NEW YORK TIMES* BESTSELLING AUTHOR
OF *HOT PROPERTY*

SUSAN JOHNSON

GORGEOUS
AS *Sin*

An erotic romance star who "takes sensuality to the edge"* debuts her new historical-romance trilogy.

Fitz Monckton, Duke of Groveland, has never encountered a woman he can't seduce—until he clashes with the beautiful Rosalind St. Vincent, whose bookshop sits in the way of Fitz's lucrative development deal. If money won't entice Rosalind to sell her shop, Fitz must tempt her in other ways—hopefully in ways mutually pleasurable, as well as profitable.

penguin.com

*The Oakland (MI) Press

SUSAN JOHNSON

DELIVERS A SENSUAL TREAT

Wine, Tarts, & Sex

World-renowned chef Jake Chambers has
special talents in the kitchen—and in the
bedroom. And local Minneapolis vintner
Liv Bell is determined to let him taste what
she has to offer.

M352T1008

New York Times bestselling author

Susan Johnson

turns up the heat

Hot Legs

With her stunning red hair and a body to die for,
museum curator Cassie Hill has no trouble turning
heads. After breaking up with her lying, cheating
ex, however, she's ready to swear off men.
But when a priceless painting goes missing from the
museum, they call in a hot-shot bounty hunter—
who drives her wild with good old-fashioned lust.

"FUNNY, ROMANTIC, STEAMY, SEXY...
GREAT READ!"
—*Best Reviews*

"FAST-PACED, HEATED ROMANCE...
ACTION-PACKED."
—*Midwest Book Review*

"JOHNSON KNOWS EXACTLY WHAT HER
DEVOTED READERS DESIRE."
—*Booklist*

penguin.com